Move Over Darling

Christine Stovell

Published 2012 by Choc Lit Limited
Penrose House, Crawley Drive, Camberley, Surrey GU15 2AB, UK
www.choclitpublishing.com

A CIP catalogue record for this book is available
from the British Library

ISBN-978-1-906931-65-0

Printed in the UK by CPI Group (UK) Ltd, Croydon, CR0 4YY

For my indomitable mum, Doris, with love.

Acknowledgements

I'm truly grateful to the following people
for their generous support:

My daughters, Jen and Caroline, my sister, Tracy,
and my stepson, Tom.

The Choc Lit team and my fellow ChocLiteers.

Frances Oakley, thank you for a memorable day
in New York.

My dear friend, Jill, and the Amazing Thursday Girls:
Ann, Hazel, Julia and Rose.

The many bloggers who have been so kind, but especially
to those who were there at the start of the journey and
gave me a nudge along the way: Maggie Christie, Gillian
Hunt, Jane Price, Jill Shearer and Fennie Somerville.

And, as ever, to Tom, always.

Chapter One

Doris Day was singing in the background, telling Coralie Casey that whatever would be would be. Coralie disagreed. Doris was a goddess – but she was wrong about fate. The future *was* yours to see. Furthermore, you could look at it, decide you didn't like it very much and do something about it.

She dragged her thoughts back to the present before they had a chance to head off like a wayward dog and poke around for something nasty festering in the corners of her mind. Instead of waiting to be dealt another bad hand she'd reshuffled the cards and laid out her own destiny. She'd swapped suburban streets for country lanes and the nine-to-five for the steady rise of Sweet Cleans, her range of natural cleaning products for body and home. It wasn't completely true to say she'd moved on, but she had, at least, moved over.

Beyond the window of her workshop the late January snow spiralled in the air like down, cushioning the gentle green slopes in soft white. In seven swiftly passing months Coralie had seen the west Wales landscape in many moods and was learning to love them all. Even the rain, which seemed to fall in epic quantities in Penmorfa, was eventually followed by pale candyfloss clouds and bright blue skies.

She stopped for a moment to gaze at the delicate beauty of her garden under its white veil. A winter wonderland. Doris Day started telling her it was magic, but Coralie knew it was all down to hard work. By taking a huge gamble and some tough decisions she'd made her own dream come true. Or was making progress towards it. Who needed a crystal ball to see that things were looking good?

And her former colleagues thought *she* was the crazy one when *they* were still holed up in their offices! As for job satisfaction? She gave a small smile of contentment. Naturally, in the early days at the management consultancy, she had really believed in what she was doing. Every night, she would turn out the light feeling good because she'd nursed another dying business back to health. Rooting out clogged-up departments, weak processes and bloated boards saved an awful lot of money. But, that was before ... Rock! Oh poor Rock! He must be desperate for food!

When she'd woken up early, unable to wait any longer to try out the idea for a new soap recipe which had popped into her head just as she was drifting off to sleep, she'd only intended to allow herself an hour before seeing to him. How could it be almost nine o'clock already? How selfish of her to lose track of time so completely when he relied on her for regular meals! Throwing on her coat, she flew quickly up the garden path as fast as its dusting of powdery snow would allow and grabbed the box off the kitchen worktop.

'Ro-ock! Rock, Rock, Rock, Ro-ock!' Back out in the garden Coralie gave the plastic box of dried cat food a hearty shake, but there was no sign of the fluffy black stray who'd adopted her shortly after she'd moved in. Although she would never have admitted it to anyone else, it had taken some time to get used to her new home. Thanks to a weight of unfinished jobs, the tiny cottage had initially felt a bit unloved. Its selling point had been the workshop – and the low price, of course. The holiday let next door might have put some buyers off too, but, touch wood, all the visitors she'd encountered had been very well-behaved.

The relative isolation of the pair of cottages, which she'd found so attractive when she'd viewed them, could also exclude them from the village's warm embrace. They were accessed by a long, narrow road trailing off from what passed in Penmorfa for a main thoroughfare. By day, it was merely The Lane That Time Forgot; perfect for a bygone age when a pony and trap might have trotted merrily down to the village and back, but less suited to modern requirements and any car without a 'thin' button.

However, once the light – and her initial excitement – had faded, there had been times when the trees seemed to scratch at the sky, the dark sockets of potholes appeared to be lying in wait for the unwary traveller and the night air felt still and expectant. Having Rock squeezing through the hedgerow and bounding towards her whenever she appeared made her feel welcome. She paused to listen out for his little chirrup of greeting. Where was he? Perhaps he was in hiding from one of the farm cats who regularly tried to bully him? Poor Rock, you only had to look into his worried gold eyes to see how pathetic he was.

'Ro-ock!' She tried again, jumping to add a bit of extra impetus to her cat-food maraca.

'Hey! Little Red Riding Hood! I take it this is yours.'

The box of dried food went flying from her grasp as Coralie came close to finding out how it would feel to jump out of her skin. The Big Bad Wolf was tall, dark and stubbled, with a voice that could lead a nun astray. His eyes glinted like blue diamonds that cut right through her as he held Rock up from the other side of the fence. He was also, Coralie couldn't help but notice, wearing a black waffle bathrobe, which gaped open to reveal just the right amount of dark hair over smooth skin. Alys had recently given the cottage a makeover, hoping, she said, to appeal to the boutique hotel set, so if this holidaymaker was typical of the new breed, life was about to get interesting.

'Where did you find him?' she asked, wondering why she

was feeling so self-conscious when *he* was the one standing there half-naked.

'On my head,' he said, tucking Rock into the crook of his arm. 'He took advantage of me whilst I was sleeping.'

That would account for why Rock was looking so pleased with himself. 'He's very insecure,' she explained. 'Sometimes he just needs the comfort of being close to someone. The first time he did it to me I dreamt I was in a sauna wearing a Davy Crockett hat. I woke up with Rock's tail in my mouth and his little legs dangling down either side of my head.'

The Big Bad Wolf's mouth was set in a straight line above a granite jaw and the blue eyes regarded her with weary irritation. 'Would you like to take your cat or not?' he asked impatiently, 'because I'm freezing my balls off here.'

'Try not to drop anything until I get close to the fence, then,' Coralie advised, wondering if she should feel offended by a total stranger discussing his testicles with her. Good Sense Of Humour distinctly lacking, even if he was very good-looking. Pity. Safely back in her own home, he probably wouldn't seem that good-looking, either. One downside of Penmorfa was that a surplus of crusty old farmers made it easy to get overheated about any man lacking an abundance of nostril or ear hairs. On the other hand, standing in a frozen garden in just a dressing gown was likely to make it harder to see the funny side of things. Either way he was a fleeting visitor, not her concern, unlike Rock, who was beginning to get restless.

'Don't worry, Rock, darling, I'm coming to get you,' she said soothingly, just in case the nervous little cat thought the impatience was directed at him.

Except getting close to the fence was slightly harder than she'd anticipated. Gardening hadn't been her highest priority since moving in; the first job was to set the workshop up and get the business running smoothly and the winter had proved far too wet and cold to entice her out to tidy up the borders. The hawthorn bushes the previous owners had planted had been beautiful with their lacy white blossom when she'd moved in, but now they were armed and dangerous with prickles. In one sense that made her feel safe, on the other she didn't especially want to snag her lovely red vintage coat. Picking her way delicately through to a gap in the clearing, Coralie reached the fence, leaned across and lifted her arms to take Rock from the man the other side before his voice went up several octaves.

'There, there!' she cooed, as much to reassure herself as the nervous stray. For all his claims to the contrary, the brief touch of the man's hands against hers as he started to transfer his unwelcome hostage over to her suggested there was plenty of hot blood in him.

'Got him?'

'Yep!' she said, as she lost her footing on a patch of ice.

The silence of the normally peaceful and tranquil garden was rudely broken by a cocktail of sound comprising some fine old-fashioned expletives, yowling and hissing and a few whimpers of fear. Once it had subsided and Coralie could bear to look, Rock was nowhere in sight, but at least there were no track marks down her neighbour's chest to show where he'd been.

'Oh, I'm so sorry! Are you all right?'

'I should have looked around for something more substantial to put on my feet than open-toe hotel slippers, that's all.' He winced.

Spa slippers, too. Coralie was impressed; she wouldn't have guessed that there was any market at all for corporate businessmen looking to chill on the remote Welsh coast, but Alys had obviously done her research. Perhaps she should have done something about blocking the cat-flap, though?

Still, the stylish make-over had evidently attracted at least one weary executive to her holiday cottage. Except the man on the other side of the fence was looking more chilly than chilled.

He'd gone quite pale, but she couldn't tell if his adrenalin was priming him for fight or flight. Either way it wasn't going to do wonders for his sense of humour. If he did keel over there was no way she would be able to catch him, assuming she could even pole-vault over the fence in time.

'Just stay right where you are and I'll be fine,' he said, reading her mind and scowling at her. 'Now, if you'll excuse me, I'm going in before I catch pneumonia.'

'Don't exaggerate,' she said, hoping a bit of levity might help. 'I'm sure a fine big man like you can handle a bit of cold.'

As his dark eyebrows rose, she noticed, at the same time, that in all the excitement his bathrobe had come completely undone making her wonder exactly what was on the other side of the fence from her. She felt the deep blush, despite the freezing air, and was mortified when a flicker of amusement danced across his eyes and the corners of his mouth lifted briefly. It was some small comfort that at least he didn't have lockjaw.

'Have pity,' he said, cracking a smile at last. 'It's still four in the morning according to my body clock. And if that's not cruel enough, various parts of me are in danger of getting frostbite out here,' he added, as if she hadn't noticed. 'So you won't mind if I go in to warm up.'

Coralie stared doubtfully at him, 'Are you quite sure you're okay? You know where I am. Don't hesitate to ask if you need help.'

He drew his bathrobe round him and gave a short bark of laughter. 'Thank you, but don't worry, I've got a cell phone.'

Now was probably not the time to tell him that anything higher tech than a yoghurt pot on a string was wasted in Penmorfa. Instead, she made an attempt at a bright and cheerful smile so their encounter would end on a pleasant note and before he wrote anything like 'peaceful cottage, shame about next door's cat' on TripAdvisor. 'Right, well I'll let you get on,' she said. 'Bye then! Oh and enjoy your holiday! You couldn't have picked a lovelier part of the world to visit.'

He turned hastily and made the sound of someone stubbing a toe. Coralie decided not to look over the fence to see if she was correct. She hung around just in case her limited first-aid skills were required until she heard his back door slam, when she deemed it safe enough to go back inside her own home. Rock was stretched out in front of the wood burner looking at one with the world, but Coralie knew she wouldn't be able to relax. Everyone had accused her of running away to live in a fairy tale; now it was complete with its very own Beast.

Gethin limped inside, trying to decide which of his feet to attend to first. *Tawelfan* was the name of the holiday cottage, Alys Bowen had told him when she'd handed him the key. *Quiet place*. Well, it wasn't especially peaceful so far. One split toe was now bleeding over the kitchen's tiled floor whilst over on the other foot his little toe had turned purple and was looking sulky.

When he'd woken up in a strange bed and discovered his even stranger new headgear, his original intention had simply been to get to the back door and forcibly eject his furry intruder. The guest robe and towelling slippers had been conveniently to hand so saved him the bother of getting dressed just to see off his unexpected guest. But

7

then the commotion had started up in next-door's yard and he'd caught sight of the back of his neighbour's head. Her copper hair was coiled in a quaint up-do that bounced as she bobbed up and down the other side of the fence, her breath cloudy in the cold air.

The cat, in his arms, started wriggling in response to her bellowing, so putting two and two together, it didn't seem exactly gallant to give it a gentle boot or the opportunity to nip back inside behind his back, when he could easily hand it straight over. Besides, he was curious to get a better look at the *front* of his neighbour's head.

Well, the cat, presumably, had escaped unharmed but *he'd* certainly suffered for his curiosity. The new guest slippers had been trashed, but it was only good manners to avoid staining the new white grouting pink as well. A rummage in the kitchen cupboards unearthed a first-aid kit containing a giant roll of crepe bandage and a box of Gruffalo plasters. Fortunately, his essential supplies did run to aspirin and a bottle of Jack Daniels. Since he was sure he'd read something about aspirin thinning the blood, he poured himself a medicinal measure of JD instead. What the heck, his body clock was screwed anyway.

Lovely part of the world to visit, indeed! Alys had asked him if *hiraeth* had brought him back. The Welsh word described a deep longing for home; a silent call which could only be answered by the waves and the rocks and the mountains. No, not *hiraeth* so much as a last-ditch attempt from beyond the grave to control his behaviour. So if anything had called to him when he'd crested the hill in his hired car and caught his first glimpse of the cluster of limewashed cottages below him, bound by the pewter ribbon of the sea, he'd quickly turned a deaf ear.

Resting his foot on a kitchen chair, he sipped his drink

and stared at the Gruffalo and the mouse looking at each other on his toe. Like the girl peering cautiously over the fence at him, her tawny eyes widening in shock, and her Cupid's bow lips rounding in alarm. And suddenly all the anger and frustration of being dragged back to the place he thought he'd left for good diverted itself into something far more surprising; his shoulders started to shake and he threw his head back in a great shout of laughter.

A clean getaway, he reminded himself. No complications and certainly no local girls. Hell, if he'd let his father tell him what to do, he'd still be up to his knees in mud and cow muck and coming home every evening to the bitter face of the girl from the nearest farm slowly realising he'd only married her for her land. All that weight of expectation on a young couple; everyone in the village relying on them to work the land, fill the schools and keep the shops open. No pressure there then. So the local girls were strictly off-limits, he reminded himself, even if his cute next-door neighbour came round and offered to kiss every single part of him better.

More to the point, he'd promised Ruby that wild horses wouldn't stop him making sure that everything would be in place for the show – including him. Whilst he had every confidence in her abilities, it wasn't fair to leave the kid holding the fort all by herself. Especially not with Laura Schiffman, Pamala Gray's chillingly efficient senior director, breathing down her neck.

'Let Pamala down and it won't just be your father's cottage no one's touching,' Laura had warned. Pamala Gray was not the kind of art dealer anyone messed around, especially in a tightening market. Every exhibition in each of her three galleries had to repay its outlay. If he was a less successful artist, he'd be concerned, but his gold-plated sales record insulated him from any such fears. Not that he'd take advantage of his position; he'd play the game for Ruby's sake so when the time came for her to strike out on her own, she'd be able to cash in from his patronage.

He hobbled upstairs, holding up his big toe stiffly so as not to mark the pristine beige carpet, and picked his phone up from the side of the bed, wondering if was too early to give Ruby a quick call just to reassure her. Great. No signal. Leaning out of the window to see if the reception was any better, he caught the sound of someone singing 'Just Blew In From The Windy City' in the kitchen below. Somehow it didn't come as a surprise when he cracked his head ducking back in.

Chapter Two

A little later, gazing round at the winter sun lighting up the whitewashed walls and gilding the oak A-framed rafters of her shop, Coralie felt restored by the sight of her neatly stacked shelves. *Sweet Cleans, Dream Body* for beauty and skincare on one side, *Sweet Cleans, Dream Home* for household and utility on the other. It was a comfort to see the battalions of gleaming bottles and tightly packed jars and imagine them all primed and ready to bring a little shine to so many neglected places. She shrugged off her red coat, smoothed out her pleated skirt with its fifties' geometric print and switched on her music. 'Secret Love' filled the air and Coralie quickly forwarded it to something that didn't make her think of anything messy, like half-naked strangers in the garden.

When Alys tapped at the door, she was glad of the diversion. Alys, who, with her husband, Huw, ran the Penmorfa Garden Centre, had inadvertently helped her to make up her mind when Coralie was still weighing up the pros and cons of moving to the area. Coralie had been exploring, following the winding road up and across the hill to where emerald fields sloped down to a turquoise sea, when she'd first come across the garden centre. It had been a gloriously hot day and noticing that there were signs for a café and something called the Craft Courtyard, she called in for a cool drink and the chance to nose around.

The converted stable buildings, clustering round the garden centre's pretty Victorian cobbled courtyard, housed an eclectic variety of both crafts and craftspeople and seemed to be attracting a healthy flow of visitors. With hindsight, she'd probably let her heart rule her head when she'd noticed there were units to rent. The Craft Courtyard in winter was a much quieter affair, but the attraction of such a lovely setting and an instant 'family' of friendly faces so close to her prospective new home had been too strong to resist.

Coralie waved Alys in. Even in her garden uniform of old jeans and black polo-neck, covered today with a black pea-coat, Alys looked stylish and chic, a bit like Helen Mirren, with her silver bob and slim figure. Alys had a lot of oomph, too. Considering her daughter, Kitty, was quietly causing havoc, she was also managing to stay very calm.

'I don't suppose Kitty's said anything to you about the baby yet,' said Alys. 'Not that I'm asking you to break any confidences.'

'No, and I know,' Coralie told her.

'I just wish she'd open up to me,' Alys sighed.

'How's Huw taking it?'

Alys fingered a bar of soap from the *Dream Body* range. 'He's having a late mid-life crisis. It doesn't suit him to think that his little girl is all grown up; he hasn't got the faintest idea what's going on under those loose tops she's wearing. He still thinks of *her* as a baby so he certainly doesn't think she's capable of being a mother.' She stroked her hands across the label on the wrapper. 'Mind you, I sometimes wonder what's going on inside his head these days. I could stand in front of him stark naked and I swear Huw wouldn't notice.'

Stark naked reminded her of her new neighbour again, so Coralie was relieved when Alys closed her eyes to raise the soap to her face and inhale the vanilla scent. It gave her a chance to rearrange her expression before Alys read the guilt there. She'd rather not have to own up to disfiguring one of her holiday tenants. 'Ah, but that's because you're secure with each other,' she said. 'Huw's just comfortable with you.'

Surely you couldn't keep feeling the way she had when her neighbour had appeared over the fence? Excitement like that every day couldn't be good for you, could it? And yet something in Alys's expression as she replaced the soap and stood up suggested that comfortable wasn't all it was cracked up to be.

Outside in the courtyard, Willow, who sold silver jewellery to the sounds of dolphin calls and rainforest music from her little shop, had arrived after everyone else as usual, but appeared to be having trouble with her door. Coralie and Alys watched as she drifted in to Rhys, the chair maker, as big and solid as one of his products.

'Oh, hello,' said Alys. 'Seems like Rhys's number has come up.'

Coralie did a double take; privately she thought that Willow, with her very faded pre-Raphaelite beauty, was well-named since she did an awful lot of drooping.

'I hope she doesn't frighten him away before the Valentine's raffle,' Alys said, folding her arms. 'Rhys has promised to donate some hand-carved plant labels. We had a weaver here once – lovely man he was, beautiful work – but Willow would keep pestering him. I think he was all for the free massages she offered to start with. Quite happy to have his pressure points relieved and that, but once she cornered him with her Tarot cards, telling him they were meant for each other, it all got a bit heavy for him. Last I heard he'd changed his name and was working up at B&Q near Llandudno.'

'Surely not?' Coralie blinked.

'Well, I might have misheard the bit about B&Q, but it was something like that,' said Alys, her laugh sounding very like Kitty's. 'But Willow is very fond of men who are good with their hands. Blacksmiths, potters, sculptors, gardeners,' she continued, sounding more serious. 'Treats them all as if they're superheroes. She forgets they're just ordinary men and like ordinary men they'll take what they're offered and then they move on.'

The throaty gurgle of an engine alerted them to Huw, oblivious to them watching, trundling past on a quad bike with Edith, his wire-haired Jack Russell looking full of her own self-importance, perched at the back. Alys watched him disappear, her expression hard to read. Gardeners, she'd said. Not Huw? He was certainly good-looking in a rumpled, lived-in way, but why would anyone who had Alys waiting for him need to play away from home? Just as she was starting to feel quite glum, she noticed Alys smiling again. 'I'll tell you what, though,' she said admiringly, 'Willow will certainly bite off more than she can chew if she has a go at this one.'

Coralie took one look over Alys's shoulder and quickly turned the sign on the door to 'Closed'.

'Oh, you've met your new neighbour, have you?' said Alys, raising an eyebrow. 'I knew he had something of a reputation, but I didn't think it was that bad!'

The closed sign didn't seem to be putting him off; he continued to bear down on them, although his progress did seem to be hampered by a barely perceptible limp.

'It's all right, Gethin,' said Alys, switching the door sign over again and beckoning him in. 'You don't have to press your face against the glass, there are plenty of warm rolls in the oven.'

She looked rather pleased with her selective misquote from *Pillow Talk*. Coralie had lent her the DVD of the film in which Doris Day was cast as an independent interior designer forced to share a temporary telephone line with a philandering composer. As Alys stepped back, Coralie took a look at the man standing in her shop and decided that some of his pillow talk was probably quite lively, too. The late morning sun slanting through the windows caught the intense, blue-black of his hair, the twinkle of his dark eyes, a glint of white teeth as he smiled. No wonder he had a reputation. Going round looking like that, he only had himself to blame.

'Little Red Riding Hood, it's you again!' He laughed, shaking his head in disbelief at her. 'Just keep your distance, will you?'

Coralie was starting to feel that simply being on the same planet as Gethin Lewis was too close. Seven months of immersing herself in the practicalities of Sweet Cleans meant she had almost blotted out the messy memories of undertaking gladiatorial combat in some very risky arenas on behalf of corporate emperors. All the whisking, heating and blending of simple, chemical-free ingredients was highly therapeutic; every batch of marigold and lavender foot balm or Squeaky Clean window cleaner gave her a sense of achievement and of brighter days ahead.

In some small way, the products she created were soothing the weary and banishing the dreary. Maiming the man next door on first meeting felt like a retrograde step. Towering over her now, his broad shoulders blocking out the light from the door, he looked like a dark deed in her pure, pristine world. Shame she couldn't just give him a quick squirt of something and pretend he hadn't happened.

'Have I missed something?' asked Alys, looking from one to the other.

'Apart from a suspected broken toe and hypothermia?' responded Gethin mildly, picking up a bottle of Glow Surround, Coralie's all-purpose kitchen cleaner from the *Dream Home* range. 'I nearly cracked my skull open on the window too, thanks to your singing.'

'My voice isn't *that* bad,' said Coralie, feeling slightly miffed.

'Nothing wrong with it at all,' he agreed, pleasantly. 'You just took me by surprise when I was trying to pick up a phone signal. Although, if I was being picky, I'd say maybe stay away from the Doris Day numbers.'

For Alys's sake, she was prepared to keep the peace and tone the singing down for a week or so. She was even prepared to compensate him for his injuries. She pointed to the bottle he was holding. 'Please accept that, then, by way of an apology. It's very good on hard surfaces.'

'Oh, you *have* been getting to know each other,' said Alys, sounding impressed. 'Looks as if I can skip the introductions.'

'I'm Gethin Lewis,' he said, smiling and offering her his hand.

'And this is Coralie Casey,' said Alys for her, which was good because something had got her tongue.

'Coralie?' he said in a voice like brown sugar on a Welsh cake. 'That's unusual.'

The blue eyes turned on her speculatively. 'It suits you,' he nodded, 'especially with your colouring.'

'Gethin's a successful artist,' Alys explained, whilst Coralie stood dumbstruck, wondering if he would have felt so free to comment about the old Coralie in her sober black suits. 'He came from Penmorfa originally.'

'So, are you back here on holiday?' asked Coralie, recovering her powers of speech.

'Holidays are where you go to have fun, so I'm afraid that rules Penmorfa out for me,' he said, looking reflective.

'It depends on your idea of fun,' said Coralie. Personally she got a lot of satisfaction from trying out ideas for new products, but he looked the sort who might have very different expectations about soapsuds and body lotions. 'What about all the gorgeous coastal path walks? Surely you'll want to remind yourself of all those glorious views?'

The corner of his mouth just lifted. 'I appreciate the suggestion, but I'm very familiar with the local beauties.'

Beside her, Alys turned away to stifle a cough that sounded very much like a muffled laugh. Coralie narrowed her eyes at him. So why was he here? Decorative as he was, she hoped he wasn't back for a prolonged period. She could just about handle the idea of having him as a neighbour for a couple of weeks, but now she'd got used to it, she liked the seclusion of her cottage. She relished being able to pop out to her workshop at the bottom of her garden whenever she liked and mix up an experimental batch of something when the idea struck. A neighbour who was a permanent fixture complaining about noise and smells would certainly cramp her style. Especially someone who wasn't fond of Doris Day and little black cats.

Successful artist, Alys said. Coralie was beginning to think that anyone who could hold a paint brush in west Wales regarded themselves as a successful artist. Just as anyone who could string a sentence together was writing a novel or a collection of poetry. She thought she could be forgiven for not identifying Gethin Lewis as one of them since he'd managed to steer clear of the usual accessories like a ponytail or a loud, hairy jumper. Although a silver hooped earring – the perennial favourite with a certain type of west Wales artistic man, generally old enough to know better – would have rather suited him, giving those dark good looks a distinctly piratical edge.

'So,' she said, trying not to dwell on the dark good looks bit, 'do you exhibit your work anywhere?' Most would-be artists in the area had a sign outside pointing at a shed marked 'Gallery'.

'New York,' he said, with a gleam in his deep blue eyes.

'Ah,' said Coralie. At least he wouldn't be distracting her with any more half-naked appearances across the fence for very long. 'I expect your girlfriend's missing you.'

His dark eyebrows rose, making Coralie wish she'd thought more carefully before opening her mouth, but with looks like that he had to belong to someone. Despite the battered leather jacket, which gave his appearance a touch of louche edginess, he was quite different from most local artists; especially the ones who looked as if they dressed from a fancy-dress box. Carefully dishevelled hair, designer stubble, expensive jeans, black tee shirt under charcoal jumper; that understated style suggested he didn't need any gimmicks to attract attention.

'The only woman anxious to see me is the art dealer who's about to show my work, but she'll just have to learn to be patient,' he said, amiably. He returned his attention to the bottle in his hand. 'Sweet Cleans. Some kind of hobby?'

Coralie ground her teeth. Cath Kidston must have heard that one a few times, too. 'Like painting you mean?' she said, and heard him laugh. 'I'm providing a complete range of natural, eco-friendly cleaning and beauty products because there's a growing demand for them.'

'From people who can afford to pay through the nose for bleach in a fancy bottle, you mean,' he said, returning it to the shelf. 'Good luck with finding many of those round here.'

'Gethin!' Alys chided gently before Coralie could protest about his quick dismissal of her environmentally sensitive ingredients. 'A lot's changed in recent years. You should go up to Abersaith and take a walk along the high street if you want to see what I'm talking about; there are individual shops selling handmade stationery, exclusive knitwear, coffee shops with a choice of pastel-coloured macaroons ...'

He shook his head. 'I've seen it all before, Alys. And been back enough times to watch all the false dawns; too many of those businesses are here and gone before you blink. They seem a good idea when the sun's shining and the few holidaymakers that bother with this part of the world are about, but most of them don't survive the winter.'

'Not this time,' Alys said firmly. 'A permanent change is happening, thanks to people like Coralie who are deliberately choosing to live and work in the area.'

'Ah, I wondered why I couldn't place you,' he said, studying her face again. 'Not a local girl then?'

Coralie could imagine what he was thinking. Anyone born in Penmorfa had probably heard enough from incomers 'finding themselves' or making fresh starts to wonder if it was worth advertising the place as a centre for reincarnation. The 'muck and fluff' image of west Wales that suggested it was largely populated by farmers and hippies was hard to shake off. Even her well-meaning friends had accused her off running off to Penmorfa to live in a fantasy. All the amateur psychologists amongst them had nodded sagely at her fledgling business and made knowing comments about wiping away the past. Nevertheless, she wasn't about to let *him* get away with writing her off as some kind of fantasist.

'I didn't come here on a whim,' she told him. 'When I accepted voluntary redundancy it occurred to me that with an internet connection, I had the freedom and opportunity to start my own business in a place that had always attracted me.' Even if her parents had thought she was in the throes of a nervous breakdown.

'I tested the demand for my products by taking a stall at a couple of summer fairs to see how they'd be received, and when I'd sold out by lunchtime, I realised I was on to something. I haven't looked back since. The Craft

Courtyard's the ideal complement to my online business and how many people get these kind of views from their work place?' She gestured at the window. 'It certainly beats climbing the corporate ladder.'

'Hmm,' he replied, darkly. 'I'm not sure the poor sod who has to get up at four in the morning to milk cows, before he goes to his other job because he's at his wit's end wondering how to pay his fuel bills, would agree.'

'Oh, Gethin!' Alys wailed, throwing her hands up in despair. 'Don't be such a misery! Are you deliberately trying to frighten Coralie back to the city?'

He rubbed a hand across his stubble and managed a rueful smile. 'Don't take any notice of me, Coralie. I'm sure you'll prove me wrong with Sweet Cleans, but nothing in your shop's going to help me clean up the mess my father left behind. Besides, I prefer the countryside from a distance. Call me a bad Welsh boy, but that green, green grass of home business doesn't do it for me. If I ever get the urge to look at grass, a run through Central Park suits me fine.'

Coralie didn't need an invitation to call him a bad boy; it was etched all over him. Opinionated with it, too. But soon he'd be back on a plane and back to New York where he belonged. 'I escaped to the country and you escaped from the country,' she said out loud, earning herself another penetrating glance from those deep blue eyes.

'Exactly,' he said, before turning to Alys. 'So if times have changed, why is it still so hard to get decent mobile phone coverage? As if trying to find a builder to come out and give me some quotes for work on the old cottage isn't going to be enough of a challenge.'

'Oh, that's easily remedied,' said Alys. 'Come over to the farmhouse with me and I'll get you the number for our builders and you can use the landline, but don't forget about the Pembrokeshire promise.'

'Eh?' said Coralie.

'Promise we'll do it tomorrow. Unless there's something better to do,' said Gethin, shaking his head. 'Since my phone's refusing to play, I suppose it's too much to expect that there's an internet café in the village now, is there?'

'You can get twenty-minute slots on the two PCs in the library, provided you've got a ticket and you're prepared to take turns with Wilfie, our nearly famous local poet who's trying to find a publisher, and Edna Harris, who's looking for a man on "My Single Friend",' Alys told him.

'Or, if you promise to be nice to Rock, you could come in and try my router,' Coralie heard herself say, wondering how she'd managed to make it sound like a sinvitation. Two faces turned to her in surprise. 'What?' she said. 'I was only trying to help.' Trying to help mattered to her these days. Besides, the sooner Gethin Lewis finished whatever he'd come to do, the sooner she could get on with her nice, neat life.

'Excellent idea,' said Alys beaming, but Gethin looked doubtful.

'I appreciate the offer,' he said, taking a step backwards, 'but you nearly finished me off just looking over the fence.'

'Actually that was Rock,' she felt compelled to point out, 'and it was an accident.'

'Sure it was,' he agreed, 'and thanks, but with the hours my body wants to keep at the moment, it'll be less trouble for both of us if I can find an alternative.'

'I'll get that number then,' sighed Alys, going out of the door.

'And safer,' he added with a smile, before following.

Coralie felt her face fall and was glad no one could see. He wasn't wrong about that.

Chapter Three

That evening, at the farmhouse, Alys tucked her white-blonde hair behind her ears and decided that she'd had enough of sitting at the kitchen table listening to the clock ticking her life away. Left to Huw, who'd started the business with an acre of land adjoining the Lewis farm, the garden centre would have remained little more than an expensive hobby. He'd been persuaded, when the chance came, to expand the acreage, but it had been up to Alys to come up with diverse ways to make it pay. She was pleased with how the Craft Courtyard was taking off and even the investment in the holiday cottage was beginning to look as if it would pay dividends. But instead of Huw and Kitty supporting her, as she had hoped, she was starting to feel as if she had left them both behind along the way.

She eyed them now; Penmorfa ought to be the perfect spot to create a family-run series of businesses and she had hoped that Huw and Kitty would share her vision. But far from engaging in a lively debate about it over dinner, both her husband and daughter were doing an excellent job of pretending not to have lost their appetite, each of them mesmerised by their chicken casserole as if it contained the secret of the universe. When had she become less interesting than a dead chicken?

'Well, isn't this nice?' she said, brightly. 'All of us sitting down together again – just like old times.'

There was a clattering of cutlery as both Kitty and Huw stopped eating to cast suspicious looks at her, as if daring her to go on. Which one should she start on first? Kitty had been difficult and moody since she'd come home so something was bothering her. Apart from the obvious. Alys eyed her over a glass of supermarket Cabernet Sauvignon which Kitty had turned down, claiming to have a headache. 'So, Kitty, what's the latest on the job front then? Heard anything from that agency yet?'

Kitty picked up her fork and poked at her food as if the answer was hiding under a dumpling. When she failed to find inspiration there she addressed her thoughts to something else with a soft centre – her father.

'I thought I'd take a bit of time out, so I don't make the mistake of rushing into anything.'

Huw smiled and nodded and withdrew into his own thoughts again, mechanically lifting food to his mouth. In the summer months he enjoyed giving talks to the tourists at the garden centre, but during the winter no one in Penmorfa needed a lecture on 'Vegetables for Beginners', which tended to make him feel a bit redundant. In the environs of the nursery, Huw could coax just about any plant to life, but at home he was a bit like a bulb that had withered away and shrunk underground. Alys thought the time for him to emerge from the hard soil to bloom and thrive again was long overdue.

'But you've already been here a month, Kitty,' she said, willing her husband to join in. 'It's lovely for your dad and me to have you here, but it's not going to do wonders for your career, is it?'

Alys was beginning to run out of patience. Huw was becoming so introverted that at this rate he wasn't even going to notice that Kitty was having a baby until she went into labour. Since her daughter had gone to live in Cardiff in September, she guessed that they only had until June or July to get their heads round the idea. She looked from one to the other and waited to see if Kitty would finally give in and admit that she wasn't planning to return to work any time soon.

'I'm getting a bit of work experience with Coralie,' Kitty said, making big sad eyes at her father.

'Uh-huh. And how are you going to support yourself on that?' *Not to mention the baby*, she was sorely tempted to add. Kitty, as Alys bet to herself she would, managed to squeeze out a few tears. 'Are you saying I'm not welcome? Most parents would be glad to have their daughter home. Wouldn't they, Dad?'

'What?' said Huw.

'It's called tough love,' said Alys, trying not to lose her rag. 'You're twenty-two years old and you haven't stuck at anything yet. You can't be an adolescent forever. At some point you're going to have to decide what you want to do with your life.'

'Fine,' said Kitty, pushing her plate away as she had done when she was a toddler. 'If you don't want me here, I'll move into the holiday cottage out of your way.'

Alys shook her head, 'I'm sorry, Kitty, but that's not possible. I've just let it out to a paying customer. We've got to pull together and bring in the money where we can.'

Huw brightened up. 'Oh, fair play to you, *cariad*. Where did you find a holidaymaker at this time of year?'

'I didn't,' Alys said. 'He found us, but he's not exactly a holidaymaker. It's Gethin Lewis. He was planning to stay at Gwyn's old place, but there's been a burst pipe and it's uninhabitable so I said he could rent the cottage whilst he sorts out what needs to be done.'

'I suppose he's come back to get shot of the place, has he?' said Huw, stabbing a mushroom. 'I mean, if Gethin Lewis could barely be bothered to come near the village whilst his father was alive, he's not going to hang on to the cottage now his father's gone, is he?'

'It wasn't as simple as that, you know. He must have had his reasons. Look how busy he's been for a start; crucial exhibitions, interviews.' She sought in vain for Huw's face against the glare of the pendant light. 'Gwyn was a hard man. He liked everyone to dance to his tune. Maybe Gethin needed to put himself first at some point.'

'Selfish,' said Huw. 'Like too many people today, putting their own pleasure first.'

'Not so selfish,' Alys said, sharply. 'He did the right thing by his father when it counted. He couldn't have found a better nursing home for Gwyn, the finest in Pembrokeshire. Anything he needed, Gethin saw that he had it.'

'Anything except his time!' Huw observed crossly. 'He could have helped put his father's cottage right sooner.'

'Do you really think so?' she asked. 'Can you imagine Gwyn welcoming a raft of renovations? Do you think he would have agreed to a travertine-tiled bathroom? Or a Shaker-style kitchen? You know how careful he was. He would have seen any attempt to modernise the cottage as a complete waste of money. Lord knows he only accepted help from Gethin when he was too feeble to refuse.'

And he drove a hard bargain. Goodness knows she and Huw had had to pay the full price when they bought the old farmhouse from him, together with the swathe of land that hadn't been sold for grazing. Huw had been a bit reluctant to take on such a big financial commitment, but Alys could see the advantages of living on site rather than to-ing and fro-ing from their previous home on the other side of the village. Lately, though, she had started to wonder if she would have taken the same decision again had she appreciated quite how much stress it would bring.

'Besides,' she said, reaching across to collect plates since everyone seemed to have stopped eating, 'it's in our interest to keep Gethin Lewis sweet. Don't forget that the track to the old cottage goes right past this house. You don't know who he might sell it to. Or what they might do with it. Now, if you've all had enough, I'm off to the *Merched y Wawr.*'

'Daughters of the Dawn,' sighed Kitty, 'Don't you just love the way they try to make the WI sound exciting here? Like a bunch of loose women.'

Alys shot a quick glance at Huw, but he was too busy staring at the space where his plate had been. 'I'm glad you're so interested, Kitty,' she said. 'You're coming with me.'

With too much jetlag keeping him awake and not enough Jack Daniels to help him sleep, Gethin put on his jacket and boots, ignored his throbbing toes and followed the narrow lane up through the snow-covered banks to where it joined a wider road. Instead of turning right towards the village, he took the left-hand fork across the land which had once been part of his father's estate, past Penmorfa Garden Centre.

The old farmhouse where he was born had been given a considerable makeover by Alys and Huw. What he'd privately dubbed the Amityville Horror now looked cosy and welcoming against the frozen fields. The cottage his father had retired to five years earlier, built at a later date for one of the more fortunate farm hands, lay hidden away up a steep unmade track that disappeared to the side of the main property.

In the fifteen years since winning first prize in a national art competition, as a nineteen-year-old, the course of his life had changed dramatically, but inside the cottage time might have stood still. His father had clung on to the farm for another couple of years after his mother's death, but gave it up in disgust when Gethin sold the work that had made him an overnight name. Contempt at the apparent ease with which Gethin had made his fortune also made him spurn financial help for as long as he was strong enough to do so.

On the hideous mottled-brown tiled fire surround in his father's old sitting room a porcelain shepherdess his mother had cherished, because it was a rare gift from his father, was still flirting with the porcelain shepherd a family photograph away. If she was anything like his temporary next-door neighbour, the china lovers were best kept apart. The woman had as good as broken his toe just looking at him. Those vintage clothes were a menace too, turning his thoughts too dangerously towards black satin and the siren sigh of seamed silk stockings.

Gethin shook his head and concentrated on the black-and-white photograph in the centre of the mantelpiece. There he was, a skinny little kid with glasses, leaning into his mother, his back to her stomach, her arms crossed over his chest to protect him. His father, just apart from them, one hand on his hip, one on his wooden staff, looking at the camera as if it would cost him money to smile.

All the helplessness of that small boy, his inability to protect his mother against his father's dark mood swings, brought a bitter taste to his mouth. Why the hell had the old hypocrite kept the picture on display when his family meant so little to him? And the old man expected him to perpetuate the misery by bringing up his own children here! If his mother had still been alive it might have been different. How she would have loved seeing grandchildren running about the place!

He almost left the pale shepherdess where she'd stood for Lord knows how many years, but then he took pity on the lovers who had been apart for so long and placed her next to the young shepherd. Let them enjoy some time together whilst they could, before the house clearance guys turned up and separated them for good.

Closing the front door behind him, he took a deep breath of fresh air, noting that, yes, it really was warmer outside. Ready for sleep at last, he made his way back down the hill, the beam of the torch Alys had thoughtfully left for her guests picking out diamante clusters of snow. In his opinion, the holiday cottage's hotel-style makeover had wiped it of all personality, but it was clean, warm and the double bed was comfortable. All he had to remember was the sloping ceiling above it.

A shaft of yellow light shining into the lane from his neighbour's bedroom window reminded him that he wasn't quite alone. The village's isolated position created the worst of all worlds; long-term residents with a deeply ingrained way of doing business and all kinds of eccentric outsiders desperately seeking some rural nirvana. Wind farms, wind-chimes, woolly jumpers and crazy cat ladies – who needed it?

Before he could get to his front door, there was movement at his neighbour's bedroom window and there she was, dressed for bed, in something sleeveless and mint-green that flared from her shoulders, billowing to somewhere just below her bottom. It was also, Gethin noticed, as she bent forward and came up with her cat, very sheer. He froze, wary of doing anything that might alert her to his presence and give her completely the wrong idea. 'Samba Artist's Sordid Secret' was exactly the kind of story the British red tops would relish and whilst the New York press barely acknowledged the UK's existence, he didn't feel like putting his theory to the test.

Nevertheless he couldn't quite drag his eyes away as his neighbour kissed the cat's head and did a little twirl with it before putting it down again. With her curls loosened and touched with flame by the light behind her, she looked like a wayward angel, and when she finally reached up and drew the curtains, Gethin didn't know whether he was disappointed or relieved. Except that this wasn't Heaven, he remembered, this was Penmorfa.

'It's out of the question. The chairman of the Local Business Association has always drawn the Penmorfa Valentine's charity raffle,' insisted Delyth Morgan, clearly unable to support anything that would deprive her creepy husband, Hefin, of his moment of glory. The couple ran The Foundered Ship, and were responsible for more evil Sunday roasts of shrivelled meat and overcooked vegetables swimming in grey gloop than Kitty could bear to imagine.

Staring at the grandfather clock in the Vicar's front room, Kitty longed for an end to her evening with the *Merched y Wawr*, especially since her numb backside was making her regret her choice of a straight-back chair in the corner of the room. Her knitted tunic fell in soft folds that hid the swell of her stomach, but for all the notice anyone was taking of her, she might just as well have stretched on the sofa, sporting a 'Baby on Board' slogan tee shirt. Except that she would have been stuck between Delyth and Mair, the double act of doom. There were many good women in the room, all trying to do their best for each other, she thought, but not Delyth and Mair, who were only interested in themselves. They had been trying to stamp their collective authority on the meeting all evening, but it was Alys, Kitty noticed, who drew most of their scowls.

'But we're talking about an internationally acclaimed artist,' Alys said, looking shocked. 'Wouldn't it be marvellous publicity for the village if he could do it instead?'

'We're talking about Gethin Lewis,' said Mair, folding her skinny arms. 'I had to give him more than one smack when he started Sunday school. I'll never forget the time he tried to bite me when I prised him away from his mother. She was always too soft on him. As soon as she'd gone I made sure he was sorry. He soon got the message, I can tell you. He didn't dare play me up after that.'

And they were surprised that so few young people stayed in Penmorfa, thought Kitty, wondering wildly if she would ever have a social life again. Her rented room in a shared house in the student heartland of Cardiff had been minging, but there was always someone to have a laugh with. Her job in Events and Leisure Management had been fun whilst it lasted and her social life had been brilliant. And all that gone, thanks to being stupidly lazy about contraception.

'Quite right, too,' Delyth was saying, looking faintly amphibious in her leaf-green fleece. 'It may be marvellous publicity, as you put it, Alys, but for whom? What's he done for us? He can hardly even bring himself to acknowledge his roots. This village made Gethin Lewis what he is today and all he's done in return is throw everything back in our faces.'

'Don't you think that's a little unfair?' asked Alys, giving the older woman a despairing look over the rim of her reading glasses. 'Especially given the demands of his career. I'm sure if we approached him, he'd be only too happy to help.'

'We can manage without help from the likes of Gethin Lewis, especially when he's shown the whole world exactly what he thinks of us!' Mair insisted, tucking a handkerchief into the elasticated waist of her flora dirndl skirt. 'When you've lived in Penmorfa as long as we have, you'll understand these things. Gethin Lewis thinks he's far too good for us. He couldn't wait to get away and I'm surprised he's got the nerve to show his face again now.'

Now they were getting to the real issue, thought Kitty; Alys could never win in their eyes because she hadn't been born in the village. Most people in the room had moved with the times, but Delyth and Mair still expected everyone to defer to their decades of experience about the way things were done.

'It's Penmorfa I'm thinking of,' said Alys, getting cross.

The Duo of Doom exchanged a look to suggest that Alys was no judge of character. 'Well, he's certainly got you on his side.' Delyth puffed her cheeks and looked even more like a disapproving frog. 'He always was a little devil with the girls. Perhaps it's just his pretty face you're finding difficult to resist, Alys?'

Now you've done it, thought Kitty, longing for her mother to explode. Her parents had their ups and downs like any couple, but they never faltered in their support of each other. If Alys, with her drive and energy, was like a restless wave, her father was the constant rock absorbing the poundings, forever enduring. Looking at it from the outside, there might have been an element of predictability about the arrangement, but there was a permanence about her parents' relationship that made Kitty feel rather wistful. It was difficult to imagine being in a partnership of some thirty years when, in her experience, most blokes found it hard to stick around for thirty days. She waited for the fireworks, but Alys just shook her head at the paperwork on her lap and settled back in her chair, her mouth set in a tense line. Even her mother, it seemed, found it difficult to tell Delyth and Mair where to get off.

In the frosty silence all Kitty could hear was a mint rattling against someone's false teeth until a log cracked in the wood burner and made everyone jump. Just then the sitting-room door opened. The Vicar, who'd already been delayed because she'd had to run her husband to the station when his car refused to start, only to be called to the phone on her return, finally surfaced.

'So sorry, ladies,' she said. With her chic dark hair and lovely high cheekbones she was, Kitty was surprised to see, a bit of a babe. For a woman who had five churches to look after, she was remarkably serene, too. 'That was the Bishop.' She smiled. 'I'm afraid there may be a slight problem with the Valentine's dance.' She settled herself between Mair and Delyth, dividing the Red Sea of Remonstration nicely, Kitty observed.

'But first, I don't suppose many of have you have undergone Criminal Record Bureau checks, have you?'

'I don't know what you're implying, Vicar,' huffed Delyth, her chest beneath the green fleece swelling with indignation.

The Vicar gently patted her arm and looked round the room, searching in vain for raised hands. 'Oh, dear. That's what I thought.'

'What difference would it make if we had?' asked Alys, leaning forward.

The Vicar gave a ladylike sigh. 'Well, because the mother-and-toddler group use the church hall twice a week, it's raised what the Bishop is calling "legitimate concerns" about the safety of the toddlers.'

'Meaning?' said Alys.

The Vicar spread her pale hands in a gesture of helplessness. 'Meaning that unless all of you have CRB checks, it's simply not reasonable for us to guarantee the safety of any toddlers you may come into contact with. The Church has to ensure that any organisation undertaking regulated activities within the hall has made the necessary checks and registrations. '

'But most of them are our grandchildren!' a plaintive voice from the other side of the room cried.

'I'm afraid that doesn't give you any legal rights in this case,' the Vicar said, shaking her head. 'We must be seen to be putting the necessary safeguards in place not just to protect and promote the welfare of children, but also to enhance public confidence. I'm very sorry to be the bearer of bad news, but it simply won't be possible for the Church to allow you to use the hall until this issue is addressed.'

'Yet another example of Health and Safety gone mad!' protested Alys, accompanied by mutinous murmurs.

'Alas, it's more than bureaucratic zeal,' said the Vicar as heads turned her way. 'I'm sorry to report that there's an additional concern. A recent inspection of the building has revealed that it falls seriously short of modern standards. The heating's inadequate, the loos are beyond antique and there's no disabled access. Unless the means are found to carry out the necessary work, it will have to be closed anyway. The Bishop did point out that when Abersaith was in a similar predicament, their historic market hall was saved when funding was secured to match the sum raised when everyone agreed to buy community shares.'

'Our church hall's not exactly an historic landmark.' Alys sighed, gathering up her paperwork. 'And there's still the immediate problem of the Valentine's dance. Doesn't the Bishop realise how not being able to use the church hall will affect Penmorfa? Unless he reconsiders the matter, there's simply nowhere else to go.'

'Actually, Mam,' said Kitty, anxious to go home and congratulating herself on coming up with a brilliant idea that would mean Delyth and Mair having to be grateful to her mother. 'What about our Summerhouse Café? It's just about big enough. Is there any reason we couldn't hold the do there?'

Chapter Four

'Thanks for helping me this morning,' said Coralie. 'I'm pleased with how this *Dream Home* range is selling, even in the current climate.'

'Beats me how you came up with the idea for all this,' Kitty said, unpacking a bottle of Squeaky Clean window spray.

'It's all thanks to my fairy great-godmother,' Coralie explained, taking a box cutter to the next parcel. 'My grandmother was evacuated to a family near here. Unlike so many children, her story had a happy ending. She grew very close to her Welsh family and returned for years for holidays after she'd had my mum. Aunty Elinor, as she called her, had been in service here; she got my gran to practise her handwriting by dictating all her cleaning secrets to her.'

'Hmm, maybe something life-changing like that will happen to me,' mused Kitty, standing back to admire her handiwork.

Something life-changing *was* happening to her, Coralie nearly pointed out, except that would slow Kitty down even more and at the rate she was working they'd be there all day. Kitty had returned to Penmorfa at Christmas, apparently after a temporary work contract had ended in Cardiff. That was one reason she'd given for coming back. She still wasn't talking about the other, the little baby bump she was trying to hide. Everyone was playing along with Kitty for now, pretending nothing had changed. Not that Coralie had a problem with that approach; most people had something they didn't particularly want to talk about. And whilst Kitty wasn't going to be able to keep her secret to herself indefinitely, it would be a relief for all concerned if she turned to her mother first.

'I don't really know what I want to do,' Kitty went on, pulling at her crinkle tunic top where it was trying to hug her stomach. She was still at the stage where most people wouldn't have noticed her condition, but most people hadn't had Alys pacing their room, tearing her hair out over her daughter's determination to remain close-lipped.

Coralie took over with the unpacking, unobtrusively speeding things up whilst Kitty wandered over to the *Dream Body* sample bottles and helped herself to a dollop of hand cream.

'I keep hoping something will come to me, see. I worked in the garden centre last summer, but I get terrible hay fever and it ruined my nails,' Kitty said, flexing her fingers. 'Perhaps Gethin Lewis will spot me whilst he's here and ask me to be his next muse?'

Coralie bent over the box. She'd woken up far too early, full of the usual four-in-the-morning worries, and then found herself wondering about her neighbour. Her grandmother's notes recommended tucking a piece of muslin sprinkled with lavender oil into a pillow case to combat sleeplessness. Although Coralie lay back and tried very hard to conjure up lavender fields, she couldn't quite dismiss thoughts of alternative cures involving the man next door, possibly reclining just the other side of the wall.

'Is his work any good?' she couldn't resist asking, whilst Kitty blatantly unscrewed one of the non-samples and waved it under her nose.

'Oh, that smells lush!' Kitty eyed her over the bottle. 'I can't believe you're asking that! You must have heard of *Last Samba before Sunset*.'

'That's not him, is it?' Coralie was shocked. Posters

and cards of the elegant yet deeply sexy portrayal of a couple dancing on the beach in late light, oblivious to the disapproving stares of two frumps crouched behind a windbreak and a pair of old farmers assessing them like horse flesh, adorned living room walls and student bedsits everywhere. The male figure was in shadow, his back turned, so that the attention centred on the sensual beauty of the woman with her arms outstretched moving towards him. It was an iconic image and to think, its creator had been practically naked in her back garden!

Kitty grinned and nodded. 'Watch, there'll be a run on any magazine with a free lipstick in the express supermarket, now he's back. Even if they do offload all the rubbish colours on us here. Got to be worth a try, though. I wouldn't mind letting him have a good look at my finer points.'

The weak sunshine filtering in through the stable door, which was open whilst they went to and fro with boxes, was temporarily blocked as a shaggy-haired, good-looking blond guy leaned in at them. 'Talking about me again, Kitty?' he said, raising the shovel he'd been using to clear the paths like a trident.

'In your dreams, Adam,' Kitty sniffed, turning away to get on with the stacking.

Adam grinned, showing a chipped front tooth which, together with a slightly crooked nose, only added to his rakish charm. Coralie shook her head, puzzled by Kitty's sudden froideur. It was hard to find anything to dislike about Adam, even when he didn't turn up for work at the garden centre because he was down at the bay trying to catch a wave. She could see why Alys always forgave him.

'How are my two favourite girls, then?' he went on. 'Coralie, did I ever tell you how much I love redheads?'

'He's also quite partial to blondes, brunettes, girls with

36

straightened hair, spiky hair, short hair, long hair, and he isn't averse to a touch of silver either,' said Kitty with a touch of vehemence that made Coralie blink.

'Cheers, Kitty,' said Adam, with a flash of his emerald eyes. 'I thought you might be pleased to see me for once, especially as your dad and I are running around like blue-arsed flies thanks to your bright idea for the Summerhouse Café.'

'Oh, have you found someone to take it on?' asked Coralie, still wondering why the air was crackling between Kitty and Adam. Surely it was a good thing if the place was being reopened? The Polish couple who'd been running the café and who'd seemed so determined to make a go of life in Penmorfa had taken off shortly after she'd moved in, but then austerity Britain had been quite a different place to the one where they'd started their optimistic new life. Alys, she knew, worried about the loss of winter trade, but had been forced, for lack of staff, to leave it closed.

Coralie listened whilst Kitty gave her a potted history of events at the *Merched y Wawr*. 'So, the Summerhouse Café's just a stop-gap, whilst the Vicar discusses permanent provision of a community space with the Charity Commission,' Kitty concluded. 'She says that if they go down the route of restoring the existing church hall there are several funding pots we can try.'

'Cheaper to build a brand new hall,' said Adam, raising his eyebrows.

'Except there's no money for a new build!' Kitty told him, as if he was stupid. 'By saving an existing building we get points for sustainability, like they did at Abersaith.'

'Penmorfa always loses out to Abersaith,' mused Adam. 'It's because nothing ever happens here. It's a pity Wilfie isn't better known. If he was as famous a poet as Dylan Thomas, we could claim that he wrote his best poems in the church hall and ask for funding to preserve it for the nation.'

'But,' said Coralie, who was still getting used to the idea, 'you do have a phenomenally well-known artist. Surely that has to offer some possibilities?'

Kitty and Adam exchanged glances, back on common ground.

'He's a bit controversial, see,' said Kitty. 'There are some people who hate that painting. They say he's poking fun at rural life, making us all look like yokels. Delyth and Mair will never forgive him – they say it's them behind the windbreak!'

'There's that, of course,' Adam agreed, 'then there's the fact that the smooth bastard's shagged half our women. I daresay he'll have a crack at a few more whilst he's home.' He cast a sour look at Kitty.

'Oh, you're not afraid of a bit of competition, are you?' laughed Kitty. 'Don't worry about it, Adam. I mean what sort of woman would give in to a fabulously wealthy, drop-dead-gorgeous hunk when she could have a young stud of a garden-labouring surf-bum?'

'At least I've got a job,' he shot back. 'You're still a lazy cow who runs home to mam and dad every time the money runs out. One day you're going to have to grow up.'

Sooner than he thought, Coralie predicted, taking a step back and getting ready to protect her stock. All that was thrown, though, was another bitter look from Adam before he nodded a curt goodbye and took off.

'Really,' Kitty tutted, her face a picture of innocence as she turned back to the shelves, 'some people can be so touchy.'

By mid-afternoon the Courtyard was deserted and a cold front had closed in. A couple of cars had rolled across the tarmac of the car park earlier, spilling out the hardier variety of holidaymaker, those who didn't mind a spot of wind and weather. But most of them had been in search of shelter and some respite from the bone-chilling temperature which refused to lift despite the deceptive sunshine. Coralie didn't need to tell Kitty twice that she might as well find something more useful to do than hanging around in an empty shop.

Eventually, even Coralie decided that rather than standing there doing nothing she would go home and see what she could do to increase internet sales instead. Willow, with her pale face and cascade of dyed red hair, was looking woefully out of one panelled window like a latter day Lady of Shalott, although Coralie suspected that she was keeping her eyes peeled for Rhys rather than paying customers. She gave her a little wave as she crossed the courtyard and received a wan smile in return.

Most of them don't survive the winter. Gethin Lewis's stark conclusion about the new start-ups in the area nipped like the cold air. What *would* she do if she'd mistaken that tingle of excitement that had changed her life when she'd opened the dusty journal and started to read her grandmother's neat script? Coralie used to be able to claim that one thing she did understand was business, but how could she say that when it had all gone so spectacularly wrong?

She stopped to take some deep, steadying breaths, the raw air stinging her nostrils and making her eyes water. Across the car park the sight of Betty, her Atlantis-blue Rascal van, standing alone in a thin layer of almost untouched snow, gave her a focus and helped draw her back to the present. Poor Betty, not half as prestigious as her previous car, a luxury Audi that made light of the many business miles she used to drive, but ideal for trundling her boxes from the workshop to the Craft Courtyard and back.

Coralie jumped in and switched on the engine, the cold vinyl seat making her teeth chatter as she waited for the windscreen to defrost. Given the rather basic heating, this could sometimes be a lengthy process. Eventually a big enough gap appeared for the long wooden shed of the garden centre shop to come into view. Alys was probably poring over catalogues inside, planning for the future. Gardeners had a wonderful ability to see the potential in the most barren, unpromising ground, thought Coralie, releasing the hand brake. It wasn't a bad philosophy, although some days she looked at her own life and wondered if she would ever see green shoots again.

Realising that she was clenching the steering wheel so hard that her fingers were numb, she relaxed her shoulders and found something to listen to. Comfort music. Something to chase away all the dark thoughts before she got home and had to try to drum up new outlets for Sweet Cleans. The bass notes started and Coralie nodded. 'Move Over Darling', Doris's 1964 hit about irresistible temptation, one of her favourites. Perfect, although the line about waving her conscience goodbye almost set her off again.

A bone-jarring jolt, as one of the potholes in the road still waiting to be filled after the previous year's snow made its presence felt, brought her back down to earth. Coralie slipped down a gear and managed to coax the van over what felt like the foot-slopes of Snowdon. However, the operation appeared to have cost a front bulb which flickered weakly. Whilst Betty's compact size and manoeuvrability meant she could squeeze past tractors without too much difficulty, some caution was needed to ease her along the pock-marks and craters of the narrow lane leading up to her cottage. To negotiate those, what was ideally required was a big, solid car with a powerful engine. Like the one steaming far too fast towards her.

Uncertain condition, thought Gethin, pressing his shoulders against the supple leather of the heated driver's seat as he set off down the lane. The legal term, apparently, for the clause his father had inserted in his Will in an attempt to control him from beyond the grave.

'The meaning's clear enough,' his solicitor had told him, once the Will had rumbled through the due legal processes. 'You'll only have the benefit of your father's house if you reside there personally for the next five years. But no court in the land will enforce that condition because it's impossible to apply.'

'What about a challenge from the other potential beneficiary?' Gethin had asked, wondering how quickly he could get shot of the place.

'Litigation, litigation, litigation. It's a costly old business challenging a Will. And once the wheels are set in motion they can be very hard to stop. Especially when the costs are coming from the claimant's own pockets.'

Perhaps, somewhere, his father had sensed he'd found a loophole because he'd certainly left something behind; an unsaleable cottage and no builder to sort it out. A scramble, it seemed, for soon-to-dry-up funding streams meant that anyone who was any good was heavily involved in regeneration work up at Abersaith.

'Any progress with the other business? The "Art in Your Home" stuff?' he asked. Just to add to the fun, and his legal costs, the company responsible for all the posters of his famous painting had recently gone into liquidation owing him money, another victim of improved digital printing technologies crowding the art market.

'You know there's a strict order for creditors: tax authorities, banks … These things take time, but we're doing all we can to pursue your royalty payments.'

Was no one in a hurry these days? At least he'd found a builder who could spare him half-an-hour to give him a quote, albeit with a few caveats about his very busy schedule.

Gethin put his foot down. Might as well give the smart, hired Land Rover a run for his money; that's what potholes were for, wasn't it? He was just beginning to enjoy himself when he caught sight of a single light coming towards him in the dusk and hit the brakes. Almost instantly, he realised that the single light didn't belong to a motorbike, but a van whose offside light was winking so feebly that he hadn't spotted it at first. Swerving into the hedge, he winced as he heard the hawthorn branches scratching at the pristine paintwork and pulled up just a nanoparticle short of disaster.

He opened the door and heard music. Not the angels playing their harps, luckily, but bloody Doris Day telling him how much she yearned to be kissed.

'Move over, darling!' he snarled to his temporary neighbour, Coralie, when she wound down the window. 'That's what you should have done, instead of wrapping yourself up in your bloody music!'

'You were the one hogging the road!' she said, looking taken aback. 'And going far too fast!'

'I managed to see you in time and stopped,' he went on. 'If I'd been some old farmer in a tractor, you might not have been so lucky. If you'd have checked your vehicle before setting off, you'd have noticed that offside light's on the blink. Your windscreen's iced up, too.'

'The heating's dodgy,' she mumbled.

Gethin shook his head. 'It's not the only dodgy thing, is it? This has got to be one of the ugliest vans I've ever seen.'

'Oh, don't start on Betty, too!' she said, sounding so vexed that he peered into see who else was in there.

'Betty Blue, because of her colour,' she offered with a weak smile.

'Well, I'm glad you think it's funny,' he said, seething. 'I just hope my builder appreciates the joke when I tell him why I'm late. Let's get moving, shall we?'

She didn't seem especially keen on the idea, then he worked out why. 'Oh, I get it!' he said, leaning over her again. 'Women drivers can't reverse, can they? Well, don't you worry your pretty little head, I'll do the gentlemanly thing.'

He stomped back to the Land Rover and reversed it back, hard. The butt-ugly van showed no signs of following, but then he saw the driver's door open and a pair of Wellingtons drop beneath it. Shortly after, Coralie stood up in them and, with the door still open, applied her shoulder to the frame.

'Why didn't you tell me you were stuck?' he asked, running back and noticing for the first time that she'd steered into a pile of slushy snow at the side of the lane to avoid him. The Land Rover would have slid out of it comfortably, but Coralie's heap of rubbish needed some coercion.

'Get in,' he said roughly. 'Now put it in second gear – you do know which one that is, do you? Then, when I say, let the clutch out very slowly.'

Marching round to the back of the van, hoping that she really did know where second gear was and didn't find reverse instead, he hefted his shoulder against the bodywork and with a bit of brute force, the van was free. Coralie gave him a wobbly thumbs-up sign which did little to improve his mood, especially when he returned to the Land Rover and realised that it was only possible for her to get home if he reversed all the way back to the pair of cottages.

And now he was running late for the builder, too. 'Sodding mobiles!' he muttered seeing the 'service unavailable' message, having got out of the car in the vain hope of picking up a signal. Willing the guy he was supposed to be meeting to hang on at his father's house until he got there, he decided to save the lecture he was going to give his neighbour about the state of her van for another time. 'You can come in and use the landline, if it helps,' she offered, quietly. 'You might stand a better chance of getting through.'

He glared at his useless phone in frustration. 'I've only got a mobile number for the builder I'm supposed to be meeting. If he's up at the cottage there's no signal there. Besides, he's never in a hurry to answer his voicemail.' What a backwards place this was!

He shoved the phone back in his pocket. 'Thanks anyway,' he said, remembering his manners and looking at his neighbour for the first time since she'd got out of the car. 'Coralie?' he said, shocked at the sight of her. 'What's wrong?'

Chapter Five

Even in the fading light, he could see how pale she was, her lips drained of colour. And shaking; he could hear her keys jangling in her hand. Either she felt the cold far more than him, or he'd frightened the life out of her. He mentally replayed their near miss in the lane and all he could hear was his hectoring tone, a soundtrack of constant criticism: her music, her car, her driving. No wonder she was scared. He'd behaved like an utter bully; cruel and overbearing when she was in no position to fight back. Hell! He was no better than his father. Yet another unwelcome legacy.

'Are your house keys on that bunch?' he asked, self-disgust making his voice gruff. She nodded and his stomach lurched at the distress in her eyes.

'I think we should get you inside, that's all,' he said, more gently, 'before you're frozen solid.'

A gentle bump beside them, as her cat jumped down from wherever it had been hiding, seemed to reassure her.

'Hello, Rock,' she sighed, as the little animal rubbed itself against her Wellingtons.

'Your key, Coralie?' he reminded her. She offered it to him and he felt the cold brush of her fingers before she bent to scoop the cat up in her arms. It seemed only natural to place a guiding arm round her shoulders to usher her inside and he tried to ignore his inner voice observing what a good fit she was. None of that leaning-over problem he had with very small women, or stretching up to accommodate tall ones.

'It used to feel very cold here,' she explained, turning and catching his bemused expression as he looked around at the cosy room with its eclectic blend of junkshop finds and vintage fabrics. 'The oranges and red just warm everything up.'

'They do that all right,' he agreed, comparing it to the stream-lined minimalism of his New York apartment, somewhat necessitated by its compact size admittedly, and wondering how any man could put up with all the girlie clutter. 'But standing there won't stop you shivering.'

When Rock jumped out of her arms and strutted over to the wood burner, Gethin helped her shrug off her coat. Her feminine, floral scent and her hair in its forties' style rolls put him in mind of old-fashioned glamour and movie stars like Rita Hayworth and made him curious about whether or not she had a leading man. Then a glance at her pinched face reminded him that rather than worrying about who was or wasn't sweeping her off her feet, he ought, at least, get her to sit down.

'Shouldn't you try to catch up with your builder?' she reminded him, before perching on the edge of the oversized red sofa.

'Another time.' He shrugged. The least he could do after bawling her out was to make sure she wasn't in a state of shock before abandoning her. 'Let's get you sorted out first. This is my fault for forcing you off the road. I'm sorry if I was hard on you.'

'No.' She shook her head and hunched over her folded arms. 'You were right. I should have made sure my windscreen was completely clear before setting off. It's just that it's such a short drive from the garden centre to here. I often walk it, especially when I'm not carrying stock. I thought I could get away with it. But if anyone *had* been walking along the lane, I probably wouldn't have seen them. I could have killed someone.' Her face looked even more pallid against the blaze of colourful cushions behind her.

'But you didn't,' he said firmly. 'We both made mistakes, but there's no harm done. You're just shaken, that's all.' Mainly by his brutish behaviour, he thought, with another wave of self-disgust. 'Got any brandy here?'

'There might be a bottle at the back of the cabinet.' She waved in the direction of a dark oak thirties' sideboard. 'Help yourself.'

'I meant for you,' he said, smiling in spite of everything. 'But now that you've mentioned it ...'

The embers in the wood burner were turning silvery. He added another log from the basket beside it, patting Rock, who he'd had to disturb in the process, by way of an apology, then turned his attention to the cupboard.

'Babycham?' He threw her a look of disbelief over the Deco-patterned door.

'What?' She frowned. 'I like the Bambi glasses.'

'Well, I don't.' He shuddered. Glasses with faces? That was definitely a girlie touch too far. Tia Maria it was then, although the last time he'd drunk the syrupy liqueur was probably for a bet. He poured a couple of measures and accidentally took the seat next to her on the sofa, instead of the armchair as he'd intended.

'You really do like everything to be pre-loved,' he teased, handing her one of the Schooner sherry glasses just like the ones his gran used to own.

'Not everything,' she said, eyeing him warily as he sat back next to her. 'Some things have gone through too many hands even for me.'

Man, thought Gethin, scratching his head. The grapevine had been busy, even if the phones didn't work. Kiss the wrong girl in Penmorfa and you were branded as a philandering Lothario for the rest of your days. The gossips would try to carve him up whatever he said. Instead of aftershave, maybe he ought to sprinkle himself with a little salt and pepper before venturing out in future?

He thought of his last visit, the previous March; a bright spring day at the modern crematorium twelve miles away. Daffodils nodding and the few villagers who had made the funeral service shaking their heads that Gwyn Lewis's only son had buggered off immediately after the ceremony. Even though they'd been more than happy to drink themselves sober again at his expense on the money he'd left behind the bar in The Foundered Ship, for the wake. Just as well his hectic schedule had kept him so busy since then or he might have been tempted to remind one or two of them about that.

'The vintage look just suggested itself when I did my first craft fair,' Coralie continued, reclaiming his attention. 'It works well with the products and it's popular with customers, too. They like the association with old-fashioned values and the nod to more innocent times.'

Old-fashioned values were overrated in Gethin's opinion. Despite Alys's claims to the contrary, he was willing to bet that if you scratched at whatever visitor-friendly face Penmorfa tried to put on the same long-held petty resentments would still be festering underneath. Fair play to Coralie for believing she could tap into the tourist market, but he didn't want a bottle of over-priced bubble bath, and all his memories of the place were unhappy. He couldn't think of a single thing that would draw him back to the village.

'Besides, we throw too much away,' she said, furrowing her brow. 'Sometimes it's good to save what other people might have rejected or discarded.'

Was she speaking from experience? Had someone broken her heart and put *her* on the scrap-heap? He glanced at her and thought about what she'd said to him in her shop; if she'd escaped to Penmorfa, she must have left something pretty bad behind. Not that he had any intention of asking her what it was, because that would be dumb.

'Like Rock?' he suggested, before she got too serious.

'I suppose so,' she agreed, nodding.

'And butt-ugly vans and Bambi glasses.'

'Hey!' She shot him a look. 'You were doing really well for a while there.'

He was pleased to see some colour returning to her cheeks; that had to be a good sign.

'All right,' she admitted. 'So I might have developed a bit of taste for kitsch, too. When I was a little girl, my grandparents had a glass-fronted cabinet in their front room which was filled with all kinds of treasures: blown-glass animals, dolls in national costume, souvenirs from their holidays. I longed to open it and handle the contents, but I was never allowed. Perhaps I'm making up for it now? What started as a marketing strategy is at risk of becoming a serious eBay habit.'

A small smile lifted the sad set of her mouth. Then she raised her hand to a disobedient curl that had uncoiled and was brushing her cheek. The soft swell of her breasts beneath her black angora cardigan caught him off guard and made him catch his breath. She wasn't a little girl anymore. She turned to him and he found himself meeting her questioning tawny gaze.

He was dimly aware of the hiss of the wood burner and Rock purring to himself, but they were being drowned out by the sudden thudding of his heart. Her eyes held his and the room grew still. Gethin swallowed and dropped his gaze to her mouth. A voice inside his head ordered him to back away before things started getting messy. Even the sofa creaked a warning as he shifted his weight to get comfortable. Jesus! He really had become a monster, he decided, leaning back quickly and reaching for his glass of Tia Maria. The poor woman was in shock and here he was thinking about making a move on her!

'"Less is more" can be good, too,' he advised before draining his glass. 'Possessions only make life complicated.' So did families and one house too many. And women. He stood up to leave, but she got up at the same time and he nearly walked into her. And there was her mouth again, all soft and enticing. Keep it simple, stupid, he reminded himself and wished her good night.

Pausing on her doorstep to allow the cold air to dissipate some of the heat he'd built up, he reflected that little had he known, as a small boy, that he'd have reason to be grateful to Mair for drumming the Welsh alphabet into him. When Coralie had looked at him with eyes he could have drowned in, it was only by reciting the letters very slowly in his head that stopped him confirming everything all the gossips had ever said about him.

When Coralie closed her front door behind her the next morning, she was dressed for the cold and prepared with a can of lubricant to ease the screws of the casing that housed Betty's broken headlight. She was unprepared, however, for the flat tyre that was also waiting for her. Terrific. She cast a longing look at the drawn curtains of the house next door, before quickly dismissing the thought.

Gethin Lewis probably wouldn't appreciate a summons at this hour. Besides, she could tell from the way he'd shot off at the earliest opportunity that he wasn't the kind of guy who'd welcomed having to come to her rescue. He struck her as someone who was far too self-contained to think about help at all, either giving or receiving it. She, on the other hand, was compelled to rescue stray cats, glasses with faces, forgotten recipes, and any amount of unwanted and discarded flotsam and jetsam because she needed to. Because, after everything that had happened, she liked to feel that she was still capable of saving something.

Opening the back of the van, she dug out tools and some old carpet to kneel on whilst she found a jacking point for the wheel. A stiff wheel nut almost had her weeping with frustration before she composed herself, flexed her aching fingers and freed it. Leaning panting against the wheel arch, she hoped fleetingly that Gethin Lewis would look out of his window and take pity on her. After an hour, she had finally changed a tyre, a headlight bulb and a set of clothes and was sitting in the driver's seat waiting for everything to warm up when Gethin came down his front path and waved to her.

'Need a hand with that front bulb?' he asked, when she opened the window.

'Yes,' said Coralie, inwardly sighing at what the last hour would have done to his expensive jeans. 'Tell me if it's working, will you, please?'

'But –'

'Humour me,' she insisted.

His eyebrows rose as she winked both lights at him.

'And slow down in these lanes, if you're taking your new toy out,' she advised before reversing out, 'you're not in New York now.'

The smile on her face died when the post van flagged her down at the other end of the lane. Along with the junk mail was an envelope which she knew contained more unwelcome post. Another month, another visiting order, but familiarity didn't make the routine any easier. Coralie checked the mirrors and drove away carefully. However difficult it was for her, it was so much worse for him. Ned needed her.

Hurrying past the Summerhouse Café on her way to her

shop unit a few minutes later, Coralie stopped short at the sight of Kitty inside and went in to see what she was up to.

'I was thinking about how to cheer this place up for the Valentine's *Twmpath*,' Kitty said, taking a tentative stab at an enormous cobweb with a broom. 'It's lost something since Marika and Jerzy left. Jerzy mainly,' she added with a grin.

'Well, yes he *was* a good reason to drop in at the café,' Coralie had to agree, fondly remembering Jerzy, with his soulful dark eyes, floppy hair and ready smile. She pulled her Fair Isle jumper down over the waistband of her wide-leg forties' trousers and considered the matter. 'But I'm guessing for this place to keep itself it needs more than good-looking staff. How about using it for informal wedding receptions? The setting would be great for photos.'

'It would have to be a small one,' Kitty said, undoing a packet of Love Hearts. 'There's the fire certificate to consider; we're likely to be close to the maximum number for the *twmpath*.' She sighed and held out the sweets.

'"Marry Me",' laughed Coralie. 'No offence, Kitty, but you're not my type.'

'So who is?' Kitty said, slyly. 'Who are you hiding from us then? Who do you go sneaking off to meet? Anyone special?'

Guessing that she'd been the subject of some speculation, Coralie pulled a face and crunched on her Love Heart. Alys had once done some fishing on the subject of lost loves. If only it was that simple. On balance it was better to let everyone assume that she was broken-hearted than having to explain about the broken lives. 'I wish,' she said at last. 'I just about keep up with my family. My previous job took me all over the country. I used to help other companies run their businesses more efficiently. I was never in one place long enough to meet anyone and now I'm too busy.'

Kitty narrowed her eyes at her; they both knew it was all

a bit glib and rehearsed. '"Will you?"' she mused, reading out the motto on the next Love Heart.

Looks as if she already had, thought Coralie, watching the way her hand fluttered lightly over her stomach.

Adam sidled in, rubbing his hands. 'Getting excited about the *twmpath* then, girls?'

Wearing a perma-tan and a red twill Superdry lumberjack shirt over scruffy jeans, his bleached-blond hair casually tousled, he clearly fancied himself as a right little Jack-the-Lad. She glanced at Kitty to see if she was sneering and was taken aback by her wistful expression.

'What is a *twmpath*, anyway?' she asked, still looking at Kitty and wondering what was going on.

'It's Welsh for hump,' said Adam evilly. 'As in hillock,' he added as Coralie blinked at him in alarm. 'It's a reference to where the musicians sat when they were playing for dancers on the village green. Now it's just the term for a Welsh barn dance.'

'It's just the kind of thing that gives Wales a bad name,' said Kitty, visibly pulling herself together and glaring at Adam to make it plain that included him, too.

'So you won't be going then?' Adam asked, coolly.

Coralie watched as Kitty held his gaze then straightened her top before turning away. 'Only in so far as that I'm helping Mam,' she said, her bangles tinkling as she picked up her broom again.

'You mean you're getting paid by your parents to do bugger all as usual?' he taunted.

Kitty swiped at the floor and when she looked up again her face was flushed with annoyance. 'Well, I certainly won't be going for the dancing, especially not with you clumping on everyone's toes in your gardening boots.'

'You know, I liked you better before you went away,'

53

Adam said softly, going up behind her, 'when we could still have a laugh and a joke.'

'You can't be a clown all your life,' Kitty muttered. 'Some of us have moved on.'

Coralie heard Adam swear under his breath and felt a bit sorry for him. His assessment didn't seem too wide of the mark. Kitty had moved to Cardiff in September, a few months after Coralie arrived in Penmorfa. Her experience in the city had apparently made her feel that in terms of sophistication, she had left Adam behind. Getting herself pregnant there had probably made her a bit prickly, too.

'Now Coralie,' Adam went on, turning his back on Kitty, 'isn't the kind of girl to look down her nose at us like that. She's got some manners.'

'Oh no, you leave me out of this,' said Coralie, backing towards the door. 'Three in this row would make it crowded.'

'Who's rowing?' said Adam. 'You're not too proud to be seen with me, are you, Coralie? You'll dance with me, won't you?'

Coralie waited for Kitty to rescue her; she'd happily agreed to donate a basketful of her products for the raffle, but was less enthusiastic about putting herself on show, too.

'You should go.' Kitty shrugged, pushing her long dark hair away from her face and lifting her chin. 'You won't have to worry about getting stuck with Adam all evening. Everyone gets to dance with everyone else. Plenty of variety, just what Adam likes. It's another of those quaint Welsh customs everyone has to try once.'

'A bit like me.' Adam grinned.

'You'll be single forever at this rate,' Kitty told her, making Coralie feel she was seventeen years older rather than seven. 'You can't keep shutting yourself away. We've seen enough incomers who want to escape to the country and then don't like the reality. Besides, you know how pleased Mam would be to see you there. She needs a bit of cheering up.'

Coralie gave a shrug of resignation. The last thing she wanted was for the people who had accepted her into their community thinking she was too proud to join in. As for Alys? She could think of many reasons for a certain amount of tension in the Bowen home, one of which was right in front of her. Or rather, right in front of Kitty. Going to the *twmpath* wasn't going to ease that particular difficulty.

Chapter Six

In the garden centre, a few days later when the bitter weather had given way to a milder spell, Alys moved over to water another display and brushed some soil from a label. Their plant of the month was Hebe, chosen for its range of varieties and because it was such an accommodating shrub happy to grow in a patio pot or in open borders. She particularly liked the stunning pink foliage of 'Heartbreaker' although the name was a painful reminder that, like frost under hedges, some cold spots took longer to thaw.

'Alys?'

A tentative hand touched her shoulder, sending a jet of water from the hosepipe in her hand arcing over the raised bed. A small stream, bubbling down the concrete path, revealed how long she'd been standing there.

'You were in another world,' said Gethin, scrutinising her. 'Are you all right?'

'Gethin!' she said, putting her private sadness away and pasting on a smile as she went to turn the tap off, 'any luck with finding a builder yet?'

He shook his head. 'They must all be millionaires round here, no one seems to want to quote.'

Alys wondered if there was more to it than that. Penmorfa hadn't exactly rushed to kill the fatted calf for this prodigal son, although his reappearance in the village had certainly attracted attention. With those looks he was impossible to miss. She watched as he put his hands in the pockets of his old leather jacket and shifted his glance to where the spangled frosty fields tumbled down to the cliffs and ivory foam fringed the turquoise waves.

'There's no rush with the holiday cottage, you know that,' she said. 'You can stay for as long as you need.'

He shook his head. 'If I don't get back to New York for my next exhibition soon my reputation will be in shreds.'

Alys opened her mouth and he grinned.

'Yeah, I know – home from home.'

She reached out and touched his arm. 'It's not really like that, Gethin. Believe me. Most people are very proud of what you've achieved and anyone else isn't worth bothering about. Look at how you've made a name for yourself in the big wide world. Next thing you know everyone'll be clamouring for a permanent exhibition here to celebrate your achievements.'

'Achievements!' he said, shaking his head. 'I don't think so, Alys. As far as Penmorfa's concerned, people are still waiting for me to get my come-uppance for daring to believe there *was* a bigger world for me than the family farm.'

'Life moves on, even in Penmorfa, Gethin. Attitudes change.'

He laughed as he reached past her to pull up a weed that was interloping in one of the pots.

'No, really,' said Alys. 'There are all kinds of initiatives springing up in the village: Neighbourhood Watch—'

'That's not new,' said Gethin.

Alys pressed on. 'Keep Penmorfa Tidy, Welsh classes, the Quilting Group—'

'Stitch and bitch,' muttered Gethin, shaking his head.

Alys glared at him. 'And following the success of last year's Valentine's *Twmpath*, there's even a demand for dance classes.'

Gethin grimaced. 'Nice try, Alys, but you're not tempting me to move back.'

She flicked a toe at the hosepipe curled up at her feet, in

frustration, dodging a tongue of water as it spurted out at her. She couldn't let Gethin leave without at least trying to get him on board.

The Church's surprising decision to hand the church hall over to a management committee for use as a community resource was a poisoned chalice, even the Vicar agreed. On first sight, it was great news that the everyday use of the hall was in the hands of the people who mattered, the people of Penmorfa. Looked at closer, though, and there were onerous duties, not just for financial responsibilities, but requirements to get the building up to scratch, and then to keep it in an acceptable state of repair.

'I'm not asking you to move back, Gethin, but I do need your help.'

His eyes narrowed. 'With what?'

'Don't look like that.' She laughed. 'It's just a small favour. At the moment, we don't even have a suitable building for all these community activities to take place, but there are a number of grants we can apply for if we renovate the church hall. In the meantime, we're hoping to secure a short-term loan of say, about thirty thousand pounds.'

'A bridging loan? Won't that be too expensive?'

'Not if we get it from ACORN, a charity offering financial support to rural communities. And it would enable us to kick-start the rebuilding work until the grants come through. We're looking at total costs in the region of about one hundred and fifty thousand, but we'll need some willing volunteers and a lot of fund-raising events to pay for it. We're making a start with this year's Valentine's dance and all I need you to do is to come along and draw the raffle.'

She saw the shutters come down and his lips start to form the refusal. She took a deep breath. 'Please. We've a huge task ahead of us for a small village and right now we can't even agree on the membership of the Hall Management Committee.'

'Let me guess who's causing all the problems.'

'Well, Mair's made it plain that she expects to take the Chair, whereas other people have hinted they'd like to see someone with, shall we say, a more forward-looking approach.'

'Someone like you, you mean?'

Alys nodded. 'Obviously, if you have to return to the States before the raffle, we'll work round it. I'm sure Delyth will be only too happy for Hefin to step in, but it's not much to ask and a community hall on the doorstep would serve such an important role in reducing isolation. Think of what it would mean to those vulnerable, frail and elderly people who would otherwise be stuck in their homes.'

People like his mother, she didn't need to spell out. Gethin had moved away but had yet to make his name when Katrin became ill. Unkind voices sometimes linked the two events, even though Gethin had visited as often as his father would allow. Poor Katrin, overruled by her husband even during her final illness; she'd been so grateful for the respite of the occasional coffee morning, despite the painful chill of the draughty church hall which was so hard for her gaunt frame to bear.

'It's a win-win, isn't it?' she continued softly. 'You can prove to the doubters that you're not such a bad guy after all, and the publicity will help draw attention to our cause.'

She watched as he gave a wry smile and held up his hands in resignation. 'Yeah, all right, Alys, next thing you'll be telling me I can walk on water, too. I'll draw the raffle for you.'

'Good.' She nodded. 'And I'll get Huw to chase up the builders for you. He ought to be able to find someone who wants to do the job.'

Her reassuring smile faded as Gethin gave a short laugh before thanking her and walking away. Yes, Huw ought to be able to help, but the question was, would he? She touched her hand to the deep pink leaves of 'Heartbreaker'. These days she was no longer sure.

Another advantage of moving to Penmorfa, thought Coralie, as she sat watching the sea after work, was that she'd saved a fortune on gym membership. The beach was a short walk away, a steep descent past the ever-changing hedgerows of the country lanes on the way down, and a challenging push uphill all the way back. If she'd ever toyed with the idea of getting a bike, the sight of even the fittest cyclists having to dismount had quickly put her off.

As for running? There were two very good reasons why she'd never been much of a runner and they were sitting right in front of her; until someone invented the sports bra that would control the bounce, fast walking was a far more comfortable activity. Her waist and hips, though, were noticeably slimmer than in her consultancy days when the sober black suits had been good for hiding the inches that had crept on during the long working weeks and too much snacking on the run.

Noticing feathery grey clouds gathering and staunching the red seep of the setting sun, Coralie lowered herself stiffly off the rock and set off across the beach for home and warmth. Reaching the top of the stone steps, she saw a figure, barely more than a silhouette in the fading light, waiting by the old lime kiln. Walking briskly to the footpath, she was startled as something she quickly recognised as a wire-haired Jack Russell shot out in front of her and gave a bad-tempered growl.

'Edith, you monster,' she muttered knowing better than

to risk a finger or two petting the grumpy, pompous little dog.

'Edith!' shouted Huw. 'Come back this minute! Sorry, *bach*, I didn't see you down there. I was just watching one of the dolphins. See there!'

A black coil rose up and disappeared again under the slatey sea and they turned to each other in childlike satisfaction.

'I've been watching them since I was a little boy,' Huw said, grinning. 'And I still feel that same sense of wonder every time I'm privileged enough to see one. '

'Me, too,' agreed Coralie. 'The day I don't, I'll know it'll be time to move on.'

Huw glanced at her. 'You're not thinking of leaving us just yet, are you, lovely?'

'Oh no,' she said, crossing her fingers in her pocket and hoping it was true, 'I'm very happy here. It feels like home.'

'Pity more young people don't think that round here,' he said sadly. 'But what can we offer them? The youngsters don't have anywhere to meet up or to build a sense of belonging and when they grow up they can't find jobs or houses so they have to move away. Take us, we've got young Kitty home at the moment. She'll want to make her own way in the world, but she's got an uphill struggle from what I can see.'

How much could Huw see? Was he really as unobservant as Alys seemed to think? Coralie wondered. They both turned at the sound of footsteps and Coralie sighed inwardly at choosing rush hour in Penmorfa Cove for her quiet break.

'And here's another one who had to leave the place where he grew up to make his way in the world,' he told her, sounding not altogether pleased about it. He turned to the younger man whilst Edith yapped round his feet. 'So, Gethin, you don't get sights like this in the Big Apple, do you?'

'No, not quite the same,' Gethin agreed, his gaze travelling lazily over Coralie. Probably making sure he wasn't about to come to any harm, she thought, still feeling a bit embarrassed at how close she'd already come, on two occasions now, to mutilating the man who'd created *Last Samba before Sunset*. Although, from what she'd read, it looked as if one or two art critics might be cheering if she'd managed to prevent him picking up a brush.

'How's it going up at Gwyn's cottage?' Huw asked gruffly. 'I understand you're looking for a builder. There's not that much needs doing to it, surely? Or you'd have known about it sooner, wouldn't you?'

There was the briefest of pauses before Gethin replied. 'I can see how someone might be fooled by the outside of the cottage,' he said slowly. 'But the real damage occurred after I'd moved my father out, during that cold snap when he started to go really downhill. It's pretty much uninhabitable at the moment.'

'*Duw, duw!*' said Huw.

'Good God, indeed. It doesn't quite capture it, but it's close enough,' Gethin agreed. 'It's a waste to have the place standing empty like that when it could be a great family home.'

'Yes, that's what this place needs,' Huw said, sounding much more cheerful. 'Young couples, children. A bit of life in the community. You'll need someone reliable to do the work. I'll put the word out. See who we can find.'

'I'd appreciate it,' said Gethin, his stomach rumbling loudly.

'No, not you, Edith,' Huw went on, dragging her off Gethin's jeans. 'We know there's plenty of life in you!'

Gethin was looking quite frisky too, Coralie couldn't help notice.

'Well,' said Huw, 'Alys and I were planning a meal at The Cabin up at Abersaith this evening, but Alys isn't feeling too good.'

'Oh that's a shame,' said Coralie, genuinely concerned, but scenting an opportunity to escape. 'It must have been sudden. She seemed fine when I spoke to her earlier. Would a visitor cheer her up?'

'I think she's got a bit of women's trouble,' Huw said, neatly halting further lines of enquiry. 'Anyway, the hotel restaurant – wonderful food they do there now, Gethin. You wouldn't recognise the place.'

Even in the half-light Coralie could see he wasn't convinced, but then he was used to New York and schlepping down to Buddakan or a trendy bistro in Manhattan's meatpacking district or some other hip and happening joint, she thought, running out of *Sex and the City* hotspots. Welsh cuisine probably wasn't sexy enough for him now, but once you got over the sight of laver bread and cockles, all that iodine was supposed to do wonders for your love life. On the other hand, Gethin Lewis didn't look like a man who needed any chemical crutch to boost his libido.

'It would be a terrible shame to waste the table,' Huw went on slyly. 'Why don't you two take it? You haven't been there, have you, Coralie?'

Coralie knew she could lie, but she was out of practice and Huw had caught her off guard. Anyway, Gethin wouldn't want to go so she didn't have to worry.

'Excellent idea, Huw,' said Gethin, making her blink. 'We'll do that.'

'Eight o'clock suit you?' said Huw. 'I mean, it's eight o'clock we booked for.'

What else could she do? 'Eight o'clock,' she repeated, neatly trapped.

'Right you are then,' said Huw. 'Enjoy! Edith!'

He strode off into the gloom with Edith scampering along beside him. Coralie made sure he was out of earshot before she turned to Gethin, who stopped her with a smile before she could speak.

'Do you get the impression Huw's desperate to make sure there's a family living next door to him?' He grinned. 'Seems as if he's not averse to trying anything to stop me selling the land for development or something like a caravan site. Even a spot of matchmaking.'

Coralie was glad that, pulled up, the collar of her tweed jacket hid at least part of her face. 'Oh dear,' she said, squirming. 'He's not very subtle, is he? We'll just have to make up some excuse, won't we?'

'No.' Gethin rubbed his jaw. 'Think of Huw's feelings. He genuinely believes he's doing everyone a favour. He'll be racing back to the farmhouse now, drumming his fingers whilst someone at The Cabin trots off to find an appointments book they never need, because, hey, when was the last time there was a rush for tables at any restaurant round here? Think of how foolish he'll feel if he thinks we've seen through him.'

Coralie stared at him with new respect. Some of the stories circulating in Penmorfa suggested that Gethin Lewis's sole concerns were for himself. She silently wondered if she'd fallen into the trap of believing the gossips.

'You're right.' She nodded. 'I think poor Huw feels a bit like a spare part during the winter, anyway. He's been a bit grumpy since Potato Day.'

She heard Gethin choke back a laugh.

'He set up an all-day workshop on all things potato after reading up about successful winter events at other nurseries,' she went on, unable to hide her own amusement.

'It was a terrible failure. Hardly anyone turned up apart from our poet, Wilfie, who wrote a Potat-Ode to celebrate the occasion.'

'Only in Penmorfa,' said Gethin who was shaking his head at the thought of it. Even in the fading light, she could see the big smile on his face when he stopped and stared at her. 'I'm grateful to you, Coralie, thanks for saying you'll come to dinner with me.'

Coralie smiled down at her boots and started to think that, possibly, she could get through an evening with Gethin Lewis without too much trouble after all. She could even feel the faint stirrings of her appetite returning. Then he ruined it by speaking again.

'Just as well you reminded me how prickly Huw can be. I've got to keep on the right side of him because he's my last hope of getting a builder. And the sooner I get a builder, the sooner I can decide what to do about the cottage. Maybe then I'll finally be able to put Penmorfa behind me.'

Chapter Seven

'Why not keep the cottage as a holiday home?' Coralie asked once the waiter had taken their order. Far from being as humble as its name suggested, The Cabin was a rather splendid pastel-coloured Georgian building up at Abersaith. Once a run-down bed and breakfast, new life had been breathed into it by its current owners: a woman who had been a runner-up on a TV cookery programme and her husband, a former professional rugby player.

The revamped hotel, described on its website as cool, chic and classy, was another sign of a rising tide of gentrification creeping across the once-forlorn town. To Coralie's surprise they were far from being the only diners; maybe Huw was right to anticipate a stampede of food tourists?

'Holiday? I don't have time for holidays,' Gethin said, topping up her glass. Coralie reminded herself that just because she was feeling nervous didn't mean necking a strong Shiraz in double-quick time was a good idea. She had offered to drive, not least because it would have given her some control over the evening, but Gethin had raised an eyebrow and told her he liked a more comfortable ride. She assumed it was a reference to her van rather than some frank over-sharing.

'I've got my hands full at the moment trying to be in two countries at once. I can't see it ever being any kind of home for me,' he said, the look in his deep blue eyes growing wintry. 'With all the trouble the old place is causing, it might have been easier if I'd just let it fall down.'

Coralie thought about it. Maybe all his memories and sentiment were invested elsewhere? 'Alys told me their farmhouse used to belong to your family.'

He shrugged and she felt a pang of recognition and involuntarily leaned a little closer; that show of indifference hid a few raw spots.

'That's right,' he said. 'My parents ran it as a dairy farm, but milking a hundred grumpy, smelly, enormous animals all determined to kick you to kingdom come was never my idea of fun. Good luck to Alys and Huw, they're welcome to it.'

'So you're really going to cut every tie with the place where you grew up?' Coralie twisted a corner of her neatly pressed napkin. Was it possible for anyone to walk away from their past? Hadn't she tried to do just that? But, for every step she took forward, someone was always ready to remind her of what she'd left behind.

'Look at everything you've sacrificed,' her mother regularly lamented. 'That salary!'

So where once she justified spending far too much on clothes for work on the pretext they were investment pieces, she now scoured eBay and charity shops for bargains. Hardly a sacrifice.

'... Your old friends.' Another of her mother's favourite woes, forgetting that a day spent pulling a boardroom of directors back from a lemming-like surge towards organisational destruction hadn't always left her feeling very sociable.

'... Status.'

Coralie closed her eyes; she'd never felt comfortable with that slightly deferential attitude on the first day of work at a failing company.

'You know you could go back to your old job at the drop of a hat.'

When she came to her senses and gave up playing at a new career being the subtext here. Her parents still hoped she would go back to 'normal', as if stress, burnout and dreading going to work was a good thing. But her moral compass had shifted irreversibly and her former values of what was right and what was wrong belonged to someone else.

She looked up again and found Gethin studying her face. 'It's easier to go when they don't want you to stay,' he said, quietly. 'Over here, I get slated because my paintings are popular. In New York, they respect me for it.'

Coralie hoped a sympathetic nod would do. All that studied eroticism seemed a bit overworked and obvious to her; an easy way for lazy buyers to create a certain ambience or chosen because the colours matched the decor. Personally, she much preferred rootling through junk shop boxes for old frames or discarded prints to create something original for her walls. Even so, just because Gethin Lewis's work was popular didn't mean he lacked talent or wasn't a master in his *oeuvre*.

'People can say what they like about what I do because I'm doing it on my own terms,' he continued, folding his arms and looking altogether too dark and brooding to be contained by the ordered constraints and austere lines of the modern dining room. 'No one gives a damn about who you've been or where you've come from in a big city. They're all too busy getting on with their own lives.'

There was a pause whilst the waiter arrived with their first courses. The more she thought about it, the sadder it seemed that Penmorfa was missing the chance to celebrate one of its own by allowing another country to take all the plaudits. And for all his show of indifference, surely Gethin must secretly wonder how long he would have to wait for recognition in his birthplace? Wasn't a living, successful artist at least as valid as a dead poet? There was Alys trying to drum up enthusiasm to raise funds for a community space when, it seemed to Coralie, there was a fundamental breach between the village and Gethin crying out to be healed. Perhaps the money would roll in more quickly if the villagers learned to love their most famous son? The first mouthful of grilled goat's cheese with honeyed fig was a rallying call to her jaded appetite, perking her up enough to put forward a suggestion.

'Perhaps people in Penmorfa don't feel they have a stake in your success? Maybe the perception is that it's something happening in a glitzy art world that's nothing to do with them?'

'There's nothing I can do about small-mindedness,' Gethin muttered at a spoonful of spicy seafood chowder.

'Ah, but maybe if you were minded to give something back to Penmorfa the villagers would feel more inclined to share your achievements?'

'To hell with that.' He stopped to scrutinise her. 'Like what?'

'What do you think?' she asked, sitting back. 'Something more substantial than a set of mugs with a Samba print on them, obviously. I was thinking about a painting, of course. Something to hang in the new church hall, perhaps?'

'Coralie?' he said, setting down his spoon. 'Have you even seen one of my paintings? I'm not sure that the good people of this parish would regard my work and the church hall as a good match!'

It was true, from what she'd Googled, there didn't seem to be an article on Gethin Lewis that didn't include the word 'sexy'. Although the term was liberally applied to the artist as well as his work.

'Couldn't you just paint a landscape?'

'Something that captures an authentic Welsh identity, I suppose?' His dark eyes looked thunderous then, to her relief, he laughed. 'Huh! The hard truth is that pretty ladies sell. The bleak imagery of moody skies, desolate hills and the realities of farming the land don't.'

As his eyes held hers, she saw the sparkle return to them. Her fork trembled a little under such close examination and a trickle of honeyed syrup went straight down her cleavage.

It took every shred of Gethin's self-control to make a pretence of studying his food when he would rather have leaned back and enjoyed the show, thanks to that accidental spill. Really, Coralie Casey was the kind of woman calories were made for; that dewy peaches-and-cream complexion, glossy cherry lips, the succulence of her body beneath that orange, silky dress. A cornucopia of curves, you could say, except it was probably better not to think about horns of plenty. Especially when he was having enough problems keeping his mind off fantasies about a warm finger, preferably his, dipping into that soft, inviting cleavage.

He'd been acutely aware of her from the moment the evening had started. Even when she'd turned to close her front door, he'd noticed how the light from her hall, spilling out into the lane, briefly illuminated her bright, piled-up hair, and an orange ribbon that clashed with her red coat. An alluring flame flickering in the dark, except he was old and wise enough to know not to play with fire. Of course, there was no harm in just looking.

Judging that he'd given her enough time to regain her composure, but returning his eyes to her face rather than looking for glistening traces of honey, he found her watching him thoughtfully.

'We should be doing more to celebrate what's unique about the village,' she told him. 'How can we build the community when we don't even have a functioning community hall?'

Yeah, good luck with that, Gethin thought, paying more attention to her low, slightly breathy voice, with its Home Counties accent, than what she was saying. No matter how hard she tried, that pattern of speech would always mark her as an outsider in Penmorfa. One, he was willing to bet, who'd arrived in the village with a pre-conceived idea of the countryside almost entirely informed by magazines. Funny how there was never any mention of the stink of slurry on the fields in those glossy pages, or the sound of farm machinery working long into the June nights. Nothing about the kids getting trashed on Saturday night or the ones who hanged themselves because there was no hope for the future. Some idyll.

'Coralie, I'm sorry, but you're mistaking me for someone who cares about what happens in Penmorfa. I stopped feeling any attachment to the place many years ago.'

She dropped her gaze in apparent disappointment, but the arrival of the waiter turning up to fuss around clearing away their plates forced her to smile and make suitable noises about their starters. He didn't blame her for trying; she was still in the honeymoon stage of her new life in the country. Perhaps all that enthusiasm would rub off on him, too? He was certainly in need of it; his productivity had slowed, although that wasn't necessarily a bad thing. No point in flooding the market. But he was occasionally aware of something else stilling his hand.

It wasn't that he was intimidated every time he set a blank canvas on his easel. Nor did he feel a sense of trepidation whenever he picked up a brush. The problem – one that he would have shaken his head in disbelief at back on the farm – was that everything had fallen in his lap so easily. All the hurt and hunger that had once fuelled and inspired him simply didn't exist anymore; somewhere along the line his grand passion had become nothing more than a pleasant pastime. Getting the work together for his forthcoming show had almost been a chore. What he needed was some reinvigoration, something to shake up his ideas.

'Maybe I should paint you?' he suggested and watched her head jerk up in surprise. 'How would you like to be the star of the village hall?'

'Paint Alys then,' she replied without missing a beat. 'She's the Chair of the new Hall Management Committee. And she's gorgeous.'

'And married,' he added, as his dish of Welsh Black beef arrived.

'Excuse me, but I thought we were discussing a painting, not an elopement,' she said, looking up from her fish and breaking into a smile.

'Some husbands don't appreciate another man looking at their wives that closely,' he explained. Some girlfriends weren't too thrilled about that kind of intensity either, he could have added. Whatever his girlfriends said at the beginning about giving him space to work, none of them were quite so understanding when it came to him being holed up in his studio with a beautiful woman.

'Well, how do you know I don't have a significant other?'

'Rock doesn't count,' he told her, grinning to himself when her pursed lips confirmed his guess. 'And no man in his right mind would put up with so much Doris Day,' he added, laughing at her scowl.

'Mm, I don't know what goes on in your studio and I don't want to know either,' she said, quickly. 'So you can forget about trying to gauge the size of my nose or deciding what colours to mix to match my teeth whilst we're here and concentrate on your meal.'

He shrugged and picked up his fork, but now the idea had

taken root, he couldn't stop thinking about how he might portray her. For the first time in longer than he cared to remember, he itched to pick up his brush.

Paint them and forget them had become his mantra. Not one that he ever said out loud about the paintings or the women, admittedly. The intimacy of painting the beautiful women he met was a kind of exorcism; by the time he'd noted every freckle and mole, the hollow at the base of a throat, the bone structure beneath the skin, the infatuation was over. And every time he managed not to get involved, it stopped him turning into his father, who'd treated his mother more like part of the furniture with every passing year.

In the Summerhouse Café on the morning of the *twmpath*, Kitty looked up as Coralie came in.

'Wow! It looks amazing in here!' Coralie said, sounding genuinely impressed.

Kitty was pleased with herself for creating such a transformation with such basic accessories. Perhaps she ought to play fairy godmother to Coralie too, since today she was wearing what appeared to be a pair of men's twill trousers with a striped cotton shirt and a pair of braces that strained either side of her ample chest. Whilst Coralie was beautiful enough to carry it off, it was the kind of look that women admired and men didn't get.

Her dad had insisted that Gethin was renovating his father's cottage to make it family-friendly, but her mam had said counting on Coralie persuading Gethin not to sell the place to the highest bidder was a bit much to expect from one date. For all Huw's scheming, Coralie didn't look like a woman celebrating her engagement. Neither was she wearing the dazed, satiated expression of someone who'd just enjoyed a few nights of vigorous horizontal romping.

Kitty straightened a gingham table cloth. She might have been a bit envious of Coralie if she had.

Kitty, who had now given up any hopes of being whisked off her feet by a handsome stranger – and at the rate she was putting on weight he'd have to be quite a powerful stranger – was a bit disappointed for Coralie who had clearly missed the boat. Drawing the raffle at this evening's Valentine's dance was Gethin's last duty before flying back to America. Whilst Kitty admired Coralie's entrepreneurial spirit, she couldn't help feeling that, at pushing thirty, Coralie was wasting valuable time burying herself in the country, especially if she wanted to stand any chance of meeting someone who wasn't already in a relationship.

She eyed Coralie's outfit doubtfully. Perhaps she should offer to lend her one of her denim mini-skirts for the evening? Although there probably wasn't enough stretch in any of her lacy tops.

'I thought I was meant to be giving you a hand,' said Coralie, 'but it looks as if you've done everything. Has all the cleaning been done? Do you want me to check the loos?'

Such a waste, Kitty thought regretfully, Coralie was kind too, always ready to roll up her sleeves and pitch in wherever help was required. No wonder everyone liked her. 'If you could just give me a hand with the bunting, that would be great.' She might have imagined the briefest of glances at her stomach before Coralie quietly took over any work that required use of a stepladder.

'Oh, it looks very romantic,' Coralie said when they'd finished festooning the room with cheery bunting and strings of fairy lights. She nodded at the tables now dressed in their checked tablecloths and the flowers that Kitty had arranged in old French jam jars wrapped in raffia. 'Have you done anything like this before?'

'I worked for the Leisure and Events Manager in my last job,' Kitty told her. 'Being back here makes me realise how much I miss the challenges. Pity it was only a short-term contract. I was only the admin assistant, mind, although I did get to try the sample menus before some of the dinners. It's amazing what you can pick up about organising large groups of people just by keeping your eyes open.

'It's a bit like being a nanny,' she went on. 'I was a bit intimidated by all the important business people at first and then my manager told me to imagine them as children. After that it was easy. So long as everyone was sat at the correct table with the correct menu in front of them and the vegetarians didn't get tofu too often, everyone was happy. Well, most of the time.' She grinned.

'Morning ladies,' Adam said, breezing in, his strong arms wrapped round a stack of chairs. 'I gather the Boy Wonder's going to grace us with his presence tonight. Good of him to condescend to join us.'

Kitty shook her head. 'You've lived here so long, Adam, you're even sounding like one of the gossips.'

'Whatever,' Adam said, setting down the chairs. 'He did all right for himself though, didn't he? Made a shed-load of money painting beautiful girls. Can't be a bad way of earning a living, can it? Maybe I should have a go?'

'I think it takes some talent to be as successful as Gethin Lewis,' Kitty said, setting the silver bangles on her wrists jingling as she folded her arms. 'Still, given your penchant for drifting, I suppose you could always become a professional surfer.'

'He always did have an eye for the ladies, didn't he?' Adam went on, ignoring her. 'I mean look at the girl in that *Samba* picture – she was a bit of a babe, wasn't she? I wonder where she is now?'

'Not in Penmorfa, that's for sure,' Kitty said, thinking of the life she'd left behind in Cardiff.

'Well, just watch yourself, ladies, if he offers to paint either of you. You never know what it might lead to, eh, Coralie? Coralie?'

But somewhere during the discussion, Coralie had quietly left the room.

Chapter Eight

Gethin got fed up of listening to fiddle music on the night air and reached for his leather jacket. It sounded as if some people were having fun, but it must have been some latent masochistic streak that had made him agree to join them. Why else had he allowed Alys to cajole him into drawing the winner of the Valentine's raffle?

Alys was one of the few villagers he had time for, he thought, standing in the crowded Summerhouse Café, as she gave him a wave and made her way through the throng towards him. Not least because she was one of the handful of people who'd bothered to make the long journey to the crematorium for his father's service.

Talking to her earlier, when he'd called in to discuss timings for the evening, in the kitchen of the farmhouse where he'd grown up, he'd felt unexpectedly moved by how different the atmosphere in the old place was now. As soon as he walked in he'd felt a homely warmth that just hadn't been there when he was a child. All the little details his mother never had time to add, like a pretty collection of blue-and-white china, the jug of early daffodils on the windowsill, and handmade gingham curtains, transformed the room into the beating heart of the home. Some of his old anger returned too, when he saw a new red Aga and thought about his mother struggling with the temperamental old range that had once coughed in the alcove. All his success had come too late to save her.

He kissed Alys's cheek and felt the tension fizzling from her, as if she were guarding her secret self with an invisible electric wire.

'Anything wrong?' he asked.

'Red tape again!' Alys shook her head. 'The Gambling Act this time – we can only sell tickets here at the event, so we don't fall foul of it. I'm beginning to wonder if we'll make *any* money for the church hall.'

'Well, never mind, I've brought this, if it helps,' he said. He'd been surprised to find the unsigned pastel sketch of the farmhouse, one of many he'd painted whilst still living at home, framed and hanging in his father's cottage. A cheap box of twenty-four crayons, a can of fixative and a sketchbook had enabled him to work fast, making the most of every valuable break from farm work, teaching him about colour and composition. This little sketch probably wasn't quite what Coralie had hoped for, but it ought to help shift a few more raffle tickets.

'Oh,' Alys said, looking both touched and saddened, 'that's beautiful. Are you sure you want to part with it?'

'I doubt very much that my father kept it for sentimental reasons so I have no reason to, either.'

Alys gave a small frown, but maybe it was because she had caught sight of her daughter. Kitty, pretty as a picture in a sweet little frock that did something low and tight around her breasts, was doing a pretty good job of selling tickets. The cocky guy from the garden centre was certainly interested in something; he'd draped his arm round her shoulder and was twisting a lock of her hair round his finger. In contrast to Alys, who was thinner these days than he remembered, Kitty was positively blooming. In Manhattan she'd be regarded as outsize, but she was proof that you didn't have to be rake-thin to be beautiful.

'Well, if you're quite sure, then thank you. I'll put it on the table with the other donations but I'm going to make it our star prize,' said Alys. 'Now, why don't you go and help yourself to a drink?'

Gethin decided that was a very good idea; a couple of beers would also stop him wondering where his next-door neighbour was. So would a distance of three thousand miles; that would certainly help to put her out of his mind. Then he spotted her. Her sherry-coloured curls swinging in a fifties-style ponytail secured with an orange silk bow that matched the peaches printed on her crazy yellow cocktail frock. Despite his best intentions to keep away, it cheered him up just to look at her.

Kitty, leaving her admirer casting longing looks at her, swept over with her raffle tickets to Coralie, who had her arms full with a hamper of Sweet Cleans products. The sight of the two women provoked a palpable surge in male hormones all around him, but he was quicker off the mark.

'Here, let me,' he told Coralie, taking the hamper. 'And Kitty, I'm coming back for some raffle tickets.'

He carried it to the prize table where Alys received it gratefully and Coralie gave him a 'your work is done now' look. But he was just beginning to enjoy himself.

'If anyone asks you to dance, you're taken.' He laughed. 'I'm coming back the minute I've bought my raffle tickets.'

'Think of the danger,' she reminded him, when he returned. 'I have no co-ordination and your feet will be sorry. You'd be a lot safer dancing with someone who knows the steps. Ffion's looking for a partner.' She pointed to a young woman, with hair bleached and straightened to within an inch of its life, standing awkwardly by the bar.

'Maybe,' he said, stepping close enough to catch the floral scent of Coralie's distinctive perfume. 'But I remember her when she used to follow me along the beach with a nappy full of wet sand hanging round her knees and now she's heading this way!'

'I think she's outgrown the nappy,' said Coralie still hell-bent on getting away from him.

Was he losing his touch? He took both of her hands in his and looked deep into her eyes. 'Yes, but has she forgiven me for dating her sister? You're the only one who can help me, Coralie, everyone else's memories are way too long and I don't know who's going to accuse me of what next!'

She sucked in her bottom lip as if trying to frame a tactful refusal, so he could have cheered when the caller shouted out for everyone to take their partner for the next dance. 'Don't worry, I'll take care of you,' he said close to her ear, grinning as she threw him a suspicious look. 'And, no, I don't say that to all the girls.' Well, only the pretty ones.

Maybe she'd been a bit quick to congratulate herself for staying out of trouble, thought Coralie. For all his cheeky comments, Adam hadn't been so hard to handle. After a couple of dances which revealed them to be entirely out of step with each other, she'd excused herself in order to collect her contribution to the raffle prizes and watched him head towards an over-excited cluster of teenage girls like a little boy in a sweet shop. Gethin Lewis, as her body urgently reminded her, seeing the challenge in his animated blue eyes, was all man.

Having trodden all over Adam's toes, she also found herself a bit reluctant to let Gethin partner her for another reason. The woman in a backless wisp of a red dress, all long legs and flicky dark hair dancing towards her partner in his most famous painting, was depicted with the passion and tenderness of a lover's eye. What might he read into her own limited dancing skills measured against that?

She looked around for someone else to take her place, but Kitty, in a breathtaking about-turn, had withdrawn her claws and agreed to partner Adam. Willow, looking like a cut-price Florence Welch in a purple tie-dye maxi dress that clashed with her hair, was swaying provocatively in front of an embarrassed-looking Rhys and Alys had finally persuaded Huw to take to the floor.

'Farmers' Fancy – *Ffansi Fermwyr!*' instructed the caller and, before she could do anything about it, they were off.

Gethin took her hand and placed the other round her waist, his fingers warm and firm through the thin fabric of her dress. Bad idea, she thought, as her skin tingled and every atom in her body whispered, 'Yes!'

'You owe me this one!' he told her in his low, lilting voice, bending close to make himself heard over the music before spinning her away.

'Oh?' Concentrate, she instructed her legs, as she raised her head and met his eyes.

'That authentic Welsh landscape,' his palm scorched against hers, 'you asked me to donate for the good of the village?'

'Yes?' Just one dance, her brain was ordering, despite every cell in her being getting interested and calling out for more.

'It's over there on the prize table,' he murmured as he circled round her. 'You might win it, if your number comes up.'

They turned to face one another before linking hands again.

'So,' he said, watching her face closely. 'Do you feel lucky?'

The mischievous look in his eyes sent a jolt through her that was so shocking she missed a step and was forced to think about what her feet were doing until she'd recovered herself. He'd been standing beside her when she'd bought her raffle tickets; but surely he couldn't fix the result?

'Right hand turn!' the caller shouted, compelling her to focus on what her body was doing rather than his beside her, moving in beautiful synchronicity.

'Left hand turn!'

Kitty was smiling up at Adam, looking genuinely relaxed for once.

'Both hands turn!'

Alys and Huw were dancing self-consciously, like two people who'd forgotten the steps they'd once known so well.

'And do-si-dos!'

Poor Rhys was trapped.

'And swing!'

Coralie's head was spinning even before the rest of her joined in. Gethin Lewis had listened to her. Maybe the little unsigned picture wasn't exactly what she had in mind to engage the village in its famous son's success, but she'd asked him to give something back to Penmorfa and he had. And now he was hinting it could be hers if she wanted it. What did that mean? A little voice was whispering that such a small, apparently insignificant, picture would make a wonderful souvenir of Penmorfa if she was ever forced to leave, but she made herself ignore it. A sketch of the farmhouse, a significant landmark in the village, and, however humble, a Gethin Lewis original, deserved to stay where it could, she hoped, be admired and appreciated.

It occurred to her that whilst the picture might be staying, the artist was about to leave, which was probably just as well given how her feelings had changed in a few weeks. From actively resenting having someone next door, she couldn't help but check her appearance in the hall mirror if she heard movement in the adjoining property, just in case he happened to be leaving at the same time. She'd grown accustomed to her own thoughts and company, but now she came home disappointed on the days when her path hadn't crossed with Gethin's or if they hadn't swapped a few neighbourly words.

Coralie was afraid of losing her grip, and not just because of the rising temperature. She hoped Gethin was holding on tight because staying cool in the heat of that smouldering glance was quite a challenge. Her hands felt as if they'd been greased as she clung on to him. The tempo of the music gathered pace, becoming more frenzied and creating a contagious sense of wild exhilaration. Reverberating in the background, like the high note of a plucked string, was the matter of the raffle draw, as she wondered whether to be flattered or worried by what Gethin might do. She was beginning to see just how seductive that kind of attention could be. Gethin, it struck her, as he shot her another burning glance, was quite like his art, really: decorative, sexy and probably found in lots of bedrooms.

'Now make your final promenade and prepare to take a new partner,' the caller instructed. 'Gentlemen you may kiss your girl farewell!'

Out of breath and laughing, Coralie forgot herself and leaned into Gethin, resting her hand on his chest as she lifted her face to his dark gaze. Something about them getting sweaty and breathless together fooled her brain into thinking that something far more intimate had taken place. Just as she was about to stand on tiptoes and stretch up to him, she became aware of people watching and quickly pulled away so that his lips missed her mouth and brushed her cheek instead. He raised an eyebrow to show that he knew she'd just chickened out, making her grateful for the heat in the room that hid her embarrassment.

But, along the line, another couple did seem to have forgotten that they were in a public place. The man who was supposed to be her new partner had taken the caller's final instruction to extremes. From the way Adam's mouth was locked against Kitty's he seemed to be anticipating not a temporary split but a lengthy separation. More of a French Fancy than a farmer's fancy, thought Coralie.

'Looks as if you're with me again,' said Gethin. But just as she decided that dancing with Gethin was a burden she could bear, Alys tapped him on the shoulder.

'Sorry to break in,' she said, 'but I think this would be a good time to draw the raffle.'

Coralie took it as a sign that it was also a good time for her to head home.

'Don't even think about going anywhere,' said Gethin, winking. 'We're only just getting started.'

'And now a special prize ...' Gethin glanced at the prize table. From the lower-value prizes, the bottles of wine and spirits had been picked first, the craft prizes had gone in dribs and drabs and a delighted Wilfie had won a voucher for a massage from Willow. Just his pastel sketch, which Alys had kept aside as the star prize, to go.

Scanning the room, he saw Coralie clutching a blue ticket. He smiled. Here was his chance to ensure that his painting went to someone who appreciated it. 'John Singer Sargent meets Jack Vettriano' a critic had once said of his recent work: flattering, sexed-up portraits of Manhattan's most beautiful and wealthy. Not in a good way.

'But first a few words,' he said. 'I'm sure everyone would like to join me in thanking Alys and Huw for hosting this evening and I know the funds raised tonight will be going to a very worthwhile cause.' Community hall fund, Alys had confirmed. Well, good luck with that. 'With that in mind, I would like to present this,' he held the picture aloft, 'to Alys as a gesture of thanks for all her hard work.'

Alys looked at him questioningly but there were tears in her eyes as she accepted the work, almost too choked to speak. As she reached up to kiss him, he could see Delyth and Mair exchanging sour looks.

'And to tell you about this evening's top prize.'

Mair was glaring at him, which he took as a sign that no love was lost there. Well, never mind, the feeling was entirely mutual. For as long as he could remember, Mair had done her utmost to make his life miserable. As a very small boy, he'd once sunk his teeth into her arm, retaliating in the only way he could for all the times she'd laid into him with a ruler behind his mother's back for reasons he was too young to understand. Although sticking her – or someone very like her – together with someone who looked a lot like Delyth behind the windbreak in *Samba* probably hadn't helped the situation. The look she had given him when he'd walked into the room suggested that given half a chance and a metal ruler, she'd probably like to have another go at him. Except they both knew that now he had the means to fight back.

'Many years ago, as a keen amateur artist, I won the prize of a short art course. This, as you know, gave me the opportunity to turn my hobby into a profession.' He saw Delyth curl her lip at Mair. 'That profession has taken me far away from Penmorfa, and maybe one or two of you think that I've forgotten where I come from, so tonight I'd like to say a small thank you in the best way I can.'

The room grew quiet and he could feel everyone waiting.

'I'd like to make a contribution to the renovation of a hall for the village by donating one of my works for auction, with all the proceeds going to the community hall fund.'

There were low murmurs from some quarters of the room and he paused to see if anyone was bold enough to put up a protest, but Coralie, bless her, was beaming at him and had just clapped her hands together when he resumed his speech.

'This will be a new piece, especially created for the sale. My reputation, as some of you will know, rests on a painting inspired by ...' he lingered whilst Mair gave him a furious stare, 'an image I set on the beautiful cove at Penmorfa, so it's Penmorfa I'd like to pay tribute to now by taking, as the subject of my painting, the winner of the Valentine's raffle.'

There were more murmurs as people in the room cast nervous glances at each other.

'And that winner is ...' He picked out a blue ticket and pretended to read it. 'Number eleven!'

Mair screwed up her ticket. He saw Coralie suck her peach-stained lip and felt like sucking it for her, although he'd definitely get another rulering from Mair if he did. He watched the emotions flicker across Coralie's face as she studied her ticket and seemed to be on the point of shoving it back in her bag. Then Rhys, the chair maker, looked over her shoulder at it and cheered, starting a ripple of applause that gradually got louder as everyone showed their approval. As the noise started to die down, smiling faces started to turn to Coralie expectantly, except for the corner of the room where Kitty and the guy from the garden centre – Adam? – were having a discussion that was becoming increasingly heated.

'So,' roared the guy, standing up and sending his chair flying, 'when did you think *would* be the right time to tell me what you've been up to!'

Alys quickly signalled for the music to start again, grabbing her husband to lead the next dance only, as Huw gave an exaggerated shake of his hips as he got up to join her, a jolt of pain creased his face and then he was clutching his back in agony. With all eyes on Huw – insisting that he didn't need medical help – and Alys enlisting the help of a couple of burly bystanders to get him over to the farmhouse, he just caught sight of Coralie sidling towards the coat lobby and pushed through the crowd after her.

Chapter Nine

'Not so fast,' said a familiar voice behind her, just as Coralie thought she was safely outside. 'I'm coming with you.'

She looked up at the bright constellations and congratulated herself for not being the type to be easily dazzled. 'No,' she said. 'You stay here and find someone else to paint.'

He gave a short laugh and stayed by her side anyway. 'Have you any idea how much women pay me to immortalise them on canvas?'

'I pay men for things that are useful to me. Like fixing my septic tank or re-pointing my chimney,' she insisted. 'Look, I don't know what kind of game you're playing, but whatever issues you've got with this village, it's not fair to involve me.' She started to walk down the lane, picking her way carefully because it was slippery and her shoes didn't feel as clever as when she had first put them on. He muttered something under his breath, then took hold of her arm, steering her away from a frozen pothole.

'You asked me to be a little more philanthropic and I've obliged,' he pointed out, still keeping her close. 'I thought you'd be pleased to help with the fund-raising effort.'

She shook her head, trying to make sense of the swirling, contradictory thoughts that were so confusing. Part of her was beguiled by how far Penmorfa's very own bad boy was prepared to put himself out for her, but the suspicious part questioned his motives. 'You cheated!' she accused, still relying on his support to stop her sliding on the thin ice. 'I don't know how or why you did it, but that prize belongs to the person who won it!'

Even in the dark, she knew he was smiling. 'I just know what the paying public wants, that's all. A portrait of Mair or Delyth won't get you more than a tin shack for the village. Don't worry about it,' he said, patting her arm. 'It's just a raffle prize.'

But it wasn't just any old raffle prize, was it? Only one of Gethin Lewis's models had ever managed to remain anonymous. Despite intense speculation, no one had discovered the identity of the girl in *Last Samba*, but she couldn't afford to take that risk. Being in the spotlight was something she'd much rather avoid.

'You know,' he went on, 'I don't usually have this trouble persuading someone to sit for me.'

She could believe it. That voice would make a lot of women do far more than just sit for him. A sudden shiver ran through her body at the thought.

'You're not scared of letting me paint your portrait, are you?' he said, softly.

'I'm cold,' she said, which was a lot better than admitting she was shivering because she was out in the dark with the tall, dark, dangerous wolf who could gobble her up at any moment.

He unlinked his arm from hers and wrapped it firmly round her waist instead. 'Better? I believe in making my potential models comfortable,' he explained when she shot a surprised look at him. 'I'm considerate, unlike some artists who bend their sitters into difficult positions and expect them to stay there for hours. My demands are entirely reasonable.'

For a moment, her libido got interested in his demands. What would it be like to listen to the soft caress of his voice as he told her how he wanted her? To have those midnight-blue eyes roam over every inch of her body? To be passive, helpless, whilst he did whatever he pleased? Just then a barn owl skimmed past them towards the silver fields, looking for small prey to seize. Coralie was reminded that if she didn't take care, she'd be in the grip of something difficult to escape, too.

'I promise you'll be in good hands. I like to spend time with my model and get to know her, so I present a true picture.'

Just what she was afraid of. To become, once again, the object of pity, or curiosity, or even worse, blame – why risk putting herself through all that again? It was a good thing they were nearly back at the cottages where the window in her front door was casting a welcome square of light across the lane.

'And how long does it take you to get to know your model?' she asked, thinking, with some regret, of all the things she wasn't going to let him do.

'Six sittings; six sessions over six days.'

Six, six, six. The devil's number. Which was only to be expected, since he was doing his best to tempt her. Go away, she told him silently. Was this how it would be for the rest of her life? Being crippled by guilt? Living in an emotional void, a bystander whilst Kitty had her baby, Alys and Huw celebrated their lives together and green shoots marked the passing seasons in the garden centre.

'It's not too late to go back to the dance and tell Alys there's been a mistake,' she said. They were outside her front door now and the light was just glancing off his cheekbones and the curve of his lips as he caressed her with the lovely lilt of his voice, which still betrayed his Welsh roots however hard he'd tried to escape them. It crossed her mind that she must have been a teenager the last time she'd stood on a doorstep whilst someone tried to tell her about all the good things he could do for her if only she would let him.

'Finding the right winner doesn't mean you'll necessarily end up with Delyth or Mair. Find someone who'll be pleased with the prize. Even in Penmorfa there are beautiful women who'll fall over themselves to lie on your couch. What's the problem?'

He laughed quietly and stretched one arm across the doorway before bending his head to hers. 'The problem,' he said, softly, 'is that I don't want any of those other women. I want you.'

The roar of the sea from the other side of the headland made her feel reckless. No one was guaranteed a happy ever after, but what was wrong with a happy for now? Tomorrow she'd be standing there alone, watching the jet stream of every plane that disappeared over the wide blue bay. Thinking about it crossing the ocean to where the long beaches and coves were sliced open by another waterway. Dipping down towards a city of glass towers shimmering into the air, buildings humming with thousands of people sleeping, eating, making love, laughing. And one of them would be Gethin Lewis, getting on with his life.

'Someone's going to find out that you deliberately called out the wrong number,' she whispered, her gaze dropping to his mouth, naked and sexy against the black shadow of incipient stubble, filling her with thoughts of what it would it would be like to taste the tang of salt spray on his lips whilst the dark waves crashed on the night beach.

'But I didn't,' he murmured, reaching into his pocket. He took out the square of folded blue paper and pressed it into her palm.

'Number eleven. Just like yours.'

Coralie exhaled slowly. There it was; temptation in the

palm of her hand. She stared down at the ticket, letting her imagination run riot for a few seconds, daring her to claim the prize that was rightfully hers.

But that would be a terrible idea,

'There's one detail you've overlooked,' she said, ducking underneath his arm and putting her key in the lock. 'You'll be leaving soon, to return to America, and I'm staying in Penmorfa. We'll never be in the same place again.'

She stepped away from him and from thoughts of what might have been, crossing the threshold to reality and her brightly lit hall. Then she turned to face him for the last time. 'Since it's clearly impossible for me to collect my prize, would it be too much to ask you to donate a different painting? Please don't let your memories of the village get in the way of doing something good for the place. It may even help you come to terms with the past?'

His soft laughter made a mockery of her stiff little speech. How uptight did that sound? And who was she to give him advice?

'Coralie,' he said, straightening up and shaking his head at her. 'You make it sound as if I've got spare paintings lying around. All my available work is tied up in the current exhibition, and I can assure you that there's no shortage of interest. You'll just have to come to my studio in New York.'

'Very funny,' she said, dryly. 'I have a business to run, in case you hadn't noticed.'

'A week away won't make any difference.' He shrugged.

'Oh?' Coralie folded her arms. 'Because it's only a hobby, I suppose?'

'An interest in art,' he said, quietly, 'was not exactly something my father encouraged. I'm not belittling your work; in fact, by doing my bit for Penmorfa, I'm helping your business, too. The air fare and board are included in the prize, so if you really want to do something for the village, you'll do as I say. No portrait means no painting. Think about it.'

The next day Kitty woke up to a sky that was as blue as she felt and a crisp cold morning that was almost as brittle. The winter sunshine beamed onto the floral duvet warming the exact spot below which her baby somersaulted in its secret, watery world. At the beginning she'd almost convinced herself that nothing was happening; so what if her periods had stopped – she was busy at work, wasn't she? And if her breasts were tender, that was because her period was due, wasn't it? And with all that to worry about, well, no wonder she was off her food. Yes, it had been so easy to carry on as normal; even her body seemed to be colluding, her young, tight stomach muscles hugging the baby close. The neat bump and heavier breasts could, with careful clothing, be explained away as a bit of a weight gain.

But beneath it all the baby had bloomed from a blob with a heartbeat on an ultrasound scan, to someone who rolled and kicked inside her, making her back ache and her lungs feel cramped as it pushed for more space. And now she was scared: scared of giving birth, scared of the responsibility and scared of having to face the future on her own. Realising that her tears had soaked the pillow, Kitty levered herself up and groped around for a tissue. She gave her nose a good no-nonsense blow and went over to the window where, she noticed, the birds were having a fit of spring fever outside. The birds were right, of course; it was far too beautiful a morning to be moping around – especially when her days of freedom were numbered – so she had a quick shower and wrapped up to go down to Penmorfa Cove.

The inlet was enclosed by steep shale cliffs and accessed

by narrow stone steps which deterred most couples lugging toddlers in buggies or grannies on scooters. Kitty was aware of her extra burden and felt as if she'd aged several decades as she picked her way down. In summer, especially on the rare hot days, the fine sandy beach could be bustling with holidaymakers, although most of them didn't arrive until late morning and had cleared off again by early evening, pretty much guaranteeing you could always find some time to yourself there.

Except that this morning she wasn't alone. She watched the solitary surfer in his winter wetsuit snake along the silver barrel of a wave before spilling into a crest of foam and considered slipping away before he noticed he had company. But, as Adam righted himself, he spotted her on the shore and started wading towards her, creamy water lapping at his thighs.

'Hi, Mummy,' he said, his tone matching the icy chill from his body.

She winced, but found herself huddling a bit closer anyway, longing for a glimpse of the old, easy-going Adam. 'Look, I don't want to talk about it. All right?'

'You should have thought about that last night, before you let me kiss you,' he said, casting off his Neoprene gloves and striding towards his rucksack which was tucked into a rocky niche. 'Did you think you could fool me like everyone else?' He pulled at the collar of his wetsuit and reached round for the ripcord, tugging at it impatiently.

'You'll tear that if you're not careful,' she said, taking over so that she could watch his toned, tanned back appear as she released him. 'I just—' She took a deep breath because her throat was so tight it was difficult to get the words out. 'I just needed a bit of time to get my head round it. Once I start telling people they'll all be wanting to knit bootees, or buy little outfits, or they'll be asking me if I know what I'm having and if I've thought of any names. I'm just not ready to deal with all that. I can't believe that this,' she waved her hand at her stomach, 'is a real person waiting to happen.'

'And what about the daddy?' He turned to her at last, his green eyes glittering in a sudden shaft of sunlight. 'Is *he* ready to deal with it?'

She took a deep breath. 'I … The thing is …' She shook her head at the damp sand whilst he unpeeled himself from the wet rubber. 'We're not together.'

'That's not what I asked,' he snapped. 'He does know, doesn't he?'

Kitty folded her arms across herself. 'Yes,' she said, cringing, 'he knows, but he's not exactly the settling down type. Now can we just talk about something else?'

'Sure,' he said, draping a towel across his shoulders and rounding on her. 'Let's talk about what a busy time you've had in Cardiff. You know, there was a time last year when I thought that you and me might have something going for us. The way you followed me round the garden centre, pretending to be interested in what I was doing.'

'I was interested!' Kitty protested, turning her back as his hands moved to his trunks. 'I was weighing up my mind wondering if I should stay here and help Mam and Dad with the business or if I should strike out on my own. I needed to find out more about what happened here and if it was for me.'

'Yeah, well it's quite apparent you found the big city a touch more exciting.' He buckled up his jeans and pulled on his hoodie, before pushing his fingers through his sun-bleached hair. She followed him as he bent to pick up a pebble, throwing it viciously into the soaring spray.

'Yes I did, in fact,' she said, feeling the anger rise. 'I worked in a great office, and I learned new skills and I had a great social life. And I met a wide range of interesting and exciting people who had more to talk about than the neighbours' business and whether or not the weather was right for planting.'

'Well, you don't need to worry about the weather when you're planting indoors, do you?' he said, with a soft laugh. 'You didn't waste any time replacing me with Mr Casual Fling, did you? Was it because you were in such a hurry that you forgot all about contraception?'

Kitty spun away from him, stomping through the wet sand that made the going tough. Sheer anger took her up the first steps, even though she was finding it hard to catch her breath, but somehow she misplaced her foot and found herself falling heavily.

'Oh, fuck!' She groaned, waiting to see what was hurting most. And then she thought of something worse and braced herself for the sweating and nausea and the abdominal cramps to begin. Staring up into the wide azure sky she watched a seagull's lonely flight as it soared away from her and listened to the roar of the waves before they crashed against the cliffs. Cradling her stomach, she wondered if that was the closest she would get to holding the shadow child waiting in the wings. The baby seemed to feel her anxiety and reassured her with a lazy stretch, as if waking from sleep, little limbs pushing against her stomach. It wasn't going anywhere, the baby, she thought, with an unexpected twinge of relief, which made her laugh.

'What are you grinning at, you fuckwit?' said Adam, his face like a worried sun appearing in the sky above her.

'The baby's all right, Adam!' She reached up as he knelt down to her and wrapped her arms around his neck. 'I didn't think I cared, but I do!'

'Of course you do, you silly mare.' He smiled gently at

her, making her feel that everything might work out after all. On impulse she nuzzled in and kissed his neck only to feel him stiffen and pull away. 'Come on,' he said, sounding strained. 'Let's make sure you're in one piece and get you home.'

Maybe he did care about her? Perhaps a glimpse of what could have happened had shaken him, too? He helped her up the stone steps with more tenderness than she'd have thought possible, so she made the most of it, holding tight to him for as long as she could.

'So, are you going to tell Alys now?' he asked as he turned her hand to inspect a graze on her palm.

Looking down at his fingernails, broken by all the outdoor work he did, she got distracted by the thought of how nice it would be to see them every day, before she realised he was waiting for an answer. 'Not just yet, eh?' she murmured. 'I can't stand the thought of all the fuss.'

'Up to you.' He shrugged. 'But don't leave it too long or it'll be too late.'

The track leading towards the garden centre lay before them. 'Your surfboard,' she reminded him. 'Go on, I'll be fine now.'

Adam stopped and took hold of her hands again. That had to be a good sign. 'You need a friend,' he said, with a small smile that revealed his chipped front tooth and made her feel all warm inside. 'I'm here for you, if you need me.'

Kitty nodded and tried not to cry. Friend. That would have to do.

Chapter Ten

In the workshop a few weeks later, Coralie pressed a button and Doris started singing 'Bewitched, Bothered and Bewildered'. Bittersweet remembrances soared around her, making Coralie tut-tut at some of the more ludicrous lyrics. She had no intention of worshipping any man's trousers, she told herself, quickly dismissing a fleeting mental glimpse of Gethin's dark denims hugging thighs that were lean and hard and pressed firmly against hers. She had far more self-control and her pressing concerns ought not to be about a man she was never going to meet again.

For a moment the tantalising possibility of being Gethin Lewis's latest muse floated up in front of her, before she dismissed it. The prize had been a PR stunt, something to do away with that residual ill-will that dogged him in his home village. With distance, she hoped that he would realise that he could make an equally grand gesture by simply presenting them with a work that didn't involve anyone from Penmorfa. Especially not her.

'Do we have to listen to this?' asked Kitty, tossing her head in a way that made Coralie fret about future customers unravelling long dark hairs from the mixture she was stirring.

'It's happy music,' said Coralie, pointing her wooden spoon in a warning gesture to silence her. 'Doris Day is wise and good, so leave her alone.'

Kitty frowned and picked at a loose thread on her top. 'Wasn't she a bit of a goer?'

Coralie huffed but managed to hold her tongue. Kitty had been tetchy and miserable since the Valentine's *Twmpath*.

Coralie couldn't decide if it was Adam's kiss or the subsequent spat that was getting to her most, but Adam's happy-go-lucky attitude was bound to have made Kitty even more aware of the responsibilities she couldn't escape.

The loose thread dealt with, Kitty was now apparently all set for work. 'So what are we on today, then?'

'Goats' milk and ylang-ylang – very good for dry skin.'

'Do you drink it or bathe in it?' Kitty said, peering into the pan.

'Neither,' said Coralie, nudging her out of the way and making a mental note to dig out a spare scarf from the growing collection she used to tuck up hair whilst working. Today hers was silk with a jaunty nautical design of which she was particularly fond. 'It's soap. It'll need to cure for about a month and then it'll be ready to go.'

'Oh, I'm disappointed now.' Kitty took the hint and moved back to settle herself in the armchair by the stove. 'I was hoping it was some sort of essential nutrient. I'm that hungry. What have you got out here that I can eat?'

'Well, you can make us a pot of tea if you'd like and if you're very good I'll tell you where the cakes are hidden.'

'Nah!' said Kitty, pulling off her biker boots and wiggling her feet in their striped socks at the wood burner. 'I can't be arsed.'

Lowering the heat under the saucepan, Coralie watched Kitty getting comfortable and wondered if she'd come to work or talk. Sweet Cleans was ticking over at a rate she could cope with in her workshop, she had a roof over her head and she could pay the bills. However, she was gradually realising that drawing anything like a salary was some way off. Taking her little cottage industry to the next level would mean more than just sharing her recipes. Making it worthwhile would take her away from the very aspects of the business she relished and perilously close to the world of commercial cut and thrust she'd left behind.

'Unless one of us is arsed,' Coralie pointed out, 'there won't be anything to sell so I suggest *we* get on with some work then.'

'Oh look, here comes Mam,' observed Kitty, staying put. 'Probably needs cheering up. What with Dad's back playing up and him not being too thrilled with her getting so involved with this Hall Management Committee thing. You could cut the air with a knife at home lately.'

Who'd have believed it, thought Coralie wiping her hands and opening the door.

'Busy?' said Alys, giving Kitty a bit of Beady Eye Factor.

'Depends,' said Kitty, stretching contentedly.

'I've just had some good news,' Alys said, wringing her hands and waving away Coralie's offer of a seat. 'I've just had a call from ACORN, a charity that helps rural communities in need. They've approved our plans!'

'Fair play, Mam,' said Kitty, not sounding especially interested. 'What does that mean then?'

'It means we're eligible for a sizeable loan from them which means we can get on with the work until the bulk of the money from the grant is approved,' said Alys, still looking, to Coralie, very tense.

'The revamp of the church hall, you mean?' she chipped in, applauding Alys's dedication. Coralie was more than happy to support any fundraising efforts that didn't involve her, although she always found that she was particularly busy whenever Alys mentioned anything about her joining the *Merched y Wawr*.

'So, how will you pay back the loan?' she asked. Perhaps there was a similar pot of gold for rural businesses, too?

'It seems that hall management committees are generally

very conscientious about repayments,' Alys replied, her uneasy body language belying her nonchalant tone. 'Once the grant money arrives it won't be a problem – we can pay it back then. Thanks to Gethin, we have a painting to sell which will guarantee that even if the grant takes time to go through the system we won't default on the bridging loan.'

'Oh, that's great!' Coralie was delighted that her faith in Gethin to do the right thing hadn't been misplaced, even if a very small part of her lamented the lost opportunity for further contact with him. 'What's the painting like?'

Everyone listened to the gas hob hissing until Doris Day moved on to 'High Hopes' and Alys cleared her throat. 'Well, we know what its subject is, don't we?' she said, giving Coralie a worried look. 'I understand that Gethin's so keen to do this to support the village's cause that he's even prepared to pay to fly you out there. I must say that's one in the eye to everyone here who's ever written him off as a totally selfish man. And given how busy he is with his current exhibition, it's very good of him to spare us his time.'

'Oh, no!' Coralie banged her wooden spoon against the pan as two eager faces turned to her. 'You must see that it's totally impractical for me. I can't just drop everything here.' Gethin Lewis might have made her feel as if she could fly again, but that didn't mean she was having her portrait painted for anyone.

'We'd take care of Sweet Cleans for you,' Alys insisted.

'And keep an eye on Rock,' Kitty joined in.

'Penmorfa's whole future depends on you!'

Now that *was* being melodramatic, thought Coralie, opening her mouth to protest. 'Wait,' she said. 'Why can't we just redraw the prize? I don't see why it has to be my portrait when the painting's being sold anyway. It could have been anybody in that room that night. '

'Not really,' said Kitty, getting up and prowling round the soap mixture. Coralie shushed her away. Was this the moment when Kitty had to admit why it couldn't have been her, why jumping on a plane would have been out of the question? She stared at her pan rather than at Kitty, afraid of doing anything which might make the younger woman think twice about her confession.

'I don't know if I should tell you this. I kind of promised to keep it to myself,' Kitty said, eventually.

Too late, already, thought Coralie. But she was sure Kitty would feel so much better once she'd unburdened herself about the pregnancy.

'The thing is, the other half of your strip of tickets was never included with the rest of the draw that night. Gethin asked me to give them to him. He told me he'd been thinking about something you'd said to him about giving everyone a stake in his work, so when I saw he'd donated a painting to the raffle, I just assumed ...'

'He must really want to paint you,' Alys finished.

'Or something,' Kitty mumbled, before breaking into giggles and setting Alys off, too. 'Oh come on, Coralie!' said Kitty. 'Don't look so disapproving. He is lush and he's obviously dead keen on you. Don't tell me you're not tempted. I so would if it was me he'd invited to lie on his couch!'

'It's not you, though, is it?' Coralie protested, a sudden constriction of her throat making it quite hard to speak. Not that Alys and Kitty were listening. They were too busy cackling and leaning on each other for support, all differences between them apparently forgotten, leaving Coralie feeling even more isolated.

'Sorry, Coralie,' said Alys, straightening up and wiping her eyes, 'we're just jealous that we didn't get a free holiday in America and the devoted attention of a red-hot man. You'd need to sell an awful lot of soap to buy that much excitement.'

'What makes you think I want that?' said Coralie, stung. 'I came to Penmorfa to live quietly and to do something creative and fulfilling. It's not about how much I earn, but that I'm enjoying what I do. That's all the excitement I need.'

'And we respect that, of course.' Alys nodded, pulling a straight face, even though the amusement still danced in her eyes. 'You've settled seamlessly into the village. Everyone admires the way you've joined in and made a real effort to be part of the community. No one's ever had a bad word to say against you – even Delyth and Mair think you're a quiet, hard-working girl. Thirty thousand pounds is a lot to repay through cake sales and coffee mornings alone, but thanks to you we can be relaxed about the loan. I promise you that we won't let the business suffer whilst you're away.'

'Thank you, but that won't be necessary,' Coralie said, slowly lifting her eyes to face Alys. 'Aren't you forgetting that I'm not a bowl of fruit or a flower arrangement? You can't just push me around for this painting as if I were some inanimate object. You might be happy for me to drop everything, but what if you'd been in my shoes? Would you be quite so keen to jet off to the other side of the world if it meant leaving everything in the garden centre to Huw and Kitty?' She shook her head. 'I'm very sorry, Alys, but I can't help.'

Gethin was sitting in his favourite diner trying to convince himself he was pleased to be back. Today, New Yorkers were wrapped up to beat a wind chill factor so cold that, anywhere else in the world, it would have cleared the streets of its citizens. The lovely brunette passing the window clearly didn't have far to go; she was bare-headed, her glossy hair just bouncing gently on her shoulders as she walked. As if sensing his interest, she turned her face towards him. Beautiful grey eyes under perfectly groomed brows met his. Her rosy lips parted in a flawless smile and then she winked and sashayed away.

Normally that would have been enough to remind him how he loved this city.

'Only takes one dumb animal,' reminded his apprentice, nodding at the woman's fur-clad back.

'Good morning, Ruby Arnold!' he said loudly, making her wince. 'Good of you to drop in. Caffeine kicked in at last?'

Ruby mumbled something inaudible before returning to her pancakes. Gethin shook his head. So the kid partied hard, but some internal switch flipped to 'on' as soon as they were working. 'Is that the thanks I get for making sure you were registered for the Brave New Artists' Prize?'

'You did what?' Her head jerked up. 'I wasn't going to bother. You know, with the fee and all.'

'All taken care of.'

He caught a glimpse of the part of her she kept hidden, the softer, vulnerable Ruby, before the guard went up again.

'Thanks, but you should have saved your money. They won't pick a nobody like me.'

'Speculate to accumulate, Rubes,' he said, fondly. 'If you can't even be bothered to enter then you definitely won't make the cut.' He'd never imagined himself permitting anyone to share his studio – God knows, plenty of people had tried to flatter their way in – but dogged little Ruby had chipped away at his stone heart. He'd been quietly impressed with her raw talent, but it was the wounded look in her eyes that had really got to him.

Once upon a time … well, those early days had gone. And,

if anything, the lean times had made him more determined to prove himself. He'd had his lucky break and Ruby had more than repaid hers, proving herself an able assistant with an almost intuitive knack of giving him what he needed before he realised he needed it and always putting her hand up to a mistake. No nasty surprises with Ruby; she was a quick learner.

'Hey, Mr Jones? Can I get you a refill?'

Gethin put his cup down, 'I'm good for coffee, thanks, Max,' he said to the manager. 'Come on, Rubes, I think we've let Pamala wait long enough.'

The art dealer's exacting standards were well-known. Some people survived the ordeal of working with Pamala Gray and came out the other side with enhanced reputations; others slunk away wounded, barely able to exhibit again.

'You might have shaved,' Ruby reproached him, looking up at his jaw as he got to his feet. 'You ought to at least try to keep up the good impression, for my sake if not for yours. I might need her when I win that big prize.'

Gethin laughed. 'So now you're not just in the competition, you're going to win it. I like your thinking. Listen, if Pamala Gray gets close enough to inspect my stubble, she's close enough not to care,' he said, running his hand across his chin. 'We're fine-tuning my exhibition, not going on a date. Besides,' he added with a grin, 'she's the one chasing me.' More people than ever were clamouring for his flattering portrayals of sophisticated couples and strong, beautiful women. If one or two of the stuffier art critics lifted their eyebrows at the mention of his name, what did he care? Everything was going his way, so why was he feeling so miserable?

'Here, I'll take that for you.' The manager leant over and took his tray. 'You have a nice day now, Mr Jones.'

Gethin flung his bags across his shoulder and turned up his collar, before gently shoving Ruby into the cold.

'Shouldn't he know your name by now?' Ruby tugged a beanie over her peroxide crop and fumbled in the pockets of her faux-leather jacket for gloves. Gethin handed her the lightest of the bags.

'Jones as in Tom – Max's little joke when he found out I was from Wales.'

'Whatever.' Ruby shrugged. 'But talking of the old home town, what's happening about that portrait you asked me to fit into the schedule?'

'Bad idea,' he said, shouting above the noise of a truck which had pulled up beside them, its brakes hissing noisily. 'The only way I can do it would be if we were both in the same place and the model's still refusing to come out here.'

'New York's an awfully long way to travel for a sitting,' Ruby bellowed back. 'Did you take that into consideration?'

'Jetlag,' he mumbled. Snowflakes were falling between the tall buildings and settling on Ruby's hat; he brushed them off and pulled her out of the way of an oncoming umbrella. It wouldn't do for his assistant to lose an eye now.

'Is she pretty?'

That was the other thing about Ruby; she had a really big mouth. 'I just want to paint her and help the old place along the way,' he said, hoping to shut her up.

'Sure you do,' she said, not hiding her smile very well. 'So why don't you just give her a call and ask nicely?'

Rock didn't rush to greet Coralie when she walked up her front path; perhaps he'd heard about her refusal to co-operate and was giving her the cold shoulder, too? The black windows of the next-door cottage were as lifeless as her workshop after all the laughter had died away and it was obvious to everyone that Coralie was going to stand her ground. Kitty had threaded her arm through her mother's, leading her away without a backwards glance, as if Coralie no longer existed.

The front door was cold against her shoulder as Coralie let herself in and flopped down on her sofa without taking off her coat. She switched on a lamp which did nothing to lift her gloom and only seemed to deepen the shadows in the room. True friends would surely accept her decision, she thought, chewing her lip. Wasn't all the emotional pressure a bit unfair? She replayed the moment when Alys's white bob folded briefly across her face as she stared at the floor and how, when she looked up again, her eyes had been unusually bright.

'I really thought I could pull this off,' Alys stated quietly. 'Prove to that dreadful Delyth and Mair that Penmorfa needn't be stuck in the past, that we *can* change and grow together. But without your help, Coralie, I can see it all slipping away.'

They thought she wouldn't help, when the truth was she *couldn't* help. It was arduous enough keeping up with her regular visits to Ned along with everything else, but she knew how much they meant to him. What would the consequences be if he thought she'd abandoned him like everyone else? But if she went to New York for a week, how could she also fit in a visit to him and get all her work done?

Coralie wilted back on the sofa and only noticed she was crying when she saw teardrops falling onto her tightly clasped hands. She wiped her nose, wishing that like her fingers still scented from the essential oils she'd been working with, she, too, could come up smelling of roses. Somewhere next to the sofa was a box of tissues, and as she groped around for them, Rock slunk out with a tiny brown mouse still struggling in his jaws.

Coralie had found out during the first of the cold weather that mice were an inescapable fact of country living, albeit one that no one boasted about. Since she was surrounded by fields, there had seemed little point in catching and releasing them only to have them re-home themselves in her loft at the earliest opportunity. Having Rock about the place acted, she hoped, as a deterrent, but she wasn't about to condone torture and murder, especially when it was going on right under her feet. Grabbing Rock in a surprise attack, she got ready to catch his victim before it shot off and hid somewhere so she wouldn't be able to find it again.

The tiny creature was frozen in fear. Coralie snatched at it, hissing at Rock to keep away and fending him off with her foot. The fluffy black cat she'd come to love looked more like the spitting, feral stray who'd vigorously defended himself against her attempts to clean him up when she'd first rescued him.

'Get out!' she roared, sinking back in triumph when, after a long, baleful stare, he finally sloped out of the room. She knelt there for a moment taking slow deep breaths, before daring to look at the fluttering, fragile, flicker of life in her palms. Slowly, slowly, she uncupped her hands and took a peep at the pitiful thing inside them. To her huge relief the little body was unmarked; really, it was quite lovely when you looked at it closely: the glossy brown-grey pelt, the delicate paws and bright, beady eyes. Satisfied that the little mouse was safe, Coralie smiled to herself and savoured what felt like a hard-won achievement. She'd done it! Just one, tiny heartbeat of a life – but she'd saved it!

Lifting herself up on her knees, she was looking round the room, pondering her next move when a sudden sense of unease stilled her. Opening her hands again, she felt the small body shudder and the light leave the bright eyes as the mouse gave its last breath. No! Please no! She'd only been trying to help. Utterly wretched, she sank back and let the tears flow freely. No matter where she went or how fast she ran, there was always someone she couldn't escape from, the one person she couldn't shake off. If she could only save just one thing, maybe, just maybe, she could learn to live with herself.

Chapter Eleven

Pamala Gray had finished with Gethin by lunchtime and had passed him on to Laura Schiffman, her Senior Director. Laura wanted to catch one of the temporary exhibitions in town by a Lithuanian-born artist who did something clever with string, so Gethin found himself sitting in a museum restaurant, a temple to glass and light where, on first sight, only beautiful worshippers were admitted. Laura was talking, but her earnest, monotone delivery soon sent his attention wandering. After the rough edges, sullen faces and frustrations of Penmorfa, he'd been relieved to get back to New York, yet now the good manners and smooth service made him yearn for something that made life a little less predictable.

Even his meal was flawless: four halves of hard-boiled egg arranged on a slate, looking very much like one of the art exhibits. Each half was a thing of beauty; a glassy set white, a perfect creamy swirl rising from the dip where the yolk would have been and a glistening, miniature spring of caviar bubbling from each delicate peak like black lava. He thought of The Cabin and the generous Welsh Black beef filling the plate and his stomach rumbled in a disappointed lament at how very empty it would be, even if he drank all of the endless refills of iced water.

'... and of course we're hoping to attract interest from all those collectors hoping to add to their ego-seums,' said Laura, arranging her spoon by the side of an artistically wonky bowl.

'What?' he said, looking at her worthy and almost untouched lentil soup and thinking of Coralie, sighing with satisfaction as she rounded off her chocolate pudding with more chocolates and a double espresso.

'You know,' she said, waving perfectly manicured hands, 'the new status symbol for the super-rich. Instead of leaving their art collections in storage for lack of space, or donating their collections to public museums where they might not be put on permanent display, they're buying up bus garages and underground bunkers so they can show the world what great taste they've got.'

Or not. Leaving the restaurant behind, they started their tour. Gethin began to notice collections which ought never to have gone on display but for the patrons who'd donated them insisting they be viewed in their entirety. The results said more about conspicuous consumption than love of art or good taste. Oh, there were always lots of big egos about.

Making an offer to Penmorfa that he thought Coralie couldn't refuse – wasn't that just him flaunting his great big ego? Or something? Perhaps that's what Coralie thought, too, since she'd turned out not to be the pushover suggested by her soft-heartedness. The only reason he could see for her to reject his offer was that she'd seen him for the conceited prick he'd become. What other reason would she have for not playing nicely when her refusal risked hurting Penmorfa?

'Now, this is a wonderful example of what Fuller meant when she talked about lines as being points in motions,' Laura murmured, looking at the string exhibits with great reverence. Everyone else in the gallery seemed equally enthralled. Gethin noted that whilst they represented many different ethnic backgrounds, all were linked by a particular kind of well-bred, well-educated upbringing and a certain self-conscious cool. He felt a great wave of nostalgia for Delyth and Mair and had to pull himself together.

Laura hadn't noticed his lack of response. 'One day, your work could be rubbing shoulders, so to speak, with a Quinn, an Ofili or a Koons,' she whispered, pressing a pale fingertip to the space between her clear grey eyes as if trying to erase any imminent frown-lines.

Now why didn't that make him jump for joy?

'Pamala takes the long view, she's not there for the shock of the new,' Laura went on, smiling to show white, even-spaced teeth. 'She really takes care of her artists. What she sees in you is tremendous ability along with huge imagination and a touch of edginess. She has great expectations for your exhibition.'

Gethin stared past her at the courtyard below with an artificial tree, an amoebic blob of a sculpture, a square pond and some paving slabs and found himself thinking about the crashing exhilaration of the waves breaking on the cliffs at Penmorfa; their wild, untameable energy. How come he kept getting the feeling that he'd left something important behind? As if he was living in a monochrome world and waiting, like the wisteria arbour in the Shakespeare Garden that he had passed through that morning, for a change of temperatures to bring him some colour and life.

Laura was wearing a clever grey jumper that managed to be both flattering and tasteful; something the aesthetic part of his brain appreciated. Yet all he could think of was Coralie: the copper curls, eyes flecked with gold, a peachy-soft mouth and all the glow of whatever colour combination of crazy clothes had taken her fancy that morning. How would he set about capturing all her changing kaleidoscopic character and setting it on canvas?

Forget about Coralie, he told himself. Be smart and keep following the money. Like this guy who was literally pulling the wool over the critics' eyes with string, he thought, shaking his head at another meaningless installation. Except trying to be smart wasn't making him happy, so perhaps it was time to do something crazy?

'Laura,' he said, surprising them both. 'Would you excuse me? I have to make a phone call.'

In the lobby he paced the floor whilst a phone on the other side of the Atlantic rang itself off the wall. Just as he was about to give up, he heard her soft Home Counties voice say hello.

'What do you want me to do?' he asked, rubbing his hands over his jaw. 'Beg?'

Kitty waited until Adam had got most of the way round the greenhouse he was cleaning, then set up at one of the long tables. His eyebrows rose, but at least he didn't object to her company. Good start.

'I'm getting ahead with some early sowing,' she announced, separating the plastic seed trays. 'You never know what Mam's going to come up with next.'

Kitty had always looked up to Alys and admired her for her energetic, no-nonsense approach to life, but part of her wished that her mother would simply admit that she was backing a lost cause. 'Why she's putting herself out to rebuild the church hall for the benefit of people like Delyth and Mair, who're always looking down their noses sneering at everything she says, beats me. I don't know why they always have to take a pop at her.'

'Well, she looks half her age,' said Adam, 'and she moves with the times. But she shouldn't let those two get to her. Everyone else appreciates her hard work.'

Kitty sighed. Had Coralie been willing to play along with Gethin, her mother might not have had to have worked quite so hard, but Alys, undeterred, had carried on seizing funding opportunities with as much tenacity as Edith grappling Huw's socks.

'I'd just wish she'd save some of that energy for home, where it's needed. Dad's already being treated for high blood pressure – I found his tablets in the bathroom cabinet.'

'Then at least you know he's doing something about it,' Adam pointed out. 'Besides, it's not fair to blame Alys when she's trying to do something positive. Your dad might have other worries.'

Kitty refused to meet his eyes. All she knew was that with the usual work of the garden centre to be carried out and concerns about finding anyone suitable to run the Summerhouse Café when it reopened in the spring, it was little wonder that her father was becoming increasingly withdrawn.

'I know Mam was delighted that so many people turned up for the St David's Day event last week,' she said, on a more conciliatory note – after all, Adam had gone out of his way to help set up the garden centre when Alys had decided to turn one of their regular garden events into something much grander – 'but I never want to hear the Abersaith Male Voice Choir or smell another Welsh cake ever again.'

Battling another wave of nausea just thinking about the pervasive scent of warm cakes that seemed to suck out all the oxygen in the marquee where she'd been stationed, Kitty swallowed hard and turned her attention to Adam. Chucking-up was not the way to convince him that whilst her body might have been taken over her mind was still very much her own.

'I'd have lugged that compost in for you,' he said, tutting at her.

'I don't recall you being so worried last year.' She smiled, determined to remind him of those long, hot summer days.

'Sleeping all right?' he asked, stretching up and showing an inch of tanned, toned stomach.

Perhaps he was about to volunteer to help tire her out? She pretended to fiddle about with the first cell tray.

'Only my mate, Flat Sam – the guy with the dreads I surf with – he was telling me that when his sister was at your stage of the game, you know, when the mother and baby are sharing limited space, she found it much easier to sleep on her left side. Keeps all the blood flowing to your extremities, apparently.'

Kitty resisted the urge to tell him it was not the blood flow to *her* extremities she was interested in. 'Uh-huh,' she said, resigning herself to firming compost rather than Adam.

'Some gentle activity's good, too.' He nodded at her. 'But if you're going to be standing there, make sure you squeeze your toes from time to time. You don't want to faint, do you?'

No, thought Kitty, she wanted to scream. All this fussing was precisely why she'd tried to keep the pregnancy to herself. Although she'd called a truce with the baby, she still wasn't ready to let it dominate her. She scowled at her cell tray and the packets of seeds, feeling that it was rapidly becoming her lot to be the bringer of new life. At one time she'd hoped Adam would worship her, but she hadn't foreseen him casting her as a fertility goddess.

'Have you made a birth plan yet?' he asked, a splash of water across his cheek giving him a look of shiny-faced enthusiasm.

'Pain free,' she snapped. 'With lots of drugs.' She looked up, grateful for a change of subject as Alys ambled in with the cordless house phone and beckoned at her.

'Someone for you. Sheena Milsom?'

Oh God, she hoped it wasn't an ante-natal appointment. Kitty took the phone and held it to her chest, waiting for her mother to leave, but Alys picked up the seeds instead. 'Greyhound,' she noted. 'A good do-er. Oh, yes, Sheena's the editor of *West Life Journal*,' she added, pressing a seed into the compost. 'She wants to talk to you about your *twmpath* photos – the ones of the Summerhouse Café all dressed up for the evening that I posted on the garden centre website.'

Kitty went over to the open doorway away from her mother and Adam who, she noted, had fallen into easy conversation whilst Alys picked up a spare cloth and wiped off a smear Adam had missed.

'It's very *Country Living*,' the editor told her, after a brief preamble. 'It's just what we're looking for, just right for the bride on a budget – all those flowers in jam jars and homemade bunting. So we'd really like to use the photo, for a fee, of course.'

She mentioned a sum and Kitty's sharp intake of breath drew concerned looks from Adam and her mother. Kitty waved her free hand to show that she was ok, although she was very tempted to stand over one of Adam's window-washing puddles and pretend her waters had broken just to see what he would do.

'Who was the stylist?' asked the editor, making her frown. 'Did you bring in anyone special?'

'Oh, that was me,' said Kitty. By now Adam and her mother had stopped talking and were shamelessly eavesdropping.

'Fantastic!'

Kitty glowed at the praise. At last there was someone in the world wanting to talk about the person she was rather than the one she was creating!

'Well I must say you're very talented. What's the name of your business, so I can include it in the article?'

Kitty did some rapid thinking. 'Flair on a Shoestring,' she announced confidently. 'And I'll give you my email address too.'

'Wonderful!' the editor trilled. 'Thank you! I do hope it creates lots of interest for you.'

'Who or what is Flair on a Shoestring?' said Alys, grinning at her as she took back the phone.

Kitty couldn't help but laugh. 'The idea just came to me! I wanted to convince that editor that I knew what I was talking about. Then it occurred to me that this is something I could actually do. I'm not flustered by all the preparations for big events and I reckon I've proved that I can make an ordinary room fit for a party. Put the two together and what have you got? My new styling business: weddings, birthday parties and celebrations. A-list styling on a Z-list budget.'

Adam threw his cloth into the bucket at his feet and laughed. 'Brilliant! You won't even have to get off your backside. I mean, who's going to want anything like that around here?'

Kitty felt the flush of annoyance. 'I'm serious, Adam. Everyone's worried about spending cuts and the loss of public sector jobs. They'll be plenty of potential customers in Cardiff looking for ways to cut the cost of big celebrations.' At least her mother, perching on one of the benches, had sat down to look at her thoughtfully.

'Do you know, I think you might be on to something, Kitty. And it's a business you could grow from home. Even when you were a very little girl, you had very firm ideas about your birthday parties,' she observed, looking, thought Kitty, a bit misty-eyed. 'What do you think you'd need to start up?'

'Well, the money the *West Life Journal*'s going to pay me for the photo will buy me a few mismatched plates and some trinkets,' she volunteered, thinking aloud.

'Half your gran's stuff is still in the loft,' Alys said, leaning forward. 'We brought it with us when we moved and I never did get round to sorting it out. You should have a look at that, too.'

For the first time in months, Kitty began to feel some control over her life. She would start small, do plenty of research, accumulate some stock, maybe try an ad in the local paper. It was a really great idea and would show Adam that she wasn't going to slob around waiting for her parents to bail her out. She glanced over, hoping to catch a look of approval, just in time to see him pick up his bucket and trudge past her with his mouth set in a grim line. The baby joined in with a little kick of protest. Too bad, thought Kitty; her life-changing moment had arrived and nothing was going to stop her.

Penmorfa, thought Coralie, spotting the small gathering in the glasshouse, had been a safe haven, at least until Gethin Lewis showed up, but unless she wanted a very lonely life, there were risks she would have to take. It seemed to her, on her last visit, that Ned was dealing better with his situation. She was less afraid of what he might do. It would be a relief to send the occasional letter and maybe it would help her own compulsion to turn up in person every month.

Sullen clouds threatened rain and a stiff wind shook the life out of some of the display plants. As she quickened her pace, Adam came storming out of the glasshouse, looking as if he'd like to shake someone too and she just managed to jump out of the way as he flung a bucket of dirty water over one of the raised beds.

She was already feeling jittery about what she was facing, but no one could say that she hadn't done her bit to save Penmorfa from going the way of so many small villages dying for lack of resources. Alys, sitting on one of the benches, looked up and scowled as she came in. It wasn't quite the reaction she was hoping for. Looking at her expression, Coralie felt quite sorry for Kitty. If she'd been on the receiving end of that a few times no wonder she'd been a bit hesitant about telling her mother she was pregnant.

'I thought we were friends,' Alys said, wagging a finger at her. 'You've been living here for the best part of a year now. We thought you were one of us.'

'I am.' Coralie blinked, feeling some of the wind leave her sails. 'That's why I need to talk to you.'

Kitty stopped pretending to fiddle around with a seed tray and scuttled over to sit next to her mother. Leaning back, she forgot to hide her stomach and Coralie could see that although the exceptionally cold weather meant that outside only a few buds were swelling, Kitty didn't seem to have been affected.

Now two pairs of eyes blazed at her.

'Does the Hall Management Committee still have access to the ACORN loan?' she asked, quietly.

Alys folded her arms, and Kitty laid a protective hand on them.

'I've been thinking it over and I can't not help, can I? Not when this is the only way to pay off the loan quickly. So, I've told Gethin that if you can take care of Rock and Sweet Cleans for me, I'll sit for a portrait.'

Alys rushed over and gave her a hug, then Kitty joined in, too.

'Oh, thank you,' said Alys, pinching her cheek. 'That's brilliant, I'm so glad you've agreed to help the village. Just think of all the people who'll benefit from this, all the coffee mornings, cake sales and classes that can be restarted – you won't regret it.'

No, thought Coralie, crossing her fingers. But they might.

Chapter Twelve

'Welcome to New York, Coralie,' said Gethin, looking pleased with himself as he bent his head to kiss her lightly on the cheek. 'I knew I could count on you to do the right thing.'

'For Penmorfa,' Coralie added, still trying to catch her breath. Hardly surprising then that her head was spinning. And if her legs felt unsteady, she told herself, it was nothing to do with the rough touch of his stubble setting her skin tingling, nor was it the low, delicious murmur of his voice as he said her name. Gethin's cramped diary had meant squeezing the sittings in during the week leading up to his new exhibition. Alys might have been delighted with the speed of events, but it had meant a frantic three weeks for Coralie, who'd scrambled to leave the business in a state that someone else could manage whilst she was away.

'That's understood,' he murmured, with a smile. 'Why else would you come all this way?'

'You didn't leave me much choice,' she pointed out. 'Not if I wanted to carry on living in the village.'

'Shape up or ship out.' He laughed softly. 'Why do you think I left the place?'

Stay calm, she ordered herself, taking a deep breath. She had to keep a sense of purpose about this trip. All she had to do was sit in a studio, what was the worst that could happen?

Her sudden urge to flee became more urgent when she noticed what was going on over Gethin's shoulder. Some half-a-dozen students – all attractive women, Coralie noted – a stunning naked female model and Gethin's spiky assistant,

Ruby, were all looking at her. The collective message seemed to be to wish her back to the other side of the Atlantic. It wasn't a great starting point, but what really bothered Coralie was the naked model.

'Didn't anyone mention that you'd signed up to being painted in your birthday suit?' teased Gethin, following her glance.

'That "Calendar Girls" stuff is a fund-raising cliché,' she replied, her nonchalant tone rather ruined by the blush she could feel creeping across her face.

'It certainly is if the *Merched y Wawr* are involved. You'd want more than a few strategically placed buns to hide that lot,' he grinned. 'Let me finish up here and we'll compare notes on what we're going to do for this painting. Naked doesn't have to be clichéd, you know.'

Coralie's stomach growled at him. At least one part of her still had some sense left. She took a seat, trying to be inconspicuous whilst the lesson proceeded.

'I love this here. The way you've captured the curve of the hip is really beautiful,' Gethin was saying, sweeping his hands across one easel in a gesture that seemed to have the entire class holding their breath. 'Good work.'

At this praise, his student, a brunette wearing large silver hoop earrings and a small camisole top, despite the frigid temperature outside, ran the tip of her tongue over her wet lips, as if they were indulging in a spot of foreplay rather than discussing a picture. Bewitched, bothered, and bewildered, thought Coralie, although it was difficult not to be moved by a man who did such wonderful things for a dark pair of jeans and had a voice that could make the electoral register sound like *Under Milk Wood*.

'Hey, lady! New York ain't a postcard. You gotta do it, not look at it,' the taxi driver had advised earlier as they arrived outside the historic art school. It was true that she *had* spent the entire journey gasping at the cityscape unfolding before her. Privately, she'd been convinced that there were few surprises in a city she thought she knew from so many films and television series, but the screen images were no preparation for the real thing.

Penmorfa was beautiful, but this was breathtaking in a way that she just hadn't anticipated. The early spring sunshine gilded ten thousand windows of the modern skyscrapers, turning the glass to pale gold mosaics against a clear blue sky. Byzantine arches on the older buildings soared upwards to where the dark tracery of balconies, pinnacles and water towers stretched out into the distance. Yellow cabs buzzed through the streets and lights blazed in all kinds of bars and restaurants.

Yet all that exhilaration and energy couldn't quite stop her feeling of nervous excitement whenever she thought about the reality of coming face-to-face with Gethin again. It wasn't just the sight of the art school, with its imposing stone façade and splendidly ornate window arches, that had made her so reluctant to leave the cab.

Gethin had offered her the choice of meeting him during his morning class or later, for lunch. Coralie reasoned that seeing him at work would give her an idea of what it was she was letting herself in for. She hoped he wasn't arrogant enough to believe she'd only turned up so early because she was impatient to see him, as it clearly wasn't true. She glanced up now to prove to herself that that really was the case and to demonstrate her interest in the lesson, but found her gaze straying to the teacher. Except that Gethin had beaten her to it and was studying her with amused interest.

Now she remembered that she wasn't the only one with an agenda. What was he up to? Mentally mixing colours to match her skin tone? She could feel her cheeks beginning to burn again as the reality of being under such close scrutiny started to kick in. Then his face broke into a smile that made her heart skip with pleasure before she ordered it to calm down and behave.

'Okay everyone, that's it for today,' he said, clapping his hands and ignoring the disappointed groans. 'Ruby will take over and answer any questions whilst you pack up. Same time next week.'

He picked up his leather jacket and strode towards her. Her stomach rumbled another loud warning and he laughed. 'Come on, there's a diner on the corner of the block.'

Where hopefully the coffee was served in the bucket-sized cups she'd need to clear her head so she could talk sensibly to Gethin. A stack of fluffy pancakes and a lake of syrup wouldn't hurt either; imagine how her depleted blood sugars and flagging metabolism would thank her for it.

Behind his back, Ruby, her head on one side and her startled white crop giving her the look of a small, fierce budgie, had been making Angry Bird faces at her since she'd met her in reception. She seemed to think that one of her duties was to defend Gethin from all-comers and had taken Coralie's bag with a very suspicious look. Coralie ignored her. Anyway, she hadn't come all this way to be liked, but to help seal the deal for Penmorfa's Hall Management Committee, Alys in particular. If anyone had a right to be worried it was Alys. Securing a large loan was one thing, making the repayments quite another. What would Alys do if anything went wrong?

Coralie's mouth went dry just thinking about the prospect. As a businesswoman it was in Alys's interest to rebuild the community; how else could the garden centre expand and grow without local people to work and shop there? But Coralie sensed there was more to it than that, that somewhere Alys had a personal investment in this project. Coralie comforted herself with the thought that all she had to do was make sure that Alys ended up with a painting. She could do that, couldn't she? It wasn't as if she'd been asked to bungee jump off the Empire State Building. Hey, the model today had managed to stand there stark naked without being the slightest bit self-conscious. Then she glanced at Gethin, who gave her a wolfish grin and she remembered that she didn't have to take her clothes off to feel exposed.

Gethin couldn't wait to get Coralie in his studio. Just looking at her closing her eyes whilst she sucked the last of the syrup off her spoon made him feel good to be alive.

'Oh, that's better!' she said, offering him a quick, grateful smile across the table. 'Looking at all those hot dog and pretzel vendors on the streets this morning from the taxi must have made me really hungry. I was starting to feel quite light-headed.'

Must have been something in the air affecting him too, thought Gethin. Why else would he have struggled to stay grounded when Coralie appeared in the doorway of his class, turning all the monochrome to colour with her dishevelled chestnut hair and short, flared turquoise jacket?

'How was the hotel?' he asked. 'Did you get any sleep?'

'I wondered if they were expecting any princesses when I saw the size of that room and that huge bed.' She smiled, shooting him a mischievous glance that made him have all kinds of thought about the huge bed. 'Are you sure you're not about to be landed with a right royal bill?'

Gethin frowned, but only because Max, the manager, was finding every excuse in the book to hang round their table.

'Call it a small thank you for agreeing to bunk at Ruby's place for the rest of the week. Are you all right with that?'

Coralie played with her empty cup. 'It was very hospitable of her to have me to stay whilst her roommate's out of town, and besides, you've been more than generous.'

Max, leaning over the table making a show of collecting plates, turned his head so Coralie couldn't see and winked at him.

'More coffee, ma'am?' he asked, returning seconds later with a refill and placing a neatly wrapped package on the table in front of her. 'Chocolate muffin, ma'am. On the house, from the best diner in town. Just so's you'll come back and see us again,' the older man added, looking dazed when Coralie rewarded him with a smile that lit the room. What did he have to do to make her beam at him like that?

'I'll get the bill,' she said, reaching for her purse.

'You making a profit on that business yet?' he asked. 'Because unless you can look me in the eye and tell me you've got money to burn, I'm getting this.'

She opened her mouth to protest and then shrugged.

'Better,' he told her. 'Don't struggle, just give in.'

She threw him a startled look and he had to agree he could have phrased it more subtly. On the other hand, wasn't that exactly what he was thinking? It was all he could do not to reach out for her as she ducked under his arm when he opened the door for her. He couldn't quite believe she'd crossed an ocean to see him, come all the way from Penmorfa. He'd have to be made of stone not to have wanted to pull her to him and kiss her. Steady, boy, he reminded himself, just because she was standing there didn't mean she'd come to see him and certainly not of her own free will. Given half a chance, she'd be off like a shot.

Nevertheless he couldn't help noticing the glow of her

cheeks still pink from the crowded diner, where the red vinyl bench seats never had a chance to grow cold. Nor could he miss that small contented sigh as she lifted her face to the fresh air in a way that made him smile and gave him a nice warm feeling.

'Eating is not a problem in this city, but there aren't too many of the true diners like that left,' he said, trying not to think too much about the nice warm feeling. 'Not those comfortable, lived-in kind of places where the food's good, the service is fast and every table's set with Frank's Hot Sauce and Aunt Jemima's. Not in Manhattan. They've torn most of them down and put up fake ones instead. They look the same, but all the heart and soul's been knocked out of them.'

He pointed to a restaurant on the corner. 'Think that's a genuine Italian restaurant? All the Italians have made their money and moved on, so it's somebody else's turn. They're all run by Mexicans now. All is not what it seems here.'

'If that's true, why do you love it here so much?' Coralie asked.

Realising he was in danger of leaving her behind if he walked at his usual pace he slowed down to give her a chance to keep up.

'Why not stay in Penmorfa if you're looking for something down-to-earth and authentic?'

'What? So everyone can tell me how easy I've got it, playing with paints instead of fighting a losing battle running a farm? That's never going to happen.'

Penmorfa had to be really important to her because why else would she fly all this way? All *he* cared about was having an excuse to study her in detail. He allowed himself a good look at her, appreciating the way her rolled bronze curls gleamed and bounced as she tripped along beside him, the concerned compassion creasing her brow. Wait a minute! He followed her line of vision and spotted one of the city's 'Adopt me' dogs, a skinny little hound in its distinctive orange vest, looking up gratefully at its elderly carer.

'Fosterers slip those on the dogs that need a home before walking them,' he explained, as Coralie cooed over what looked to him like an overgrown bony rat showing off with an extra spring in its spindly legs as it passed them. 'It tells potential adopters that the dog's available.'

'Poor little fellow,' she said, looking stricken.

It was almost worth offering the dumb mutt a home so that her eyes would follow him with the same interest.

'I hope there's a happy ending for him,' she went on, still watching the dog sadly. 'He's very cute.'

'But not your type,' he told her, rolling his eyes. 'You can't take him back on the plane with you. The world is full of dumb creatures, Coralie, not all of them have happy endings.'

And not every home was loving.

'You said you'd escaped to the country,' he mentioned, giving in to his curiosity about what she'd left behind. 'But you never said why. What did you escape from?'

'Why does anyone choose to live in the country?' She smiled, a little too brightly. 'For a better quality of life, of course.'

Bullshit. There was a bust-up behind her, he'd bet on it. 'Having your portrait painted can be very therapeutic,' he told her. Next time Ruby wisecracked about his interest in Coralie, he could confidently reply that she was barking up the wrong tree. The last thing he needed was someone crying on his shoulder over some clown who didn't appreciate her.

One of many advantages of being single was that he didn't have to bother himself with anyone else's concerns, like who did the floral arrangements for that elegant wedding at the Plaza Athénée, or whose fortieth birthday went from wake to baby shower when, at the eleventh hour, she'd found a straight man and got pregnant. Hell, if he'd wanted to listen to emotional problems, he'd have become a hairdresser. At least he could tell his clients to shut their mouths.

'Coming face-to-face with yourself like that shows you all kinds of stuff about yourself.'

A shadow flickered across her face and some of her liveliness and energy abandoned her. Definitely a broken heart. No wonder she went around half the time looking so haunted, but he could take her mind off that.

'Don't worry about it.' He smiled, offering her his arm. 'It's going to be fun. First sitting tomorrow. Early.'

Coralie woke up in a tiny apartment in downtown Manhattan the next day, after a short night of not so much drifting as diving into sleep only to paddle around in the shallows from around three in the morning when her body started telling her it was time to get up. The springs of the sofa bed twanged as she wrenched herself upright, but the room remained disconcertingly black and silent.

She pushed up her eye-mask and winced as the light came flooding in. Ruby was mouthing something at her. Coralie pulled out her earplugs; there was no cure for New York City noise, especially when the apartment was situated on a busy street, but two wodges of pink foam did a lot to absorb it.

'You want coffee?' Ruby repeated.

'Yes, please!' Coralie said, with what she hoped was a grateful, thank-you-for-thinking-of-me smile.

'Get to it then.' Ruby cocked her head towards the tiny windowless kitchenette crammed into an alcove leading off the living room with a hint of sadistic pleasure. 'Gethin doesn't like to be kept waiting. Especially when he's being so generous.'

If he was that generous why couldn't he just put his hand in his pocket and buy Penmorfa a new community hall, thought Coralie, ignoring the distrust with which she was being regarded. She straightened up after digging out her wash bag from her suitcase stashed under the sofa and found Ruby raising her pierced eyebrows at her bargain stripy-cotton gents' pyjamas.

'You know, Gethin never has to ask a woman twice to sit for him, so I'm just wondering what your game is?'

Bunching her fingers into her towel, Coralie chose not to say something she might regret and marched over to Ruby's narrow bathroom. It couldn't have been more of a contrast to her hotel suite, where the vast bathroom was equipped with a gigantic white bath and a silver fountain of a shower. No free samples of bathroom goodies for her to compare with Sweet Cleans products, either. She frowned, temporarily distracted by thoughts that the packaging she'd picked for her range looked somewhat rustic and naïve compared to the sleek toiletries that had been on offer at the hotel. That was something to think about later. For now she had to deal with Ruby.

Coralie was pretty sure she hadn't been doing anything antisocial in her sleep because she was certain she hadn't been asleep for long enough. Maybe the reality of being lumbered with a complete stranger in such proximity was starting to hit home. Recharged by her shower, Coralie had just resolved to try to be extra nice to her hostess when she heard a voice outside the door.

'Hey, I hope you didn't help yourself to any of the hotel's towels. Some of them come with hitchhikers,' Ruby shouted. 'There are no bedbugs in my life and I'd like it to stay that way.'

Strangely enough, there hadn't been any mention in the hotel literature of the bedbugs that had invaded so many of the city's biggest names. It wasn't, apparently, something Manhattanites liked to boast about. Little wonder then that the hotel air, a notice on the wall explained, had been infused with calming, restorative aromas to revive the weary traveller. Pity she couldn't have chucked some of that into her suitcase.

'So why did you take the risk?' Barging past in a cloud of steam, Coralie dragged on her clothes, shook out her curls and did some quick sums. 'Listen, I appreciate you putting me up, but it's obviously not convenient for me to stay so I'll look for somewhere else.'

'No can do. If you're modelling for Gethin, I want to know where you are.' Ruby scowled. 'Gethin's a great artist. He's got a big exhibition coming up and he doesn't need to chase round Manhattan looking for you. He's really put himself out to fit this portrait into his schedule, you know, and it's my job to see that you jump when he tells you to.'

'No problem,' said Coralie, reaching for her short turquoise jacket. 'Believe me, I want to get this over with as much as you do.'

Ruby stuck a piece of gum in her mouth and chewed on it thoughtfully. 'So why *did* you come all this way if you didn't want your picture painted? Did you think you could get a bit closer to the artist?'

'I'm doing this,' said Coralie, with as much patience as she could muster given that her body was telling her it didn't know which way was up, 'for the sake of the village I love.'

'Playing hard to get, eh?' Ruby nodded. 'Smart tactic. Just don't kid yourself it'll work.'

Chapter Thirteen

The Foundered Ship was in full swing. Or it was if you stared at the vicious swirls of the greasy red carpet for too long, thought Kitty. Dark panelled walls and fake beams were enough to give you cabin fever if there were more than five people in the saloon, and a stingy little fire burnt the leg off anyone sitting right next to it, leaving everyone else freezing. According to the calendar it was almost spring, but in Penmorfa the icy winds still gusting across the west Wales coast were keeping tourists away from the Craft Courtyard.

As bored as she was feeling, the novelty of trying out Coralie's products having completely worn off, it was easy to act casually when Adam had put his head round the door of Sweet Cleans to propose knocking off for a quiet lunchtime drink. The Foundered Ship had all the pizzazz of a weak shandy, but the atmosphere was marginally warmer there than at home. With her mother embracing the whole community hall fundraising thing almost to the point of obsession she'd initially felt a bit sorry for her father. Now, she was proud of what her mother had achieved and thought she deserved better than her father's curmudgeonly comments whenever she left the house to attend a committee meeting.

Hefin, behind the bar, looked meaningfully across to the corner where Kitty was trying to hide and winked lasciviously at Adam who was getting the drinks. 'Some pork scratchings for the lady?' he suggested. What a charmer, thought Kitty, shaking her head as Adam turned and raised his eyebrows at her.

Adam hitched his shirt up to dig his wallet out of his

back pocket and Kitty stared sorrowfully at his backside and thought how lovely and taut it was, what with all the gardening and surfing. Not that she would be seeing it any time soon. She managed a smile as Adam came towards her and placed a diet cola on the beer mat in front of her. Something, she supposed, that had been put there so that the punters didn't have to chip their glasses off the sticky table. 'Cheers,' said Adam, raising his glass of Brains Dark beer. 'Your very good health and—'

'Yeah, thanks,' she said quickly, conscious that Hefin, leaning over the counter, was making no attempt to hide his shameless eavesdropping. She turned her attention back to Adam, giving him another smile so he wouldn't think she was being grouchy. She'd had time to nip into the loo and had managed to make a passable stab at looking glamorous without seeming to have tried too hard. Just the two coats of mascara, foundation, blusher and a slick of pink lip gloss.

Adam was fussing round, asking if she was warm enough and if her chair was comfortable. 'You know, that diet cola stuff has a lot of rubbish in it, artificial sweeteners and all that. I don't think you should be drinking it anymore. Let me get you some fruit juice instead. You ought to be thinking about the—'

'I am!' she hissed, nodding at Hefin who was still hanging on their every word. 'Flip, I've barely drunk anything but water for months now.'

'I think you've been cheating on that diet,' Hefin called over. 'Looks to me like you've put on a few pounds.'

Kitty was about to tell him what he could go do with himself, but she knew that part of her anger was sheer disappointment that there was no chance of Adam even making a token gesture to get her into bed. She was heartily sick of being treated like a pregnant Mother Teresa. The door creaked open, and Wilfie shuffled in, both hands deep in his trouser pockets, jangling his change. He wasn't a pretty sight, but Kitty was delighted to see him because whilst he was droning on about real ale to Hefin, she could concentrate on trying to show Adam she was still a woman.

'Will you let me have a feel?' Adam asked, his eyes shining.

Not perhaps the most romantic approach she'd ever had but a good sign nevertheless. 'What, in front of all these people?' She laughed, looking round the almost empty saloon.

'Well you don't have to take anything off, do you?' Adam smiled.

'Depends what you're trying to feel.' She giggled.

'You know.' He eyed her stomach. 'I just want to feel the baby kicking. That would be wicked.'

Kitty looked round in alarm, but one of the beer pumps running dry was causing a diversion over at the bar.

'Can we not talk about this here?' she begged.

'Sorry,' he said, with a sheepish smile that revealed his chipped front tooth. 'You're the first girl I've felt I could ask. Couldn't exactly go up to any of my mates' wives or girlfriends and put my hands on their stomachs, could I?'

'Why not? You're not usually afraid to cop a feel, are you?' The hurt flared up in his eyes and her pithy comment felt plain mean.

'Yeah, thanks, Kitty. Nice to know how little you think of me, like I'm some kind of low-life.' He put down his glass and started to move away, but she managed to get a hand across the table in time.

'Please don't go,' she said quickly. 'I was out of order.' She took a deep breath and wished she could explain just how depressing it was that she only had his attention because he was interested in the baby, not because he'd changed his mind about her. She stared down at his hand beneath hers, waiting for her vision to stop swimming with tears.

'Hey,' he said, touching his other hand to her chin and lifting it so he could look at her. 'What's all this?'

'Hormones,' she whispered, because she knew that's what he'd want to hear.

'Got to be.' He pressed his knuckles very gently into her cheek. 'You're not usually so sensitive about calling me names.'

'Yeah, well. You're not usually so sensitive when I do. You are allowed to say stuff back, you know. I'm still the same person I was last summer.'

He dragged his green gaze away from her and when he turned back his expression was bleak. They both knew it wasn't true. Kitty did a quick check – Hefin and Wilfie were still farting around trying to restore the flow of Old Blue Tongue, or whatever the guest beer happened to be, so she sidled closer to Adam and grabbed hold of his free hand.

'There,' she said, placing his palm over her stomach just in time to catch the ripple of limbs moving inside.

'Whoa!' said Adam, his delight infectious, making them both break into giggles.

'What's going on over there?' Hefin called over sharply. 'We don't want any petting in this pub, thank you.' Another flaccid, frothy sound from the recalcitrant pump spared Kitty having to tell him that chance would be a fine thing. Even so, Adam moved away again, putting some distance between them and ruining their moment of intimacy.

'You're not serious about this Flair on a Shoestring stuff, are you?' he asked, looking worried. 'I mean, it's not just a question of arranging a few bits and pieces, is it? You've got to lift boxes and climb ladders, too.'

Anyone would think he was the one carrying the baby, she thought mutinously. 'So? Look, I'm not going to take any risks, am I? I can't afford to put myself out of business before I've got started.'

'I wasn't thinking about the business.' He glared at her.

'It's a good job that I am then,' she said, glaring back. 'How do you think I'm going to provide for – what you're thinking about – if I don't start planning for the future? I can't live on thin air. Besides, you're the one who's always accusing me of sitting around on my backside, sponging off Mam and Dad. I thought you'd be pleased for me!'

Adam looked beaten. 'What about the father?' he asked, flatly. 'Whatever you think about him, he's involved. Surely he ought to face up to his financial responsibilities?'

'Ha!' she said, nastily. 'He wouldn't know what a responsibility was if it hit him in the face. Trust me, Adam, it's better that I do this on my own.'

'Sitting comfortably?' Ruby asked over Gethin's shoulder.

Coralie harrumphed at her and concentrated on the morning sun rosily reflected in the tall buildings she could see from Gethin's rented Upper West Side studio. Having overcome her initial nerves, she wondered what she'd been so worried about. So long as she sat there and did as she was told, no one really took any notice of her. No wonder portraiture was peopled by so many serious subjects; Whistler's mother, probably bored out of her mind, Ophelia turning blue in a cold bath unnoticed by Millais, Lucien Freud's benefits supervisor, not exactly having a laugh a minute. Kitty said Gethin was known as a fast worker. Coralie hoped she was right.

Leaning back a little, Coralie could just see a roof garden

in miniature below, with tall grasses and shrubs and a palette of flowers from white through to pale pink. Whilst she was looking, a doll-sized woman appeared, apparently in her dressing gown, and arranged herself on a cushioned lounger. She looked far more comfortable than Coralie, who was sitting on a rag-covered stool. Especially since the stool was balanced on a plank placed across two crates.

'Eyes to me,' Gethin ordered. 'Or you'll fall over.'

'I thought you said you didn't expect your sitters to assume difficult positions,' she grumbled.

'What's difficult about sitting down?' If he was hoping to sound innocent, he'd blown it with a flash of those wicked blue eyes. 'You're the right height for the light, that's all. Just do as you're told and it'll all be over with before you know it.'

At least Ruby appreciated the joke, grinning and shaking her head as she handed him a new brush. If doing what she was told meant the painting would be finished quickly, then fine. So, if Gethin wanted her to look at him then, dammit, she'd do just that. It wasn't so hard to do. He was wearing old jeans that had seen much better days, but hugged his hips attractively, and a loose-fitting shirt that had once been navy blue. If she knew more about paint colours she might have been able to name some of those decorating it, but she was more interested in the fact that a couple of the top buttons were undone. When he leaned forward her lofty position afforded her the odd tantalising glimpse of his chest, which was entertaining even if it did remind her of their first meeting.

'I do hope Rock's all right,' she said out loud. He'd been a bit cool with her since the mouse incident and she hadn't really had time to make it up to him.

'Hudson?' said Ruby, wringing out a rag at the surgical-looking steel sink. 'Didn't you know he left the building with Elvis?'

'This Rock was reborn as an alley cat.' Gethin stood back and frowned at her when she moaned in protest. 'Coralie, he's almost feral. He foraged for himself before you came along, and he's smart enough to know a soft touch when he sees one.'

'He was in a very sorry state when he first started hanging around,' she remonstrated. 'His eyes were runny, he wasn't keeping himself clean and he was practically starving.'

Gethin shook his head. 'And now you think you've got him eating out of your hand – except he knows it's the other way round.'

Good teeth too, thought Coralie, sighing as he gave her a wry smile before returning to his work. Kitty had joked that the real reason Gethin had left Penmorfa was because he'd run out of women. 'Likes his freedom too much, see. Plenty of farmers round here, desperate for a wife, but not Gethin Lewis. Well, not one of his own, anyway.'

It was true that the iron bedstead with its crumpled sheets standing at one end of the studio looked as if it had seen plenty of action, although with no blinds at the long windows it was very public, even this high up. Gethin, seeing her giving it a wild look, like a frightened horse, when they'd first entered the long, stripped-back room, had raised his eyebrows at her. 'Relax,' he'd told her. 'It's a prop. Now go behind the screen and take your top off. Ruby will make sure you're decent. Oh, and I'd like you to wear your hair down, please.'

So much for all that stuff about the erotic tension between artist and model, the voyeur-painter with his sexualised gaze reducing his sitter to an object of lust. Anything less erotic than her hard perch was hard to imagine and, for all the tension when he studied her, she was beginning to wonder if he'd even noticed she was a woman.

Also, whilst he was undeniably decorative, Gethin wasn't stopping her bottom from going to sleep. She shifted a buttock and the plank wobbled.

'To me!' Gethin growled. So much for all the fun he'd suggested it might be. Outside, the sunlight had turned pale lemon, but the studio remained cool. The white walls and white-tiled splashback behind the sink were made more clinical by the metal tables which looked as if they'd originally been intended for use in an operating theatre. Even though they were laid out with brushes and paints rather than forceps and retractors, the effect was equally daunting; both sets of tools could open you up in strange and unexpected ways.

She caught his eye and he smiled at her lazily and almost sent her flying.

'You look as if you're on a throne,' he explained. 'Penmorfa's Queen of Clean.'

Why did he make it sound as if she was repressed? Ruby guffawed.

'What's wrong with that?' Coralie complained. 'It keeps a lot of local suppliers busy. I source wax from a beekeeper near Cardigan, lavender flower heads from a grower on the Pembrokeshire borders and herbs from the garden centre.'

'Everything you ever needed right on your doorstep, then?' he said, dabbing at the canvas.

Coralie bit her lip. Why did it sound so unadventurous when he said it? It wasn't as if she hadn't taken any risks; doing her accounts often made her pulse race. And she had plans – just looking at some of the window displays in the huge department stores on 5th Avenue had given her fresh ideas for the business. Having her own doorstep was a good thing; most of her single friends were still renting, but because she'd been prepared to move to an undiscovered area, she'd been able to stretch to buying. And what a beautiful area it was too, with a breathtaking coastline and stupendous view from the cliffs of dramatic churning surf. Of course she was happy!

It was just occasionally, when one of her friends announced her engagement or if she received another excited call about a new baby, that the evenings in Penmorfa seemed especially quiet. And once in a while, when she scattered confetti over another happy couple, she felt a lump in her throat and wondered if there was a man out there who could love her for who she was. There was always Wilfie, she supposed, if she needed some male company, although thinking it over, she didn't need male company *that* much.

Gethin came out from behind his easel. His ruffled dark hair made her thoughts stray to wondering how it would feel to push her fingers through it. What would it be like, she tried to imagine as he lifted his chin and ran his hand across his stubbled jaw, to feel the hard, rough touch of his skin against hers? Now, if she was more like Kitty, she wouldn't be wasting time thinking about it, she'd be grabbing some excitement whilst she could. Coralie came to and found him glowering at her with passionate intensity. Had the sight of her, wobbling on a stool, with her bra straps pulled down beneath some orange sheet thing Ruby had wrapped round her, pushed him over the edge?

'Your shoulders are drooping and you're fidgeting around all over the place,' he complained, throwing his brush down. 'No wonder I can't get this right. Okay, everyone, we'll have to leave it there.'

'Not going so well, eh?' said Ruby, once Gethin had sent Coralie off to explore the stores, because he couldn't stand the frustration of looking at her and not being able to paint her any longer. 'Why's that?'

Gethin scratched his head to see if it would stimulate his brain into coming up with an answer he liked better. 'Post success stress?'

Ruby laughed. 'That's a new name for it.'

He pointed to the brushes in the sink, indicating that she should get on with it. 'I'm serious. Everything's ready for the exhibition, but there'll be the usual merry-go-round with the press to deal with afterwards.'

'The press come with the joy of being the people's painter,' Ruby said above the noise of the running tap. 'Remember that when you get your next print royalties.'

Make that 'if', he nearly admitted. According to his solicitor, the administrators who'd taken over the firm that had handled all the reprints were still doing their best to avoid settling up with him. 'Of course,' he acknowledged airily, 'but it makes it hard to concentrate on a new work.'

'Something's hard,' Ruby muttered.

Gethin strolled over, leaned against the sink so he could glare at her more easily and folded his arms. 'I beg your pardon?'

'Making a decision,' she said, shaking out a wet brush so that it sprayed over his shoulder. 'You see, I've spent many hours watching you in this studio. You flirt, charm, pay compliments so the sitter relaxes, but all the time, you're watching and working. A brush stroke here, a retouch of colour there – you're fast, perceptive, you flatter them with a sheen of glamour so they'll tell their friends, who'll want the same. But this time,' she looked at him with an amused grin, 'you don't even know where to begin.'

'Don't be ridiculous!' He snorted. 'I'll just have to study her more closely.'

He turned his back on Ruby whose penetrating gaze had all the innocence of an Exocet. Yep, that's what he'd do. The more opportunities he had to study his subject, the better her portrait would be. And once he'd painted out his current obsession, he could get back to his normal, untroubled life and stop thinking crazy thoughts about Coralie Casey.

Chapter Fourteen

'This sitting's cancelled,' he told Coralie when she turned up at the studio the next morning, ignoring Ruby who was smirking at him knowingly.

'We'll run out of time if we don't get on with it,' said Coralie, not looking best pleased.

'Not all guys can perform on demand,' Ruby butted in, shrugging her shoulders and rolling her gum round her cheeks.

He fixed her with a death-ray glare. 'If you'd just let me explain,' he went on, 'I'm cancelling the sitting because we're going out for the day instead. It's just as valid a way of building up a picture of you as studying you in my studio.'

Better, in fact, he thought, ignoring Coralie's doubtful expression, because he wouldn't have Ruby psychoanalysing him or sniggering at him behind his back.

Battery Park was one of his favourite places. As much as he enjoyed the hustle and bustle of the city, he liked the breezy walk along the waterfront, enjoying all the contrasts like the juxtaposition between the upscale condos and the monuments to the past. Once upon a time important visitors arriving by sea were heralded by enormous jets of water pumped into the sky by fireboats from Pier A. If, like him, those crews could see Coralie's hair making such a vibrant splash of colour against the shimmering blues of the Hudson River, the big sky and the glass towers of New Jersey glinting on the opposite bank, he was sure they'd be out there again today, queuing up to pay tribute.

He'd taken her to the National September 11 Memorial first; the water, like so many tears, cascading down into the pools where the Twin Towers once stood. So many lost and fractured lives. In a palpably sad and sombre atmosphere, they'd stood to pay their respects before moving on. Now, drawn by the bright sunshine on another freezing cold day, they joined the couples strolling along the Esplanade, the joggers and dog-walkers proof that ordinary life and simple pleasures could and should resume after tragedy.

He turned to her, hoping to see her big smile widening with pleasure and was taken aback by her glum expression.

'Oughtn't we be getting back to the studio now?' she asked, an anxious frown creasing her brow. 'Six sittings, you said. This is my third day here – how are we going to fit them all in?'

'You know, your haste to get away from me is a little indecent,' he told her, slightly miffed that he wasn't making half the impression on her as she was on him. 'Especially since you kept me waiting so long in the first place.'

'Why draw this thing out any longer than is necessary?' She shrugged, with another frown. 'Shouldn't you get it out of the way so that you can concentrate on your exhibition?'

'The more I concentrate on you,' he reminded her, 'the quicker we'll be done. Just relax, will you, or you'll risk missing what's so fantastic about this city. Take a look at that, for example.' He pointed to the waterfront.

'Oh! It *is* beautiful,' she said, and he could see some of the tension leave her shoulders. 'It's a vast stretch of water, so much bigger than I expected! And it's wonderful to smell sea air again!'

She pushed her hair back as the spring breeze lifted it in a ripple of copper waves.

Nope, he thought, trying to frame the image to keep in his mind's eye, he definitely wouldn't have been able to catch that joyous expression in his studio. The idea of simply walking round with her was a stroke of genius, except that everywhere they went would always be indelibly stained by the memory of her, which didn't seem quite so clever. He was willing to bet there was nothing in the Sweet Cleans range strong enough to wipe away anything like that.

'Anyone would think you'd been away from it for weeks,' he told her. 'You're not feeling that cooped up already, are you?'

A pair of cute girls in running vests jogged towards them, but he was too busy watching Coralie, waiting for her to wrinkle her nose, or tilt her head on one side whilst she thought about it. All the funny little expressions he was learning about.

'This city's amazing, but I wouldn't want to move away from the sea,' she said, with a quick, shy smile that made him catch his breath. 'Not now I can walk to the beach every day.'

And he wouldn't go back to Penmorfa, not once he'd discharged his duties there. He'd made his mind up about that a long time ago, only now when he thought about it, it made him feel depressed. He shot a quick glance at Coralie just to prove to himself that it was nothing to do with her and saw that she was rapt at the sight of a Chihuahua dressed in a pink frock and sitting in a buggy being pushed by an elderly Japanese woman. Another dumb mutt had beaten him to her affection.

Not that he was looking for her affection, he reminded himself. She wasn't even his type, he thought, taking a quick mental note of the way her eyes crinkled with amusement. His preference was for women who knew how to play the game. Who wouldn't bug him in the morning, or nag him for an engagement ring. Coralie was just a lovely, uncomplicated woman trying to live the good life in the countryside –

although once she woke up to the reality, she'd find, like all the rest of the incomers in search of the dream, that you couldn't spin gold out of straw. It still peeved him that she didn't even seem to notice he was there.

Still, it wasn't all bad if he experienced the odd frisson. In the studio it would add something extra to the painting and Ruby would have to eat her words and praise his dedication to his work. But something was upside-down when he was starting to take account of what Ruby thought, he frowned to himself. Who was the master and who was the pupil here? Besides, he had the rest of his life to think about work, but less than a week to think about Coralie. It was plain good manners to see that she got the most out of her visit.

She suddenly grabbed his arm. 'Look!' she said, as if he'd never noticed it before, 'the Statue of Liberty! And I was so determined not to be impressed,' she said, darting in front of another jogger for a better look. 'I've seen it so many times on screen – but it just takes your breath away, doesn't it?'

'You think it would survive as such an enduring symbol if you could pin it down so easily?' he asked, trying to ignore the voice that was asking him if he wasn't trying to do just that with the real live woman in front of him. 'Everyone thinks they know New York from the movies, but you have to be here to know how it really feels.'

'No wonder so many immigrants have been so inspired by the sight!' She leaned out across the rails, trying to get a better view of Ellis Island, where the ships bringing new arrivals had once docked.

'Nearly twelve million people have passed through the gates there,' he told her. 'Some of them probably came from Penmorfa. When the railways came in the nineteenth century, it put the old cargo ships that used to dock at Abersaith out of business. The industries that served them declined, meaning hard times for the surrounding villages, too. The next wave of ships to dock at Abersaith came to carry Welsh emigrants away to New York. The architect Frank Lloyd Wright's family was amongst those who made the long Atlantic crossing.'

Leaving the life blood of the little towns to drain away ever since, as men like him turned their backs on the old ways. 'You've got to ask yourself why they all left,' he added, more for his own benefit.

'Looking at this, they must have believed they really were on the brink of a brave new world.' Coralie turned to face him so that the vivid seascape glistened behind her.

'Yep,' he said, drawing her back from the rail to sit on one of the benches. 'Once they were off that boat, they could be whoever they liked.'

'Is that what you did?' she asked. 'Left the boy behind in Penmorfa and became a famous artist here?'

'Coralie,' he said, 'I came by plane. It's not quite the same.'

'But you've made your name here,' she insisted. 'I can see how anyone could fall for all this, but surely there must be part of you that still belongs in Penmorfa?'

He took a long, hard look at her and shook his head. 'Not one little bit. Not now. Not ever.'

Coralie was deeply concerned about how little there was to show for what felt like hours spent sitting on a stool, wrapped in an orange sheet.

'Will there be any value in a blank canvas if I persuade you to sign it?' she asked, chewing her lip. After a second and then a third session during which Gethin freely distributed his scowls between her, the canvas and Ruby, whose mission seemed to be to wind Gethin up, the portrait had barely progressed. With only two full days of her trip left to go, she wondered if they could hoodwink the art world into believing it was a bold step in a new direction.

Even Ruby's pierced eyebrows raised when he called yet another halt to the sitting and proposed a further sightseeing tour instead. 'It's too good a day to miss the view,' he'd insisted, when she'd been half-hearted about seeing the Empire State Building. 'And look, there's not even too much of a queue.'

Coralie followed him in to the marble-lined entrance lobby with its towering relief image of the skyscraper superimposed on a map of New York State. All that glitz only made her suspicious that it was designed to soften the blow that the view probably wasn't all it was cracked up to be.

'All this trailing round the tourist traps,' she said, looking up at him. 'You're not trying to tell me something, are you? You haven't changed your mind about donating a painting to Penmorfa, have you?'

'Indulge me, Coralie.' He shook his head as he handed her her ticket. 'Pander to my artistic ego. If I have a yearning to show you the view, that's what we'll do.'

A small observation deck right up in the sky couldn't possibly offer many places to hide. If he thought he could wriggle out of answering her question, she decided, smiling to herself as they piled into one of the first set of elevators, he'd have no choice but to hear her out once they were up there.

'We can go outside on the 86th floor observation deck, but I wanted you to see this first,' he said, leading her over to more elevators.

The highest observation deck was closed in, wasn't it? That was good; he couldn't even pretend that the wind was carrying her words away.

'All the way up to the tippy-top!' the operator announced, shutting the doors behind them.

The only problem was that standing beside Gethin, as the old-fashioned lift cage climbed steadily to the 102nd floor, she was beginning to lose sight of her goal. It was getting harder and harder to keep her feet firmly on the ground. Gethin had spent an awful lot of time with her; was it only because he was serious about his work? And when he grinned down at her like that, exuding excitement and danger, was it simply because he needed to get a better look at her? The Empire State Building's Art Deco spire was once intended as a mooring mast for airships, but if she wasn't very careful, she'd also be floating on air. The operator pulled open the doors and Gethin led her outside to the observatory.

'The view here's even more spectacular and it's less crowded. Three hundred and sixty degrees of the Big Apple.'

Coralie sucked in her breath, all her preconceived ideas about hype blown away by the reality of seeing the city spread out before her.

'Now tell me you're not impressed,' he said, triumphantly. 'You think you've got views in Penmorfa, but they're nothing like this.'

'You may have a point,' she admitted, giving in. The Chrysler spire looked fabulous glittering against the Manhattan skyline and the backdrop of the East River. And from here, she thought, turning and looking down, she could see how the distinctively shaped Flatiron building got its name, too.

'There's the Great Lady again,' said Gethin, leaning over her shoulder and pointing to the Statue of Liberty rising from New York Bay. 'I bet you're glad you let me take you all the way now.'

Kitty would have said they hadn't even got off first base.

It was a difficult thought to ignore, especially when he was close like that. A young American woman, her rich brown hair tied up in a ponytail, waiting by the elevator with a couple who could have been her parents, caught her eye and smiled.

'Hey, you guys look happy,' she said, pointing at Coralie's camera. 'Want me to take a picture of you, before we go?'

Judging that it was less embarrassing to simply submit rather than explain, Coralie handed her camera over. The worst that could happen was that she might have been suckered by a camera snatcher, but since it was an entirely average piece of kit, this seemed unlikely.

Vertigo, she decided when Gethin pulled her nearer, forcing her to meet his twinkling blue eyes. That must be why her stomach had given a little lurch.

'Aw! That's great!' cooed their new pony-tailed fan. 'You guys make such a cute couple!'

'That's very kind of you,' Gethin told her as she handed the camera back. 'Now we'll always have something to remind us of today, won't we, sweetheart?'

She gave him a look and he grinned back at her, deep blue eyes full of mischief. Definitely vertigo, she told herself. What else would explain that giddy feeling when he leaned close to her? Or the tingle of excitement when he rested his fingers lightly on her shoulder? In case of a sudden fit of light-headedness, she decided it was wise to hang on to him whilst he pointed out all the famous landmarks. There was Brooklyn Bridge, 800 acres of Central Park, iconic buildings like the New York Times everywhere she looked and beyond, in the distance, Connecticut, New Jersey, Pennsylvania and Massachusetts. All the places which had just been names to her but which she'd forever associate with one day in New York when she felt as if she was on top of the world.

A lick of black glass nagged at the corner of her vision for attention. Kitty's voice told her to ignore it and concentrate on the good feelings, but curiosity got the better of her. Leaning forward for a better look, she recognised it as the hotel where she had spent her first night in the city and she came back down to earth. Playing the tourist was all very well, but imagine what would have happened at the consultancy if she'd allowed herself to be so distracted from the task in hand? What would Alys do if she returned to Penmorfa empty-handed?

Gethin frowned at her. 'Something bugging you, Coralie? Why can't you just relax and enjoy me showing you round?'

'I guess I'm just not very good at relaxing,' she said, trying to smile.

'Then I'm going to have to find a way to make you.' He sighed. 'These sittings are going nowhere. For a start you're going to have to trust me.'

He took her arm as she raised it in protest, moving her along as a tall, pale-skinned Russian couple, exotic in their expensive designer sunglasses, came up to look out of the window beside them. 'Stop trying to control everything, Coralie. Not everything's neat and tidy or sweet and clean, but that's what makes it exciting. Why don't you let go and see what happens?'

He reached over and took both of her hands in his, rubbing his thumbs over her short, neatly manicured nails. 'What are you scared of?'

'Nothing.' Coralie took her hands back. 'I just want to do my best for Penmorfa, that's all,' she said, stubbornly.

'But that's not why you're afraid,' he said, leading her towards the elevator. 'Do you want to be like the kid on the beach who watches everyone else have fun? Put it behind you, whatever it is. Sometimes you've just got to accept that you can't build sandcastles without getting your hands dirty.'

'Going down,' the operator announced as the elevator doors opened.

A bit like me, thought Coralie, feeling her spirits sinking along with her stock. Producing a range of cleaning products didn't mean that everything about her was necessarily snow white.

'Look, we'll give it another shot tomorrow morning,' he said, as they stopped again at the 86th floor. 'Then I'll have to put in an appearance at the gallery, before the reception for the new show.'

Coralie nodded, determined not to let her bruised ego spoil the opportunity to experience that amazing view of the city from the open-air observatory. Raw air rushing towards them and people jostling for the best views made conversation difficult, giving her a few moments for reflection whilst she waited. For all her protests, she had started to feel quite intrigued about her portrait. Surely, you'd need to be made of granite not to be a bit curious about what that deep-blue gaze would reveal? Except she'd been secretly hoping that the person he could see was more like the glamorous, free-spirited dancer in *Samba* than a prim, buttoned-up nobody, afraid of getting creases in her skirt.

By the time they were back in the street again, she'd managed to rally her flagging spirits. With his show about to open, Gethin really didn't need a temperamental model on his hands, too – or any excuse to call off the final sitting.

'I'm really looking forward to the reception, even though it will be my last night here,' she admitted, dredging up a smile. 'It's coming round quickly, isn't it?'

Too quickly. In a very short space of time, she'd got used to being by his side, enjoying the quiet thrill of listening to that wonderful voice, feeling the pride he took in the city he adored. Seeing his new works would be a real privilege – assuming she felt relaxed enough about the painting's progress to enjoy it.

'You're booked for tomorrow evening, too,' he said, rather formally.

'Yes, I suppose we'll need another sitting,' she agreed with relief. Six, he'd told her at the beginning. She hoped that he could produce a finished work in fewer. Penmorfa's future depended on it.

Chapter Fifteen

In Penmorfa, Alys, returning from another committee meeting, was just about to open the back door when she caught sight of movement in the kitchen and stopped, feeling terribly sad. The man she could see through the kitchen window, as she stood on the outside looking in, was still her own dear Huw – strong and solid, with warm, brown eyes and silver hair curling into the nape of his neck. But Huw, the man she had loved for all her adult life, no longer pulled her to him.

Their move to the farmhouse, with a bigger mortgage, all the legal costs, and the strain of the recession, had taken its toll on Huw's health and sent his blood pressure soaring. As the one who'd pressed for them to make the change, Alys felt it was her responsibility to do whatever she could to ease their financial burden. But although she was optimistic about the future of the garden centre, especially now Kitty had come up with such an innovative idea to add to their family businesses, it all seemed a bit futile if she'd lost Huw along the way.

She had tried to be understanding when, increasingly, he'd been unable or unwilling to make love, but sometimes she despaired of ever hearing the rise and fall of his breathing beside her in bed again, or of feeling the fortress of his arms wrapping round her.

'Just leave it, will you?' was all he would say when she'd begged him to talk about the problem. But the most hurtful moment had been when he'd taken himself off to the spare room the previous summer, when Alys's hot flushes were keeping them both awake, and just when she was feeling especially insecure. It had been a painful and difficult time.

A dark chasm had opened before them, yet somehow they had both, separately, looked over the precipice and had decided to step back from the edge. But even their most casual moments of intimacy were still forced and unnatural.

Nevertheless, Huw smiled as she padded into the room in her socks, having kicked off her boots at the door. 'Your fingers are cold,' he told her, catching her hand just briefly, before turning to pour her a glass of wine. 'Go and sit by the stove and warm up. Kitty's turned in for an early night so we didn't wait for you to eat.'

'Is she unwell?' Alys worried.

Huw pulled a face. 'She's just tired, you know, thinking about this wedding styling scheme of hers. I've saved you some lasagne.'

When Huw placed it before her, she chewed a forkful and forced herself to swallow.

'The meeting went on a bit, didn't it?' he said, wiping his hands on the red check tea towel.

'Mair took a bit of convincing before she signed the paperwork. She still can't believe that Gethin's work is worth good money. She's obsessed with how we're going to make the repayments on the loan. What she refuses to see is that it's little more than a paper exercise with the sum we're about to raise from the sale of the painting.

'And then I stayed on to talk to the Vicar. I think she's finding looking after five churches a bit of a struggle. It doesn't help that her husband's academic research has taken him away from home so much lately, of course. I know she misses him when he's not there. Oh, and we've confirmed the date for the official handover of Gethin's painting and the date for the charity auction.'

'Alys, you don't need to account for every minute,' he said lightly.

He ran some hot water and began scraping at the empty lasagne dish. Alys gritted her teeth as the noise went through her and fought the urge to tell him just to leave it to soak. How many more times would she have to remind him that he'd waste less water dumping everything in the dishwasher? Thirty years of marriage and he still made a ritual out of hand washing dishes at the sink. She stopped pushing pasta round her plate and put her fork down.

'Finished?'

She watched his back as he worked at the sink, wiping her plate and rinsing it under the tap. More waste. 'Oh, for goodness sake!' she begged, 'why don't you stop doing that and sit down with me?' He dried his hands again, screwing up the tea towel and leaving it in a damp heap beside the sink. Alys resisted the urge to march over, shake it out and hang it neatly on the stove. Or maybe it was Huw who needed a good shake. Finally, he lowered himself into the Windsor chair at the other side of the long pine table. One of the cats jumped into his lap and Alys watched as his strong fingers burrowed into the soft fur behind its ear as Edith looked on jealously.

'All right, let's talk.'

Alys waited, suddenly nervous.

'When are you going to get round to telling me that our daughter's expecting our first grandchild?'

Alys breathed again. This was not the conversation she would have chosen to have, but it was one they needed to have. Soon she would have to face up to Huw and talk to him about the other problem on her mind. Delyth and Mair might only be stabbing in the dark, but some of their comments were keeping her awake at night. For now, this was a more immediate issue. One thing at a time.

'I haven't discussed it with you, Huw, because so far Kitty

hasn't even been able to tell me.' She laid her hand on the table, hoping that he would take it. 'I wanted to give her the opportunity to discuss it with us in her own time. We have to let her come to terms with the changes she's facing in her own way, Huw. She's always worked her problems out by herself, ever since she was a little girl. I'd rather give her some space here, where I can keep an eye on her, than press her and have her take flight. Just try to be patient ...'

'Don't you think, Alys,' he said, standing up suddenly and sending the cat flying, 'that my patience has been tried enough?'

Alys heard the cut of his breath as he sat in the back lobby and changed his slippers for gardening boots. Edith scampered after him. There was a rasp as he zipped up a fleece, the rustle of waxed cotton as an outdoor coat was shrugged on, then the slamming of the door.

Gethin glanced down at Coralie, who was subdued, at his side. When he'd taken her by surprise that morning and invited her out for an evening date, he'd been secretly hoping for a warmer response, but instead she'd been rather fretful about the lack of progress on the portrait. He had to admit to some mild feelings of concern himself. Great apes had produced superior artwork to his clumsy daubs. Nothing he applied to the canvas came close to capturing Coralie. How tough could it be when those colours and curves just invited themselves to be traced in sensuous strokes?

'So now you've got it so bad you can't even be in the same room as her when you paint,' Ruby had commented that morning, when she'd found him alone in the studio staring impotently at his failed portrait. But Ruby talked a load of rubbish; all he needed was to get a proper look at Coralie. Some talent would help, too.

'I'm taking her to the opera. I think it'll help to catch her off-guard, when she's not so aware of being watched. I can always finish the work later.'

'You're going to have to. There's a lot of setting up to do before the reception. It'll take both of us to keep Pamala Gray happy,' she'd scolded, shaking her head. 'Opera? You said those Puccini arias all sound the same.'

'It's Bizet,' he informed her, trying to gain the upper hand. 'Carmen, acclaimed for the brilliancy of its melody and harmony.'

'"Love is a rebellious bird"', said Ruby, mysteriously, adding in response to his raised eyebrows, 'It's a line from one of the show's big numbers.'

'All right, you proved you know more about opera than me,' he admitted. 'I just want to show her the Met.'

'Just the Met?'

Ruby was always ready to speak her mind, but Coralie was probably too kind to wonder out loud if his skills really were as limited as some critics had suggested. He realised how much her good opinion mattered to him and he was fast running out of time to earn it.

'Now, that's what the tourist guides would recommend you do for a romantic date,' he pointed out as they skirted the corner of Central Park and saw the lines of horse-drawn carriages waiting to take couples on a tour.

She looked at him warily, but at least it was nice to see her face rather than her cold shoulder.

'And it'll part you with your cash pretty smartish,' he added as an aside, before they turned into West 63rd Street, the constant pulse of yellow cabs just slowing for the lights at Columbus. 'But I think a ride in the park is overrated,' he felt her stiffen beside him, 'compared to this.'

Coralie slowed to a halt and her hand flew up to her

mouth as the Lincoln Center and the white façade of the Metropolitan Opera House, with its five distinctive arched windows lit up, appeared in front of them. Gethin wasn't a great believer in guardian angels, but he offered up some silent thanks to his, just in case. If his artistic powers had deserted him, his observant eye served him well. He'd run an inquisitive eye over Coralie's music and film collection, the evening he'd nearly run *her* into a ditch in Penmorfa. One film in particular had attracted his attention because it wasn't anything to do with Doris Day.

'Thank you,' she said, stopping him as they reached the top of the steps before crossing the plaza. 'This is very special. I know this is going to sound silly, but I've always wanted to do this ever since I saw that film, *Moonstruck*. One of my favourite scenes is when Cher, as Loretta Castorini, and Nicolas Cage, as Ronny Cammareri, all dressed up in their evening clothes, are searching the crowds for each other in vain, then catch that first sight of each other by the fountain here.'

'What a coincidence.' He grinned. 'Shame it wasn't a premiere or the season's opener, or we could have done the whole black tie thing.' He thought of her in a strapless evening gown and a waterfall necklace of diamonds and pearls warm in her cleavage.

'That would have been fun, but I'm glad I didn't wear my ball gown tonight, I might have felt a little overdressed,' Coralie admitted, looking at the people swarming towards the doors and the predominantly smart but casual vibe.

Gethin rather wished she had. Somehow it made him think about undressing her; peeling back that cashmere wrap would be a start so that he could see what it was that was silky and sleeveless and floated from her shoulders and swung just above her knees. As it was her distinctive perfume was giving him ideas about nuzzling her neck and burying his face in the feminine, floral scent of her.

'What is that perfume you're wearing?' he asked, lightly, glad that she was too busy soaking up the sights to pay too much attention to his question.

She gave him a quick, wry smile, 'Je Reviens.'

Yep, he ought to be able to see the funny side of that, too. She wouldn't be returning, would she? A couple of days and she'd be out of his life for good. No complications. Just the way he liked it. Since they were just by the fountain, radiant with white light and sparkling in the middle of the plaza, he stopped and stepped back to look at her.

'Coralie, you look beautiful. Thank you for coming with me tonight.' Then he took one of her hands and kissed it. 'How's that, Loretta?' He winked, and felt ridiculously pleased that he'd mugged up on the film when she raised her eyebrows and gave him a delighted smile. The next thing he knew he'd wrapped a hand round her waist, pulling her towards him so he could feel the sweet warmth of her body close against his.

In the maelstrom of voices and footsteps surrounding them, there was a moment of stillness as her smile faded and her soft tawny eyes held his.

'So,' she said, slipping out of his arms, 'are we going inside or is this as far as we get?'

He wanted to tell her he'd like to go much further, only the show was about to begin and her eager glance towards the arched windows showed him how keen she was not to miss it. If the only way he could get her to look at him for any length of time was in the studio, he was certainly losing his touch.

Coralie shuffled forward with the surge of people squeezing through the door behind a silver-haired Japanese man, who was keeping a protective hold of his petite, beautiful wife. At least she could pretend that her burning face was due to the crush of bodies all around her. She must have imagined that seductive message in Gethin's dark eyes.

What would a man like him see in her anyway? She'd overheard one or two cruel comments, back in the days of the management consultancy, from men who'd stereotyped her because of her job and the serious dress code that went with it. And Gethin had already decided that her idea of a good night was the ten o'clock news and a mug of Horlicks, making sure, of course that she'd removed her makeup and brushed her teeth first. The really depressing thing was that he was right.

Once inside the opera house, the sight of the huge Chagall murals each side of a stunning starburst crystal chandelier made it impossible for her to dwell on wistful thoughts about Gethin Lewis. Instead, she quietly enjoyed the feel of his hand on the small of her back as he gently guided her through the crowds, up the curving white marble staircase carpeted in plush red, to the front row balcony. As she sat there, feeling the strong, comforting pressure of his arm against hers, under the golden glow of the auditorium's gilded ceiling, she made up her mind to forget about the disastrous sittings, to forget about Penmorfa and the church hall fund and simply enjoy every moment of the evening.

'It's about to begin,' Gethin said, leaning closer and pointing at the elaborate crystal chandeliers gracefully rising upwards to open the view of the stage. The excited murmurs and last-minute coughs from the audience reached a crescendo then abruptly died away. Fizzing with pleasurable anticipation, Coralie smiled up at Gethin, who surprised her by reaching across and laying his warm hand over hers. Before she could decide what to do about it, the curtains opened to reveal two figures under an intensely vivid gash of crimson. And as the dancers moved across the stage in a thrilling and tempestuous *pas de deux*, anticipating the love affair between Carmen and Don José, she simply sat back and surrendered herself to the whole experience.

'Oh, that was amazing!' she said, fighting to be heard above the sustained applause which split the dramatic silence at the end of the performance. 'What a production! So professional and such wonderful voices. Mind you, the story's depressing. Poor Don José, he paid a heavy price for falling in love with the wrong girl, didn't he?'

'Yep, they should have listened to Doris. Their lips certainly shouldn't have touched!' He laughed. 'Now, would you like a drink, since you didn't have one in the interval? We can get one here?'

Back to reality. She'd been too busy people-watching, laughing and chatting with Gethin and simply absorbing the atmosphere of the occasion to want to leave her seat during the intermission, but the evening was rapidly drawing to a close. She shook her head, gaining herself some time to squash down the sudden lump in her throat that was making it hard to talk.

'No, you're right.' He reached for her hand as they stood up to squeeze along the row of seats. 'We'll go somewhere quieter.' He started to edge his way forward. 'Isn't that what always happens in opera?' he asked, over his shoulder, as they waited for a gap. 'They were two people from different sides of the tracks. They were never going to settle down in a cottage with roses round the door and have babies together.'

He could have been speaking about them, thought Coralie, a sudden sense of anti-climax making her feel glum.

'Just because you can see it coming doesn't mean you have to like it,' she mumbled.

He stood back to allow her to thread her way into the queue of people squeezing towards the stairs and fell into step behind her. Imagine if she'd fallen for Gethin Lewis, she thought, trying to ignore the warmth of his body against hers as he ushered her through the throng.

Two people from different sides of the ocean. What chance could there be for them when the place of her dreams was the place of his nightmares? Move over darling? Not a hope; of course it would never work.

'Thank you for tonight, Gethin,' she said, making a determined attempt to compose herself once they were outside. 'I'll always remember it.'

'And so will I, Coralie.' He smiled. 'You may be a lousy model but your face was a picture there. You lived every moment of that story, didn't you?'

Not the opera, she wanted to tell him, the evening. To put all her problems to one side for a few hours and to sit there, daring to dream that the attractive man holding her hand was someone who cared for her, had given her a glimpse of how life could be. She closed her eyes before the shimmer of tears she could feel welling up were caught by the sparkle of the strings of white lights in the trees and betrayed her.

'Hey.' He lifted her chin. 'I was joking about the model bit. It's not you. It's me.' His hand was warm against her cheek and it took all she had not to lean into him when she was so aware of how very lonely her life had become.

'Coralie?'

The lilt of his accent almost made her knees buckle. She swallowed hard and opened her eyes to find his dark gaze on hers, full of yearning. In her head, she could hear Doris Day singing out a warning, telling her that their lips shouldn't touch, but Coralie ignored her. Who cared about the rest of the world? Who cared about tomorrow? Then her arms went up and she lifted her face to meet his lips as his mouth came down on hers. All that mattered was the heat of his hands through the silk of her dress and his hot, hard body pressing against hers.

Oh, the relief of giving into what every fibre of her being had been crying out to do was all the sweeter for the agony of waiting. This was Gethin. Gethin Lewis, who'd branded himself on her imagination ever since that first unforgettable glimpse of him on the other side of her fence. She pressed her hands to the hard planes of his face, breathing in his citrus cologne blended with the warm, clean male smell of him, the rough brush of his stubble against her fingertips confirming he was real. Just for a fraction of a second, she almost laughed at the novelty of what she was doing – kissing *Gethin Lewis*, the man she'd almost maimed in her garden – but then his mouth moved against hers, demanding her attention, sweeping her away on a raft of delicious sensations and dark promise of what might come.

'Coralie?'

She pulled away reluctantly. That he'd even been capable of breaking off in the middle of a kiss to her was a bit depressing. Maybe she wasn't getting it right. Just the way his tongue teased her lips made her gasp with pleasurable anticipation and set her skin tingling. If she'd been having half the effect on him, he wouldn't have been able to come up for air. But then he thought she was prim and proper, neat and tidy. She'd have to try harder to banish any lingering impressions he might have had about her preferring a cup of tea to making love.

'We're becoming a sideshow here,' he said, gently, when

she looked up to meet his eyes. 'Would you like to go somewhere a bit less public?'

Still wrapped in his arms, she peered round him. Yup, they were still in the Lincoln Center, weren't they? No wonder people were grinning at them or walking away shaking their heads. She buried her face in his chest before looking up at him and nodding.

'My place?'

'Yes,' she said, looking him in the eye and leaving him in no doubt that her intention was not to do the dishes or push the Hoover round.

Chapter Sixteen

Gethin managed to rustle up a taxi with impressive speed, but a couple of blocks might just as well have been a trip to the moon, so giant a leap was it for Coralie and her stretched nerves. Before she managed to take control of her breathing, she was also worried that it would take a life-support pack for her to climb the grey marble steps up to his third-floor apartment.

Inside, he drew her close. 'Are you quite sure about this, Coralie?' he murmured, stroking the soft nape of her neck.

From somewhere unbidden, the dark memories welled up – the life lost, the lives wasted. Then something wonderful happened; as unexpectedly as they had appeared, the doubts faded and the worried voices fell silence. She felt as if she belonged in his arms.

'What do you think?' she asked softly, smiling up at him. Then he kissed her, his lips moving gently and slowly with hers, and the heat began to build. She closed her eyes, shivering with the thrilling sensation of his skin grazing hers as he bent his head to kiss her throat.

Her hands moved to unbutton the rest of his shirt. Somehow it was mostly undone and hanging loose anyway. Of course, that didn't mean that he didn't still consider that she was the one who was buttoned-up. Maybe there was a chance he'd think she was removing his shirt because it was crumpled and she wanted to iron it? She decided on the direct approach and reached for his belt buckle. His sharp intake of breath indicated that she'd hit the spot, but before she'd managed to congratulate herself, his hand slid under her dress and she forgot what she was thinking.

'That's a yes,' she gasped a few minutes later, lying on his bed, just in case he was in any doubt, 'I'm sure.'

Straightening up, she pushed his shirt off his shoulders and enjoyed getting acquainted with the sight of his lean, hard body that she'd only previously glimpsed. She made him lie down and traced the fine dark hairs across his chest, then followed to where they formed a dark line from his flat stomach downwards. Retracing the path her fingers had taken with her lips, she teased him with fluttery kisses and delicate nips, whilst her hands restrained him.

'I'm a patient man,' he said huskily, breaking free and rolling her on to her back, 'but I have my limits and you're pushing them.'

His mouth moved to her throat. 'I've waited a long time for this ...'

His breath was warm against her skin as he moved slowly down her body.

'You have?' She shuddered as the relentless progress of his tongue set off wavelets of pleasure rippling across her body.

'Uh-huh.' He propped himself up to look at her. 'Ever since the moment I saw you doing your Little Red Riding Hood act out in the garden at Penmorfa.'

Her only answer was a soft, involuntary moan, because his lips, following his fingers to explore her inner thigh, were doing something strange to her breathing pattern. She lifted her head at the same time as him and found herself looking into his deep, dark, midnight gaze. The Big Bad Wolf, all lean, hard and hungry, a slow smile playing across his face.

Gethin propped himself up on his elbow so that he could get his fill of Coralie in the morning light: silky dark lashes, the pale, smooth skin of her back, her chestnut curls contrasting with the white pillow. It was a room that he'd always thought of as tranquil, the sliding shoji doors dividing it from the living room maximising the light and enhancing the apartment's understated opulence. But now he was feeling anything but tranquil.

Flashbacks of the night before fast forwarded through his brain: his hand on Coralie's thigh, the slipperiness of silk sliding under his impatient fingers, her soft mouth hot against his. The soundtrack, too: whispers turning into moans, her breath in short, urgent gasps by his ear and then nothing but sweet, mindless oblivion.

Coralie stirred in her sleep and turned towards him, her amber eyes trusting as her lashes fluttered and she glimpsed the first sight of him. When she reached up and traced his jaw with her fingers, he dropped his head to kiss her shoulder before anything in his expression betrayed his confusion. His body felt wonderful, as if it had only just experienced what it really was to make love, but his brain was telling him to wrap up everything quickly. His brain had a point. Any minute now, Pamala Gray would be setting her terrier, Laura Schiffman, on him, reminding him that he was meeting her at the gallery at lunchtime to go over the final details for the evening reception yet again. Although, why they couldn't just get on with it without him, he didn't know. The paintings could practically sell themselves.

In which case …

'Hey, you,' Coralie murmured, winding her hands round his neck. He pulled her towards him, feeling his pulse leap at the sweet morning smell of her. God, how he longed to plunge into all that luscious heat and softness! Somehow, he managed to find enough willpower to hold back. He knew enough about her to realise that this wasn't her usual style; there was a shyness about her which made a refreshing change from some of the women who commissioned him to paint them and acted as if they'd bought his body along with his talent.

Coralie's reticence made her more of a challenge, too; made him eager to discover the part of her she was withholding. Time had to be marching on, but he couldn't bear the thought of losing what might be the last opportunity to feel her soft curves against his body.

'Thank you for last night,' he murmured, running his fingertip across her lips. 'It was very special. You're lovely – do you know that?'

But when he stole a glance at her to see if her thoughts reflected his, he was alarmed to see her eyes brimming with tears. Oh, not now; he didn't have time for a scene.

'I'm not,' she whispered, her pupils contracting as the cold daylight glanced across her pale face. 'There's something I need to tell you.'

Uh-oh! The on-off boyfriend was back on the scene, perhaps, and now she was recriminating herself for giving in to temptation? He didn't know whether to be relieved at the lucky escape from more emotional involvement than he could cope with or insulted that she'd used him.

'Whatever it is,' he said carefully, 'it shouldn't affect what's taken place between us. There's nothing you need feel guilty about.'

'You sound like my mum,' she said with a weak smile. 'She's always accusing me of punishing myself for something that wasn't my fault.'

'Well, you should listen to your mother. I wish I could still listen to mine, but it's too late now.' Where had that come from? This really wasn't the moment to air his family's misfortunes. Especially when he had such a full day ahead of him. But something about the woman lying next to him seem to fit so well, as if she were part of him, and it was making him drop his guard. He lifted his head just enough to catch a glance of his bedside clock. Ten-thirty already and he was supposed to be at the gallery by one o'clock. Heck, where was the morning going?

And then he felt Coralie's body quiver and saw the tears starting to spill down her face.

'Come on, *cariad*,' he said, holding out his arms and gathering her up. 'Nothing's that bad.'

He lay still, rubbing her back until she cried herself out. Could he take the day off? Tell Pamala he was sick? Something was making his head swim and confusing his thinking. One thing at a time. First he'd try to find out what was causing Coralie so much distress. Probably best just to let her get it off her chest.

'So, tell me about it,' he said gently.

After a deep breath, he heard her gather herself ready to speak.

'Before I moved to Penmorfa, I used to work for a management consultancy, in the Process Improvement Unit – that means axing jobs to you and me. It's easy to make struggling firms more efficient; you either get them to run better computer systems or lose staff. Most of the time you can pat yourself on the back and tell yourself that the human sacrifices are worth it. Another company is saved and people's jobs are secure – until the next round at least.'

'Quite a responsibility,' he observed, sympathetic but at the same time willing her to get to the point.

She nodded and went on. 'Only this time, the company I was sent to was close to home. My boss assured me everything would be fine. Except that I knew one of the employees through a mutual acquaintance, a guy called Ned Wallace. Ned was a nice enough guy, a bit of a lad, liked all the trappings, you know? Designer suits, go-faster car – all bought on credit, it transpired later. He never believed for one moment that he was expendable, but the management level there was far too top-heavy so it was the obvious place to cut. Ned, of course, was then faced with the reality of not being able to finance his extravagant lifestyle. That was the moment when all the careful calculations I'd made in the seclusion of a tidy office became a messy, uncontrollable reality.'

She paused to collect herself again. 'On the surface Ned took it quite well. Joked about how he was going to blow the redundancy money on the holiday of a lifetime, but no one realised that he was far from being all right.'

'So?' He stroked her shoulder. 'You can't make everything better, Coralie. Sounds like the guy was a loser, carrying that amount of debt. You might even have done him a favour.'

She cleared her throat so that she could carry on. Fresh tears started sliding down her cheeks on to the pillow. 'No. He lost everything he had, but he wasn't the only victim. He was distressed about how his fiancée would take the news that he'd lost his job. So, he drove round aimlessly, screwing up the courage to go home, and he completely failed to notice a pedestrian crossing. He didn't see a young trainee teacher, Hayley Butterfield, returning to her flat from the convenience store across the road.'

'Oh, no.' He stared at the ceiling feeling helpless.

'Hayley was killed instantly, although Ned Wallace didn't know that because he just kept driving. Somehow, he convinced himself if he didn't stop, it hadn't really happened, so he just kept going until he got home. It took three days before his conscience got the better of him. Even then he only handed himself in because he realised he'd been found out. He'd had his car repaired, you see, the day after the accident. He guessed, correctly as it transpired, that the mechanic would see the appeal for information and put two and two together.'

She paused to swipe at her tears. 'Three days, imagine that. And a young woman lying dead and her family's lives in ruin because of what I'd done.'

'No.' He sat up and drew her to him. 'You can't blame yourself for that. It was him, the driver, who killed that girl, not you.' He looked at her pinched face. 'Oh, Coralie. That's the burden you've been carrying all this time? The reason you took yourself off to the middle of nowhere? So you could hide away from it all?'

She took a deep, shuddering breath. If he could have stayed there with her, he would have, but that would mean letting too many people down. The gallery assistants, Ruby, everyone who was working so hard to make this day a success for him. So he tried to make it better as far as he could. He took her face gently in his hands and made her look at him. 'Listen, Coralie, you have to forgive yourself or it'll ruin your life, too.'

'But it wasn't just Hayley's family who suffered that day. My decision cost Ned Wallace dearly, his family disowned him, his fiancée called off their wedding. He was left with no one.'

'Some people would call that retribution.'

'Not me, I—'

'Forget about it, Coralie,' he said, letting her go. 'You've lived with this for long enough. It's time to move on.'

He couldn't help stealing another glance at his clock. And she saw him. He groaned inwardly; the fact that he'd been smiling and trying to sound friendly and reassuring didn't make him feel any less of a bastard for not giving her every bit of his attention.

'Coralie, I'm sorry—'

'No, really, it's fine.' The vulnerability in her eyes, when she stared at him as if trying to convince herself she'd been mistaken, could have broken his heart. Really, she didn't know how much better it was this way.

'I really shouldn't be going on at you when you've got so much to do.' She turned on her side before swinging her legs to the edge of the bed. Her shoulders drooped as she paused, very briefly, and he began to register how much she was hurting. He longed to pull her back to him and cradle her against his chest. Except he was so afraid that eventually he'd only end up hurting her more.

'Perhaps you'd call a cab for me?'

'Hey, look – let's both shower and have breakfast then we could go together, if you like?'

Jesus, he was gabbling, but with that vulnerable expression she was wearing he was afraid that he'd fill a gap by saying something stupid, like ordering her to tear up her ticket and asking her to stay with him. He wished he could make everything all right for her.

'I don't think that's a good idea, do you, not when you've got such a busy day ahead and the reception this evening.'

The reception! Maybe that would be his chance to put things right?

'You are coming tonight, aren't you?' he asked desperately. 'Only, I'd like you to see the new work before you go.'

Go. He looked past her, at the black metal fire escapes snaking down the yellow brick apartment blocks opposite and tried not to think about how much he'd miss her. Otherwise, he'd start wondering why he'd utterly failed to paint her portrait, and why all that heat and intimacy had only left an increasing craving for her. Not looking at her made it easier for him to inject the right note of cheerfulness into his voice. The mistake he made was glancing at her and seeing how the lovely soft morning smile had vanished from her face to be replaced by something shadowed and hidden. He almost relented and reached out for her.

'Just one thing,' she said quietly.

He held his breath.

'The portrait …'

'I'll scrap the whole idea, if you like,' he said, lifting his hands. 'You were never very happy with the whole idea, were you?' he pointed out, trying to sound like a reasonable man rather than a guilty one. 'So, it's not fair to put you through that kind of ordeal when it's not really working for either of us. I'll sort something out for the charity auction. I won't let Penmorfa down.'

'Well,' she stood up, giving him a tight little smile, before gathering up her clothes, 'you're all heart.'

At the sound of the shower he flopped back on the bed and let out a long breath.

There had been no other choice, he thought, after the taxi had driven her away. Penmorfa was renowned for its outstanding natural beauty, but however lovely Coralie was, it didn't mean he wanted to spend the rest of his life there. It was better that he forgot about her. Every time he thought about the place where he grew up it reminded him that according to precedent, Lewis men weren't good to their women. Hadn't his father shamelessly taken all the love his mother gave him and worn it down in the cold and mud and the long, hard hours at the farm? He thought he'd escaped his destiny by leaving Penmorfa behind; the last thing he'd expected was that it would follow him.

Now Coralie's absence was all around him. He couldn't face Ruby's sarcasm, either, so he tapped out a text telling her he'd meet her at the gallery and set off. Outside, he crossed a grating and the ozone smell of the subway rose up beneath him, the accompanying hot air feeling uncomfortably like a forewarning that there'd be hell to pay for behaving so badly. Crossing the roadway into the Park, he was so busy trying to convince himself that all he'd done was neatly sidestep a difficult obstacle that he was almost hit by an oncoming roller-blader.

Having dodged past the cyclists and joggers, he hoped that looking at the scenery would make him feel more at peace. The cherry trees were still waiting to come into blossom, but the last of the daffodils, that always reminded him of home, now turned their heads away in another rebuke.

Even the birds seemed less than harmonious: sharp-beaked starlings, so much more aggressive looking than their European counterparts, made a thuggish crew, strutting in their shiny green-and-black, two-tone plumage. A huge pigeon, clumping along like a dinosaur walking the plains, watched stupidly as a cluster of sparrows stole the scraps of bread from under its feet. Somehow Gethin couldn't help but identify with it; he was pretty sure that he had just allowed something to be snatched away from under his nose, too.

Chapter Seventeen

Forty-five minutes, thought Coralie, feeling dazed. Not even a full hour to get out of Gethin's apartment. She'd once seen a programme about low-temperature surgery. A reduced need for food and air was supposed to keep the patient comfortably numb and preserve the vital organs. Maybe the frozen feeling around her heart would prove to be similarly protective?

So much tidier this way, she tried to tell herself, as the taxi dropped her outside Ruby's apartment block. *Surgically* clean. No hanging around like a persistent stain. Why pretend it could be any other way? It wasn't as if they had a future together, but if all Gethin Lewis had been after was a one-night stand, he could have saved her a lot of time and effort by dropping the pretence that it was all about art.

Letting her forehead rest lightly against Ruby's aquamarine door as she inserted the key, she stared down at the oily-green linoleum lining the communal spaces. Except that no one had forced her into his bed; she'd gone to him gladly. Ruby's Uncle Sam poster pointed at her accusingly as she opened the door. Deep down, hadn't she always accepted that part of his attraction was that there *was* no future for them? Maybe she'd even tried out her confession for precisely that reason? So that she could say some of those troubling words out loud *because* there was nothing to lose?

Coralie closed her eyes and exhaled slowly.

'You okay?'

Since her good luck fairy had clearly taken the day off, it wasn't surprising that her wish to be alone so that she could bury her head in a pillow and cry her eyes out hadn't been granted, either.

Ruby, dressed to go out in tight leather trousers and a short, white tee shirt, stopped checking her hair in her hand mirror to give Coralie the full benefit of her bright, beady-eyed gaze.

'I'm still trying to decide,' Coralie said, taking off her evening shoes and sitting on the sofa bed next to her. There was no point at all in rushing into the bathroom to change when it was obvious to them both that she was still wearing the clothes she'd gone out in. 'It's been a night of seduction, conflict and tragic resolution.'

'That *Carmen*, it's a hell of an opera,' said Ruby, padding out to the kitchenette and returning with two cans of Coke. 'What about you and Gethin?'

Coralie choked out a laugh and pressed the cold can to her cheek. The shock stopped the laughter spilling into tears. 'He's giving up on the portrait and donating a painting to the charity auction instead.'

Ruby chewed her gum, thoughtfully. 'He's not finishing the work?'

Got it in one, Coralie agreed silently. Finishing work clearly wasn't Gethin's strong point. 'He's got the exhibition to think about now. That'll keep him busy.'

'He's always busy,' Ruby said cheerfully, stretching her legs and admiring the black nail varnish on her toes. 'There are a lot of beautiful women to paint in Manhattan.'

Boy, did that make her feel good. Coralie plucked at her dress whilst her blurred vision cleared. Since she had company she'd have to wait until she was in the shower to cry her eyes out now.

'And by the time he's finished painting them, he's sick of the sight of them,' Ruby added, strapping up her studded gladiator sandals, before picking up her jacket. 'Don't look like that,' she said laughing at Coralie's disapproving expression. 'It may be an intense relationship for a short time, but it's only paint. It's not love or death. He's not inviting anyone into his studio promising them a big white dress, two kids on the porch and a happy ever after.' She seemed to be about to leave but stopped and cocked her head on one side. 'So he's really not going any further with your portrait, eh? That's different.'

Inside the smart Chelsea gallery that evening, Coralie was surprised to find Ruby had been looking out for her.

'I can always say you had a headache or something,' she suggested.

Coralie shook her head and swallowed hard. She almost preferred the rude Ruby incarnation to the one suddenly taking pity on her; perhaps clearing up after Gethin outside the studio as well as inside was one of her regular duties? She was brazening out the evening in her favourite peach-printed cocktail dress and kitten heels. All she had to do, she thought, whipping out her compact mirror, was to retouch her painted-on coral smile. Gethin might have drawn a line under their relationship, but she was determined to make her exit in style.

Her courage nearly deserted her when she looked around the stark room and saw what everyone was wearing. Any colour within the range grey to black seemed to be the dress code for the evening, she noticed, wondering how many variations of grey there were and feeling like a fruit display in her brightly coloured dress. If Lady Gaga was going to put in an appearance, as Ruby had suggested, she would certainly liven the place up.

Ruby grabbed a drink from a passing waiter and handed it to Coralie. 'Get this down you quick,' she advised, watching her with a trace of pity. 'I'll see what's happened to Gethin.'

Coralie decided it would be better to soak up the paintings, rather than draining her glass. Even if her relationship, if it could be called that, with Gethin was a non-starter she hoped that his work would leave a lasting impression. Would his style have altered much since the surreal glamour of *Last Samba before Sunset*? And which of the pictures, she pondered, would he send to Penmorfa's Hall Management Committee?

But, as she moved round the room, it occurred to her that she would probably have felt more comfortable back in a boardroom discussing figures than taking a view on the kind of figures before her now. Where were all the abstract paintings when you needed them? With every beautifully depicted curve of back, buttock and breast Coralie yearned for a landscape drawing to break up all the flesh.

'Oh, look! A brown painting,' she overheard a well-dressed elderly lady confide to her young male companion. 'I'm looking for a brown painting to go in the new apartment.'

Coralie examined the brown painting and noticed a pattern emerging through the umber, cinnamon and walnut tones. It was a bit like looking through a wooden blind, because the artist *was* looking through a wooden blind at ...

'Oh my!' exclaimed the elderly lady, spotting it too. 'Am I looking at someone's *ass*?'

Having wondered if it was fair to form a true impression of Gethin as an artist from the ubiquitous reproductions of his most famous painting, it seemed to her that the works on display were quite lazy, as if Gethin had taken the easy route and returned to the same old theme. No wonder he'd found her difficult to paint. Plenty of people seemed to like them though, since the gallery was becoming increasingly full. And with the buzz of so many fans clamouring to talk to him, Coralie judged she had all evening to frame a tactful opinion.

She was just beginning to relax when a row of fashionably thin women parted like corn waving in the breeze, only the force parting them was Gethin strolling towards her.

'Coralie! Thank God, you're here!' He took hold of her arm and started to steer her away. 'I was worried you wouldn't come. Can we talk?'

'Don't wander off, Gethin, you're wanted,' said a glacial-looking, Grace Kelly look-alike, grabbing his elbow.

Again, thought Coralie, feeling somewhat mollified when he shook his arm free and stood his ground.

'Laura, this is Coralie Casey, my guest from Wales. Coralie, Laura Schiffman, Pamala Gray's Senior Director.'

'How lovely to meet you,' Laura chimed, scanning her face, presumably against a mental check list of the great and good on the guest list, then turned back to Gethin. 'Pamala would like to speak to you. Now. You will excuse him won't you, Coralie?'

That rather suggested she wasn't on the VIP list.

'Let me walk you round instead,' Laura insisted, erring on the diplomatic side, just in case. She dragged Coralie away, whilst Gethin, his mouth set in a tense line, marched off the other way. Two attractive gay men waved to him as he passed.

'Show of hands,' she heard one of them say, as a young woman walked in wearing a black gown that revealed most of her ample assets. 'Do we think those are for real?'

'Gethin's spontaneity is unsurpassed,' said Laura, pointing at a turgid-looking painting of a bored couple. 'Everything he turns his gaze towards transcends the ordinary.' She kept rubbing the back of her hand where a rough, red patch of skin was blooming angrily. 'Must have exhausted everything in Duane Reade trying to fix this one,' she said, seeing that Coralie had noticed it.

Coralie fished in her bag and found a small pot of her

Happy Hands cream. 'Try this,' she said, offering it to her, 'it's very gentle, mainly beeswax and almond oil, but it's very soothing.'

The other woman looked doubtful. 'I don't think ...'

'I make them myself,' Coralie added, meaning to reassure her but seemingly causing further alarm. Laura smiled bravely and rubbed the tiniest amount on her sore hand. No doubt it would be washed off as soon as she could get to the ladies'.

When Gethin reappeared, he was engulfed by well-wishers. Although he caught her eye several times, he never quite seemed to be able to extricate himself for long enough to talk to her. In a way, it made it easier for her to remain detached. What was there to talk about now? Apart from the charity auction? Her only worry, judging from the number of people at the reception, was that the exhibition might be so successful that all the paintings would sell.

Ruby appeared, flushed with heat and excitement, but her face dropped when she saw that Coralie was on her own.

'I'll text Gethin from the airport tomorrow. Don't disturb him now, he's still busy,' said Coralie, staring at his back whilst the next potential candidate to commission a portrait flicked her long hair at him.

Ruby looked so tearful when she opened her arms to give Coralie a stiff hug and wish her well that it almost set her off, too. She was pushing through the crowd when Gethin grabbed her arm.

'Just hang on, will you? My driver will take you home.'

'What, all the way to Penmorfa? He must have quite a car.'

Gethin's brow creased and he swore softly under his breath. 'Look, I know I've messed up really badly,' he said, following her towards the door. 'I've never been unable to paint a woman before. I was scared I was losing my touch.'

'Your touch is fine,' she assured him. 'But your bedside manner leaves a lot to be desired.'

'I'm sorry.' He bent his head and seemed to be struggling for words. 'Please wait. When I've finished here, we'll find a place to talk.'

'About what?' she said, feeling her chest tighten. 'This is as good as it gets. You live here and I live in Penmorfa. There'll never be a place for us.'

He let out a long sigh and stared at the ceiling and when he looked at her again, the blue-black eyes were wretched.

'What?' She caught her breath.

'Try not to think too badly of me when you look back on this.'

'Why would I do that?' Coralie gave a short laugh and was surprised to feel her anger slipping away. How could she remain angry when he'd turned the key and given her a glimpse of what life could be like without the fear and guilt?

Smiling, she reached up to hold him for one last time. 'I've finished looking back. From now on, I'm only moving forward.'

She closed her eyes as his warm, rough jaw touched her cheek and kissed him goodbye. No looking back, she reminded herself. And kept walking.

Someone was making a heck of a racket in his head, thought Gethin, coming to on the sofa where he'd cosied up with a bottle of Jack Daniels the previous evening.

'Open the fricking door!' someone was bellowing. Ruby; he'd recognise her dulcet tones anywhere, but how had she got inside his head? He levered himself up and then wished he hadn't, especially when the hammering went on. A door chain rattled, more distant, but still loud enough to set his teeth on edge. Then another voice, a deep juicy drawl, added to the cacophony.

'Hey, lady! Keep the noise down, will ya?'

Gethin groaned; the apartment opposite belonged to a now-reclusive actress who'd been a huge Hollywood star in the eighties. Whilst the actress had withdrawn from public life, she and her minder regularly starred in his. Generally it was via a billet-doux from his landlord, accusing him of some imaginary infringement of his tenancy agreement. Occasionally, like today, the minder would put in an unwelcome cameo appearance and invite him or his guests to remain silent on the landing, or tiptoe on their way out down the stairs. When the time came to move on, Gethin was going to buy himself a vuvuzela and play them a farewell salute so they'd always remember him.

'Butt out of this, buddy,' Ruby snarled, 'before I give you something to complain about!'

'Oh yeah? That's really funny! Come on then, surprise me.'

Okay, that was enough. Ruby could talk the talk but the guy across the corridor was built like a truck and the medical bills would be enormous. For the guy. Gethin got up, opened the door and pulled his bristling assistant in before she got carried away and started swinging punches.

'How dumb are you?' she roared at him, making him wince.

'Not so dumb that I pick a fight with a guy three times my size.' He grinned.

'Oh, that's right,' she sneered, trying and failing to push her face in his, 'I forgot. You like to humiliate them into submission, don't you?'

'Eh?' The Jack Daniels wasn't helping him here. He edged his way back to the sofa and lay back and looked at the ceiling as if it could give him a few clues as to why Ruby was so mad.

'You moron!' Ruby threw off her khaki jacket and sat down heavily beside him, cruelly bouncing the springs. The tee shirt she was wearing proclaimed her to be very, very happy. The one that said she was very, very mad was probably in the wash. 'You know, snubbing Pamala Gray in her own gallery was a terrible idea.'

Gethin would have shaken his head only it hurt too much. He had done that, hadn't he? But when the art dealer had clicked her fingers at him to get his attention, as if he was one of the waiters, just as he was beginning to realise that Coralie had walked out of his life for good, he was damned if he could switch off and obediently come to heel.

'But, hey, I guess when you're a big shot, you can afford to behave badly once in while.'

Gethin breathed out. 'I'll send flowers.'

'Good luck with that,' Ruby snorted. 'So what are you going to do about Coralie?'

'What did you *want* me to do?' He wrenched himself up. 'Propose to her?' Self-disgust was making him tetchy.

She shook her head, and the white spikes of her hair quivered. He had some sympathy with them. 'You dragged the poor woman all this way on some flimsy pretext about painting her portrait and you didn't even manage that?'

'It wasn't working,' he said flatly. 'She wouldn't relax; what kind of portrait will it make?'

Ruby sneered at him. 'Hey, you're the one with all the talent; don't blame the sitter. Or maybe you were so busy trying to get her to relax, that you lost sight of the fact you were supposed to be *painting* her.'

Gethin shuffled under her intense scrutiny, trying to get

physically if not emotionally comfortable. 'I tried the usual tourist stuff.'

'Yeah, sex and the city – but not the official tour, right?'

'I liked you before you turned into my mother,' he grumbled.

'Your mother would be ashamed of you!' Ruby said, her voice shaking. 'If you'd used your eyes last night you'd have seen how brave Coralie was being and taken pity on her. What the fuck were you thinking of? Couldn't you see how much she was hurting? Or maybe you were *too* busy thinking about the f—'

'Careful!' he warned.

'Well,' she remonstrated, 'anyone could tell she wasn't like those other women, the ones who *hope* you're going to screw them when they commission a portrait.'

'Don't.' His head was hurting too much to listen to this stuff.

'Or what?' Ruby shook her head. 'You've been running away from getting involved all the time I've known you. Anyone would think you're afraid of making a commitment. Then someone comes all this way to be with you and you let her slip through your hands.'

'The only thing I know I've got in common with her is Penmorfa and we can't even agree about that! Nothing flourishes there except gossip and that includes Sweet Cleans. I've seen more incomers fail at their idealistic attempts to start a new life in the country than you've had hot dinners. I'm right about that business, you wait and see.'

'Gee,' she said sarcastically, 'that'll keep you warm at night. What's wrong with you? You're not getting any younger, you know. You'll end up a lonely old man.'

Like his father. Gethin narrowed his eyes at her. 'When you've quite finished chewing my ear, there's a hot shower waiting for me.'

Ruby sniffed at him. 'Yeah, and you could do with it, too. You'd better freshen up because it's gonna be a long day.'

Gethin raised his eyebrows. Pamala Gray, he supposed. And a large slice of humble pie.

Ruby looked at him beadily. 'Have you seen what the critics are saying about your show?'

Chapter Eighteen

In her parents' house in Surrey, where she had broken her journey for a few days, Coralie smiled as her mother returned to the living room with a box of chocolates. 'I must say, darling, it's been lovely having you back,' Susan Casey said, sitting next to her.

Coralie leaned back against the deep cream-and-gold cushions. It was a comfortable room: soft neutrals with touches of gold and pale pink, tasteful landscapes on the wall and Carol Klein's *Life in a Cottage Garden* bookmarked on the glass coffee table. She ought to at least try to relax. A quick phone call to Alys should have taken care of her immediate concerns and staved off some close questioning. And yet ... No, it wouldn't do to dwell on what wasn't to be. Coralie made a conscious effort to make the most of her brief respite. She watched her mother affectionately, noting that she'd added a few copper lowlights to her regular colour as a nod to what was once flame-red hair.

'It's been very quiet since you've been gone,' Susan said, laying one hand lightly on Coralie's knee.

'I'm not dead,' said Coralie, the sudden almost-tears spilling into a splutter of laughter. 'And I'm only a drive away.'

'A *long* drive,' her mother said reproachfully. 'Your dad finds the motorways tiring now. We're neither of us getting any younger.'

'Mum, you're fifty-four and regularly attend Pilates classes!' Coralie frowned at her. 'You're hardly a candidate for Dial-a-Ride. Besides, you and Dad are perfectly capable of tracking down obscure graveyards, so you're not exactly housebound.'

'You make us sound like a couple of body-snatchers,' her mother grumbled. 'It makes a good day out, that's all. It's far more meaningful to see a moss-covered headstone than simply looking online.'

Tracing their ancestry was a hobby her parents embraced with equal enthusiasm, although, thankfully, they were less inclined to regale her with blow-by-blow accounts of their discoveries these days.

'Well, *I* think we have more time to talk now. We can speak to each other at any time of the day,' Coralie said, hoping to avert the Too Far Away conversation or the inevitable discussion about the family tree. With so many of her cousins adding twigs to it, her mother was growing more concerned about the future of their own branch.

'I suppose so,' sighed her mother. 'And we can text each other. Well, we could if you had a signal. At least we can send emails.'

'You're pleased with that new iPad, then?' Coralie laughed, seeing her mother's glance stray to her latest toy sitting next to Carol Klein on the coffee table in front of them. 'See? There's really no need for anyone to be out of touch. Everyone knows where everyone is these days.'

'If you two are going to sit there nattering, you won't mind if I go and watch the football in the kitchen, will you?' her father said, winking at her as he rose from the armchair.

'So tell me, is Gethin Lewis as sexy in real life as he looks in his photos?' asked her mother, as soon as he'd left the room. Coralie's heart, which was supposed to be convalescing, leapt into her throat, and she had to pretend to think about it so as not to leak any clues her mother might spot.

'He's certainly what they'd call "lush" up our way,' she agreed, concentrating on the box of chocolates her mother had just opened. 'But there's an unbelievably gorgeous queue of New York women who think so, too. Hmm, is this tiramisu?'

'Coralie, *this* is your way, this is where you're from, remember?' Her mother frowned, poring over the illustrated guide to the contents.

As if she could forget! Even the drive back from the airport had raised ghosts. Sitting in the back seat, she was glad that her parents had been chatting about nothing in particular when they passed the Old Mill. Taking the project there had seemed such an attractive option; a young company, lovely offices in a beautiful riverside setting and located close to home so that she'd have more time to catch up with her friends. At the time she'd congratulated herself on a lucky break, but how she wished she'd turned it down.

'Fund-raising exercise, you said. I suppose you were the best person to talk to him in New York given your managerial skills,' said Susan, abandoning progeny for posterity in the apparent hope of distinguishing the family history by any means.

Coralie shifted uneasily. She hadn't exactly lied about why she was going to New York, she'd just been sketchy about the precise details, knowing what a fuss her mother would make about her daughter being painted by a famous artist. But now there would be no portrait anyway, so it didn't matter.

'It must have been good to think on your feet again. Don't you miss using your brain?'

'Don't worry about my brain, Mum, it's fine.' It was just her heart that wasn't doing too well. 'I've been thinking it over and I'm seriously thinking about outsourcing some lines to a contract manufacturer, so I can expand the business. I know it's early days, but it looks as if the demand's there, so I ought to think about how best to keep pace with it.'

'Bugger!' Susan raised a hand to one cheek. 'That was toffee not coffee. I'll have to watch my crowns. Look, wasn't the whole point of this exercise for you to do something less stressful? I mean, you've got a perfectly good career waiting for you here, if you're bored. Oh, Coralie,' she went on with a sigh that was only slightly muffled by the toffee, 'please don't tell me you're still wasting your time on that dreadful man! It just makes me feel so angry. I feel as if we're all paying for what he did. When I think of you, burying yourself away in the back of beyond ...'

Her pained expression was replaced by a look of concentration as she steered the toffee past her crowns. Coralie quickly picked up the iPad to take advantage of the lull. 'This is brilliant,' she enthused, 'the images are so sharp and clear!'

'Aren't they just?' Her mother leaned in, enveloping her with the warm, woody scent of Estée Lauder's Knowing. 'Oh! Why don't you show me something from Gethin Lewis's exhibition?'

Coralie could think of many reasons why, nevertheless a small, masochistic part of her wanted to remind herself of everything she'd walked away from. 'Hmm, okay.' She tapped in a search, 'Pamala Gray Gallery ... Chicago ... Paris ... ah, here we are ... New York.'

'Very swish! *Did* Lady Gaga turn up?'

'If she did, it was after I'd gone,' Coralie replied, clicking on the list of current exhibitions. 'That's strange, it's not listed. I wonder why?' She quickly keyed in another search, which produced a flurry of reviews, and clicked on the *New York Times*.

In New York Gethin was engaging in his new favourite pastime of sprawling on the sofa. He hit the remote control and watched the TV adverts; each and every one of them a warning of the possible woe betiding any American omitting to take out insurance. Here's granny lying on the floor with no one to hear her cries, here's the charred remains of your house, here's your sick pet. Health? Man, that was another minefield! Don't buy the cheap tablets or your cholesterol will kill you, your asthma will choke you, your heart will fail. In comparison, a little thing like his exhibition bombing didn't seem so bad.

'Derivative,' had been one of the observations. 'More originality in a painting-by-numbers kit.' From the same critics who not so long ago had been declaring his work to be 'dynamic, well-composed with an agreeable tension'. Who did these people think they were? Yet, deep down, he couldn't help feeling he'd been found out. By sticking to the tried-and-tested formula he'd painted himself into a dead end. If he'd reached the point when he could barely be bothered to pick up a brush, why should anyone else care?

In Penmorfa, the morning air was still cool as Kitty, panting with the effort, hefted another box into Alys's capacious Berlingo. Letting it go with some relief, she was just gathering strength to push it into a better position when someone asked her what she thought she was doing. She steadied herself with a deep breath before turning round. Adam's arms were folded across his broad chest and there was concern in his sea-green eyes. Kitty gave an inward sigh. He looked better in an old tee shirt, tatty jeans and boots than most men did when they were dressed up; no wonder so many female visitors to the garden centre were always finding reasons to get him to carry stuff to their car.

'I've taken a stall at a wedding fair at Llandrindod Wells,' she told him, resting on the boot for a second to let her swimming head settle. 'I'd like to spread the word about my low-cost wedding styling solutions to a few more brides-to-be and show them the kind of themes I can offer.'

'Jesus, Kitty, that's nearly a hundred miles away! Does Alys know what you're up to?'

'Mam's doing Hall Management Committee stuff again today and I can't be bothered to chase after Dad. He's a miserable so-and-so lately, always moaning about his back but never doing anything about it. I don't know how Mam puts up with him.' She stood up and closed the tailgate with some effort.

'Kitty!' He stood in front of her and rested his fingertips on her shoulders, ensuring he had her attention. 'You really shouldn't be doing that journey on your own. Not at this stage of the game. You know what that road's like through the mountains. What happens if something goes wrong?'

'I'll call the AA.' She shrugged, looking away.

He shook her shoulders gently. 'You know I wasn't talking about the sodding car!'

Kitty reached up and placed her hands on top of his. 'Don't try to stop me,' she said softly. 'Can't you see, I have to get used to coping on my own? I have to learn to be a grown-up now for this one's sake,' she added, nodding at her stomach. 'There are all kinds of reasons why I could skip this fair today. It would be so much easier to find an excuse and not go, but where's that going to get me? Yes, I am nervous about the drive and I'm worried that the fair will be a complete waste of time and money, but I'll never know what I can do until I try.'

Adam pulled her closer and rested his chin lightly on her head. 'Let me come with you. I just want to see you get there and back in one piece.'

For a few moments she let herself enjoy the comfort of

being in his strong arms, being held against his chest and breathing in the warm, masculine scent of him, then she wriggled out his grasp and put on a brave smile. 'Thank you, but it won't help me in the long run. Besides,' she grinned up at him, 'you've got work to do. Mam's sloped off, Dad's nowhere to be found. Someone's got to keep this place going.'

Adam gave her a resigned smile, showing his chipped front tooth. Funny how all the scuffs and imperfections in his face only gave it more character. 'Okay, but just let me give the car a quick once over before you set off.'

She stood back and watched whilst he refilled the washer bottles and checked the oil. 'The tyres look all right for now too, although I think the front two will need replacing before long. How's the spare?'

'Adam!' She pushed him away gently. 'At this rate, the fair'll be over before I get there!'

She eased herself into the driver's seat and wound down the window. 'Don't look so worried!' She blew him a kiss then set off, watching him in the rear window until he was out of sight, trying not to think about how much more she would enjoy the day if he was at her side.

Gethin dragged a hand across his face as the weatherman came on with a warning about falling temperatures. Perhaps if he'd been less preoccupied thinking about Coralie, he might have felt the winds of change blowing across his reception, the cluster of critics gathering like storm clouds to rain on his parade. The reviews had been so toxic that the gallery might just as well have been at the centre of an exclusion zone it was so empty.

Pamala Gray, minimising the risk from fall-out, had taken the unprecedented step of closing the exhibition, bringing in a newly trendy Dutch artist specialising in avant-garde sculptures as a hurried replacement. Gethin had always brushed aside any suggestions that in New York, at least, the world of art and fashion was inextricably linked. Easy to do when everyone was scrambling for a piece of him, but what else would explain why he'd fallen so dramatically out of favour when all he'd done was to produce more of the same?

And what would Coralie say? Not that she could think much worse of him. He couldn't believe how much he missed her; his world, which was already black and white without her, had now faded to a depressing shade of grey.

Wasn't this exactly why it had been such a bad idea to get involved with a girl from Penmorfa? Now he couldn't even walk round New York without looking for her. The city streets were full of people but seemed empty without her, and every famous landmark and tourist postcard only served to taunt him about what he'd lost. He missed her mad clothes, the coils of chestnut hair, her laughter and, even though she'd only been there for one night, he sure as hell missed the sweet warmth of her in his bed.

Yep, it was payback time all round. The sting in the tail for thinking he could get away with taking what he wanted and giving the bare minimum in return was the unpleasant discovery that for all his efforts to escape his fate, he was no better than the man he least wanted to become. Utterly defeated, he buried his head in his hands, wondering what he could possibly do that wouldn't have Coralie thinking he was a desperate man, just trying to impress her because he'd fallen on hard times. And then a voice on the TV broke through to him.

'Prices for Gethin Lewis peaked last year,' some clever dick so-called art consultant was telling the camera as news of his humiliation reached the screen. 'So anyone thinking of buying his work as an investment would be wise to place their money elsewhere. It's not that the big money buyers aren't there – pre-sales estimates for a series of landscapes by Lewis's compatriot, Sheri William, were smashed by collectors. Of course, Lewis remains very popular with the public, reprints of his most famous painting *Last Samba before Sunset* are said to have made him a fortune, but the selective buyer is now looking elsewhere.'

'Oh, man!' What was any painting of his worth to the people of Penmorfa now? Any dealer or collector watching the press releases and seeing that his exhibition had been closed prematurely would be worried that he had lost impact in the art world and be nervous about his work. Mair and Delyth had always wanted to wipe the floor with him, and a floor sander would probably be all they could afford out of the auction proceedings to reinstate their precious community centre. But was it too late for him to do something about it?

A lane closure on the motorway meant that Coralie's journey home took far longer than she'd anticipated when she set off from her parents hoping to get back in the light. By the time she reached the narrow lane that curled down to Penmorfa, the village was in darkness and she was shaking with fatigue. Not that there were any guarantees that she would sleep. Not only was she was apprehensive about how Sweet Cleans had fared in her absence, although she was sure Kitty would have done her best, but now there was Alys to face, too.

As she persuaded Betty up the hill through the other side of the village, a shadowy canopy of branches loomed over the dark lanes. The road dwindled to a thin strip, slowly unravelling in the car's headlights. But, outside the farmhouse, the beams picked up something worrying, a shape in Alys's Berlingo, as if someone was slumped over the steering wheel. She pulled up beside it and wrenched open the driver's door.

'Kitty!'

'I'm fine.' Even in the artificial light Kitty's face was very pale as she lifted her head and pushed her hair back. 'It's been a long day, that's all.'

'I hope you're doing a better job of convincing yourself than you are me!' Coralie muttered fiercely as she crouched down beside her. 'What's happened?'

Kitty explained that she'd been driving back through the Cambrian mountains after a wedding fair, when she had to pull over for a pee. She'd been compelled to stop twice more on the way home, once at a public loo and once to use the facilities in a supermarket, and had been alarmed to find a trace of blood as she wiped herself. Her back was hurting, too.

'Don't worry, everything's going to be all right. Stay calm, and I'll get help.' Coralie put her arm around her in comfort.

'No, don't go!' Kitty said, looking scared. 'Oh, frigging hell, I'm tired, Coralie. I'll probably feel better in a minute. I've just got to take this as a warning, a sign to take it easy for the next few days and let everything settle down.'

They both looked up at the sound of footsteps coming towards them. Kitty's bottom lip started to tremble and a tear ran down her cheek.

'I think the baby's coming, Mam,' she said, reaching out towards her.

Coralie shuffled out of the way so that Alys could get closer.

'What baby's that then, love? This one here?' Alys asked gently, rubbing Kitty's hard tummy. 'The one you haven't been telling us about?' She turned anxiously to Coralie before touching her lips to her daughter's forehead.

'Now try to relax as best you can whilst we get you inside. It's probably a false alarm and it'll settle down once you've rested. After all, you're not due yet, are you?'

Chapter Nineteen

Rock's rapturous welcome and mewling cries broke the silence of the lonely lane and went some way to making up for the emptiness of the adjoining holiday cottage. Once Alys had appeared Coralie had made a tactful withdrawal, leaving mother and daughter to handle their new situation in their own way. Crouching to stroke Rock, Coralie felt unexpectedly weepy and was grateful that he was ready to overlook being deprived of first his mouse and then her company. Whereas some cats would be a bit standoffish after being deserted for a week, Rock was far too needy to play games, greeting her as if she'd returned after years of absence.

Picking Rock up, since getting to her front door with a small cat threading through her legs was hampering progress, she allowed herself one brief glance at the neighbouring windows just to confirm that there was really no one at home.

'Just you and me then, Rock.'

She opened the door which led straight into her living room and all the warm colours and vintage fabrics she had chosen to please herself. Instead of cheering her up, the bright colours jarred and her clever charity shop nostalgic nods to domestic bliss looked shabby and second-hand. What was wrong? This was her home, the place she'd come to find her own slice of the Good Life. Why did she suddenly feel like chucking everything in a skip and starting again? Why, instead of feeling peaceful, did her home feel empty and quiet? She pressed a few buttons and music flooded the room; Doris started singing 'Lullaby on Broadway' and

Coralie stomped over and switched her off. From now on she was going to listen to Tinie Tempah or Plan B. Anything but Doris.

Kitty let everything go in a frightened rush of tears. Alys led her inside, holding her close and letting her sob out her fears. 'There, there, it's all going to be fine. I must say, I thought my grandchild was in danger of going off to school before you let on,' she said, trying to keep her own emotions in check.

'I just thought everyone would think I was stupid. I mean me – getting pregnant! I couldn't believe it myself at first. I mean, we did use contraception ... most of the time.'

'After you'd had a little practice run without first, I suppose,' Alys said, giving her a squeeze. 'I hope you've given him hell.' She felt her daughter stiffen as she tried to hold back more tears and knew there was worse to come. 'You haven't told him? Or he doesn't want to know?'

'Both,' Kitty mumbled into Alys's tee shirt. 'I didn't tell him because he wouldn't want to know.'

Alys couldn't help the sigh that escaped.

'Oh, Mam,' said Kitty pulling herself up with difficulty. 'I'm not completely stupid. I have been doing all the other things right; not drinking, being careful with my diet. I've been seeing Nurse Williams regularly, too.'

'I know,' said Alys. 'She told me she was looking after you.'

'Isn't that illegal or something?' Kitty frowned.

'So sue us,' said Alys. 'Someone needed to keep an eye on you.'

Kitty opened her mouth to reply, but her retort was stifled by the spasm of pain that made her double up.

'Breathe through it,' said Alys. 'There's a good girl.' She

waited until the contraction had passed and Kitty managed a weak smile. 'I think we'll ring the hospital just to be on the safe side, but I'm sure there's no need to panic; it's often tricky to tell what's happening with first babies. Then I'll wake your dad up so he comes, too. Just in case he has to drive.'

'Mam? Whilst you fetch Dad, I just need to make a quick phone call.'

Gethin dragged himself into the bathroom and stood under the cold shower to wash away the last of his hangover. The cold jets of water, like acupuncture needles in his skull, were supposed to take his mind off the pain, but did nothing for his guilty conscience. When he looked in the mirror, the same dumb prick stared back at him; the one who'd taken advantage of a good-natured woman who'd trailed all the way out to America for the sake of others. He should have given her the attention she deserved when she needed it, and should have addressed her fears instead of brushing them aside, but he'd behaved just like his father, who'd never listened to his mother. Whenever his mother had tried to express her concerns for the farm, her father had rubbished them and made her look small. As for all that selfless devotion to him? Had his father respected it? Had he, hell! All he'd done was take her love and trample all over it.

Maybe it would be better for Coralie if he did keep away, but there was something he could still do to prove he wasn't all bad. Gethin picked up the old jeans and shirt he wore when he was working. He'd promised that there would be a painting for the handover ceremony at the end of April when everyone in Penmorfa would have an opportunity to see the work. And if he wanted to avoid letting everyone down, there'd be an awful lot of midnight oil to burn if he was to meet the deadline. He squared his shoulders and rubbed his hands together, eager for the challenge. A Lewis man by name, but no longer, if he could help it, in nature.

The first faint blush of dawn was illuminating the sky when Kitty and her parents arrived at the hospital. By the time the midwife had finished her initial checks, a pale sun cast a lemon light over the white walls. At first Kitty clutched at the daylight, grateful that she wasn't hemmed in by inky-black squares of night. But, as her contractions racked up in strength and frequency, even the sight of clouds scudding across the blue began to annoy her and she jumped every time the door opened.

'It's all right,' said Alys, who was looking much happier now that the midwife had reassured her that the baby was doing well. 'Your dad's waiting outside until it's all over.'

'I wish I bloody could,' Kitty said, as the screw of pain in her back tightened again.

'Try to relax,' said Alys, smoothing the hair from her brow. 'I know it's easier said than done, but believe me, fighting it won't help.'

Her mother was clearly too old to remember that this was seriously painful.

'Fuuuck!'

'Nice greeting!' she heard someone say as the contraction subsided. Good, she thought, resting back on the pillow, now it can begin.

'Adam?'

Kitty grinned at the surprise in her mother's voice.

'Oh good,' said the midwife following him into the room, 'your partner's arrived!'

'Birthing partner!' Adam added quickly. 'A spare one at that since she's already got her mum here.'

'Shame,' muttered the midwife, looking disappointed. 'Lovely looking man like you. I'm not sure you should be here, in that case.'

'Don't you dare go!' Kitty bellowed, finding some strength.

The midwife thought about it. 'Hmm, well, Mum seems to want you here …'

'Yes, I sodding do!' roared Kitty, feeling like a huge monster baby herself.

'Well, since we're not busy …'

Kitty saw Adam twinkle at the nurse, then quickly wiped the smile off his face when Alys gave him her hard stare. Was it something genetic that made him flirt with every woman he met?

'You got round to telling your mum at last then,' he said, bending down to drop a kiss on Kitty's forehead, as she reached for the gas and air. 'I offered to be here just in case,' he explained, pulling up a seat next to Alys. 'Although, I never seriously thought she'd take me up on it,' he added, grinning back at Kitty.

'I'm just going to check to see how she's progressing,' said the midwife.

'Do you want to swap places?' Kitty heard her mother offer. 'You're very close to the business end.' She was glad that Alys refrained from making any further comment; Adam was looking quite self-conscious enough. Then, as the next contraction broke over her, Kitty reached out and grabbed his hand as if someone had just thrown her a lifeline.

'I want to push!' she yelled. She was sorry for swearing at the midwife when she suggested she might not be quite ready, but it was very fucking annoying, to say the least, to be advised to stop, and highly satisfying when she finally got the green light. Kitty gave everything she had into one almighty push and nearly as much to a second. By the time she'd got to what felt like the tenth or possibly the twentieth, her initial enthusiasm was beginning to wane.

'I can't do this anymore,' she wailed.

'You got to!' said Adam, sounding horrified.

'I want to go home now!'

'Don't be silly,' said Alys, suddenly not sounding so reassuringly like mummy. 'Working yourself into a tantrum isn't going to help any of us.'

She heard a small muffled sob and sensed someone quietening her mother. Then Adam was there, holding her face, making her look into his eyes.

'Come on now, sweetheart,' he said gently. 'Just keep calm and think of how close you are to seeing your beautiful baby. Stick with it, girl.'

'You're doing really well,' said the midwife. 'I can see baby's head now. Baby's got lovely blonde hair.'

Hair? For a split second, she forgot the pain. A real baby with real hair! And then she sensed something like the first ripples of a distant tsunami heading her way and braced herself for it to break. Kitty grunted and the grunt turned into a roar of pain and triumph. Suddenly everyone in the room was crying.

'You beauty!' said Adam, wiping away the tears to kiss her and then Alys. Alys managed to stop him kissing the midwife, who was just wiping the baby ready to pass to Kitty.

'Well done, Mummy,' said the midwife, handing him over. 'Here's your beautiful son.'

Kitty took her eyes off her baby just long enough to smile at Adam. 'What do you think of him, Daddy?'

'So that's what all the bickering between Kitty and Adam was about!' said Coralie the next afternoon when Alys called into the shop with the news.

'"My only love sprung from my only hate",' quoted Alys, sending Coralie's thoughts off in a direction she didn't especially want them to follow.

'I could see the sparks flying between them last summer, but I was a bit slow on the uptake,' Alys continued, looking thoughtful. 'No wonder some of the flower beds were looking a bit neglected.'

'But why didn't Kitty tell Adam about the baby sooner?'

'I think she assumed he wouldn't be able to handle it; with good reason, I guess. He's never going to be an easy dog to keep on the porch.' Alys perched on the stool next to the counter. 'This way at least she knew he'd be there for the birth of his son.'

'I wished I'd seen his face, I bet it was a picture.' Coralie smiled, thinking how unfair it was that she was about to spoil Alys's happy mood.

'Well, fair play to him, he didn't faint, not even when he realised what Kitty was saying. He looked over the moon, actually.' Alys sighed and shook her head when her eyes met Coralie's. Adam settling down? However lovely it seemed, they both knew it was unlikely to happen.

'Have they chosen a name yet?'

A shadow flitted across Alys's face. 'I think she feels she wants to get to know him first. I'm worried that she's spent so long denying this baby's existence that she's finding it particularly hard to accept he's here. I'm thinking about putting her and the baby in the holiday cottage. Would you mind? Adam's still sharing a place with his brother, but I thought it would be a way to encourage the three of them to get to know each other without me and Huw cramping their style. Who knows if Adam will stick around for the long haul, but let's give them all the best possible chance. I think Kitty's got enough to cope with just getting her head around being a mum.'

Whilst it would be nice to have company again, Coralie wasn't convinced that a screaming baby would make up for Gethin's absence. 'Well, Kitty can always give me a shout if she needs anything. Though I can't say I'm an expert on babies.'

Nor was she ever likely to be, she thought, feeling glum.

Alys gave her a sharp look, 'I must say, you're looking very sleek. Something to do with New York?'

Coralie acknowledged the compliment with a smile. Alys didn't look entirely convinced by the silky black shirt teamed with black jersey boot-cut trousers. Since she'd brought them back with her though, it seemed a waste not to wear the clothes she'd been storing at her parents. Especially when she'd spent so much on them in the first place. Her hot brush had been amongst her things too, so she'd straightened out the kinks and swept her hair back in a simple pony tail rather than fiddling around with scarves.

'Well, it did make me think twice about where I want to go with Sweet Cleans. I'm thinking about redesigning the brand, maybe going for something a bit more sophisticated. When I approached Tessa at The Cabin at Abersaith about my range, she thought it looked a bit amateurish. Different styling might make it a better fit.'

'The Cabin *is* a very upmarket hotel,' Alys said frowning, 'though there's a high chance that someone like Keira or Sienna or one of those other actresses will discover you, if Tessa agrees to stock you.'

Coralie hesitated. When an email had arrived from the Pamala Gray Gallery her hopes had been raised then dashed. Her dejection was somewhat mollified when she read on. Laura Schiffman, who'd done such a good job of fielding

Gethin on the night of the disastrous reception, had written to send warm thanks for the sample of Happy Hands which had apparently soothed her eczema like no other cream.

So impressed was she by its efficacy that she'd even ordered a dozen more to give to her stressed-out colleagues and friends. The interest had caused Coralie to wonder yet again if she could muddle on with Sweet Cleans on her own, or if it was time to think big. She decided against sharing her thoughts with Alys, putting off the discussion that would certainly cause the older woman additional worry.

'But are you sure that's the direction you want to follow?' Alys went on. 'Most people are trying to save money. I mean, we're even pushing plants for austerity Britain now. Some of our customers are uneasy about buying roses which have racked up air-miles, so there's been a real resurgence of interest in grow-your-own cut flowers like dahlias, roses and gladioli.'

The sound of R&B blasting from a white van crunching down the road beside the garden centre from the old cottage made them both look up.

'I haven't seen any of those for a while,' said Alys. 'They can't have very much left to do.'

'I suppose it will go on the market, will it?' Coralie asked casually.

Alys, who'd picked up a pot of Happy Hands, removed her glasses to give her a close inspection, making Coralie feel she'd rather revealed her less-than-happy hand. If there was any chance of running into Gethin she wanted to be prepared.

'It doesn't look like the same place now, that's all I can tell you,' Alys replied. 'Mind you, it should never have been allowed to get so run-down. Nothing to do with Gethin, by the way,' she added, reading Coralie's expression. 'He did his best for Gwyn, even though the old boy could be so stubborn and difficult.'

Maybe it was a family trait. Coralie pretended to tidy her greetings card display, something she'd taken on trial because she felt sorry for the artist. If Alys couldn't see her face, maybe they'd stay on safer ground.

Coralie blew out a long breath and, omitting the details, explained that Gethin was planning to substitute the portrait with one of his existing works.

'Oh, that's all right!' Alys laughed. 'I'm sorry that it was a wasted exercise for you, although –' she shot Coralie a quick smile – 'I hope you *did* manage to enjoy yourself. And I daresay there'll be a few comments about lowering the tone, but the point is that an original work by Gethin Lewis, however, erm, racy, will sell for an awful lot of money! Besides, there's nothing the rest of the Hall Management Committee can do but grumble. ACORN have already approved the loan.'

Coralie folded her arms. According to what she'd read online, the reason Gethin's work had sold for such extravagant sums was mainly due to investors hoping to make money from another *Last Samba before Sunset*. Everyone loved a winner, but how would they feel about an artist whose work had so dramatically fallen out of favour?

Chapter Twenty

Gethin's shoulders were burning, but at least his stomach had stopped complaining. His back ached from standing for so long and his throbbing brain was warning him that he was going to have one hell of a tension headache when this was all over. But still it wasn't fucking right. He swiped at the canvas again, frustrated that his hands just couldn't translate what was in his head, repeatedly reverting to the cynically sensual crowd-pleasing oeuvre that had swollen his bank account and left him emotionally bankrupt.

He'd painted through sunset, oblivious to the glass windows turning to gold in the late light. The neon signs above the bars and clubs winked unnoticed by him as the last commuters hurried home and the first pleasure-seekers arrived in search of something to take their cares away. He'd been painting too urgently to think about food. As for drink? He'd had such a bad taste in his mouth for so long he wondered if there was anything that could ever wash it away, although his imagination was telling him he could smell coffee.

'She's worth it, you know.' Ruby, a cardboard cup in each hand, kicked the door shut behind her and looked round for a flat surface that had escaped the worst of the paint.

'Hi, Rubes, what are you doing here? Haven't you got work to do? There's a big exhibition ahead, you know.'

She shook her head. 'I still can't believe I was shortlisted! "Brave New Artists: Rising Stars". And one of them's me! Oh, man!' She slid down the wall and sat cross-legged on the floor, as if the weight of everything that had happened in such a short space of time was too much for her.

'It's great news, Rubes.' He passed her a coffee and then sat down beside her to rest his aching shoulders. 'I want to see you get the prize for the best painting, too.'

'I feel bad,' she said, plucking at the silver dog tag round her neck. 'It should have been you getting all the attention.'

'Oh, I'm not short of attention.' He patted her knee. 'And I couldn't be happier for you. So the judges approved of the digital image then? That's terrific.'

'Yes, now I have to submit the physical painting for judging.'

Ruby gave him a rueful smile and he shoved gently against her shoulder. 'You should get out of here now then, before someone spots you hanging around with a loser. I'm finished here, you know that.'

She pulled a face. 'I owe you. You were the one who took me on when I had nowhere to go. I would have had to leave school if you hadn't paid my fees and found me somewhere to live.'

He rose stiffly to his feet. 'I was shrewd enough to spot talent, that's all.' He shrugged. 'Besides, none of the other applicants ticked the boxes about being able to lift five gallons of paint or work off ladders. For a tiny girl, you punch way above your weight.'

'People should be more loyal,' she said, getting up and shoving her hands in her pockets. She stared moodily out of the black windows at her reflection. 'This isn't about fashion, it's about an artist creating something fresh and original.'

Gethin raised his brows at her. 'So tell me, when did I last do that? The fact is, Rubes, I've been playing the system for too long, rote-producing stuff with no heart and soul. I've been found out.'

She lifted her eyes to him, meeting his in the glass. They

both knew it was true. 'So take your chance and make the most of it. Don't go down the same route as me.'

'At least you'll always have *Last Samba before Sunset*,' she said, trying to cheer him up. 'That'll keep you off the streets.'

Yeah, maybe, but what did that painting mean to him now? The royalties from shelves full of *Samba* merchandise – the prints, coasters, mugs and mouse mats – had enabled him to set up in New York. They'd also helped to keep the old man in comfort in an expensive private nursing home where he could be certain that the well-trained staff could cope kindly with the frailties of his failing mind and body. For where was the good in making a dying man suffer for past hurts he struggled to remember?

And even if the administrators for his art publishers paid up, as he was assured they would shortly, sales had to be reaching saturation point. He'd even watched a documentary programme about supposedly lost tribes, where one of the elders was wearing a *Samba* tee shirt with his loin cloth in a startling ancient world meets modern combo. Yup, *Samba* had been so huge he'd almost choked on it. No wonder he'd lost his appetite for producing new work when all the public was looking for was more of the same. Getting that hunger back made him feel nervous and excited all at once; a bit like falling in love.

'Go on, Rubes, it's late,' he told her, eager to get on. 'Your girlfriend'll be waiting for you.'

'Yeah.' She grinned. 'It's good to have her back. Not having her around when Coralie was there made me appreciate her more.'

'That's the way it goes,' he agreed. 'You don't know what you've got until it's gone.'

She shuffled up to him and, uncaring of the paint on his

shirt, wrapped her arms stiffly around him. From someone who'd been so badly used by her mother's partner it was a huge deal. Ruby had come a long way from the scarred, scared, borderline dropout she'd been when he'd first noticed her potential.

'When are you leaving,' she muttered into his chest.

'The unveiling ceremony's next week and I'm running out of time. So hop it.' He dropped a kiss on her fluffy blonde head and she stepped away.

'Oh man!' she said, looking at the canvas for the first time. 'You've really done it now.'

'Promise me you'll bring your children up at Penmorfa.'

His father's final words. This from the man who'd been so quick to banish him from the place. And Gethin had been happy enough to agree if it meant the old man had one fewer burden on his conscience when he closed his eyes for the last time. The voice was suddenly so clear in his head that Gethin could almost imagine his father was up at the cottage waiting.

The hired Mondeo he was driving past the garden centre and up the rutted track towards his father's cottage wasn't nearly as luxurious as the Land Rover he'd used last time, or as much fun. But it would stop any rumblings about him flashing his cash and he hoped any villagers catching sight of him the day before he was due to hand over his painting would approve of his frugal choice and feel more generously disposed towards him.

Behind him the green tracery of the overlapping trees gradually closed a veil over the little village and it was easy to forget it was there. But for the intrusive arrival of PVC windows and the occasional plastic door squatting brutishly in the once-humble terraced houses, nothing much ever seemed to change. Penmorfa was everything he'd been glad to leave and yet – maybe he had a touch of *hiraeth*? – he was almost glad to see the place again.

He could, of course, have stayed in the States, but it was time to make decisions about his father's cottage. It was as good a place as any to let the fuss about his latest exhibition blow over, which, he was confident, it would. And Coralie? Maybe this was his chance to show that he was willing to do all he could to make amends.

'What's that you're driving there, boy?' he could imagine his father saying, leaning out of the window of his ancient Land Rover. 'Some sort of girl's car, is it?'

For a moment he was reminded of the old man's cutting sense of humour, sharpened and honed by a quick and clever mind. Mam, bless her, hadn't been the brightest tool in the box, lovely as she was, and hadn't always kept up with Gwyn's voracious reading and lively curiosity. No wonder the old man had lost his rag at times, hemmed in by his land, his cattle, and with no outlet for that keen mind – and yet he'd been eager for his own son to perpetuate the misery.

'Don't think you've won,' he muttered out loud, 'this is only temporary. The whole idea of me staying here is preposterous.'

His father's aspirations for him had always been narrow: the farm or nothing. Qualifications were a waste of time; university a waste of money. 'Watch me, boy, and you'll learn everything you need to know.'

So he'd watched his parents struggling to earn a living wage, seen them buckle under concerns about BSE, Foot and Mouth disease, the withdrawal of subsidies and the rising cost of feed and fuel. What he'd learned was that he'd be better off following his passion, pursuing his artistic ambitions, instead. His father had accused him of treachery, of walking away from the fight to rejuvenate the industry and keep the local community alive. And, later, even of being the cause of his mother's early death.

The old man had never given in and admitted that he might have been right to leave. Not even after the sale of the old farmhouse, when the monies, as he'd later found out once his father had been too ill to refuse help, had barely been enough to keep him once outstanding debts had been paid. Well, it was too late to resurrect the family farm, but maybe he could do his bit for the community?

A sickly farmyard odour that he always associated with his father wafted into the car. Gethin waited to hear his dry snicker behind him and glanced up into the mirror. His harshest critics would have agreed with his father's assessment: that he'd overreached his ambition and should have stayed on the farm. But they hadn't seen anything yet. This time, he'd thrown out all the artifice and pretension and returned to first principles to paint what really moved him. At long last he could look himself in the eye and know that the work he was about to unveil came straight from the heart.

The thin smile he'd found, against the odds, was replaced by sheer amazement when he reached the cottage and wondered if he was at the right place. The practical brown-framed replacement windows his father had been forced to install when the originals had gone beyond repair, had been swapped for something far more sympathetic to the character of the building. The ugly rendering had been painted a sunny cream, the front door given a heritage paint makeover in a powdery seaside blue and a new slate roof sat snugly against the weather.

Inside, the mephitic stink of mildew mixed with plague pit had been ousted by the smell of fresh paint and new carpets. Plastered walls and new ceilings gave the rooms a clean, modern feel. Cream units and oak worktops gave the kitchen what the magazines would have described as a classic country feel, though not one that his father would ever have recognised, and the ghastly avocado bathroom – a so-called improvement installed in the seventies which his father insisted was 'good enough for me, boy; it'll get me clean, won't it?'– had been replaced with a modern white suite and a power shower. All he was missing, he thought, as it suddenly occurred to him, was some furniture. At least he'd had the sense to stop off at what he thought of as Penmorfa's shoddy goods store, where you were nearly beaten back by the smell of cheap plastic before you'd got through the door, to buy a sleeping bag and some basics.

He trudged back to the car just in time to be snarled at by a wire-haired Jack Russell as it leapt off the back of a quad bike before heading off on important business in the undergrowth. Huw Bowen, his hair sticking up from the breeze in an 'owner most like dog' moment, looked just as gruff.

'Alys saw you go past. She was worried that you might be hungry so she sent you up some lunch.' Regarding him suspiciously, Huw handed him a thin cotton bag that was heavy with a couple of foil-wrapped packages and a flask. His expression suggested that the gesture was nothing to do with him and he sincerely hoped that Alys had laced it with laxatives.

'Alys is a thoughtful woman,' he said. 'You're a very lucky man, Huw.'

Huw flushed, as if he'd hit a nerve, and glared at him. 'Just don't let her down, will you? She's worked hard trying to persuade her committee that you're genuinely trying to help the village, which is no easy task considering how many people still think that *Samba* painting was a bit of a piss-take.

Mair's been going around telling everyone you're about to present them with another painting of a scantily-clad floozy on the beach and turn Penmorfa into the laughingstock of Wales again.'

Gethin shook his head. Nothing had changed. And he was trying to help these people? He took a deep breath. Not these people. One person: himself.

The clouds, which were almost as dark as Huw's face, let loose an April shower that threatened to soak them in seconds. Gethin beckoned to the cottage and Huw and Edith hurried after him.

'Tell Alys not to worry,' he shouted above the sound of the rain echoing in the bare hall. 'It's an entirely new work, that hasn't been created for an exhibition or gallery. I hope it will have resonance for everyone who comes into contact with it.'

Huw nodded, not looking completely convinced. 'So, everything all right here?'

'As far as I can tell the builders you recommended did a good job. Trying to oversee it at a distance, I was afraid I would come in to wet plaster and wires dangling out the ceiling, but they were as good as their word. I'm grateful to you, Huw.'

Huw's expression softened and he relaxed enough for Edith to leap out of his arms and skedaddle upstairs to take herself off on a tour.

'But you've got no furniture!' Huw said, slightly out of breath from chasing after her, as he returned with Edith squirming in his arms. 'You can't stay here, boy. Where are you going to sleep? Young Kitty's in the holiday cottage – and that's another story, I can tell you. There's The Cabin at Abersaith, though it's pricey, mind you, although I daresay if anyone can afford it, you can.'

Gethin waved his hand, slightly too close to Edith who tried to take a couple of fingers off in passing.

'Thanks, I'll be all right here.'

Huw positively beamed. 'Getting a feel of the old place again, eh, boy? That's the spirit! I wouldn't want to be away from it for a moment longer than I had to be if it was mine, either. Maybe you'll decide to return to the village, after all, then no one will be able to say that you think you're too good for us.'

Gethin refrained from saying anything to darken his mood again. He still couldn't make up his mind where he stood with Huw, but that was true of so many people in the village. And one woman in particular. 'And in the meantime,' he said instead, 'your good wife has packed more food than I can possibly eat. Would you care to share some lunch?' He opened one parcel and handed a chicken salad sandwich in good, thick granary bread over to the older man who, with Edith slavering in his arms, took a huge appreciative bite.

Good, thought Gethin. If Alys had laced the food with laxatives, he wouldn't be the only one suffering.

'Pinky-winky,' announced Alys, looking over her reading glasses as the glass doors of the garden centre shop slid open. Coralie, who had wandered into the revamped former shed for company, wondered if she'd been spending too much time with her grandson.

'The names they come up with now!' she went on, with a smile, coming out from behind the counter.

'What, Kitty and Adam?' New parents sometimes got a bit carried away, but the new baby would have to grow up tough if he got lumbered with that.

'Oh no, he's definitely James, after Adam's late father.' A shadow flitted briefly across Alys's face. 'I'm relieved one of them came to a decision, and since Adam's only got his brother and sister now it seemed a lovely gesture. Do you know I had visions of that poor child starting school still being called The Baby if it was left to Kitty. No, it's one of our catalogue range of new plants. Lovely ornamental hydrangea, though.'

Coralie hoped that Alys, who could get very passionate about plant trends, wasn't going to nag her about the dominant trend in her own garden, which was mainly to let it look after itself.

'Bird Poo Remover.'

Coralie looked up.

'I must order some,' Alys reminded herself. 'Everyone'll be wanting to clean up their garden furniture soon. Have you seen how much mess the house martins have made over Willow's unit? She's having to dash for it every time she crosses the threshold. Wilfie got stuck in there with her for ages recently. Came out looking quite dishevelled. Still, nothing you can do about it once they've established their nests, of course.'

Willow and Wilfie? Coralie shook her head; she still couldn't quite believe the evidence of her own eyes.

'Poor man,' Alys went on. Although as far as Coralie could tell, whatever was going on in Willow's unit was doing Wilfie the world of good. Even his beard looked clean and tidy these days.

'Imagine how much it must have hurt Gethin to be described as an indifferent painter who'd got away with pulling the wool over everyone's eyes for far too long? It just goes to prove how little those New York critics know,' Alys continued, as she slowly paced one side of the shop, checking her stock. 'I'm confident that none of this nonsense about the current exhibition closing hurriedly will make a blind bit of difference over here. The publicity might even help. I daresay even Delyth and Mair will be on his side, now that the Big Apple's spat out one of Penmorfa's own. They all love a loser round here.'

'He certainly doesn't need to face any more criticism,' Coralie had to agree. 'Getting that from the city he loves must have come as a terrible shock.'

'Anyway, we'll make sure we put on a good show of strength at the presentation ceremony and give him the reception he deserves,' Alys called over. 'Have you managed to catch up with him yet?'

In fact, when Coralie heard he was back in the village, she *had* decided that she ought to talk to him sooner rather than later, just to dissipate some of the potential awkwardness between them. But somehow she hadn't screwed up enough courage to do it. She looked down at her feet.

'No? Well, never mind – here he comes now!'

Chapter Twenty-One

Oh no! Coralie's stomach lurched. He was just as gorgeous as she remembered. So much for telling herself that when she saw him it would be like digging out an old picture of a pop idol she'd once had a crush on. Part of her hoped to discover that her libido had tricked her into falling for someone who, in hindsight, she might be embarrassed by.

She remembered vividly her shame as a teenager after she'd got carried away at a Christmas party for the staff of the local supermarket where she worked on Saturdays. Snogging the manager of the meat counter, who'd looked almost attractive under fairy lights after a glass of Lambrusco, seemed like a particularly poor idea when he turned up at her house and offered her mum free sausages hoping to ingratiate himself with her.

But seeing Gethin again, all she could do was congratulate herself on her impeccable taste. Even in the height of summer it was never scorching in Penmorfa, due to its proximity to the sea, but today it was pleasantly warm and it was great to see Gethin without his leather jacket. She could admire his fine forearms, with their dusting of dark hair, and the curve of strong biceps disappearing under his short-sleeved black tee shirt. His thick dark hair was unruly, his jaw was set off by at a least a day's worth of stubble – though she'd have to run her fingers across it to be sure – and his dark eyes looked just as sexy in broad daylight as they did across a pillow. In fact, he looked as if he'd just rolled out of bed.

'Who died?' he said, looking from her to Alys and frowning. Coralie winced.

'Oh, we are all in black, aren't we?' Alys beamed.

It was true that Alys and Gethin were both wearing black tee shirts and jeans, and both wearing them very well in their own ways, but Coralie had resurrected another of her management consultancy outfits.

'Coralie looks well, doesn't she?' Alys nodded at the black silk vest top and straight linen skirt.

'What happened to all the colour?' Gethin asked, his scowl deepening.

'It's lovely to see you again too, Gethin,' Coralie said, miffed. 'I told you in New York, if you remember, that I was going to start looking forward. The retro clothes didn't feel right anymore.'

'So you've shrugged them off, along with the past, have you?' he growled.

Coralie went over to pick up a packet of seeds that had fallen off one of the shelves as an excuse to hide her face. Giant Red carrot seeds, renowned for their size and vigour. Gethin looked big and vigorous too, although the carrots, she hoped, were less prickly.

'Goodness me,' said Alys, 'someone got out of bed the wrong side this morning. I hope you'll be in a better mood this evening at the presentation ceremony. Come here and give me a kiss, you great brute!'

'The things I do for you, Alys,' he said, shaking his head. A smile spread across his face at last, lighting up the dark corner where they were standing as he held her, then kissed her on both cheeks.

'And don't forget Coralie,' Alys reminded him. 'She was the one who went all the way out to America to get you on board.'

'As if.'

Even that brief contact was enough to make her want to burst into tears because every pulse in her body was beating a little 'touch me' tattoo at having him so close.

'I apologise, but I'm still trying to figure out where everything is up at the cottage. Like hot water,' he added, running a hand across his stubble. 'I was so travel weary when I set the timer switch that I punched in the wrong programme.'

That explained why he looked as if he'd slept in his clothes then. And that mildly musky, wildly attractive masculine scent of him.

'Not quite what you needed after a long journey, you must be worn out,' Alys agreed. 'And although Huw and I don't usually hire out our bath, I'm prepared to make an exception if you'd like your back scrubbed. Unless Coralie wants to do it ...'

Coralie glared at her.

'Don't look so worried,' Gethin said, with the ghost of a smile. He took the seeds from her and slotted them back into place. 'I reckon a cold shower will do me good.'

'Well,' Alys said, clearly choking back a laugh, 'it looks as if we've got a really good crowd coming this evening. I'm so looking forward to seeing what you've got to offer us. Which reminds me, I need to check how many chairs we've got. Coralie, can you mind the counter for me?'

'I came back to try to make amends,' Gethin said.

'How?' Coralie wandered away and leaned back against the counter. He followed and stood in front of her, longing to touch her but afraid. The brief flare of heat of her body as he'd leaned in to greet her was the only warmth he'd felt. It wasn't just her bright clothes that had cooled.

'You made it obvious the way you felt about Penmorfa and, by extension, me, in New York. That's one bridge burning.'

'I can start by fixing it for Alys,' he said, trying not to lose hope.

'Really? I hope so because Delyth and Mair will have a field day laying all the blame at her feet if anything goes wrong.' She shook her head and he longed for just one recalcitrant curl to escape from the sleek chignon that made her seem so frosty and remote.

Gethin folded his arms. He'd given up caring about what a few small-minded people with nothing else on their minds thought of him years ago. It seemed to have escaped her notice that there was only one person he was trying to impress. 'Not in front of me, they won't,' he told her, aching for her to drop her guard. 'Don't look like that,' he said reproachfully. 'I'm not going anywhere until I've smoothed everything over here.'

'So you can lie low until all the fuss about your latest exhibition dies down over there, I suppose,' she said, tightly.

'I'm not lying low or running away from anything, Coralie. There are far more pleasant places where I could cool my heels if I wanted to. I'm running to something. I came back because of you. And I don't have any plans for the immediate future that don't include you.'

He waited for her to say something, but the silence was only broken by the sound of Edith dancing around outside the glass doors, barking her head off and trying to see off anyone thinking about going into the shop. Good work, Edith.

'Think about it. I could introduce you to some great contacts in New York,' he pointed out and got the faintest of smiles in return.

'You already did,' she said, surprising him. 'I gave Laura Schiffman a sample of my Happy Hands cream. Not only did she like it, but she bought more of it for her girlfriends, one of whom, it turns out, was rather well-connected.'

'Go on,' he said, smiling back.

'She's a buyer with one of the big cosmetic houses, though our discussions are only at a very early stage.' She shrugged. 'The thing is I've been searching for growth opportunities for the business. Involvement with a large organisation would provide marketing and research and develop opportunities I could only dream of, but I do have some concerns for Sweet Cleans.'

He nodded. 'You think it could threaten Sweet Cleans' natural, wholesome image?'

A shadow crossed her face and she bit her lip. 'No, it's back to lifestyle choices; whether to stay small in the country, or get involved with big business.' She looked at him steadily. 'Right now, I'm happy with the life I've got here.'

Gethin pushed his fingers through his hair. 'Those kinds of opportunities don't come round every day and you must know the risk you're taking if you stay here.'

'I've done my sums,' she told him, firmly.

'Yes, you're the accountant,' he said. 'But you don't know how hard it is to live here.'

'I know it didn't suit you,' she began, when he rolled his eyes. 'But there are compensations: it's a close-knit community, there's almost no crime, everyone talks—'

'Oh, they do that all right,' he shot back.

'How can you say that? How long is it since you actually lived here? Those are outdated prejudices. You think you have moved on since you left Penmorfa, but Penmorfa's changed, too.'

'Not as far as I can tell.' He grimaced.

'You haven't exactly given yourself a chance to find out, have you?' Coralie tugged fretfully at the hem of the depressing black vest. 'Anyway, surely it's easier to ignore a bit of ignorant tittle-tattle than having the New York press trash your exhibition?'

Gethin grimaced. 'Critics are entitled to their opinion. I'll get over that, but I can't live in this goldfish bowl.'

'Well, that's that then,' she said, except that made it sound as if they might have had a future, when, unless he acted fast, they didn't even have a relationship.

What if Gethin's work *had* plummeted in value? Later, in the Summerhouse Café which had once more been pressed into service for the evening, Coralie wiped her damp palms together and hoped that the ordinary buyers, the ones who knew what they liked and didn't care about critical opinion, were still out there. A good Gethin Lewis would surely still sell well? As for the artist himself? Feeling tears prick her eyes, she took a deep steadying breath and concentrated on practical matters. Coralie could feel her heart pounding as she waited to see Gethin's painting at last. At first she'd been afraid that no one would turn up to the presentation ceremony, but Alys and the Hall Management Committee had, it seemed, been quietly drumming up interest. Kitty, and a couple of young mums hoping to resume the mother-and-toddler group again, appeared pushing buggies; the woman with the jet black hair who ran flower arranging classes took a chair at the end of a row next to her husband; and some elderly residents shuffled to the front row. All the people who would benefit when the refurbished hall reopened.

The thudding in Coralie's chest moved up a gear when a local TV reporter and camera crew started setting up. If the piece was aired, news of the charity auction would reach a far wider audience than the notice on the Hall Management Committee's website. It might even ignite some competitive bidding on the day. On the other hand, if anything went wrong, there was every chance that Delyth would make sure her grandson would post the footage on YouTube so that they could enjoy the sight of Alys's humiliation over and over again.

Whatever had happened between them, Gethin had come through for the village where he grew up. Not only had he fulfilled his promise, but he'd even cared enough to arrive in person to unveil the work. For that alone, he deserved her support. She glanced up at him at last, sitting next to Alys on the raised platform, and realised with a pang how tired and drawn he was. Everyone fell silent as he stood up abruptly to make some last-minute checks, scrutinising the lighting and adjusting the level of the easel. Alys's hand fluttered to her chest and she reached for a glass of water to wet her lips. Gethin, reseating himself next to her, gave her a small nod and Alys stood up to speak. Coralie pressed her lips together, willing herself to stay calm for a few agonising seconds more. Despite everything that was left unsaid between them, she was proud of Gethin and the very small part she had played in delivering the project. And even if she detested everything she saw when the covers came off the painting, she'd be the first one cheering and singing its praise.

Gethin felt everyone's attention turning to him, as Alys concluded her short speech, but he was only aware of one face. Coralie looked amazing in a tasteful, slim-fitting taupe dress and a swept-back hairdo that made her look serious, sophisticated and even more like a stranger to him. The dress depressed the hell out of him and he longed for her to loosen her copper waves and become the woman he knew. Just when he thought he'd caught hold of her, she'd slipped out of reach again.

'I hope you can all see properly,' he said, sounding more confident than he felt. 'I have to admit that things have changed since the night when I rashly offered to donate a painting to help raise funds for this village. I was, perhaps, guilty of believing my own myth, of thinking I was better than I was. Sometimes we all need a reality check to see where we've gone wrong.'

There was some nervous laughter in the room.

'So,' he went on, 'I promised the Hall Management Committee a painting that would have resonance for everyone who looked at it, yet at the same time, I wanted to stay true to myself. Well, this is it ...'

There was yet more nervous laughter from the audience and some shuffling from the seats beside him where the Hall Management Committee were assembled. He took a long look round the room and reached for the cloth covering the canvas.

Alys could see how anxiously Coralie was watching Gethin, although he almost seemed to be avoiding looking in her direction. Maybe, like her, he missed the old Coralie and all her vintage glad rags. This new, cool Coralie, looking very chic in a Roland Mouret rip-off, was a bit of a stranger. Alys was deeply indebted to her for going so far to get Gethin on board, but whether it had put some of her inner ghosts to rest was hard to tell. She looked from Coralie to Gethin and frowned; a palpable tension in the room had put paid to the festive atmosphere as everyone grew quiet. And then Gethin pulled away the white sheet covering the canvas.

There were shocked gasps and splutters of outrage, but when Alys dared look she saw a portrait that was so infused with raw emotions, it almost hurt. If anyone had any doubts about Gethin's artistic ability, that he had somehow stretched remarkably little talent a very long way – which Alys didn't believe for one moment – *Girl in a Coral Dress*, as he had entitled it, was proof of how gifted he was.

'I thought you promised me I was going to see something a bit saucy?' she heard one of the parish council members complaining to his wife, a woman with fiercely dyed black hair who was responsible for some of the more inspired flower arrangements in Penmorfa's tiny church.

'And this so-called work of art is the thanks we get,' said Delyth, folding her arms, 'from the boy who owes everything he is today to this village.'

The one consolation was that Delyth had earned herself a reproachful look from the Vicar, who was staring at her with great sadness.

'Mrs Bowen,' said a reporter she recognised from the county newspaper, frantically opening a notebook. The young woman had to raise her voice to be heard in the rising noise. 'You're Chair of the Hall Management Committee. Had you seen the new Gethin Lewis before today?'

'Given that the object of this painting was to raise funds for a project in Penmorfa, some of us were anticipating a work more reflective of village life,' another reporter was shouting, waving a recorder at her. 'Can you explain to everyone what the link is?'

'The link,' sneered Mair, puffing up, 'is that Gethin Lewis has just unveiled another of his mistresses.'

'Not that she looks very happy about it,' Delyth agreed. 'But then I suppose she had to wait until Alys decided she'd finished with him.'

'Oh, for goodness sake!' Alys protested. 'Don't be so ridiculous!'

'Ridiculous, is it?' said Mair.

'Shut your big fat gob!' Kitty shouted, practically in tears as she pushed through the crowd to stand by Alys's side. Jamie, in his buggy, started bawling. Poor thing, Alys registered miserably. 'My mother has worked harder for this village than the rest of you put together. How dare you tell such filthy lies about her!'

Alys felt sick as Delyth and Mair exchanged glances.

'I expect you've been too busy producing fatherless children to know about your mother's weakness for younger men,' Mair said, smugly.

'You complete bitch!' howled Kitty. 'Take that back!'

'Ask your mother why that nice couple who used to run the Summerhouse Café left so suddenly then. Ask her about young Jerzy,' Delyth purred.

'You seem to know what's going on ladies,' said a reporter, eagerly. 'Perhaps you know who the woman is in Gethin Lewis's portrait?'

'Another floozy,' Mair said, airily. 'Just like the one in that *Samba* nonsense.'

Alys's legs were shaking, but the words she was so desperate to find were eluding her. Then everyone took a step back. The Vicar calmly stilled the troubled gaggle with a wave of her pale hands.

'I think you're both letting your imaginations get away with you,' she rebuked Delyth and Mair gently. 'Your view of the artist as some sort of debaucher of women is quite mistaken. I can assure you that the model for *Samba* was categorically *not* involved with the artist.'

'Charitable as ever, dear Vicar,' Mair said, talking to the Vicar as if she were a newborn lamb with no knowledge of the world beyond a spring field.

'No, not charitable,' the Vicar insisted, firm but completely untroubled. She looked round the crowd making sure she had everyone's full attention. 'I know for a fact that the model for *Last Samba before Sunset* did not have sexual relations of any description with the artist.' She paused to give a modest smile. 'I know, because I *was* the model!'

Trembling with relief, Alys turned round smiling and grateful for the Vicar's intervention, but the smile froze on her face as she caught sight of Kitty staring at her in disgust.

'Kitty,' she said quickly, as her daughter started pushing everyone out of the way. Everywhere was in chaos. No one was worried about Gethin's painting anymore; all the cameras were trained on the Vicar, who was batting questions away with a promise of a full interview in due course. After a split second's hesitation she decided to leave them to it and chased after her daughter.

'Wait, Kitty,' she said, catching up with her and clasping hold of her arm. 'It's not what you think!'

'Isn't it?' Kitty tore her arm away furiously. 'You tell me what it is then. Did you or did you not have a relationship with Jerzy?'

Alys shook her head, trying to find the right words.

'How could you, Mam? You meant everything to me; you were the person I most looked up to in the whole world, the one I thought would keep me safe. No wonder poor Dad doesn't want to have anything to do with you. Just don't ever talk to me again, okay?' Kitty pushed her away, crying. 'You make me feel sick!'

Chapter Twenty-Two

Coralie took advantage of the tumult around her to take a few moments more to assimilate her feelings. So long as she never let her hair down ever again, there was a good chance no one would associate her with the pale-faced woman with her cascade of copper curls staring so trustingly from the painting. She lifted her gaze from her nude patent court shoes to take another quick squint at the portrait.

Maybe it wasn't such a disaster; Gethin had summed her up in colour and emotion rather than a precise physical resemblance. Anyway, no one had come rushing up thrusting a mic under her nose yet. In fact, since someone had stuck their head out of the mob clustering round the Vicar shouting that the model in *Samba* had been uncovered, the members of the press had all been too busy trying to submit their stories to notice her.

And by the time he's finished painting them, he's sick of the sight of them. Isn't that what Ruby had told her? *It may be an intense relationship for a short time, but it's only paint.* Was that a bad thing? She considered how she felt about that night. How her body had tingled and ached, as if, for once in a long, long time, she was truly alive and her pulse rate took off just remembering.

That intense relationship had resulted in a portrait that was neither chivalrous nor exploitative. It was tender but not sentimental. If she hadn't known better she would have said that it revealed some pretty naked feelings for the sitter. She tried to steal a glance at the man who'd made her feel reborn, but he'd been engulfed in the crowd. Then someone tapped her lightly on the shoulder.

'Hello, Coralie,' he said. 'You missed our last meeting so I thought I'd come to see you for a change. It looks like I picked a good time.'

'Selfish as ever!' Gethin heard Delyth declare as he pushed past them in pursuit of Coralie, who he'd lost sight of whilst he'd been surrounded by the baying crowd, screaming questions at him. 'Turning the village into a peepshow once again! You always have to bring sex into it, don't you? I suppose the beauty of this landscape isn't good enough for you!'

'Poor Alys,' said Mair loudly. 'If only she'd listened to us in the first place. However will the poor woman cope with such a very public humiliation? All that effort spent grooming the artist only to be traded in for a younger model!'

'Hypocritical old bat,' Gethin snarled to himself. He gritted his teeth and walked on, knowing that anything he said to defend Alys would be wilfully misinterpreted. Besides, anyone who knew Alys would never believe their lies. Instead, he concentrated on what he was going to say to Coralie. One minute more, he thought, walking towards her front door, and she'd be back in his arms and everything would be fine again. His heart was pounding and his mouth was dry and every second apart from all the softness and heat of her made each footstep feel like a mile. All he needed was to be close to the woman who'd been driving him crazy ever since she'd set her cat on him.

He was looking round, waiting for Rock to leap out from behind a bush somewhere, doing his 'feel sorry for me' act, when Coralie opened the door. They stared at each other for a moment. From the look on her face he needed Rock to hurry up and appear to teach him a few tricks about winning her over.

'Oh, Gethin,' she said at last, her sad face pale and haunted. 'I'm so sorry but this isn't a good time.'

Gethin scratched his head; this wasn't the way it was supposed to be. One of his art teachers had once told him that he needed to face his feelings when emotions were running high rather than slamming the door on them. All right, it hadn't been easy to admit what he felt for the woman in front of him, but he'd ripped open his chest and poured his heart all over that canvas for her.

'Hey, Coralie,' someone called from within, 'tell whoever that is we're busy here. You've kept me waiting long enough.'

'Please tell me that's your brother,' he said, feeling sick. But Coralie just shook her head.

'I need to talk to you,' she said, dropping her voice, 'but this isn't the right time.'

'Why not? Don't you want me to meet your friend in there? Come on, why not invite me in so we can all have a nice chat?'

'It's Ned Wallace, Gethin, and he's very vulnerable right now.'

What about me? He was about to say before he realised what she was telling him. 'The guy who killed that girl? You felt so bad about him, you got involved with him? Coralie, let me tell you that rescuing stray cats is one thing, but you just crossed the line, baby. We're done now.'

'Gethin!' She reached out to try to stop him, but if he stayed there any longer he was afraid that he might cry, so he shook her off and walked away.

Alys, crouched on a stool out of sight in the kitchenette, closed her eyes and waited until the hubbub of voices in the café subsided and all the reporters had hurried off in search of phone signals. Then, when she could be certain of escaping curious glances, she made her way home.

Gethin's portrait of Coralie was far removed from the decadent sensuality of his usual oeuvre; it was a weighty, sober reflection of a man who was either very clever or very much in love. But what did this radical new direction mean for the charity auction? Would the collectors who were still interested in his previous paintings want to buy something so untried, so raw?

But worse than her worries about what money might be raised for the village she loved, was the fear of what this spelled for her family. With Delyth and Mair spreading their poison, was there anyone left who would believe her side of the story? Hers wasn't such a very big crime, but even if she got the chance to explain, would her daughter, fragile, flooded with hormones and struggling with a new baby, understand? Now she was afraid of what else she might lose.

There was no sign of Huw when she got in but, since he frequently took himself off to read, Alys saw no point in disturbing him. She took the stairs quietly, avoiding the squeakier treads and only felt able to relax once she'd closed her bedroom door.

She wiped off her makeup carefully, clinging to the comfort of an old routine, put away the purple silk dress bought for the occasion in a spirit of such optimism and, sinking gratefully on to her bed, thanked her lucky stars that she could escape Huw's scrutiny, at least until morning. Given Kitty's very real preoccupation when she'd first arrived back home, it had been easy enough to fob her off with the excuse that Huw had moved to a spare room because he was having trouble sleeping. Now, instead of feeling embarrassed by their separate beds, she was relieved.

Pulling up the covers, she closed her eyes, even though sleep seemed unlikely. Then the door opened and Huw appeared, lit by the landing light, his warm brown eyes creased into a smile.

'Alys,' he chided gently. 'Fancy keeping me in suspense! Aren't you going to tell me how it went?'

'I didn't think you were that interested,' she mumbled through a fake yawn.

'This place doesn't run itself, you know,' he said, perching on the edge of the bed. 'Someone's had to do the paperwork whilst you've been gallivanting at these meetings.'

When he reached across and smoothed a lock of hair off from her face, she was unable to stop the guilty tear that slid down her face.

'Oh, Huw,' she said, sitting up and reaching for him.

'Don't you want to tell me all about it?' he asked, gently.

'Do you want to tell me about it?' Coralie forced herself to put away her own pain to do what she could for the young man sitting across the room from her. Ned Wallace, driving without due care and attention, had been found guilty of killing an innocent pedestrian, but she felt responsible for the blood on his hands.

'Give me a moment, will you?' he said, closing his eyes.

Was this some kind of karmic justice that he'd picked this moment to turn up on her doorstep? Just when she was beginning to think that being happy again was a real possibility? She brushed aside her thoughts; the least she owed Ned after everything he'd endured was her time.

'Regaining my freedom was a big high – but now it's beginning to sink in that I'll never get my old life back.'

Coralie watched him with a heavy heart. If only she'd listened to her inner voice, none of this would have happened. She'd gradually become aware of a sense of unease about her career at the consultancy. The content hadn't changed, so she realised something had shifted within herself. Work that had once appealed to her strong sense of order began to feel unjust and she started to wonder if some companies were simply hiring her as a face-saving means to cover ruthless cuts.

If only she'd resigned, she might have prevented all the misery for countless unseen victims instead of swelling corporation coffers. If only she hadn't struck Ned Wallace from the payroll, Hayley Butterfield might be a qualified teacher, enjoying her pupils, her friends and her family. But if she could save Ned, convince him that he had a future worth living for, then perhaps she could help salve her own conscience?

'So, *Girl in a Coral Dress*, how does it feel to have all eyes on you?' he asked, softly. 'I wonder if there's any money in it for me if I go to the papers with some juicy snippets about the model?'

Rock ducked out of his way as Ned reached out and tried to stroke him.

'If you need money,' Coralie said, hoping her voice didn't betray her sudden alarm, 'I'm sure I can help.'

He smiled and she was conscious once again of what a pleasant face he had, something that had struck her when they were first introduced, although the soft brown hair with its natural highlights was much shorter now. There were shadows, too, under the grey eyes.

'Oh, Coralie,' he said, softly, 'what do you take me for, a blackmailer?' He shook his head. 'You gave me hope. You stood by me when everyone walked away.'

Coralie looked away, sparing him further humiliation as he lifted his hand to his eyes to rub fiercely at the tears welling there. Horribly aware that his old self would have been mortified by the thin shirt, stiff supermarket jeans and fake Timberlands he was wearing, she let pity overcome her reservations and resolved to do whatever she could to support him on the long road ahead.

'You gave me some dignity, made me feel different to the rest of them,' he continued.

'Well, you were different. It's not like you were a murderer or an armed robber …'

'Or a nonce?' he said. 'I just killed a young woman, right?'

'You didn't set out to harm anyone,' she replied, at a loss again, knowing that she was unable to make it better. 'But you've served your sentence now.'

He nodded. 'It takes a bit of getting used to, being out,' he said, looking calmer. 'It's the choice, you see. In there, once you've answered all the questions, filled in all the forms, handed over your property to be bagged and tagged, part of you doesn't exist anymore. Right now, I'm not even capable of choosing my own toiletries.'

She felt another wave of pity for him. 'If I'd have known you were about to be released, I could have met you.'

He leaned towards her. 'If you hadn't missed your last visit, you would have known, but it looks as if you've had other stuff on your mind.'

Unable to stop herself, she shrunk further back in her chair. He noticed, and buried his face in his hands before returning his gaze to her, pupils like black pin-pricks in his pale face. Rock yowled and jumped up on her lap.

'I haven't come to make trouble, Coralie. I think I've got a job lined up in a hotel kitchen in North Wales, but you were sort of on the way. In so far that anywhere's on the way when you haven't got a car. I only want to get my head down somewhere safe for the night – this sofa's fine – and a lift to the station tomorrow and then I'll be out of your hair for good.' He gave a short laugh, 'I don't think there's much of a future in this relationship, do you?'

Her throat constricted and her chest felt tight, squeezing her lungs and making her heart pound in protest. It wasn't just their relationship that was about to end. Not once the word got out that he was there. But everyone else had turned their backs on Ned Wallace; she owed it to him to make amends.

What the fuck? In the old cottage's bare bathroom the next morning, no amount of cold water splashed over Gethin's shivering body could turn Coralie's words into anything that made sense. Thinking that he might have overreacted, he'd returned to her house much later the previous evening, for what? To prove to himself that he'd been mistaken? That Coralie wasn't really inside with another man? But the welcoming hall light that usually spilled through the glass door panel across the front path had been extinguished, whilst the living-room lamps still shone brightly behind the closed curtains. The longer he'd stood in the dark lane with his imagination driving him insane, the worse he felt.

Now, hurriedly drying himself on the beach towel he'd purchased in his whirlwind shopping spree along the journey, he dragged on some clothes and rolled up his sleeping bag, along with all those romantic notions he'd been nursing. Huh! To think that he'd rejected the idea of booking a room at The Cabin at Abersaith for the duration of his stay because he liked the thought of being closer to Coralie.

With his rosy glow to keep him warm, he'd fantasised about entertaining Coralie there. Imagined the two of them, sitting in a ring of tea lights whilst they chinked glasses and drank a toast to each other, having feasted on something clever he'd rustled up for her. Going out to watch the stars, or wind their way down to Penmorfa cove to taste each other's kisses against the backdrop of the wild sea. So much for that! Might as well book himself into a hotel in London, before catching his flight home, and enjoy the nightlife there instead.

Gethin surveyed the fragments of his dreams: two glasses, two plates, a box of candles. He thought about gathering the lot up in the fleecy blanket he had bought, too, and kicking it over the nearest cliff. Since it wouldn't help him or the environment he left everything where it was. Whoever turned up at the cottage next could have a romantic tête-à-tête instead. Closing the chalky blue door behind him for the last time, Gethin couldn't help but catch his breath at the beauty of the landscape in the early morning light.

The location of the cottage was lovely; secluded and sheltered on one side by tall trees yet with superb views to the front of swathes of green unfolding to the sea. He was almost sorry he wasn't coming back. Reaching the car he turned to look at the house once more. In the soft sunshine it looked friendly and surprisingly inviting. For the first time in his life, he considered the possibility that there might have been more to Gwyn's move than downsizing to save money. Perhaps his father had simply been striving to remain in striking distance of everything he held dear?

Another message he'd got too late, Gethin thought, driving slowly past the farmhouse and making a mental note to make contact with Alys. No matter how lovely the cottage looked, it was the last place on earth he wanted to live. Not when it meant seeing Coralie with Ned Wallace, for crying out loud. Being tender-hearted was one thing, but shacking up with the guy on his release? Well, he wasn't going to stick around to find out how her pity had somehow been twisted into some sick form of love whilst the man was in prison.

Yet, whatever noises his solicitor made about the terms of the Will being too uncertain to be enforced, neither could he sit back and think of the other beneficiary, whom he detested, living there. What a mess!

Paying for petrol in the garage where he'd stopped to fill up before the long journey, Gethin's glance strayed to the flickering images on the wall-mounted plasma screen babbling in the background. 'Penmorfa's Vicar is now in the frame!' said the reporter, struggling to keep a straight face. 'Racy Reverend, minxy Marianne Parry, is under pressure as the lid is lifted on her secret past. But attention is turning to the quiet young woman who villagers say moved here less than a year ago and about whom very little is known. The question everyone's asking is "Who's that girl in the coral dress?"' Good luck with that, he thought, hardening his heart, because he sure as hell didn't know.

Chapter Twenty-Three

The pale morning light crept behind the curtains and fell across the bed. It seemed a lifetime ago that Alys had sat in the kitchen longing for her husband and daughter to notice her. To feel something more than the seconds being counted away. Now, she'd certainly got their attention and it spelled the ruin of all her hopes and dreams for her family.

Huw was curled into her, one arm across her chest, his body warm and familiar. Alys listened to the rise and fall of his breathing, whilst she lay very still, trying to make the moment last, treasuring it for as long as possible. Eventually, though, Huw began to stir. She ran her fingers through his thick hair, her heart skipping a beat as he pulled away to smile at her.

'That wasn't so terrible, was it?' He grinned, looking, despite the silver hair, as boyish as when they'd made love for the very first time on a sweet, summer night.

'Huw, it was wonderful.' But simply being by his side again was wonderful, however fleetingly.

He propped himself up against the pillows to look at her, reaching out to brush away the tears that were flowing unchecked down her cheek. 'Oh, Alys, what have I done to you? Where do I begin to tell you how sorry I am?'

'*You've* done nothing to apologise for,' she gulped.

'Oh yes, I have – I should have responded to your pain far sooner. But just when I'd got my head around going to the doctors, they replaced Doctor Thomas with that slip of a girl and I got cold feet. When I got round to seeing her about my back, she asked if everything else was all right, so I finally mentioned the problem and she changed my blood pressure tablets. If only I'd known how easy it would be.'

'You wouldn't have been on those tablets if I hadn't forced us to move.'

'You didn't force us, *cariad*, it was a joint decision, the right one for our family. You don't have to shoulder the responsibility for everything, you know. I'm only sorry you felt you had to. I was embarrassed, Alys,' he said, his soft, brown eyes revealing just how exposed and vulnerable he was feeling. 'You know what it's like here. I was sure everyone would find out what was wrong and everyone would be talking about me behind my back. So I tried to ignore it. I kept thinking that it would all get better, as if by burying my head in the sand the problem would just go away. No wonder you lost faith in me.'

'Oh, Huw.' She swallowed, her throat aching. 'I never lost faith in you. I thought it was me. I felt so old and unattractive – I didn't mind not making love, but you wouldn't come near me, wouldn't hold me ...'

He studied her face. 'How could you have doubted your beauty when that boy from the café was so taken with you? Someone who was young and vigorous – not like me.'

'Huw,' she said, desperate for him to believe her, 'I was never unfaithful to you.'

He leaned back against the old brass bedstead Alys had inherited from her aunt, the place where they'd always been able to make up after their quarrels. Until now. 'Infidelity isn't always a physical act. I used to watch you laugh and talk to Jerzy in a way you hadn't done with me for months.'

Alys fiddled with the cream wool of the cover she'd painstakingly crocheted when they were first married. 'He was just a lost boy, Huw. Someone far from home, stuck in a relationship that was draining the life from him. You know how demanding Marika could be.'

'True,' Huw agreed amiably, 'but I don't suppose it helped her when she found him trying to seduce you in the potting shed.'

'Oh, Huw, hardly!' she protested, feeling herself blushing. 'He forgot himself and kissed me, that's all.'

'And you kissed him back, according to Marika. She wasn't very happy when she came running to me,' he added, sternly.

Alys shook her head in disbelief. 'Why didn't you say anything before, Huw?'

'Least said, soonest mended? I was afraid of losing you altogether,' he said, looking abashed. 'Thought if I pushed you too hard you might be off on a plane to Gdansk!'

'That wasn't even a remote possibility! Nothing happened,' she said, meeting his gaze. 'I realised immediately how foolishly I was behaving and stopped right there. It never went any further. I do admit to being flattered, especially ...'

'Especially since I'd withdrawn my services,' Huw said, dryly.

A harmless crush, she'd told herself at the time. Nevertheless, she *had* found herself watching the way Jerzy moved and wondering about his touch. So when he had held her close and kissed her, she'd wallowed in the release of that sudden, sharp, illicit thrill ... until the realisation of her own stupidity left her cold.

'Oh, Huw, what kind of support was I when you needed me? How can you possibly want me to stay?' She shook her head, swallowing tears at the sadness in his warm brown eyes. 'You know it'll be all over the village now, that I'd been having a torrid affair? Delyth and Mair will see to that. I think they've been longing to drop that bombshell when they thought it would do most damage. Kitty believes it, too.'

'Hush!' he said, moving closer. 'We've both made mistakes, Alys, but no one can hurt us unless we let them.'

Alys closed her eyes trying to stop the tears. She ran her hands across the silver hairs of his chest and breathed in the warm, male smell of him, her own dear Huw. Daring to open her eyes she found him watching her: tender, loving, filled with wanting.

'Oh, I've missed you so much,' she murmured, shivering as he pulled her close.

'I've been lonely too, love. And I know that my life's not complete without you,' he said, gently folding her to him, kissing her face and stroking her back before drawing her down to the bed.

'Huw, the curtains are still closed. They'll be wondering where we are at the garden centre.'

'If Delyth and Mair like to talk,' she heard him say as her mind went blank. 'Let's give them plenty to gossip about.'

'You shouldn't have long to wait. It's a reliable service even if the trains are few and far between,' said Coralie, letting the engine tick over whilst she waited for Ned to get out of the van. 'Are you sure you're all right for money?'

'Coralie.' He shocked her by reaching across to switch off the ignition. 'Hayley Butterfield is dead. It doesn't matter how much you try to do for everyone, it's never going to bring her back.'

She winced and took a long deep breath, but it still shuddered in her throat.

'And it's not your fault. You need to know that.' He leaned back in his chair. 'I was the one driving far too fast along a quiet shopping parade at night. I told myself I'd probably

241

clipped my wing mirror on something. And then I looked in my rear view mirror ... I panicked, drove home and – well, you know the rest. I still can't believe that I thought I could get on with my life.'

He shook his head. 'I pretended everything was normal. Didn't even tell my fiancée I'd been made redundant. I watched the appeals. I agreed what a bloody terrible thing it was that someone had taken away a young girl's life. I even said what a good person she must have been, carrying an organ donor card so that her death wasn't completely senseless.'

'You were distraught; you'd just lost your job, your income. None of that would have happened if I hadn't visited your offices in the first place!'

'An innocent girl didn't die because of a decision you took about company strategy,' he said, furiously. There was a pause whilst he struggled to compose himself. He took a deep breath then continued more quietly. 'I was – am – what they call a functioning alcoholic. Someone you'd never know had a drinking problem, because I'd got so good at hiding it. The first thing I did after work every night was to head for a bar. I would have been over the limit that night whether I'd lost my job or not,' he stated flatly. 'De-stressing, being sociable, networking, whatever spin you put on it, what I really liked to do was unwind with a drink.'

'So,' he went on, 'I didn't stop to report the accident because I knew I'd be breathalysed. I ignored that poor kid lying in the road and prayed that I'd be sober before they found me. And I pleaded guilty to hide the truth because I thought I'd get a lighter sentence. But it's not that easy ...'

Coralie covered her face with her hands, but he forced her to look at him

'It wasn't your fault; it was mine. I killed her. I'm the

one who has to live with that. But if it hadn't been for your regular visits when I was at my lowest ebb, I would have found a way to finish myself off. Two lives would have been lost, two families left without hope. By talking to me, making me feel human when no one else would, you made me see a purpose to this life. I'll always be grateful for that, but I want to forget you, and forget the past. All either of us can do now for Hayley Butterfield is to carry on living the best way we can.'

Penmorfa, on her return, was eerily calm. There was no sign, as she would have predicted, that anyone had ever been at Gwyn's cottage, no answer at the farmhouse and Kitty was nowhere to be found. Needing to clear her head, she left the house and walked down to the cove. A solitary figure in the large landscape, she stood and watched the trail of an aeroplane high above. The hustle and bustle of a once-flourishing waterway was silent now except for the occasional pleasure boat braving the shifting sands of the bar to negotiate the grey and silted-up river.

If history had taken a different course, it might have been Penmorfa pulsating with life, but the little village had failed to catch the tide of prosperity. If events had taken another course, she might be looking forward to a brave new world in America, expanding her business and, perhaps, trusting herself to love again.

'So long Frank Lloyd Wright,' she said, turning away from the sea and watching her footprints sink in the sand as she walked away from it all and went home to pack. As night fell, she loaded the van and took the winding road through Penmorfa. At the other side, she slowed down, to take a last look in the mirror at the cluster of lights from a scattering of houses disappearing over her shoulder. In the wire carrier, firmly strapped in beside her, Rock was mewling pitifully. She blamed herself for not doing enough to get him acclimatised to it. He'd been too ill to protest about it when he'd first turned up on her doorstep, and had meekly put up with the indignity. Now he was probably sitting there anticipating a trip to the vet's and wondering what was about to happen to him.

Poor Rock. Apart from doing everything she could to make it as physically comfortable for him, she couldn't do anything about making him feel emotionally secure. It was going to be a long trip unless … taking a deep breath, Coralie fumbled around for some music. Doris's singing filled the car, telling them whatever would be would be and Rock curled up and went to sleep.

'Depraved,' someone muttered, as Reverend Parry cleared her throat. Alys couldn't be sure but she was pretty certain that it came from Delyth or Mair, so she shot a withering look in their direction anyway.

'It makes my blood boil, Marianne,' she'd told the Vicar before the meeting, 'to see overpaid footballers obtaining injunctions preventing the press publishing any stories that could damage their lucrative sponsorship deals, whereas it's open season with you. You've been left defenceless.'

'Oh, Alys,' Marianne Parry had smiled, 'I'm not in the least bit defenceless. I do have a friend in a very high place.'

Nevertheless, since Reverend Parry was the one still being plagued by reporters, she had agreed to give an interview before the Hall Management Committee meeting commenced, hoping to stop any further press speculation. 'The Bishop's becoming a little weary of me being the story, rather than spreading the Word,' she said of her appearance all over the red-tops.

Whilst they waited for a couple of stragglers to settle, Alys tried not to look at the thickly painted wood-chip paper and a clashing floral border of the Foundered Ship's club room. It made her feel too depressed about the community hall which was still desperately needed.

The two weeks since the unveiling ceremony had been as bad as any that Alys could remember in Penmorfa. Even during the most horrendous crisis, such as when the last outbreak of Foot and Mouth had come perilously close to the village, everyone pulled together. Now all that united them was the search for a scapegoat and they hadn't even been able to agree on that. The press feeding frenzy for the Vicar's story had brought what many people were saying was the exactly the wrong kind of attention to the village and opened up old wounds about *Last Samba at Sunset*. Some people were cross with Alys, muttering that none of this would have happened if she hadn't 'got involved', as they put it, with Gethin Lewis in the first place. Others were annoyed with Gethin for presenting them with a portrait of uncertain value instead of sticking to what he did best. And where were all her hopes for Coralie and Gethin now?

At least Coralie hadn't had to hear one of the reporters remarking that it was a pity Gethin had squandered the opportunity to show off her fine assets. The only person to come up with an explanation as to why what had started as an act of generosity that was supposed to benefit the village had turned it upside down, was Willow, who insisted it was all to do with Mercury going retrograde.

Alys would have felt even worse about it all if it hadn't been for Huw, who'd been constantly by her side in the days immediately after the ceremony, fending off the press and mercilessly quelling any muttered criticism of his wife. It was Huw, too, who'd discovered that Kingston Gravell, the presenter of the popular art and antiques programme *Gravell's Gavel*, had a holiday cottage at Abersaith and had persuaded him to take a look at the painting.

'It's all about the quality of the work,' Kingston Gravell told them, in that deep, comforting voice everyone knew from their television. 'You don't have to be an expert to see that this is an outstanding portrait. The artist has captured his subject in all her vulnerable, sensitive beauty. Her lovely face is tilted towards the artist in a shared moment of intimacy, her bare shoulders, above the coral dress, lean towards him,' he'd said, smiling kindly. 'The only fly in the ointment is that experienced, high-level buyers only put their hands in their pockets for strong, consistent performers. Gethin Lewis's reputation has taken a big hit. There's a danger that the best dealers and collectors will avoid this auction, especially if there's any suspicion that the artist is using it as a tactic to get rid of something he wants to offload or feels is second-rate.'

He shook his head and, although Alys could tell he wished he could say more to reassure her, she could see from the expression in his eyes that he wasn't confident. 'I'll take some soundings and see what I can do, of course, but this is a considerable departure from Lewis's usual oeuvre and I don't need to tell you that we're now in a whole new financial climate. With so many needy causes, all charity functions struggle to reach their targets; the money's just not there.'

Sensing Alys's fears, Huw had been wonderfully reassuring, telling her that if Kingston approved of the painting, buyers would, too. Alys closed her eyes against the tears that sprang to them whenever she thought about how close she'd come to losing Huw. She was luckier than she deserved that he was still by her side. The only person who completely refused to engage with her was Kitty. Her daughter had stopped short of severing all contact but treated her with all the formality of a stranger. Alys didn't need Willow to read her stars to see that it would be a very long time before she was forgiven.

Now the room went quiet as Marianne Parry beamed her lovely smile at everyone and started to speak.

Chapter Twenty-Four

'When I was a little girl,' Marianne began, 'I would probably have burst into tears if someone had told me I was going to be a vicar when I grew up. Our vicar was an old man, with bushy eyebrows and a beard.'

A few thin smiles broke the tension in the room.

'I dreamt of being a dancer and for many years it seemed that my dream would come true,' she explained. 'I started when I was six and took several rosettes. Then, when I was twelve, I began entering competitions. I was working hard, doing something I loved, leading what on the surface at least seemed a very glamorous life, except that I was empty inside.'

She smiled at the people gathered in the room and even Mair didn't purse her lips in disapproval. Anyone less like a floozy than their calm, elegant Vicar would be hard to imagine. 'At about the same time, I became aware that someone was trying to speak to me, but I tried not to listen. I wanted to find fulfilment in dance, not in doing God's work. God was very patient with me, even when I kept finding reasons not to listen to Him. When I was in my early twenties even I realised that my glamorous life was leaving me overdrawn spiritually. I found time in my schedule to rent a cottage here, and when I looked into my heart, God was waiting for me!'

There were a couple of murmurs of approval, but the Vicar held up her hand and continued.

'I used to come down to the cove in the evening when it was quiet and dance, not to entertain others, but to celebrate the joy of finding my vocation. Sometimes I would see a young man there, with a sketch book. The young man and I got talking and I learned that he had ambitions of being a professional artist, but was being put under great pressure to carry on the family farm. I gave him the only advice I knew. I told him to look into his heart and trust where it led him.

'Gethin Lewis, for of course it was him, asked if he could make a few sketches of me. Later, he asked my permission to use them for a larger work. And to ask if I would mind very much if he took the liberty of adding himself to the painting as my shadowy partner to turn my little dance into a love story.

'I was very happy to agree – although I think we both might have had second thoughts had either of us known that those small sketches would take us on such an extraordinary journey – but just to set the record absolutely straight they did not lead to Gethin Lewis's bed. He was a troubled young man not yet twenty and I was already engaged to the marvellous man who was to become my dear husband.'

There was silence and then someone started to clap and soon everyone was united in their whole-hearted support for the Vicar. Alys even noticed one of the reporters dabbing at his eye, as they obediently packed up and left the meeting to continue.

Then it was Alys's turn to speak. 'I know that the work Gethin Lewis submitted was nothing like the work we were expecting or were promised. However, if we return the loan we've been granted by ACORN, we can say goodbye to our hopes of restoring the church hall and Penmorfa will wait a very long time for the community space it so badly needs. Or, we can take a calculated risk and go ahead with the charity auction ...'

'We won't get a garden shed for that now!' someone said angrily. 'His stuff's not worth a candle!'

'It's possible that demand for his previous oeuvre may have dropped,' Alys agreed, trying not to think about the possible fallout from the closure of his New York exhibition. 'But before we rush to any conclusions and reach a decision that may jeopardise something that might be of benefit to us all, I think you should listen to what the leading London art critics have to say about this latest work.'

She gave silent thanks to Kingston, who'd emailed her with the news that the tide was beginning to turn back in their favour. '"Welsh artist Gethin Lewis's true potential has been released at last. This often controversial artist is in a philosophical mood with his latest work. *Girl in a Coral Dress* – a reminder, of course, of the vivid scarlet dress that draws the eye in his earlier piece – is a poignant and inspired painting which hails a new maturity and direction for Lewis and reinvigorates the market for his work."'

'Now,' said Alys, 'I would urge everyone to remember that whatever the minority say about him, Gethin Lewis did return to his birthplace to unveil what is being heralded as an important new work and I think it's only proper that we should acknowledge a true son of Penmorfa. Let's put it to the vote.'

Kitty's eyes welled up with angry tears every time she thought about her mother. Although she was determined to keep her mind occupied, it seemed that wherever she went something was guaranteed to remind her of Delyth and Mair's smug innuendos. Even the hedgerows around Penmorfa were ripe with the heady, dirty-sexy smell of May blossom, she thought, as a few white petals rained down on her.

The hawthorn tree had a complicated mythology too – symbol of abandonment and fertility or chastity and cleansing, depending on your point of view. As a hedging plant its dense growth was thick and impenetrable and was supposed to offer a psychic shield, but nothing could expunge all thoughts of Alys and Jerzy from her mind.

She shot past the farmhouse as quickly as she could, the vibrations from the cobbled courtyard making Jamie's gurgle wobble, and found Adam filling hanging baskets in one of the glasshouses. A sunbeam was playing with his untidy blond hair, brushing the planes of his tanned cheeks with gold and lovingly gilding his muscular arms. A tray of petunias blew purple trumpet-faces at him as if he were a hero straight from a Greek myth, except of course that she knew all about his Achilles heel. As much as she wanted to believe that the smile that lit up his eyes as he saw them approaching was just for her, Kitty was sure that every woman he came across that day would get the same treatment. It was better to be realistic about these things; and if you couldn't even trust your own mother, who could you trust?

'Hey,' he said, 'who'd have believed it of Rev Marianne, eh? I hope she doesn't regret that particular confession. She's all over the papers again today.'

Typical Adam; he'd probably have a crack at her now, she thought murderously. 'Here,' she said, shaking off her backpack. 'I haven't got time to worry about that. Everything he needs is in there. I've put in plenty of nappies, there's wipes – this milk'll need to go in the fridge.'

'Kitty!' Adam rubbed her back, gently. 'Jeez! Remind me to work on those knots in your shoulders later. You're a mass of tension. Just chillax; you know I can handle whatever the little guy slings at me.'

He crouched down and made silly faces at Jamie, setting off a frenzy of little limbs waggling.

She exhaled, letting go of some of the pressure before it brought on a thundering headache. It wasn't fair to take it out on Adam, when it was her mother who was the lying cheat. 'Thanks,' she said, forcing a smile. 'If I get to do the styling for this engagement party, the money'll be really handy.'

He sighed and stood up, eyeing her doubtfully. 'I still think you're taking on too much too soon. Your body needs a chance to recover before you start dashing off all over the place.'

'Been reading the baby books again?' she teased, touched by his thoughtfulness all the same. He really could be kind. She went to brush a smudge of soil off his cheek and he caught hold of her hand and kissed her fingers. If only he knew how much she longed to spend more time with him instead of rushing off on business.

'I don't like seeing you worrying about money,' he said softly, giving her a nice, cosy, cared-for feeling. 'I mean, if you do too much,' he added, breaking away, 'your milk might dry up and then you might have trouble feeding this little fellow.'

Kitty swallowed hard, desperate not to let the tears pricking her eyes spill over, furious for allowing herself to believe that any of that tenderness was meant for her. 'Yeah and if I don't go to work, the cash'll dry up, too,' she said, snatching her hand away, 'which will have pretty much the same effect. Listen, I'm grateful to you for looking after him. Are you sure you don't mind?'

'Kitty, I'm his dad.' He frowned at her then swatted away a fly that was hovering in front of the buggy. 'Anyway, we've always got *Mamgu* at hand if we get into trouble, haven't we, eh?'

Oh, yes, good old Gran. She snorted, pursing her lips before an ugly comment tainted the sweetly-fragrant air.

'Do you want the paper?' he offered, grabbing it from the

table and opening up the centre pages. 'I've caught up with the Vicar's secret past now.'

'I really don't have the time,' she said. Or the inclination, she nearly added, unable to stop herself looking. Besides a large shot of the Vicar in her younger days looking very minxy, there was a much smaller reproduction of *Girl in a Coral Dress.*

Adam noticed what she'd seen and winked. 'Loads of speculation about Coralie too, and how she might have inspired Gethin's work to take such an unexpected direction.'

A flicker of sympathy for Coralie was extinguished as she belatedly realised what her reticence on the subject of Gethin had been about. Yet another example of the destructive power of sex, she decided wearily. What really hurt was that she'd always looked up to Alys and hated her for proving to be so fallible at a time when she really needed that strength and support.

'Say bye-bye to Mummy,' Adam said, bending down to shake one of Jamie's hands at her.

I already have, Kitty decided.

Coralie found her parents sitting in the conservatory. Her mother, in a pair of animal-print reading glasses, alternated between tapping at the iPad in front of her and frowning at the results. Her father, stretched out on his leather recliner with Rock curled up in his lap, was examining the back of his eyelids. Catching sight of her, her mother gave a small cry of relief, waking Rock who dug his claws in and almost castrated her father.

'It's okay, Mum,' Coralie smiled, sitting beside her on the rattan sofa.

'I wish you'd let one of us come with you, darling,' said her mother, laying down her iPad. 'It was awful to think of you all on your own visiting the spot where that poor young woman died.'

Coralie took her hand. 'I'm sorry you were upset, Mum. But it was something I needed to do.'

She'd gone to lay a small posy of flowers beneath the memorial plaque erected by Hayley's family, inscribed with her name and the dates of her poignantly brief life. As she had stood to pay her respects a shaft of sunlight had stroked the pale petals and she had felt a sudden sense of release.

Her mother searched her face, with a shimmer of tears in her eyes. Coralie took a deep breath and forced herself to speak, trying to keep her voice from breaking. 'I'm sorry for everything I've put you and Dad through. All the worry. You were both right to question my motives when I gave up the consultancy and moved away. I wasn't really in the right frame of mind, was I?'

She took a tissue from the box her mother was offering her and wiped her eyes.

'We wanted you to be happy, that's why we were so concerned. We wanted to be sure you were doing the right thing for you and not simply taking yourself off into some self-imposed exile. What we should have been telling you, darling, is how proud we are of you.'

Coralie looked up and saw the love in her mother's expression.

'Many people would have given up under the stress you've endured, but you found a way to cope with the terrible ordeal you suffered. Some people would say that Ned Wallace didn't deserve your kindness – a life for a life – but he's the one who has to live with the results of his actions and the consequences for the rest of his life.

'Your grandmother would have been proud, too, to think that you'd built a new life for yourself in the place where she found a loving home as an evacuee. She would have been over the moon to know that you'd created a business from her old recipes.'

They paused to remember the woman who'd meant so much to both of them.

'Mum,' said Coralie, as an idea came to her. 'Can I borrow your iPad for a moment?'

She quickly found the organ donor register online and entered her details. It wouldn't bring Hayley back, but it was a small recognition of her life.

'Oh, good idea,' Susan Casey said. 'Brian? You're next.'

Coralie leaned back exhausted, but happier than she'd been in many months.

'Just looking at the calendar,' her mother said, poring over her iPad again. 'Now, when would be a good idea for us to come up and meet your new man?'

Coralie laughed. 'There's no one to meet, Mum.'

She watched as her mother clicked on a new tab and turned her portrait towards her. 'Coralie,' she said, 'you can't hide anything from me, I'm your mother. I can see the look in your eyes in this beautiful portrait and so can the artist. Now, why are you still here when there's a business and a man waiting for you in Penmorfa?'

Coralie leaned in and kissed her so that her parents couldn't read her expression. She loved them very much, but sadly, there would be no changes to make to their little branch of the family tree any time soon.

By the time Kitty got back she was wilting after a hugely busy day. The sound of laughter from the direction of the raised beds where the shrubs were displayed made her hesitate. Treading softly, she drew closer and saw Alys and Adam having a wonderful time playing with the baby. Anyone who didn't know better might take it for a lovely family scene. Except that everyone in Penmorfa knew that Alys was an adulteress and Adam couldn't be trusted to keep it in his pants. Resenting them both for making her life even harder, she was especially snappy as she marched over and snatched Jamie from Alys's arms.

'I'll take him now, thank you,' she said, ignoring the way her mother recoiled as if she'd been struck.

'Oh, no you don't.' Adam took hold of the buggy. 'I'm sure you're tired, but that's no way to speak to us, especially not your mother. A thank you wouldn't go amiss.'

'As far as I can see you've both been enjoying yourselves whilst I've been working,' she said, knowing she was being unreasonable. 'What's there to say thank you for?'

Alys put her hands on her hips. 'Now I'm the one doubting my mothering skills.' She glared at Kitty. 'Because I swear I brought you up to have some manners. You might have the courtesy to hear what else Adam has to say.'

Kitty's head was pounding and all she wanted to do was get home and sit down, if Jamie would let her. She shrugged and Alys nodded. 'You know where I am if you need me, Kitty. Nothing's changed.'

But it had, thought Kitty, as her mother walked away.

'Wait there,' said Adam, unfolding a garden chair for her before disappearing, only to returning a few minutes later with a bottle of ice cold mineral water. Kitty opened it and took a deep drink and began to feel guilty about her outburst.

Adam watched her for a while and when he spoke his voice was tight with emotion. 'I know when I'm not wanted,' he said sadly. 'I can see you've only been putting up with having me around for the little guy's sake, and I appreciate it, but I think it's time I got out of your hair now before our relationship deteriorates any further.

'I've also been doing some thinking about what you said about work. I know I'll never be the kind of high-powered bloke you'll probably end up with, but I'm going to do what I can to make things easier for you. I've managed to get some milking work in addition to working here. I really hate the thought of not seeing the little guy in the mornings, but I guess you'd prefer the extra money to having me around.'

'But what about,' she swallowed hard, 'Jamie? When will he see you?'

'I'm sure you'll come up with a practical solution,' he said, looking utterly miserable. 'You're the big ideas woman, aren't you?'

Chapter Twenty-Five

Fat buds of shocking-pink rhododendrons were swelling in the late May sunshine, clashing gloriously with deep purple cornets of lilac blossom swaying in the fresh breeze. Coralie saw everything with a new appreciation and a sense that, like one of Alys's perennials once the brown leaves of the previous year's growth had been cleared away, she was about to bloom again.

'Whatever you did, you're looking much better for it,' Alys said, putting down the wheelbarrow she was pushing and eyeing Coralie's fifties' print skirt with the cropped summer jacket approvingly. 'I couldn't bear you in all that tailored stuff.'

The remnants of her office wardrobe were the right size, but, as she'd come to realise, they no longer fitted the person she'd become. Coralie looked down at herself with a rueful smile. 'I thought I was leaving the past behind, but now I really have.'

Before she could go any further, Willow and Wilfie scurried past, giggling, supposedly to open Willow's jewellery shop, but as soon as they were inside, the door was locked again and the blinds stayed closed.

'I think Wilfie's found true love,' Alys said as they edged away by mutual consent. 'But I do hope he doesn't start writing any sonnets about it.'

'He's found something,' Coralie snorted. 'I bet Rhys is relieved.'

'Well, not anymore he isn't, but Wilfie is,' said Alys, naughtily. 'You know, Willow's giving up her shop.'

'I did see a tall blond guy looking at Willow's unit recently. I wasn't sure if he was looking at jewellery or had come for a massage.'

Alys pulled a face. 'That's Willow's brother, Ash. He's going to keep the jewellery business going and Willow and Wilfie are taking over the café. They're planning to keep it going all year round, by supplementing the loss of income in the winter with creative writing and yoga classes.'

'Really?' Coralie felt her eyebrows lift.

'I must say, I was a bit sceptical about it, but Wilfie did hospitality and catering at college and they're both taking their food hygiene qualifications. Probably in there swotting for it now.' She winked at Coralie. 'Truly, I was surprised by Wilfie's chocolate brownies. They're lush, very moist and chewy – you should try one. I don't know if he's got a secret ingredient or a particularly deft touch.'

Their eyes met and they both giggled.

'Come here, you,' she said, pulling Coralie to her and hugging her. As she let her go she rested her hands lightly on Coralie's shoulders, her face serious. 'Gethin rang.'

Coralie closed her eyes whilst the ground steadied itself again. 'About the sale of the painting, I suppose. How are things looking for the gala auction?'

Alys looked at her in exasperation. 'I don't care if I never hear those words again! I've wasted too much time on this whole hall renovation stuff already. Displacement activity, I think they call it, trying to paper over the cracks in my own life, pretending that I was a better person than I was because I was working for the good of the community. Ha!' She shook her head. 'I only got involved because it was easier than facing up to the problems at home. I neglected Huw and was such a terrible mother that my own daughter couldn't even come to me with her problems.'

Coralie made a small noise of protest, but Alys hadn't finished. 'Don't you think it's about time you put Gethin out of his misery?'

'What about my misery? He's the one who wouldn't listen to me! The one who stormed off before I could explain,' Coralie said, her voice thick with suppressed emotion.

Alys sighed heavily. 'Coralie, that boy had a dog's life growing up, his mother was twelve years younger than his father and was always in awe of him. She was never quite strong enough to stand up to Gwyn's violent mood swings. It's no excuse, but Gwyn wasn't a well man. Gethin begged his mother to leave him but Katrin said Gwyn needed someone to look after him. And by the time he'd made his name, the money came too late to help her. She died just before the sale of *Samba*, never knew how famous it would make her son.

'Gethin's coped through the years by a combination of hiding his feelings and never standing still for long enough to let any one person get close to him. Until now.'

She caught hold of Coralie's hands and held her gaze. 'You only have to look at that portrait to know what Gethin feels about you, but if you care about him at all, you're going to have to show him.'

'So you had to drive nearly all the way to Cardiff for a feature on country weddings?' Huw shook his head at Kitty. 'It's a bit soon to be doing all that, isn't it? No wonder you've had a long day. All right, love?'

This to her mother who'd come in looking, Kitty had to admit, pretty wrung out from yet another meeting about the charity auction.

Alys hung her handbag on the back of a chair, bending to kiss Huw as she did. 'I think I've done enough to stave off the lynch mob if Gethin ever returns,' she said with a weary smile which faded when she saw Kitty's expression. She was starting to look her age, Kitty thought guiltily.

'These magazines expect a lot for their money, don't they?' Huw went on, returning to her. 'You're a new mum. Couldn't everyone have come here? To the country? That would be more authentic, wouldn't it?'

'Yes, Dad.' Kitty was too weary to disagree. 'But that's why they employed me to do the styling. To get the look without the inconvenience of actually being in the countryside. I couldn't turn them down, there's too much competition out there.'

Getting the feel of a relaxed, inexpensive wedding had been enormously hard work. The flowers, which were supposed to look as if they'd been picked from a garden, had looked weedy and dejected in the proofs, so Kitty had been forced to cheat and glam them up with some costly tall-stemmed white freesias. She still had her doubts about the rough hessian tablecloths, although that hardy perennial, the vintage fabric bunting, had wowed everyone, as usual. The tea lights in painted jam jars were very popular, too; sometimes she had to pinch herself when she thought how well she was getting paid to use such cheap, everyday props.

'I made a chicken pie before I went to the meeting,' Alys told her, washing her hands at the sink. 'Would you like to stay?'

Kitty was about to refuse, but having sat down she was too tired to stomp off again. Jamie was quiet, which meant that she could eat in peace, too. Besides, no one made pastry like her mother. Thinking about it made her mouth water and the aroma of the cooked food filling the kitchen made her keenly aware that her stomach was empty. Her evenings weren't exactly full either. With early starts at the dairy farm, Adam had taken to making flying visits in the evening, staying only long enough to say good night to Jamie, then leaving immediately. She closed her eyes and braced herself for another long night with no one to talk to.

'There are no strings,' Alys said, pushing her white bob from her face as she bent to open the Aga. 'Just food. I won't read anything into it one way or another.'

Kitty hesitated, torn between wanting to eat and bridging the gulf between her and her mother, then Huw made them all jump by banging his fist on the table. 'I've had enough of this, young lady!' he roared, making Jamie's eyes fly open. 'You've put your mother through too much already. And that young man of yours. Now bloody well stay where you are and eat.'

Jamie's bottom lip started to quiver, but Huw picked him up and settled him in the crook of his arm, jiggling him up and down whilst he poured wine for them all and Alys dished up in silence. Kitty knew that a couple of sips of wine probably wouldn't hurt Jamie. But whether it was the wine or the melt-in-the-mouth perfection of Alys's pie, or perhaps it was simply being in the warm, relaxed atmosphere of her parents' home, she wasn't sure, but she felt the brittle carapace that had been holding her feelings in check starting to crack. Had she simply not noticed the way her parents interacted before? The way her mother's gaze softened when she looked towards her father? Or her father, catching Alys's fingers after they'd finished eating, rubbing his thumb across the back of her hand? They made being a couple look natural and easy, not like the way she was with Adam which felt like walking on broken glass.

'There are no guarantees with love,' her father said, reading her mind. 'You can't hold some of it back, like a deposit, so you can get your money back if something goes wrong. You have to give yourself wholeheartedly, whatever the cost.'

Still in Huw's arm, Jamie's fingers opened like anemones at the sound of the voice rumbling beneath him. Huw extended a red, rough forefinger and Kitty swallowed a lump in her throat as her son gripped it and went back to sleep.

'Whatever you think you've heard from the gossips,' he went on, 'you've punished your mother enough. You made your mind up without letting her have her say and she's just accepted whatever you've dished out. You've got everyone running round in circles after you. Adam's working all hours, your mother's babysitting as well as trying to run the garden centre. And, despite all the thanks she's got, she's still fighting for this village and looking for funding so that the place has got a community facility everyone can use.'

'But, Dad,' she had to say it. 'How can you just pretend nothing's happened? How can you trust—'

He held up his hand to stop her. 'Because only your mother and I know what really goes on behind closed doors. You talk about trust, Kitty. Where was the trust when you came running home pregnant? Wasn't not confiding in your mother a form of betrayal? And what about Adam? Where was your trust in him to do the right thing?'

He shook his head sadly. 'Love isn't easy, but you can't keep holding back if you want to give it a chance. Just like any of those plants out there, you have to cherish it when it's delicate, nourish it to give it strength and show it some sunshine so it can blossom.'

Across the table from her, Alys was quietly sobbing. Kitty went over to her and held her very tight, breathing in the musky floral scent of Shalimar that Alys loved.

In her old bedroom the next morning, Kitty sat on the edge of her single bed, staring out of the window, pondering on what to do about Adam. Edith, looking full of her own self-importance, trotted off down the garden, followed shortly afterwards by Alys and Huw, holding Jamie in his arms. Lime clouds of *Alchemilla mollis* foamed at their feet as her parents, side by side, ambled down the path. Snippets of laughter and conversation drifted up in the morning air along with the scent of orange-blossom.

Kitty drew back from the window, conscious of not wanting to intrude on what seemed an intimate moment. No one looking at her parents now would see any outward sign of all the recent tension in their relationship. With hindsight, the separate bedrooms nonsense had been an obvious clue, but no one apart from her would have known about that.

What really worried her was how she'd failed to spot the signs; if the foundations of a relationship that she had always thought of as so constant and enduring, had been quietly slipping away under her nose, what hope was there for her and Adam? How would she know if she could trust him? She couldn't imagine him deliberately hurting her, but his naturally gregarious and sociable personality meant he didn't even have to go out of his way to attract female attention. Was she strong enough to let him be the man he was without letting jealousy and resentment come between them?

'If this is the right thing for me to do,' she said out loud. 'Please let there be a sign.'

Kitty scanned the sky searching – for what? The clouds to part? A giant thumbs up perhaps? She looked again at the garden where, as her parents walked further away, her mother brushed past a crimson camellia, the shattered blossom spilling bloodied petals over the lawn behind them. Kitty's hand fluttered to her chest and she shook her head. Was that it? That something so perfect could disintegrate at a touch? Was that her sign?

But when she dared to look again, her father was holding tight to both Alys and Jamie and her parents were staring into each other faces, looking at each other as if they hadn't seen one another for thirty years. Well, maybe they hadn't.

Leaving them to their private moment, Kitty turned away from the window, smiling a watery smile to herself and swallowing the lump in her throat. If, after all those years together, her parents could still look at each other with a love and tenderness that moved her to tears, maybe she and Adam could figure it out. When she got in she would ring him.

Gethin still couldn't work out where he'd gone so wrong with Coralie, except that some people said that his father had never worked out his feelings for his mother, either, until she wasn't there anymore. But at least he'd done the right thing by Ruby. Plenty of people were talking about her on this bright June day; everyone had an opinion. The white marble interior of the impressive stone-vaulted entrance hall of the New York Public Library had probably hosted a few remarkable occasions in its time, but today's event was something special. The photographers were everywhere, setting the marble gleaming with spangles of white light from their flashes.

Where earlier in the day the tap of every heel had rung out across the empty space, all the sharp sounds were now absorbed by the gathering crowd who, in turn, sent out new ripples of conversation and laughter. Gethin's aching heart swelled with pride as Ruby, looking amazing in black silk crêpe de Chine Vera Wang pants and black stretch tee posed for the cameras. The judges of the Brave New Artists' Prize for rising stars had picked a worthy winner.

To the right of her, Ruby's vast, prize-winning painting, the first of her dramatic interpretations of how the Pre-Raphaelite vision might look transferred to modern-day New York, was creating quite a buzz. Her reworking of Edward Burne-Jones's *The Golden Stairs*, featuring eighteen of her lesbian and gay friends who now filled the stone staircase behind her, had been inspired. Ruby had painstakingly caught the mood of the original work whilst adding her own character and spark. Looking round the room, everyone, from her models – some carrying musical instruments, all dressed in dove grey, and all desperately trying to keep straight faces – to the art enthusiasts applauding wildly in the hall, sensed that something big was happening.

Gethin was delighted by all the goodwill and support for his protégée. Satisfied that Ruby's career was off to a flying start, he caught her eye, gave her a quick thumbs up and left her to it. Although the stirrings of excitement about *Girl in a Coral Dress* were beginning to reach New York, the fallout from his previous exhibition was too fresh, so he'd deliberately kept a low profile. Even so it didn't stop someone stopping him as he tried to push through the crowd to leave.

'Hey, buddy, you're not that Welsh guy, are you?'

'No,' said Gethin walking on.

'So you're not the "Green Green Grass of Home" dude, then?'

Hell, thought Gethin, gritting his teeth and carrying on. He knew he had one or two grey hairs, but if someone really had confused him with the septuagenarian singer, it was time he got a decent night's sleep.

He stomped down the steps of the library, acknowledging the stone lions guarding the building. Patience and Fortitude, they'd been nicknamed, for the qualities New Yorkers would need to possess to get through The Great Depression. Right now, he didn't feel too cheerful and he'd pretty much run out of patience and fortitude. That probably meant he wasn't much of a New Yorker.

Deciding that a walk across the city would reconnect him, his black mood wasn't helped by a ticket tout pushing a leaflet under his nose inviting him to take a sightseeing tour. Now he didn't even look as if he belonged here. The trouble was, he thought, dropping his head and picking up his pace, he wasn't sure where he belonged anymore. The Big Apple had blown a big fat raspberry at him and, although he sometimes imagined he did hear the call of the Welsh mountains and valleys, he guessed that his longing was for the lush curves and dips of one woman who drew him back there.

'Will ya do us all a favour and call her,' Ruby had said to him only that morning, after she'd apparently spoken to him for ten minutes without him hearing a word.

At this rate he'd have to get the glove puppets out to explain to Ruby, since she insisted on being deliberately obtuse, that he and Coralie were finished. Part of him still clung on to the hope that New York might be the very place she might turn up, especially if she was exploring new options for Sweet Cleans.

'I'm sorry, I can't help you,' Laura Schiffman had said, shaking her head when he'd pressed her for information about her friend in the cosmetic industry. 'But when you do see Coralie next, I'd love you to get hold of some of her Rose Works body lotion, for me,' she'd added, brightening up.

How he longed to phone Coralie and tell her, just so he could hear her voice and imagine her smile. Sometimes he even started to dial the number so he could listen to her answerphone message, but he never pressed 'call' for fear of making the ache worse.

If anything, his thinking was muddier by the time he got

to his apartment, where the mailman was trying to negotiate his satchel-cart past a doggie-do. Gethin knew how he felt. 'How you doing today? Your wife on the mend now?' he called out.

'Not so bad. Something she ate apparently. I guess that means I'm excused cooking duties now. These are for you. Two letters *and* a parcel.'

Chapter Twenty-Six

Gethin took the steps two at time and, once inside, poured himself some iced water before opening his mail. The first envelope looked like something his solicitor might send him. Formal confirmation that the royalties owed to him were coming at last? But by the time he'd finished reading it through, he'd had to take another long drink of iced water. He needed it to cool down. A thirty-day notice to quit? How was this even frigging possible? He stared at the shoji screen room divider for a full minute because it took him that long to believe what he'd just read.

Somehow his landlord was trying to suggest that in contravention of his tenancy agreement, he was using the apartment as a second home. That his main residence was in Penmorfa, west Wales. His only proof, which would be a joke if it wasn't so frigging serious, appeared to be an article in the *New York Times*, quoting an art critic suggesting the reason his work had become so lacklustre was because of the time he was devoting to renovating his desirable country residence!

Well, that was pure garbage and he could dispute it – probably, although he resented the time and money he would waste chasing round. However, it wasn't so easy to defend himself against the second, and more concrete claim, that one of his guests made violent threats to another occupant of the building and created a public nuisance.

'Oh, Rubes.' He rubbed his jaw. She'd certainly given him a wake-up call that day. Unfortunately she'd woken half the building, too – the complaining half.

He picked up the next letter, still chewing over his predicament. Unless he took action fast, in thirty days he could be homeless. That was the reality. Out on the streets with the crazy dude who occasionally showed up on the corner of his block, rocking and swearing. Not a great place to be in New York, especially when it snowed. Jesus! Those guys had always seemed so other, nothing to do with his life, but now he was discovering just how quickly the ground beneath your feet could turn to sand. Next time he saw the crazy dude, he'd slip him more than a couple of singles, just so he'd remember him in future. In a couple of weeks they could be new best friends.

He tore open the second envelope. Might as well get all the bad news out of the way at once. A photograph dropped out, landing face down on the floor. It looked as if the landlord had set a private investigator on him, too. Photographic evidence of his 'desirable country residence', perhaps? Why would anyone bother to get photographs printed these days, unless there was something they particularly wanted to rub your face in?

He turned the print over and his breath caught at the sight.

Apart from someone who valued what other people disdained. Who didn't mind that some of her things were pre-loved. Who wanted to scoop up all the unwanted animals. Maybe she'd feel sorry for him if he lost his apartment – except she'd probably decide that the crazy dude was in greater need. There she was smiling self-consciously beside him, he with his arm round her waist, at the top of the Empire State, and he couldn't help smiling back even though the sight of her filled him with longing.

His fingers were trembling as he took out the letter inside. When he'd read it all the way through he felt like hell for not giving her the chance to explain the situation to him. Ned Wallace had turned to her because he had nowhere else to go and because of the kind-hearted person she was, she'd been unable to turn him away.

You told me once that having a portrait painted could be therapeutic, she'd written, *but coming face to face with myself in your beautiful painting just made me more aware of how bad I felt inside. I'm so sorry for hurting you.*

Why was she apologising when he was the one who was afraid of getting tangled up with messy emotions? Perhaps if he'd given her more time that morning in his apartment instead of letting her go, he might have spared them both a lot of heartache.

Ned Wallace had been imprisoned, but it was Coralie who'd been locked up. Blaming herself for what she saw as her part in a young girl's death. Putting her own life on hold out of a sense of duty to put right all the wrongs. Well, as far as he was concerned, Ned Wallace should still be rotting in prison. And yet it was because the murdering, drunken, deceitful bastard had been released that Coralie had been set free.

The parcel contained a box – Pandora's he hoped, after all the bad and sad news. He fingered it, trying to guess its contents, afraid that the expectations he was beginning to feel were about to be crushed. Opening it at last, he drew back the tissue paper and light gleamed on a glass dome. He lifted it in front of his face, shook it gently and watched silvery flakes of fake snow shimmer round the Empire State. Not quite a crystal ball, but he didn't need to look into the future to see that things were looking up.

He turned the key and the tinny notes tinkled out. Not 'New York, New York', like nearly every snow-globe he'd ever come across, but 'Que Sera Sera'. Doris Day was trying to tell him the future wasn't his to see, but she was wrong.

He may have been blind but he wasn't stupid. And he knew exactly what was coming next.

Kitty was trying to do as her father had suggested and put her whole self in. Earlier in the day she'd prepared a chilli, put some beers in the fridge and put on the dark floral hitch-skirt dress that she knew was one of Adam's favourites.

'I thought you might like to bath Jamie,' she suggested, trying not to mind that he barely flicked a glance at her before rolling up his sleeves and filling up the baby bath. Leaning against the door frame, she admired the deft way Adam managed to wash Jamie's hair without the usual trauma. Must be those strong arms making the baby feel secure, because the minute she attempted the manoeuvre it was a toss-up to see which of them ended up with a wobbly bottom lip first. Seeing how much father and son were enjoying the experience, she felt guilty for ever thinking she could keep them apart.

When Jamie was dry and sweet-smelling again and they were back downstairs, she passed Adam a beer and he sat back on one of the dining chairs, watching her on the sofa slowly unbutton the front of her dress to give Jamie his evening feed.

'You make a beautiful mummy,' he said, with a husky break in his voice.

'You don't make such a bad daddy.' It was true, she realised, smiling at how awkward and unsure of himself he looked. Just because he was never going to make great partner material, didn't mean he wasn't capable of being a brilliant dad. No one could criticise the way he doted on Jamie. Having a baby with the shaggy-haired, sexy beach-bum who struggled to turn up for work at the garden centre when the surf was right, hadn't exactly been at the forefront of her mind when she had first seen him stripped to the waist riding a quad bike on a baking hot day in late July.

Nope, the only thing she'd been thinking about from that first moment was sex. Fortunately, she soon found out, after a couple of days trailing round after him pretending to learn how to prune the spring-flowering shrubs and helping him spread nets over the soft fruits bushes before the birds stripped them, that he was a like-minded spirit. The pair of them had become quite adept at spreading and stripping activities as July rolled into August; most of them outside, working up a sweat in the steamy summer fields. Kitty let her gaze drop to the curve of his biceps beneath the rolled-up sleeves and shivered at the memory. It was when the passion had turned into something deeper and her emotions got in the way that she had started to panic.

Adam set the bottle down on the table beside him, wiped his lips and sat down next to her. Her breath slowed as he put one arm round her shoulders and leaned closer to stroke Jamie's cheek. She watched as his finger moved slowly from the baby and gently traced the blue veins of her breast, as if she was not just beautiful but desirable, too. She looked back at him and the frost that seemed to have been surrounding her heart melted.

Don't hold back, that's what her dad had said.

'You don't have to say anything back,' she said whilst she still felt brave. 'But I think I love you.'

Think? That didn't sound very whole-hearted, did it? What about the way her heart lifted at the thought of him and everything seemed better, brighter, safer because he was there?

'What I mean is, I do, love you, that is.'

'What you mean,' said Adam, grinning, 'is that you've only just realised.'

Kitty scowled at him. Later she'd have words with her father. So much for putting your whole self in; all she had done was dug a bloody great hole for herself and now Adam was laughing down at her.

'Must be quite tough for a Cardiff career girl and thrusting entrepreneur to discover she's fallen for a lowly labouring gardener,' he breathed into her hair.

'Oh, don't sound so bloody pleased with yourself,' she said, trying to keep her voice down so as not to wake Jamie. 'I forgot you get women falling for you so often you must be sick of hearing it.'

'Yeah, it's hard being me.' He sighed, making her squirm with embarrassment. 'Especially when the only girl for me is the one woman who's been holding back.'

'Anyone I know?' she muttered, doing her best to control her rising excitement.

He swallowed. 'I was beginning to lose hope. Kept telling myself that I was punching above my weight to think a woman as clever and talented as you would be interested in someone who works with their hands, like me.'

'I like what you do with your hands,' she couldn't resist telling him.

'And that's one of the many reasons why I love you.'

He leaned over and kissed her then and she grabbed hold of his hair and pulled him even closer, almost forgetting Jamie, who grunted in his sleep. Adam lifted him out of her arms and gently laid him in the carrycot beside the sofa. When he turned back, his face was serious.

'There's just one thing,' he said, looking completely defenceless. 'If you want to be with me, let's do it properly. Take my name. Marry me, Kitty.'

She swallowed hard and closed her eyes whilst she found the strength to reply. 'You're not just asking because of him.

Because of Jamie? I don't want you to ever look back and say I trapped you into a proposal.'

'Kitty,' he said, taking her face gently in his palms, 'I love *you* and I don't mind how many times I have to tell you, I'll keep saying it until you believe me. I love you with all my heart and nothing would make me happier than the honour of becoming your husband. So, what do you say?'

On the last Saturday of June, Coralie looked around her at the sunlit fields of Penmorfa rolling down to a sparkling sea beneath a perfect Pembrokeshire blue sky and hoped that the outlook would seem as bright at the end of the day. There had been a difficult moment, that morning, during the erection of the marquee for the day's gala auction, when a strong sea breeze almost sabotaged the event before it began. Thankfully, the forecast was for the wind to ease during the afternoon, staying just bracing enough to keep everyone awake rather than tearing their hats off or turning the marquee, where Adam was directing people to their seats, into a Zeppelin.

'At least if it was raining,' said Kitty joining her with Jamie flat-out in his buggy, snoozing peacefully under a parasol, 'the VIPs could see how badly we need a community hall. If they think it's like this all the time, they might think we can manage without it and only make stingy bids.'

'I'm sure they won't,' said Coralie, thinking how pretty Kitty looked in a white, floaty top that contrasted with her dark hair. Everyone had really dressed up for the occasion, all the bright colours making it a truly gala occasion. 'It's going to be fine, you'll see. Hold still a minute.' She leaned across and gently rubbed at an unblended blob of concealer where Kitty had tried to hide faint shadows under her eyes from all the broken nights. But there was no hiding Kitty's new-found happiness. Or the diamond-and-sapphire cluster on her finger that caught the light to become a rainbow of shimmering shooting stars as Kitty lifted her hand.

'Getting used to that yet?' She laughed.

'Isn't it lush?' Kitty grinned, flexing her fingers to admire all the twinkling gems. 'That's babies for you! They change everything. They can even make someone like Adam behave like good husband material. He's only proposed to me because he can't bear to be parted from this little fellow. Do you know I even drew up a list of reasons for and against marrying him: two columns, "yes" and "no"?'

Coralie shook her head, not fooled in the slightest by Kitty's feeble effort to play her excitement down. 'Rubbish, Kitty. The only one who couldn't see how besotted Adam was with you was *you!*'

For all her and Alys's fears that Adam wouldn't be good with commitment, he'd surprised everyone. Although maybe that was being unfair to him. When she thought about it, he'd only ever teased and flirted with other women right under Kitty's nose and with the sole purpose of making her jealous. His behaviour, when Kitty wasn't around, had always been entirely chivalrous.

'I wish I'd trusted him sooner,' Kitty admitted, her voice shaking a little. 'I never thought someone as sexy as Adam would pick me. I was so afraid of being hurt that I was mean to everyone.'

'Now you're being mean to yourself,' Coralie said gently, rubbing her shoulder. 'He's a good man, a great dad and this is the start of your bright future together.'

'And what about you?' Kitty asked, eyeing her from a strand of hair that had blown across her face. 'Isn't it about time you stopped being hard on yourself and grabbed hold of your bright future?'

Coralie's throat tightened. She'd written, laying her feelings bare to Gethin, asking him to come. Now it was up to him. 'I'm taking it one day at a time,' she said, reaching up to massage the back of her neck, 'so let's see what we can do to make this a good one for Alys.'

'Yes, let's.' A protest from the buggy set Kitty jiggling it frantically. 'I'm that nervous for Mam. She's worked so hard for this. You know she's got that black guy off that art and antiques programme to be the auctioneer?'

'*Gravell's Gavel*? It's great, isn't it? I love Kingston Gravell! He comes across as such a nice man. How on earth did Alys manage that?'

'It was due to Dad actually,' Kitty said, proudly. 'What's more Kingston Gravell liked the location here so much that he phoned to say he's bringing a TV crew with him in case they can use some footage from today in their show!'

Coralie gulped and reminded herself that the cameras would not be pointing at her, but at a portrait of her. One that had attracted remarkably little interest in the subject, fortunately, since it was a little more sober than all the razzmatazz of *Samba* and the sensational outing of the Vicar. Nevertheless, she was thankful that she no longer carried the burden of Hayley Butterfield's death like a shameful secret or she would have felt sickened by the thought of so much publicity.

'You've done masses, too,' she added. 'Look at all these people you've managed to get here.'

'I spent hours sending out invitations, but it was worth it.' Kitty nodded. 'And I'm glad I added one day's free styling from Flair on a Shoestring to the list of lots. Think of all the free publicity I'm going to get now!'

Coralie only hoped that it would be good publicity. The market was nervous about *Girl in a Coral Dress* because it was such a radical departure from anything Gethin had produced before. Putting a brave face on it, Alys and the Hall Management Committee had determined to raise what funds they could by extending the auction to include five lots in addition to the final lot, when the portrait would be auctioned. And whilst donations had been generous, it would still be dreadful, not to mention embarrassing, if a spa day at The Cabin at Abersaith went for more money than her portrait.

'Oh look,' she said, temporarily distracted. 'There's Derek Brockway – the weatherman!'

'He's a keen walker so I thought he'd be interested in the location.' Kitty nodded. 'I'm hoping Jamie Owen, the broadcaster, will be able to make it, too.' Her eyes widened at the sight of a clean-cut couple walking hand-in-hand and she grabbed Coralie's arm. 'That's not—'

Coralie nodded. 'Willow and Wilfie. Yes! They've bought just about everything in the Sweet Cleans range since they started seeing each other.'

In a light linen jacket over a white shirt and almost clean jeans, Wilfie, who had shaved off his beard, had gone from Bill Oddie to Ben Fogle in a dramatic transformation. Willow too, had ditched the extreme henna, an overkill of kohl and a fug of patchouli oil and looked ten years younger for it. They were followed by a stream of people making their way along the path. Behind them in the car park a minibus roared to a halt and a group of jovial-looking men spilled out, grabbing their jackets.

'Oh lord, the Abersaith Male Voice Choir again,' said Kitty as they surged towards them. 'Tell 'em you've got a partner or they'll stop and chat you up all afternoon and we'll never get on with the auction.'

It wasn't a tactic that seemed to work, since none of the

choir was put off by Kitty having Jamie, who was fast asleep in his buggy and missed all the attention his mother was attracting, although Adam, Coralie noticed, glared at one or two of the younger members as they entered the marquee.

'Oh, look over there,' Kitty said, pointing to a cluster of figures, just as Coralie's knees went weak as she spotted the familiar figure, too. 'Isn't that Gethin?'

Chapter Twenty-Seven

Gethin was delighted to have arrived in Penmorfa with sufficient time to spare so as not to have to use the short cut across the field to the garden centre, especially as it was full of cows. Paint hadn't impressed, pheromones had failed, but Eau de Farmyard definitely wouldn't clear the air between him and Coralie. Priming Huw to make bids up to the value of the ACORN loan on his behalf – the financial wrangles with the poster company administrators happily resolved – meant he had managed to get in one set of good books and ensured there'd be at least one taker for *Girl in a Coral Dress*. If he didn't have the real thing, he'd always have the painting to remind him.

And, he thought, scanning the people in an array of finery, like the two women in front of him following the chipped-stone path towards the marquee, he wasn't even the last to arrive. At the sound of footsteps crunching behind them, one of the women in front of him glanced over her shoulder, but the half-smile turned stone-cold when she saw who it was.

'I'm surprised you've got the nerve to show your face round here,' said Delyth.

The lime green feathers quivering on her head looked like a parrot had just used it as a launch pad. If that was a fascinator, it wasn't working for him.

'Lovely to see you, too.' Gethin smiled.

'Come to ruin another occasion?' said Mair, from beneath a large purple ostrich feather.

Gethin overtook and blocked their path. 'I'm here to see that plenty of money's raised for a good cause, but if you ladies came looking for a scrap, let's do it now, so as not to spoil everyone's fun. Now just *what* is your problem?'

'Don't pretend you don't know!' Delyth's shiny satin green chest swelled massively. 'I lost my daughter because of you. I never had the pleasure of seeing her married.'

'Delyth,' said Gethin, calmly, 'unless you know differently, the last I heard, Cerys was alive and well in New Zealand with three kids and a rugged sheep shearer in tow.'

'Oh!' Delyth said, dramatically, clutching hold of Mair. 'But she wouldn't have looked at that man if you hadn't spurned her! If you'd done the right thing by her, she would still be here and I wouldn't be a lonely woman.'

Gethin sighed. 'I'm sure your son and his family at Abersaith will be sorry to hear you seem to have forgotten them. Cerys wasn't running away from me; she was running away from you! That poor girl was the only kid in the village who couldn't do a damn thing without you poking your nose in. You didn't even let her join the rest of us on the beach in the evenings.'

'She was a good girl. I wanted her to stay that way!'

'I wish it had been as exciting as you seem to think. We'd listen to some music, sharing a tin of beer between us, if we were lucky. I think someone might have got hold of a spliff once, except we were all too afraid to inhale in case we became drug-crazed lunatics. Oh, and there might have been the odd outbreak of low-level snogging.'

'My Cerys was too good for any of that,' Delyth said, defiantly.

'If you hadn't set such strict rules for her, she might not have been so hell-bent on tasting forbidden fruit. She was a lovely girl, Delyth, but she was a menace, always trying to seduce one of the lads.'

'You and your filthy mouth!' said Delyth. 'She never went out after dark.'

'I hate to shock you, Delyth, but making love without the lights out is possible. She must have been in her element when you encouraged her to watch the sheep-shearing competition. All those macho Kiwi guys, flexing their muscles in public. Lucky for her, it was love at first sight when Shane set eyes on her, wasn't it? He was a smashing bloke, if you'd care to find out, but you never gave them a chance. So, if you didn't see Cerys get married, that was your choice. She's still out there, Delyth, and so are the rest of your grandchildren. Isn't it about time you got to know them – before it's too late?'

'You're a fine one to talk about it being too late,' sneered Mair. 'Did you think about the burden you placed on your poor parents, swanning off with your new art college friends? Far too good for the rest of us, you thought you were. All that extra work for your mother – you sent her to an early grave.'

'I don't think anyone sends anyone else to an early grave, Mair. My mother had breast cancer, but she ignored all the warning signs because she didn't want, as she put it, to be mutilated. She was afraid of my father's reaction. Afraid of being rejected.' He had to swallow hard to keep his voice calm. 'If anyone had a hand in her death it was you, Mair, because you never forgave my father for marrying her and not you, and even after they were married, you couldn't leave him alone, could you?'

Mair's hand flew to her mouth.

'Don't deny it, because I saw you with him once. I may only have been a child but I knew what was happening.'

'He should have married me. But what could I offer? She was a farmer's only daughter with land and I had nothing but myself.'

That part sounded like his father, anyway. Careful with money from the start.

'He paid for his decision in the end. Your father was a clever man, frustrated by the limitations of his life. We could have achieved great things together, but instead he was stuck here doing a job he hated. And, of course, once you came along, there was no escape.'

'And you've been trying to get rid of me ever since.' Gethin glowered at her. 'Well, here's the really good news, Mair. No amount of your poison's going to shift me, because I'm back for oh, let's say at least five years ...'

Mair's face was a sight to behold as she registered what he was telling her. 'That's right.' He nodded. 'We both know the terms of my father's Will, don't we? And, maybe, if you'd been a bit more subtle about conducting your affair with him, I might have felt inclined to just give up my interest in the cottage and hand it all over to you. Unluckily for you, though, I've decided I like it here, so don't go choosing new curtains for the place, will you? You might have been my father's mistress, but you'll never be mistress of his house.'

'And that, ladies,' said the Vicar, who'd been standing behind them and had heard it all, 'means that from now on I shall expect no stone throwing or mud flinging from either of you.'

Part of Gethin almost felt sorry for the two old women as, looking ashen and subdued, they retreated towards the marquee. The long shadows of the past still stained the present no matter what you tried to do to wipe it away. Then Marianne Parry laid her hand gently on his arm.

'Gethin, I visited your father at the end of his life. He was very frail by then, as you know, both in mind and body, but in his lucid moments, he was full of remorse about your mother's death.'

'He never said that to me,' Gethin said, shaking his head.

'I think he was too ashamed. He was a very troubled soul, scarred by the deprivations of his own upbringing, unable to express his feelings, who didn't realise quite how much he'd lost until it was too late. That's why he was so desperate for you to stay here, to raise children here, so that your mother's spirit would live on in some small way. I know that will never make up for his behaviour when she was alive, but I hope that makes it a little more understandable.'

He could see her kind face through his blurred vision and felt the gentle squeeze of her hand. 'Now,' she added, 'shall we raise money for a good cause?'

Inside the marquee, Alys sipped appreciatively at her Welsh sparkling Brut, supplied on such generous terms by the Glyndwr vineyard. Kingston Gravell's chocolaty tones had sweet-talked his audience and got them waving their programmes wildly; some, Alys suspected, purely for the benefit of his twinkling smile and warm gaze. But now things were getting serious. All around her handkerchiefs were being surreptitiously dabbed at moist eyes as the Abersaith Male Voice Choir concluded their set with 'The Ash Grove'.

Alys hoped that the references in the lyrics to kind faces and childhood friends would tug at some heartstrings and make the audience more receptive than a few of them had appeared when they'd taken their seats. Eyebrows had been raised at the presence of some dignitaries, like the Bishop and their Assembly Member, who, people were muttering, were only there to bask in the reflected glory. Many of those gathered had made conspicuous efforts to dress up for the television cameras with some very fixed hair-dos and a couple of dazzling home dye jobs on display, although Delyth and Mair had made predictably barbed comments about what they regarded as an unnecessary intrusion into village life.

One couple who seemed to have shed an awful lot of hair between them were Willow and Wilfie. Alys did a double take seeing them sitting in the front row. It almost looked as if a makeover programme had visited the Craft Courtyard with everyone so shiny and scrubbed up. Huw, at her side, she thought smiling to herself, had escaped, though, and looked as delightfully crumpled as ever. He reached for her hand, sensing her sudden nerves, and gave it a reassuring squeeze as Kingston Gravell took the podium once more.

She flashed a grateful smile at Huw then led the applause. Kingston's enthusiasm for *Girl in a Coral Dress* had gone a long way towards a change of heart about Gethin's work in Penmorfa, as well as some kind comments and real appreciation for what she'd achieved, too.

Kingston's beguiling manner was winning everyone over, but this was the real test. Looking round to see how his warm-up patter was being received by the audience, she caught sight of the man Kingston had pointed out to her as the art critic and newspaper columnist Jay Jewell, his arms folded and face impassive. A passing cloud sent a shadow slanting across the rows of seats and a cool breeze rippled the lining of the marquee. Alys twisted her hands together, anxious that nothing would spoil the big moment.

'Relax,' Huw said softly to her, instantly making her feel better.

The sun came out again, making the white interior glow and there was a hushed silence as Kingston paused theatrically. 'So now,' he said quietly, 'I'm going to open the bidding ...'

'Six thousand pounds!' roared Huw, making everyone jump. Alys turned her head slowly and blinked at him.

They barely had six thousand pennies. What the hell was he doing?

In the back row, Gethin released the breath he'd been holding as the gavel came down; *Girl in a Coral Dress* had just changed his life.

'Sold!' Kingston Gravell announced, smiling.

One hundred and seventy-four thousand pounds.

The marquee flaps opened and the sea mist swirled in, hanging in the air like smoke over a battlefield as a stampede of reporters charged off in search of phone signals. Gethin sat in shock whilst the Bishop and an Assembly Member argued loudly over a cab and the minibus driver made a fruitless search for the Abersaith Male Voice Choir who'd been swift to decamp to the Foundered Ship. In the cacophony of squeals and yelling, tears and congratulations, he dimly heard a couple of soft explosions.

One night with Coralie and his life had turned into a scene from the Apocalypse. Heck, he should have been forewarned the minute she looked over the fence at him.

Coralie stood in the middle of a little group, holding a champagne flute in each hand. Alys and Huw stood on one side of her, Adam, holding Jamie, and Kitty were on the other. Together they formed a small semi-circle to shield Gethin, who was slumped forward in his chair, his head in his hands.

'Well go on, girl,' said Adam, giving her a nudge. 'Don't take all day about it.'

'Gethin?'

He lifted his head slowly, his eyes taking the long route up as they first rested on Coralie's red peep-toe shoes before lingering on her bare legs and travelling over the pale green crêpe de Chine tea dress with its scattering of roses.

By the time the dark midnight eyes arrived at hers, she was blushing.

'You can put the glasses down, Coralie,' he said, with that rich Welsh lilt that had her legs turning to jelly, 'the bubbles are going to my head just drinking in the sight of you.'

'Smooth talking,' Adam said admiringly. 'No wonder you've got yourself such a reputation.'

'Just take the glasses, will you, Adam?' Gethin growled at him.

Since Adam already had his hands full, Kitty took the glasses and put them out of the way.

Gethin stood up and came towards her, never taking his eyes off her. 'I've been waiting to do this for so long,' he said, his voice breaking as he reached to stroke her cheek. Then he bent his head and brushed her lips so gently that it was all she could do not to grab at his shirt and pull him towards her.

'Well, get on with it, man,' Adam said impatiently. 'You two have got some time to make up!'

Gethin flashed them a big grin, his teeth white against the dark stubble, then planted his lips firmly on hers to a spontaneous round of applause and cheering.

A flash of light made them all turn round and everyone glared at the photographer.

'Excuse me,' the photographer said, carrying on regardless. 'You're the girl in the coral dress, aren't you? What's your name?'

'It's Doris bloody Day,' Huw snarled at him. 'Now piss off!'

'Huw!' Alys laughed.

'Well,' said Huw looking sheepish.

'Oh, Gethin!' said Alys, clearly unable to contain herself any longer. 'What a result! What recognition of your talent!

One hundred and seventy-four thousand pounds. Thank you! Now we can create a community hall to do Penmorfa proud!' The delight turned to bemusement as she turned back to her husband. 'But Huw, what did you think you were doing? I thought *we* were going to have to sell everything to pay for Coralie's portrait for a while there.'

'Yes, what were you doing, Huw?' Coralie asked, still trying not to burst with happiness because Gethin's arm was wrapped firmly round her waist. She was so close she could feel the rumble of protest as he started to speak.

'Huw ...' he warned.

'Coralie, *bach*,' Huw insisted. 'Let's just say that one way or another, your young man was determined to win the girl in the coral dress, even though someone else won her portrait. Now get yourselves a glass each will you, so we can drink a toast. Now then,' he continued, resting his gaze on everyone in turn, 'here's to love and happiness and the *Girl in a Coral Dress*!'

'I'm sure that's more than one toast, Dad,' laughed Kitty.

'I don't think you can have too many celebrations, can you?' said Gethin, turning to Coralie and smiling down at her in a way that made her glad he was holding her up. 'So, I'd like to propose a toast too, if you'll hear me out.'

He cleared his throat and looked almost shy as he started to speak. 'It's no secret that I couldn't wait to leave Penmorfa. I thought I was escaping a place with a particular mind-set, a cold, unforgiving location.' He looked around at them, as if to acknowledge his misapprehension. 'It's taken me fifteen years, since I won the art competition that showed me a different future and thousands of miles, to realise that it's not about where you are, but the people you're with.

'I'd like to say thank you to you, Alys, for understanding and for always taking me as you found me, not how others said I was. To you, Huw, I'm indebted to you for persuading some builders to transform Dad's cottage and helping me to see the place in a new light. And to you, Kitty and Adam, for so clearly demonstrating that life and love will always endure even in the smallest of villages. Together you've shown me the heart of Penmorfa and how a loving, caring family will always keep it beating. Here's to you!'

He raised his glass, but Alys interjected. 'I think you're crediting the wrong people with changing the direction of your life, aren't you?' she said softly. 'Don't leave it too late to tell her.'

'Ah,' he said, 'I was just getting to that. I think Coralie deserves my special thanks.'

'Well, it looks as if we're going to be doing much more toasting, this evening,' said Huw. 'Come on, everyone back to the farmhouse!'

Coralie would have liked some time alone with Gethin. She started to follow, but Gethin's grip tightened on her waist as he held her back.

'We've got other plans, Huw, if you don't mind.'

'Right you are, boy!' Huw said cheerfully, over his shoulder. Then he spotted an unopened bottle of sparkling wine and hurried back with it. 'Take this the pair of you; you'll get a terrible thirst on you with all that catching up.'

What was once Gethin's father's run-down cottage now felt cosy and welcoming with some simple furnishings and subtle lighting, but Coralie suspected Gethin hadn't taken her there just to admire the transformation. The planes of his face looked sharper; he'd lost a little weight, too.

'Forgive me, will you?' he said, drawing a ragged breath.

'Hush,' she said, pressing her fingers to his lips. 'There's nothing to forgive.'

'I was afraid of getting involved, of turning into someone like my father, but every time I tried to walk away from you I became more like him.'

Coralie put her arms round him and held him closer.

'I couldn't stop thinking about you,' he said, stroking her hair. 'You brightening up my life class the moment you walked in the room. You in Battery Park adding all the colour to the day. You 102 floors up in the sky. Your face at the opera. I don't know where we go from here, Coralie. All I know is that I don't want to let you go.'

'There's an awful lot we don't know about each other,' she said, pulling away again.

'I'd know the scent of your skin blindfolded,' he said. 'That's good enough for me.'

'That's just sex,' she teased, looking into his dark eyes. Her hair had started to come undone and she felt him gently release the clip that was holding it in position and let it tumble round her face.

'There are worse starting points.' He placed his fingers under her chin, coaxing her to look at him. 'Look at that portrait and tell me that I don't know you.'

'Ah, that's just paint.' She smiled.

'Paint's all I've got to show you how I feel,' he murmured.

'Paint them and forget them, Ruby said.'

'Yeah, she also told me never to let you out of my sight again, when she said goodbye to me at JFK. She wants to see us both there next time. If there is a next time …'

'I don't care where we go,' she said quietly. 'So long as we're together. We'll work something out.'

'What is there to work out?' he asked, sending her heart soaring. 'I know the tilt of your head when you look at the sea, I know that dewy-eyed look when you see some dumb animal, I know how lovely you look first thing in the morning.' He dropped his gaze to her lips. 'And I know how to make you cry out my name.'

A small sob escaped her throat and he pulled her to him and kissed her, his firm mouth on hers, his body hard against her.

'Coralie.' He laughed, touching his forehead to hers. 'Just come upstairs to my bed will you?'

He sat her on the big iron-framed bed and told her to keep her eyes closed for a minute. She could hear him fumbling with matches, cursing every so often, and wanted to laugh. But when she was allowed to look, he'd lit a circle of tea lights all round them. A little world, outside the real world. He stretched out beside her and just looked at her until she thought she'd go crazy with longing if he didn't put his hands on her.

'I still can't believe you're here,' she said, searching the depths of his sexy dark eyes. 'I'm so pleased you made it to the auction. I didn't know if you would, when I wrote to you. And I haven't even thanked you for coming,' she added, still aching for him to touch her.

'I haven't yet,' he said, with a husky catch in his voice that made her shiver with longing, 'and you will.'

'I'll start now then, shall I?' she whispered, kneeling up so she could untie her wrap dress.

'That's a good trick.' He whistled softly as the silky material slipped off her shoulders. 'It's probably just as well I didn't know about it earlier.'

Coralie was going to say something clever, but his hand cupped her breast, and his thumb stroked her nipple through the thin satin. With his free hand he reached round and unclasped her bra. 'That's a good trick, too!' was all she could gasp before losing herself in a quest to see what else they could do together.

Much later, when the tea lights had burned down twice and the chill had long worn off what was left of the sparkling wine, Coralie sat up and looked at Gethin stretched out beside her and told herself how happy she was. He had a body she could never get tired of seeing, a perfectly assembled combination of lean, hard, rough and smooth. And he knew exactly what to do with it, which was very lucky for her, too.

He scooted over and wrapped his arm across her hips and rested his head in her lap. She slid her fingers through his hair, thinking how much she'd missed him, how she would miss him again and how wrong it would be to get too used to having him around.

He jerked his head up, caught her expression and pulled himself up to sit beside her. 'Spill it, Coralie. Come on, no secrets now. Not after what we've shared. Tell me what's wrong.'

She shook her head, feeling awkward. 'Where do we go from here? That's all I was wondering.'

'Hey,' he said softly. 'If you don't know how I feel about you by now, I don't know what else to do.'

She twisted the sheet. It was stupidly insecure to ask for any more than that.

He smiled down at her, pulling her close and dropping a kiss on her hair. 'We're going to catch up on all the things we've missed, everything we didn't say and do, and we're going to be doing plenty more of this. It'll be perfect.'

'Yes, it will, won't it?' she agreed, wishing she could be certain. Something still bothered her. But when he stroked her shoulder and nibbled her neck and pulled her down beside him, she couldn't remember what the problem was.

Chapter Twenty-Eight

'Can you believe it's only six months since you went out to New York?' Alys asked, smacking her lips and pouting into the mirror. Coralie, standing behind her, tried to dodge the golden October sunlight slanting in through the bedroom window whilst she squinted into Alys's beautiful old-fashioned dressing table mirror attempting to pin up her hair.

'Bleurgh!' said Alys, applying her lipstick, 'I am *so* not used to wearing all this makeup. I feel like a clown! And next week you're off *again*.'

'Alys, you look even more gorgeous than ever. Adam's mates will all be falling in love with you.' Coralie grinned, winking at her.

'Get that clip in your hair, before I do something slow and messy with it that would ruin Kitty's wedding day,' Alys warned.

Coralie, leaning over her shoulder, laughed. 'But, it's not fair! As chief bridesmaid, isn't one of *my* duties to get off with one of the groomsmen? They'll never notice me with you around. Any chance that Adam might have gone to school with Jared Leto?'

'Jared? No.' Alys picked up one of her pink, pearl-drop earrings. 'He left a couple of years before Adam started.'

'And now Wilfie's taken, too!'

They exchanged looks of disbelief in the mirror, still unable to believe how well Wilfie had scrubbed up.

'Anyway,' Alys said, turning her head slowly from side-to-side in a last-minute inspection. 'You don't need Jared or Wilfie. Not now you've got Gethin.'

Whether anyone would ever 'get' Gethin, as Alys put it, remained a moot point, but it had been a very happy, if busy summer, she thought, straightening up before she was on the receiving end of a liberal spray of Shalimar.

'I do think it's strange though,' Alys said wistfully, 'that the events that reconnected Gethin with his Welsh roots seem to have taken you in the opposite direction.'

One day at a time, Coralie reminded herself. 'I'm so happy to see Gethin so fired up about his work again. I love the stuff he's doing now.' He'd begun working *en plein air*, painting outside to catch the light across the sea in Penmorfa Bay or making brief, lightning sketches of the faces of the people who lived and worked in the small, rural community.

'Yes, but you've done well for yourself, too. Selling your Happy Hands and Rose Works recipes to a major cosmetic house is quite a coup in these difficult times.'

'*If* I do.' Coralie tied the sash of her turquoise taffeta dress, feeling very relieved that Kitty hadn't let the little bridesmaids have their way. Purple was so not her colour. 'I'm still not sure that's what I want to do. That's partly why we're going to New York next week. Gethin's gallery have changed their tune and want to reopen talks with him, and we'll catch up with his former assistant's new exhibition, too.'

'And have some time for each other, I hope,' said Alys.

Coralie looked at herself and frowned. For all Kitty's claims that the strapless bodice of her bridesmaid dress was self-supporting, she was still convinced that unless she was very careful she could easily end up looking like the novelty act at a seedy club.

'Are you decent, ladies?'

As she ever could be, thought Coralie, chewing her lip and looking doubtfully at her reflection.

Huw, pretending to cover his eyes, walked into the bedroom.

More used to seeing him in a rather antique pair of moleskin trousers topped with a corduroy jacket of the same vintage, Coralie thought he looked incredibly distinguished with his well-cut silver hair against the black of his morning suit.

'Oh, look at you!' Alys jumped to her feet to brush some imaginary fluff off his shoulders. 'Don't you look handsome?'

Huw grinned and pulled his wife in to kiss her, despite Alys's squawks about her makeup. 'Where's the bride-to-be then? Not in here?'

'We're just going up to her room now, to help her into her dress.' Alys beamed. 'Is she getting impatient then?'

Huw scratched his head. 'Well, I don't know. I can't find her.'

'Oh, Lord!' Alys plonked herself down on the stool again. 'She'll break that boy's heart if she backs out now. I do hope she hasn't got cold feet.'

'Nope! I wore my wellies.' Kitty laughed, padding in, her feet in thick socks. 'You didn't really think I'd jilt Adam, did you? It was just that I was looking at my bouquet and it struck me that one thing was missing, so I dashed down to the garden centre for a sprig of myrtle to tie in for good luck. And when I checked the table decorations in the marquee, one string of fake pearls on the top table had given way, but the beads looked so pretty spilling across the linen tablecloth that I didn't bother to clear them up.'

'Kitty!' screeched Alys. 'Never mind all that! What about you? I know you're thrilled to be back in your old jeans, but wearing them with one of Adam's hoodies and your hair in rollers is not a great bridal look. Have you seen what the time is?'

Come on, Kitty, thought Gethin, beginning to feel nervous. To think he'd been worried that with all his secret preparations he'd be the one most likely to be late to the wedding. Everyone in the congregation was starting to lean out of their seats, wondering if they'd shelled out on all those Egyptian cotton sheets and towel bales in vain. Adam, poor sod, stood squarely at the front of the church, staring firmly ahead. He felt for him. It was hard enough for the guy anyway, with no parents to support him, although the best man, his older brother, was taking good care of him.

Whilst the organ swelled to cover the audible murmurs, Gethin reacquainted himself with the room. Penmorfa's tiny chapel was unchanged; its simple interior unadorned except for the lectern and altar cloths which were lovingly embroidered with a design of wheat and fish. As a little boy he'd thought the fishes particularly exuberant, as if, with the village being so close to the sea, someone hadn't been able to resist making them look as if they could smell the salt air and were just about to dive for freedom. He just hoped Kitty hadn't done the same.

Just then he heard heels clipping behind him and the processional music began as Alys, looking ravishing in an Edwardian-style suit in a dusky pink silk, hurried down the aisle to take her place. Alys wouldn't make a bad mother-in-law, he thought, looking at her appreciatively as she gave Adam's brother a quick thumbs up before sliding into the pew. Like one of her own garden centre prize blooms, she just got better-looking every year. Was that a tear he noticed shimmering on her cheek beneath her glorious wide-brimmed hat? Overflowing emotions, probably, on this momentous day. Joy, of course, and now that her daughter had turned up at last, more than a little relief.

Gethin turned and got a quick glimpse of Huw looking dashing in his morning suit. How hard, he wondered, had Kitty worked to persuade her father to dress up for the occasion? Not very, he guessed. 'But, Dad,' he could hear her saying, with a catch in her voice. 'Please. For me.' He could imagine the look that went with it too; any resistance from Huw would have been futile.

The bride looked beautiful but the star of the show for him was the chief bridesmaid, a girl with sherry-coloured curls and rosebud lips, who was smiling at him with tears in her lovely, tawny eyes. Gethin felt his smile grow wide and his heart beat faster, although this was probably not the moment to pull her onto his lap.

Kitty, apparently reading his mind, stopped to throw him a suspicious look beneath her veil. He was grateful to one of the little bridesmaids for recovering the situation with a swift prod to her silk-covered back. Coralie, regaining her composure, gathered them all up and shepherded the whole party towards the altar. He didn't blame Kitty for a certain amount of mistrust. He'd been doing some thinking, keeping his plans close to his chest, and the only part he'd managed to figure was that everything hinged on Coralie. It was anyone's guess what happened after that.

As Kitty reached the altar, her astonished gasp showed that Adam had been keeping a surprise of his own. He turned, grinning broadly, to reveal a real shiner of a black eye, leading Kitty to throw all protocol out of the window by fussing and cooing all over him.

The Vicar, in her own imitable style, calmly restored order, welcoming the congregation and revealing that the groom's black eye was nothing more sinister than the result of an early-morning surfing session to burn off some pre-wedding nerves. 'So now,' she continued, 'on this day when Kitty and Adam prepare to launch, well, maybe not a surfboard, but a new boat, shall we say, in which to sail through life and learn the ropes together, let us begin ...'

Letting the words of the solemnisation of matrimony flow over him, Gethin took a deep breath and looked round the room whilst he tried to refocus. Somehow the pews had managed to accommodate what felt like the whole of Penmorfa, but it was a bit of a squeeze. Kitty's Cardiff friends and Adam's surfing mates were already eyeing each other up. Some of the couples amongst them sat hand in hand, reliving their own special day; others were thoughtfully anticipating their own. And that had to be Adam's older sister, the physiotherapist, since she looked so much like her brother. He remembered Adam joking she was the brains department of the family.

All at once, the fidgeting and shuffling in the congregation seemed to stop.

In the sudden quiet the Vicar's calm voice rang out clear and true above what seemed to be a collective holding of breath. You couldn't help it, he thought, the power and poetry of the words just grabbed you, whether you believed in them or not. All that dreadful day of judgement stuff and secrets of all hearts being disclosed was guaranteed to make you feel guilty about something. But at least Coralie, smiling reassuringly at one of the little bridesmaids, had shed her secret worries about what might be in store for her when the final trumpet sounded. Unable to take his eyes off her, he leaned forward to catch a glimpse of her face in profile and had to take a deep breath when she looked over her shoulder, caught his eye and gave him a dazzling smile.

'And now,' said the Vicar, gently, 'I am required to ask anyone present who knows a reason why these persons may not lawfully marry to declare it now.'

As the newly declared husband and wife joyfully headed up the aisle to warm smiles all round, Coralie gathered up the little bridesmaids and took the best man's arm. Keeping her eyes firmly ahead until the group emerged, blinking, into the bright October sunshine; she didn't dare look at Gethin's face in case she forgot what she was supposed to be doing. The smallest bridesmaid, who was already getting twitchy, was bound to scoot off whilst she was distracted. Kitty and Adam couldn't have wished for a more perfect beginning to their married life; the ceremony had been beautiful and she didn't want anything to spoil the photos now.

Kitty was fussing over Adam's black eye again and taking every opportunity to smother him with kisses. You'd have to be very cynical indeed, she decided, to question the chance of them finding lasting happiness. Despite Kitty's slight wobble before the ceremony when she'd had a good cry on Alys's shoulder because everything was so perfect, and the attack of nerves that had given Adam such a shiner, you only had to look at the pair of them, ducking under a shower of rose petals and coming up all smiles, to see how right they looked together.

Whilst the photographer was getting them in position, Coralie shaded her eyes from the sun's brilliant gaze, unable to stop herself looking round. The little church was set on top of a hill, against the backdrop of the rolling fields and the sparkling sea, with the scattering of houses that made up the small settlement of Penmorfa roughly following the winding road. She couldn't help scanning the half-circle of fluttering, brightly coloured silks, confections of hats and smoothly tailored suits for one tall, dark figure in particular.

'Come in closer, lovely,' someone said to her, as they shuffled up for the next group picture. 'We don't bite. Well, not all of us anyway.' One of Adam's surf mates with laughing eyes and a lazy smile reached out his hand and pulled her towards him. 'Here,' he said, winking at her. 'You'll be safe next to me.'

'I think she'll be safer with me!' said a disapproving voice behind her. Coralie's fickle new friend, giving her a regretful smile, spotted one of Kitty's very pretty Cardiff girlfriends and made a rapid decision to abandon her for a damsel in a perilously plunging frock.

Coralie looked up and found herself staring straight into a dark blue gaze, like a midnight sea.

'Move over, darling,' said Gethin, slipping in next to her.

Kitty stole a look at Adam as he sat down on her parent's big brass bed beside her and her breath caught, because he was looking so sexy. She liked the way he looked at work, rough, ready, looking like a bad boy in his sweaty tee shirt and torn jeans, but this was a new, exciting Adam, a cool, sophisticated stranger in a crisp white shirt that was crying out to be unbuttoned.

'Want me to take him for a while?' he offered, reaching over her to stroke Jamie's head. Now he was making her feel weak at the knees because he was so sweet, too. He really was lush, her new husband. And he was all hers; the love in his eyes when they made their vows had reassured her of that.

'You're all right.' She smiled. 'He's just about asleep now. Once he's off I'll pop him in the travel cot and Mam'll take over.' Suddenly the idea seemed too terrifying to contemplate and she found herself choking back the tears.

'Oh love, what is it?' Adam wrapped his arms round her.

'Do you think he'll be all right?'

'He'll be fine, sweetheart. We're only leaving him for one night.'

It had taken her so long to feel like a proper mother, but now that it had happened, Kitty felt ashamed of how detached she'd felt about this poor, innocent scrap in her arms. She gulped back the tears, hoping that Jamie hadn't been aware of her initial coldness towards him and vowing to make it up to him for the rest of her life.

'We can take him with us, if you'd prefer,' said Adam, scanning her face with concerned eyes. 'We're a proper family now, after all. I'm sure they won't mind at the hotel.'

They *were* a proper family. And with the warm wishes from their friends and the good example of Alys and Huw to follow, Kitty knew that they had laid the foundations of the strongest of futures together. Everything had been perfect, but one of her favourite moments had been at the reception, after all the speeches. Alys had risen to recite Gillian Clarke's beautiful wedding poem, *Er Gwell, Er Gwaeth*, For Better, For Worse, and Huw had watched her with such tenderness and pride that the tears had started raining down again.

Kitty took another look at her husband and had to agree that they probably wouldn't bat an eyelid about accommodating a small baby in The Cabin's honeymoon suite. But she would. Jamie was snoring gently, his angelic lips puffing in his sleep, with only the slightest break in the rhythm as the cool cot sheet touched his back when she laid him down.

'I think our son will be safe and happy with his grandparents, don't you?' She smiled at Adam, who was standing over the cot beside her. 'Right now I just want to be a proper wife.' She moved into him, breathing him in and closing her eyes as his fingers traced the nape of her neck and downwards across her bare shoulders.

'Don't stop,' she murmured.

'We have to,' he told her, nuzzling her neck. 'We're neglecting our guests.'

'They think I'm changing into my evening outfit. No one will miss us for five minutes.'

'Five minutes!' Adam laughed. 'There'll be a time for fast and furious, but not tonight.'

'I suppose it would be more romantic to wait,' she agreed, sneakily stroking the gratifying bulge in his trousers in case she could change his mind. 'It is our wedding night.'

'Not just our wedding night.' He smiled, his eyes dark with desire. 'It's the first night of the rest of our lives together.'

Together. That sounded good. Kitty reached up and pulled him to her, kissing him hard, relieved, happy and looking forward to the future.

Coralie smiled at Alys, clinging to Huw as Rick Astley sang 'Never Gonna Give You Up' as they passed. Alys, looking radiantly happy, gave her a little wave over Huw's shoulder as Gethin led her away from the dance floor.

'Come on, Coralie, we've done our duty,' he said, folding back one of the flaps so they could escape from the heaving marquee, 'now it's our time.'

Chapter Twenty-Nine

'Where are you taking me?' Coralie asked, since the evening air was cool across her bare shoulders.

Gethin didn't answer, but stopped to wrap the frivolous white marabou shrug that went with her bridesmaid dress round her. Her shoulders felt less exposed but a sudden irrational fear that time was running out for her and Gethin still left her feeling chilly. She had the strongest feeling that life was about to change. She could feel the shift in Gethin. He was trying hard not to show it, but she knew him well enough now to know that he was hiding something.

Summer had been special, full of memories to treasure and take out in the cold of winter. Two people, from opposite sides of the Atlantic, who had made something precious together. So if, after their holiday together in New York, it was her fate to return alone then she would accept it, even though it would break her heart in pieces. If this was his goodbye to Penmorfa, she thought, realising that he was leading her towards the sandy cove, she wouldn't spoil the moment for him.

'Here, let me go first.' He sounded nervous, but his grip was warm and secure as ever as he took her hand and guided her down the stone steps. The black waves broke below them, whispering across the sand and the salt air touched her lips in a ghostly kiss. Then Gethin smiled up at her and hoisted her into his arms to carry her over the rocks to the flat sand. She took off her ballet pumps so they could walk along the beach together, and slipped her hand into his.

'Oh, what a pity,' she said, spotting a small driftwood fire ahead of them, being tended by a couple of teenagers. 'I was hoping we'd have the place to ourselves.'

Whilst it wasn't unusual, even on the coldest evenings, to see small groups of young people gathered together for the sake of having somewhere warm to sit and talk, it was nevertheless disappointing. She would have liked to gather up close to Gethin. *Cwtching* the Welsh called it, cuddling and protecting all in one, a *cwtch* being a private space in a room or in two people's hearts.

'Why? What did you have in mind?' he asked, squeezing her hand and settling her fears a bit more. There were just two boys sitting by the fire this evening. To her surprise, instead of passing them by, Gethin stopped and handed each of the boys a hefty tip and they scooted off, making appreciative noises about their windfall.

'Why, Mr Lewis? Have you planned this?' she exclaimed, smiling up at him and slipping a finger between the buttons of his shirt.

'I want to talk to you,' he said, removing her hand. 'But if you carry on like that I'll forget what I wanted to say. Sit down, will you?'

He straightened out the blanket where the teenagers had been sprawling and patted the space beside him. But when she leaned into him she could feel the tension in his shoulders. Should she be worrying, after all? The moon touched the oily black waves with silver, but, even feeling the warmth of Gethin's body against hers, she started to fret again that there was no bright lining but only dark clouds ahead for them.

'Gethin?'

She saw him shake his head. 'Heck, Coralie, you've got me lost for words. And have done from the moment you set your cat on me.'

'I did not set Rock on you!' she protested. 'It was your fault for letting go of him. And you weren't lost for words for very long! You weren't very happy,' she added, trying not to laugh when she thought about the look of disbelief on his face as he stood half-naked in the next-door garden.

'All right then,' he admitted, 'I was just lost.'

'You!' This time she did laugh. 'You were one of the most self-contained, opinionated men I'd ever met! You predicted Sweet Cleans wouldn't last the winter, remember?'

'I might have been wrong about that.' He shrugged. 'Is that why you didn't try to rescue me? Stray cats, Bambi glasses, forgotten frocks and broken lives … why not me?'

The low lilt of his lovely voice was getting to her. 'You didn't need rescuing,' she said, feeling her throat constrict.

'Oh, I did,' he said pushing his hands through his hair. 'I needed saving from myself. If you hadn't come along, I would have ended up a sad, lonely, old man, just like my father.'

Coralie started to dare to hope that maybe it would be all right after all. 'So what did you want to say to me?' she said, softly.

He heaved a sigh. 'Do you mind about *Girl in a Coral Dress*?'

Not quite what she was expecting. Coralie straightened up. 'Of *course* not! It's wonderful news. It's lovely to see you getting the recognition you deserve from your own country.'

Kingston Gravell had done them more than one favour when he'd persuaded his good friend Jay Jewell, the art critic, to come to the gala auction. As an avid collector too, he'd not only bought the painting for such a satisfactory sum, but he had also generously offered it on a three-year loan to the National Museum, meaning *Girl in a Coral*

Dress had been added to the collection of works by modern Welsh artists.

'Good,' he said carefully. 'I know I told you that paint was all I had to show you how I feel ...'

Coralie slid her arm around him. 'It's fine, honestly. You don't have to explain. I know how much you care.'

He exhaled deeply. 'Why is this so difficult?' He shook his head before reaching into a basket on the corner of the blanket and flicking a switch.

Not their last samba? She panicked as he pulled her to her feet. Then Doris Day started singing 'Secret Love' and Gethin drew her close to him. He smelled of sea air and firewood and his thighs were warm and hard against hers as they swayed under the starlit sky. Fireworks from the reception, still going on high on the hill above them, erupted over their head in a glittering shower. She looked up and held his gaze, wanting to stay like that forever, knowing it was impossible.

'Hey,' he touched his hand to her cheek, 'why the tears?'

'I escaped to the country, you escaped from the country, isn't that what you're going to tell me? That we're never going to be happy in the same place. Doris was right, our lips should *never* have touched. We should have stuck with our first impressions.'

She heard him laugh. 'Coralie, I hate to be the one to tell you this, but Doris Day gets it wrong sometimes. Everyone's moved over; Alys has got her family back, Kitty and Adam are together where they should be. That just leaves you and me.'

He folded her in and she grabbed hold of him, feeling the lean, hard strength of him and never wanting to let him go.

'I was so afraid of hurting you,' he said into her hair. 'I didn't want to make a commitment, didn't want to mess you up the way my father did my mother. And then, when I thought I'd never see you again …' He shook his head and his body was tense against hers. 'Coralie, we can live in the country, we can live in the city, we can live on the moon for all I care, just don't leave me.'

'I can't,' she whispered, swallowing her tears. 'I don't know what the future holds, but I only want to move forward with you.'

All the tension left his body as his mouth came down on hers, making her shudder with pleasure and her pulse race. She slid her fingers inside his shirt and heard him catch his breath. This was going to be hell on the bridesmaid frock, thought Coralie, as he pulled her towards the blanket, but when was she ever going to wear a turquoise taffeta strapless number again, anyway?

Before they could get any further though, there was bellowing from the top of the stone steps. Coralie looked up to find Kitty and Adam waving madly at them, then something came flying towards her in the dark.

'I need to ask you something, Coralie,' said Gethin, after a short pause whilst they waited for Kitty and Adam to disappear, the sound of the couple's laughter carrying down to them. 'The whole future of Penmorfa depends on you.'

Great. Alys had said something very like that to her once and life hadn't been the same since. 'Go on,' she said, unhappily.

'Coralie,' said Gethin, holding the remnants of Kitty's bouquet. 'Would you believe me if I told you that I love you?'

She looked at him, his anxious expression, his shirt hanging out and his hair untidy, the pathetic flowers shedding petals in his hand, and suddenly he didn't seem so self-contained anymore, but a real, warm, loving man. A man she would cherish forever.

'Yes,' she replied, smiling up at him. 'Yes, Gethin. I believe you. And I love you.'

She laughed as he dropped the bouquet and punched the air, before quickly pulling her into her arms to silence her with a kiss, but just when she was starting to think about *cwtching* up together again, he broke away to look at her.

'Coralie, you didn't go to Tiffany's when you were in New York, did you?'

She shook her head, puzzled. 'No,' she said, 'but I do know they don't serve breakfast.'

'You're correct,' he said, smiling as he lifted his hands and gently cradled her face. 'That's settled then, I'll take you there next week; what they do have is a pretty good selection of rings.'

About the Author

Winning a tin of chocolate in a national essay competition at primary school inspired **Christine Stovell** to become a writer! After graduating from UEA, she took various jobs in the public sector writing research papers and policy notes by day and filling up her spare drawers with embryonic novels by night. Losing her dad to cancer made her realise that if she was ever going to get a novel published she had to put her writing first.

Setting off, with her husband, from a sleepy seaside resort on the east coast in a vintage wooden boat to sail halfway round Britain provided the inspiration for her novel *Turning the Tide. Move Over Darling* is Christine's second novel.

Christine has also published numerous short stories and articles.

www.christinestovell.com

More Choc Lit

From Christine Stovell

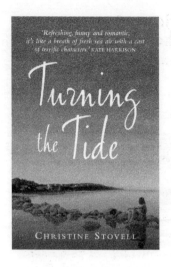

Turning the Tide

**All's fair in love and war?
Depends on who's making
the rules.**

Harry Watling has spent the
past five years keeping her
father's boat yard afloat,
despite its dying clientele.
Now all she wants to do is
enjoy the peace and quiet of
her sleepy backwater.

So when property developer
Matthew Corrigan wants
to turn the boat yard into an upmarket housing complex for
his exotic new restaurant, it's like declaring war.

And the odds seem to be stacked in Matthew's favour.
He's got the colourful locals on board, his hard-to-please
girlfriend is warming to the idea and he has the means to
force Harry's hand. Meanwhile, Harry has to fight not just
his plans but also her feelings for the man himself.

Then a family secret from the past creates heartbreak for
Harry, and neither of them is prepared for what happens
next …

Visit www.choc-lit.com for more details
including the first two chapters and
reviews, or simply scan barcode using
your mobile phone QR reader.

Why not try something else from the Choc Lit selection?
Here's a sample:

Please don't stop the music

Jane Lovering

 Winner of the 2012 Best Romantic Comedy Novel of the year

 Winner of the 2012 Romantic Novel of the year

How much can you hide?

Jemima Hutton is determined to build a successful new life and keep her past a dark secret. Trouble is, her jewellery business looks set to fail – until enigmatic Ben Davies offers to stock her handmade belt buckles in his guitar shop and things start looking up, on all fronts.

But Ben has secrets too. When Jemima finds out he used to be the front man of hugely successful Indie rock band Willow Down, she wants to know more. Why did he desert the band on their US tour? Why is he now a semi-recluse?

And the curiosity is mutual – which means that her own secret is no longer safe …

Visit www.choc-lit.com for more details including the first two chapters and reviews, or simply scan barcode using your mobile phone QR reader.

Visit www.choc-lit.com for more details
including the first two chapters and reviews

Introducing Choc Lit

We're an independent publisher creating
a delicious selection of fiction.
Where heroes are like chocolate – irresistible!
Quality stories with a romance at the heart.

Choc Lit novels are selected by genuine readers like yourself.
We only publish stories our Choc Lit Tasting Panel want to
see in print. Our reviews and awards speak for themselves.

Come and support our authors and join them in our
Author's Corner, read their interviews and see their latest
events, reviews and gossip.

Visit: www.choc-lit.com for more details.

Available in paperback and as ebooks from most stores.

We'd also love to hear how you enjoyed *Move Over Darling*.
Just visit www.choc-lit.com and give your feedback.
Describe Gethin in terms of chocolate and you could win a
Choc Lit novel in our Flavour of the Month competition.

Follow us on twitter: www.twitter.com/
ChocLituk, or simply scan barcode using
your mobile phone QR reader.